Praise for *The Cancer Ladies' Running Club*

'An inspiring read.'
Good Housekeeping

'A wise, warm and wonderful novel ... an incredibly moving,
uplifting and hopeful story that looks at the power of finding
your tribe. It will make you smile and love life just a
little bit more.'
Adele Parks

'I adore Josie Lloyd, I love her writing and you are in for an
amazing, heart-breaking, inspiring treat – read this book.'
Jenny Colgan

'[A] hopeful, uplifting read.'
The Sun

'A pitch-perfect love letter to the power of
friendship – honest, uplifting and
straight from the heart.'
Jill Mansell

'An honest read that, despite its heart-wrenching
topic, will uplift and inspire you.'
Heat

'What an engaging and life-affirming story! A page-turner,
too, with such wonderful characters. I loved it!'
Rachel Hore

'[A] homage to the power of friendship.'
Sunday Post

'Brave, bold Josie Lloyd has written an incredibly important
book. I was charmed by her light touch yet fearlessness in
dealing with the deeply emotional subject matter.
Every woman should read it.'
Veronica Henry

T0043662

'A searingly honest, but fiercely positive story about the importance of friendship and the power of hope told with Josie's characteristic warmth and humour.'
Mike Gayle

'This inspirational, hard-hitting, warm, and funny book pulsated with truth and experience. I laughed, cried, learnt a lot, and could NOT put it down. This one will be a huge summer hit.'
Louise Beech

'I thoroughly enjoyed this honest, no-holds-barred story. It is by turns funny, inspiring and incredibly moving.'
Kathryn Hughes

'An amazing story that shows us all the strength of the human spirit and the power of friendship. An inspiration!'
Magic Radio

'Beautiful and brave, powerful and emotional. An incredibly special book. I cried and laughed and fell in love with the characters, I learnt about love, humility, honesty, kindness and compassion, and to cherish every day.'
Alex Brown

'A moving and inspiring story.'
Bella

'A story as honest as it is entertaining, and as funny as it is fearless. It is a novel that celebrates friendship and the messy wonder of family, and is an inspiring and insightful story that makes you want to tell your loved ones how amazing they are and then run up a mountain shouting 'I CAN.' It made me believe in life, in love and in the power we all have to overcome the worst – an unmissable, hopeful and life-changing read.'
Katie Marsh

'Wonderful. A gorgeous, moving read.'
Cesca Major

'Josie has done a wonderful job of treating the subject matter with such honesty, and infusing the story with a great sense of courage and hope . . . She's found the perfect balance between the realities of what her characters are facing, and a very uplifting dose of inspiration and warmth . . . I think it will be so encouraging to anyone affected by cancer.'
Celia Reynolds

'Uplifting and positive, you will be cheering them along.'
Prima

'The crowning glory of this beautiful story is the network of deep
friendships that develops to sustain and hearten the women of
The Cancer Ladies' Running Club. I've laughed, cried and cheered
them on as I read. This book should be on prescription in every
oncology ward and department throughout the country.'
Celia Anderson

'This life-affirming book will make you weep – and jump for
joy. A heart-warming story about bravery and compassion,
friendship and family. Beautifully written, witty and moving.'
Freya North

'A message of positivity and hope . . . A tale of friendship and love
in all its capacities. Full of warmth that will make you glow from
your post reading workout. It will have you crying and laughing in
equal measure. This needs to be made into a blockbuster for sure.'
My Weekly

'A gorgeously bittersweet novel, unflinching and heart-wrenching – you
will need tissues – yet full of warmth, wit and joy. I was cheering
on *The Cancer Ladies' Running Club* right to the finish line.'
Eve Chase

'Beautifully written with honesty, humour and fabulous
characters – an inspiring story that's not afraid to tell the truth.'
Jessica Ryn

'I RACED through this warm, witty delight of a read about
strength, endurance and friendship. A wonderful book.'
Suzy K Quinn

Josie Lloyd's first novel, *It Could Be You*, was published in 1997 and since then she has written 19 bestselling novels (as Joanna Rees and other pen names), including the *Sunday Times* number one hit *Come Together*, which she co-authored with her husband, Emlyn Rees. Josie has also written several best-selling parodies with Emlyn, including *We're Going On A Bar Hunt*, *The Very Hungover Caterpillar* and *The Teenager Who Came To Tea*. She lives beside the seaside with her family and dog, Ziggy, and goes swimming in the sea all year round. You can find her on Instagram @josielloydwriter or on Twitter @josielloydbooks

Also By Josie Lloyd

The Cancer Ladies' Running Club

Lifesaving
for
Beginners

Josie Lloyd

ONE PLACE. MANY STORIES

HQ
An imprint of HarperCollins*Publishers* Ltd
1 London Bridge Street
London SE1 9GF

www.harpercollins.co.uk

HarperCollins*Publishers*
1st Floor, Watermarque Building, Ringsend Road
Dublin 4, Ireland

This edition 2022

1
First published in Great Britain by
HQ, an imprint of HarperCollins*Publishers* Ltd 2022

ISBN: 978-0-00-837369-6

MIX
Paper | Supporting
responsible forestry
FSC™ C007454

For the swimming gang

For whatever we lose (like a you or a me)
it's always ourselves we find in the sea
— E.E. CUMMINGS

I

Bah Humbug

Christmas Day Morning

It's only cold water. That's all. After the shitshow of this year, cold water is nothing. *Nothing*, Dominica tells herself, as she peels the Velcro closed on her neoprene gloves and strides off towards the sea, her size ten boots making a loud trudging sound over the pebbles. She's glad she's made it here and forced her sorry carcass out of bed, although it was a close-run thing. But, as usual, Helga's message on the Sea-Gals WhatsApp chat had persuaded her. *It's tradition*, Helga had written. *No excuses*.

She knows she owes Helga and Tor an appearance this morning. They're the ones who've looked out for her this year. Separately, they've both asked her to spend today with them, knowing it's her first Christmas without Chris, but she's politely declined their kind offers. She wants to be alone to wallow in her grief, although she vows now that she's going to tidy up the tissue-strewn pit of their bedroom. Chris would have a fit if he could see it.

Along the beach there are little groups dotted as far as the eye can see in both directions, most people dressed for the cold, but many of them stripping off. With the drop in church attendance, maybe the sea *is* the new religion. It's certainly a draw. Everyone is facing the water and the mood of celebration is palpable. She can hear the pop of a champagne cork (10 a.m. is a little early, but it's Christmas Day, after all), whilst a young guy contemplatively skins up on the top of the largest concrete groyne. There's a bagpiper in a kilt walking on the next beach and the reedy sound wafts over to where Dominica stands along with a tang of spliff smoke.

It used to make the national news: the nutters taking the plunge in the sea on Christmas morning, but cold water swimming has become all the rage and now the world and his wife have taken it up.

But who can blame them? Dominica thinks. There's been bugger all else to do.

There are plenty of little flocks of swimmers already in the water, lots of them in woolly hats. A couple of show-offs are front-crawling further out, dragging their red tow floats behind them. She'd love to be able to swim like those Amazons out there in these winter months, but if she goes too far out of her depth, she gets a bit panicky. She knows that the sea is not to be taken for granted – even on a calm day like today. And, besides, she's not fit enough to swim like that. Not any more. Not after a year of sitting on her arse eating biscuits.

Until the pandemic hit, Dominica had never been idle – not once during her fifty-six years. That's probably because her parents had instilled a rock-solid work ethic in her and a belief that the colour of her skin meant she needed to prove herself

2

twice as much. As an operations manager for a large travel company, she's been the consummate multi-tasker, but with the skies emptied and holidays cancelled, her whole department has been put on furlough. At least, in some ways, it's a blessing. She could never have coped with a job and losing Chris at the same time.

She's dreading going back and knows that, any day now, there'll be an email from management with the phased return-to-work plan. Her team – once thirty strong – was cut down in lockdown and she knows that a lot of her colleagues will have had a tough time too, but she dreads their reunion. She already knows that she won't be able to stand the questions… the pity, how at least one of them will almost certainly dredge up a competing story of someone they know who died of Covid too. That's the thing that gets her the most. That her Chris, with his bright eyes, booming laugh and bear hugs, has been reduced to a grim statistic for other people to comment on and chew over.

Over by the other groyne, some teens scamper across the stones in bright bikinis, squealing. Everyone is supposed to be socially distancing, but somehow the government's rules don't seem so pressing here at the water's edge. She used to get angry about joggers *breathing* and shoppers crowding the pavements with their masks on their chins, but after what happened to Chris, she doesn't waste her energy any more. The world is already full of judgers and snitchers without her joining their ranks. What's the point when the worst has already happened? Besides, it's natural for people to interpret the rules and bend them to their own making. As Chris always used to say: people are like water… they'll always find a way.

Dominica arrives next to Tor, who is ahead of her at the water's edge; Helga is coming now too from where she's slung her things on the pile of their stuff by the groyne and Dominica waves to her. As usual, Helga's dressed in her baggy blue swimming costume and retro swimming cap with a chin strap. She doesn't give a monkeys about her saggy wrinkly thighs being on show, unlike Dominica, who is body-conscious even now.

They make an odd tribe, Dominica thinks, feeling a surge of affection for these unlikely friends. There are other swimming gangs she could have joined. The women from her old yoga class swim regularly, but Dominica wanted to swim without their concerned expressions. She'd happened to arrive at the beach at the same time as Helga and Tor a few times, and, before she knew it, they'd formed a flockette of their own.

Tor is in her late thirties and is wearing a Santa hat in honour of the occasion, her bright-purple hair, some of which has turned into dreadlocks, poking out from beneath it. Dominica puts her arm around Tor's skinny tattooed shoulder and gives her an affectionate squeeze.

'Fuuuuuuuuuuuuuuuuuuuuuuuuuu,' Tor mutters, as the bubbly surf gobbles at her toes. 'It's so c . . . c . . . cold.'

'You OK, though?' Dominica checks. She knows how much Tor has suffered with her diagnosis. It's not fair on the poor kid. Dominica is always so impressed with her positive attitude and fortitude.

'Yep,' Tor says, the green diamanté in her nose glinting. 'I'm glad I'm here. Lotte threatened to come, but she's hungover.'

Dominica can imagine it. She's met Lotte, Tor's Dutch girlfriend, a few times and she's quite a force of nature. She gets the impression that Tor likes coming to the beach for a bit of peace and quiet.

'Come on,' Helga declares, in her funny accent – half Danish, half cockney – marching past them. 'Stop dallying, you two. Get in.'

In a couple of strides, Helga's surrendering gracefully to the water, bending her knees, her shoulders sinking. She sighs, as if the sea is a lover welcoming her with a caress. She flips onto her back, her face radiant. She might be the other side of seventy, but, in the water, Helga looks about seven. Her feet pop up as she floats, her arms out to her sides like a quirky otter. Dominica sees her focusing on the bandstand and knows she's working out which way the current is running from the pull on her body in the water. She's a stickler for water safety.

Dominica walks forward with Tor, concentrating on making sure she doesn't hold her breath, but it's a shock nonetheless, bringing her fuzzy brain into focus, like a camera lens. The beach, the land, every thought she had up until just moments ago, is in the past. There's only now. She's tried meditation, but this works much better for calming her scrambled thoughts. A plunge in the sea pushes her mental reset button like nothing else.

She knows that the trick is to get her hands in, so she walks in deeper, her fingertips under the surface, her gloves filling with cold water. She's aware now of the sound of the sea and the sucking shush of the backwash.

The water, which had seemed a clear green from the shore, is tea-coloured up close. A wall of milky builder's brew is coming closer now, rearing up in her vision, and she stands firm, letting the wave sweep her up in its path, lifting her off her feet.

And she's in.

She sighs out through her mouth, like a woman in labour, going through her natural reaction to gasp as the cold hits her spine. She can just see the black shadows of her gloves as she breaststrokes out towards the glittering horizon. The waves are bouncy and the exposed bit of neck at the base of her hair line tingles like a high-top drum. She's aware of her skin – the whole of it – stinging.

Chris, oh Chris, how you'd love this, she thinks, noticing the tears rising, but she's resigned to them. On land, she feels that she's a vessel full of unshed tears that might spring a leak at any time and buckle, but here, where the water inside collides with the water outside, she feels more solid than she has done for days.

She carefully puts her face under the surface, not wanting to get her bobble hat – or her hair – wet. She likes the feeling of violent, masochistic brain freeze, and she takes the opportunity to open her mouth and scream as loudly as she can, knowing that only the sea will know this secret and the others won't hear.

She comes up, the salt taste of the water filling her mouth and nose, the cold seeping into her bloodstream like the delicious relief of a drug.

Pull yourself together, she tells herself. It's been ten months since Chris died. Ten months to find a reason to carry on.

She turns back towards Helga and Tor but she sees that there's a man swimming in between and she realises it's Bill.

'Dominica! I thought it was you.' He's with two other men who look like twins with their beards and red swimming caps, like Santa's little swimmers. 'How have you been?'

'Oh, you know, getting there,' she replies with a weak smile.

She can tell that he's genuinely concerned. His kind face is as engaging as ever.

'We'd love to have you back. Any time you're ready?'

She nods. She's often thought of Bill and the team and how the phone lines must be jammed with a queue of desperate people. She can't help feeling that she's let him down, but she hasn't been able to face going back.

'Well, keep in touch. Happy Christmas.' He gives her a salute and a cheerful grin.

'Who was he?' Helga asks, in her usual direct way.

'Bill. My supervisor at the Samaritans.'

'I don't know how you do it. Other people's problems . . . ' Helga shudders.

'You're not nearly as mean as you make out,' Dominica tells her.

'They say that the path to happiness is by helping other people,' Tor says, flipping over the bobble on her Santa hat so it avoids the wave.

'Yeah, well, you're a saint, Tor, let's not forget,' Helga says.

'Oh, bah humbug,' Dominica teases her.

'Seriously, Dominica,' Tor says, 'you should do it again. You're the best listener I know.'

'I'll think about it.'

'The geese, look, look,' Helga calls, and Dominica turns to see her pointing upwards then follows her gaze. Two geese fly together at speed just overhead, their bellies impossibly white against the blue sky. A pair.

Helga watches Dominica staring at them as they disappear towards the horizon. 'They'll be off to find their flock,' she says, reassuringly, and Dominica nods.

2

The Gravy Arc

Maddy Wolfe wipes the corners of her mouth with the paper napkin, then screws it up and puts it on her empty plate. The starched linen napkins, Murano crystal glasses and Denby bone china plates are all in the dining room on the Christmas table she's so carefully dressed for her Instagram posts. Trent was surprised when they didn't eat lunch in there, but she told him that it wasn't worth getting everything dirty when it was just the two of them, so they've eaten in the snug with the kitchen crockery. She regrets it now. Maybe if they'd eaten a proper Christmas meal they'd have had more to chat about, but, without Jamie, or any relatives to fill the table, the whole festive thing feels like a hollow charade.

She's not going to tell her followers that, though. No, it's important to keep up the illusion on her @made_home channels. The carefully curated photos of the Christmas grotto in the garden and her beautifully decorated table took weeks of planning, but her feeds look gorgeous – even if she says so herself. If Manpreet, the expensive media consultant, is right, she'll soon have enough followers to make the sponsorship deals roll in. That's the plan anyway. But, *God, it's knackering* keeping up with the pressure of it all.

'Thank you,' Trent says, as she picks up his empty plate, but he doesn't meet her eye. He drains the bottle of Malbec into his glass. His cheeks are starting to match the colour of his burgundy golf jumper. His boyish brown curly hair has always been one of his best and most defining features, but he's going grey around his temples and it's thinning on top. 'That was very nice.'

Nice. The word is loaded with disapproval.

'Yes, well, a turkey crown is less wasteful. And we've got some for sandwiches later on,' she says defensively, trying to justify their unremarkable Christmas lunch. She notices, with distaste, that he's picking at some food stuck in his gum line with one of the cocktail sticks from the pigs in blankets.

Is this what they've become? she wonders, as she takes the plates to the kitchen: reduced to conversations about future meals and sandwiches? She hears the echoes of Christmases past, the ones full of relatives, the laughter, her brother's kids and Jamie careening around on new bikes or trikes, the din of new voice-activated toys, George Michael playing in the kitchen, as she and Trent juggled serving up Christmas lunch, whilst getting sloshed. But now, it's like they've turned into her parents.

Things will get back to normal once Trent's property development business is back on track and the deals start rolling in rather than evaporating into thin air, she tells herself. Who *hasn't* had a difficult year? In the general scheme of things, however, she has an enviable roof over her head, designer clothes on her back, embarrassingly expensive highlights in her glossy blonde hair. Really and truly, she doesn't have very much to complain about.

What she needs is to put her feet up on the sofa, with a large gin, she decides. In days gone-by, Trent would have already been on it, making sure she had a drink. She knows he'd pour her one if she asked, but the fact she has to ask spoils it. Like everything else, it's best to do it herself.

She opens the kitchen cupboard, annoyed to see that the Sipsmith gin bottle is almost empty. She's noticed it more now that she's not drinking so much, but Trent has been hoovering up the booze for most of December. Pre-loading, he says, before the promise of a dry January. She waggles the bottle, holding it up to the light, but she's going to need more gin than that to relax properly. She walks out into the utility corridor to get another bottle from her huge walk-in larder by the back door.

A tiny flashing red light next to the rarely used home phone catches her eye. *That's odd. Someone has left a message.* She quickly scans through the possibilities as to the caller's identity, but she's spoken to everyone. Her parents are having lunch in their gazebo with their neighbours in Shropshire, her brothers are all with their families.

How has she missed a call on the home phone? Or Trent, for that matter? He's been here all day.

She picks up the phone and presses the message button. She doesn't dare to wish it, but who else would call on Christmas Day?

Apart from him?

Apart from Jamie . . .

'Mum,' she hears, and she lets out a yelp. It *is* Jamie. Her eyes fill with tears as she waits, listening to him breathing, but he doesn't say anything else. The silence seems to stretch with all the words he can't say. She knows what Trent would want them to be: that Jamie's sorry, that he regrets their terrible row, that he's stopped taking drugs and has pulled himself together.

But Maddy can't help hearing other words in the silence: That he's in trouble; that he needs her; that it's Christmas and he's homesick and weary; that he doesn't know how to come back to her.

The message ends. There's a click.

'No, no, no,' Maddy panics, playing the message over, before realising that in doing so, she accidentally deletes it. 'Fuck!'

Hands shaking, she presses the callback button, hearing the ring tone drone on and on. She grabs a biro from the pot on the counter, but it doesn't work. She yanks open the drawer and grabs a freezer-bag marker and turns over an envelope to write on the back. She does a callback again, making a note of the unfamiliar landline number, then rings directory enquiries. It takes a while to get through, but when she finally speaks to an operator, they tell her that the number belongs to a phone box in Brighton.

Brighton? What's Jamie doing down in Brighton? She calls again, but the number rings and rings. She imagines the empty phone box, seagulls flying overhead, discarded chip packets blowing in the wind.

'Fuck!' she exclaims, smashing the phone back on its casing. She can't bear it. She's missed him. He's not there.

Her mind races with questions as she scrambles to latch on to the fact that she finally has a location for their son. It's like water in a desert.

Jamie left in February, just before the first lockdown, and she's had all year to worry herself sick about where he's gone and what he's doing. Much as she's tried to tell herself that he's a grown-up and must make his own way, his absence sometimes feels all-consuming. Today, like every other day, Jamie was her first guilty thought upon waking.

With so much time to reflect, she can't help feeling that she's let him down. She should have backed him up, but Trent had insisted that they present a united front. And, at the time, she'd agreed. But that plan had backfired spectacularly and, in the row that had ensued, some horrible things had been said that no one can take back.

She'd reported Jamie as a missing person twenty-four hours after he'd stormed out, but she got the impression from the police that they had better things to deal with than a middle-class, middle-aged woman fretting over her adult son leaving after a row. She'd been frantic with worry, but it had been an agonising five days before Jamie had called to tell them that he wasn't missing, but simply gone. She'd thought he might have mellowed, or been ready to forgive – or, even better, contrite and apologetic. But, if anything, he'd only become harder. In a steely voice, he'd informed her that he had no interest in being part of their family any longer. His words, etched for so long on her memory as justification for her letting him go, now make her feel ashamed and unworthy.

She thought Jamie had just been licking his wounds and that he'd come round and come home. How wrong she'd been. About that . . . about everything.

Mum. The word clangs like a gong in her head. What kind of terrible mother is she? He's finally reached out . . . and she wasn't there for him. Maybe he's feeling sentimental. Jamie always loved Christmas when he was little. But then, as an only child, who could blame him? He was always spoilt rotten. She longs to tell him she's bought a tin of Quality Street and is saving him the green triangles. She aches to remind him that they were once a loving family.

She runs back into the kitchen and sees Trent's black iPhone on the counter next to another bottle of wine that he's clearly just opened. She hears the downstairs loo flush.

Jamie hasn't called her mobile and whilst she knows it's ridiculous to think that he might have called Trent, if he was really in trouble, maybe, just maybe, he has.

She picks up the phone. To her surprise, it's unlocked. Trent's practically surgically attached to it twenty-four-seven, so it feels weird holding this familiar yet forbidden gadget in her hands. She looks at the unfamiliar apps and the odd layout of his screen. Seeing a number against the message icon, she automatically presses it. *Please let it be Jamie. Please. . . please.*

But there's no text from Jamie, just a long list of texts from Helen. *Her* friend Helen. Helen Bradbury. Maddy recognises the tiny picture of her face, with her long chestnut brown hair.

A kind of sixth sense kicks in as she clicks on the top text, Jamie and his call momentarily forgotten.

On the screen, there's a picture of Helen sitting in a chair taking an intimate selfie, one that's so explicit it makes Maddy recoil and drop the phone.

Saliva floods her mouth as she steels herself and picks up Trent's phone from where it's spinning on the counter and looks at the picture again, noticing it has a banner over it flashing on the screen. Christmas Surprise WAITING FOR

YOU. Miss you, Babes. There's an animated stream of kisses and heart emojis.

Her skin is pricking all over. It's a heady mixture of shock and a kind of recognition. Because *now* it makes sense. Her and Trent and the distance between them.

It's not because of the stress of work . . . or Covid . . . or Jamie . . .

It's because he's been having an affair. With *Helen fucking Bradbury*.

Holding the phone gingerly, as if the photo of Helen's minge might bite, she opens the call list. Dozens of calls. All from Helen. It's all the proof she needs.

As if propelled by some other force, she calmly replaces the phone face down and then walks over to where the dirty lunch plates are still by the sink. She opens the dishwasher and starts stacking the plates from the side. It's only when she hears Trent arriving in the kitchen that she realises that she hasn't rinsed them with the snazzy hose in the sink.

She pauses, seeing him walk to the bottle of wine, as if everything is completely normal, and she feels a shaft of rage so violent that, before she knows what she's doing, she frisbees the plate across the kitchen with a feral yell. Trent sees it in the nick of time and ducks as it smashes against the doorframe by his head and clatters to the floor in large chunks.

'Maddy! What the fuck?' he shouts.

She pauses only long enough to see that a splatter of turkey gravy has speckled the white stone tiles and blonde-wood kitchen units in a rather stylish arc, before she plucks another plate and chucks it in his direction.

It's like she's having an out-of-body experience and can see herself from the Bang and Olufsen speaker in the top corner like a wide-eyed spectator on *Gogglebox*. *She's really bloody doing it. She's actually snapped.*

'You shit. I hate you,' Maddy screams. The release of these words feels majestic. Her rage feels all-consuming – like she's plugged into an electricity socket.

'Jesus! Stop it! Calm down.' Trent inches forward, tentatively patting the air.

Maddy stares at him, seeing him for what he is – a red-faced adulterous stranger. She storms towards him and picks up his phone from the counter. She presses it so violently against his chest he falls backwards.

She swoops down and re-joins her corporal self as she plucks the car keys from the reclaimed console table in the hall and swings her tote onto her shoulder. Slamming the wood and glass front door as hard as she possibly can, she notes that the wreath that she made by hand, which got over a thousand likes on her feed, has sprung off the door in solidarity and tumbled to the floor. She stalks out to the Porsche Cayenne on the gravel drive, opens the door and gets in, only realising then that she's still in her Ugg slippers. It's no matter. Her gym kit is in the boot.

Trent is on the front doorstep shouting, but she doesn't wind down the window as he kicks the wreath. A string of lights – one of the twenty that Maddy put up single-handedly – falls and he battles with it like Indiana Jones being attacked by a snake. She beeps the electric gates and drives out of the driveway.

The white-hot anger still radiates from her.

She turns out of the lane and heads south. She's going to find her son.

3

Everybody's Having Fun

Tor mainly works out of the cramped Home Help office in town, coordinating the food bank donations and the charity admin, but thanks to Brexit and Covid, she's lost most of her volunteers and runs the outreach catering van herself with Greg and Arek.

Now she gives out the last mustard-coloured polystyrene carton from the thermal bag in the back of the van and stamps her feet. The temperature has plummeted, and she blows into her cupped hands, wishing she had thicker gloves than the cheap fingerless ones she has on. Having come straight to her shift from her swim earlier, she hasn't had the chance to properly warm up.

She jumps down from the van and starts to clear up. She knows she needs to get in the warm soon, remembering now, too late, that she's forgotten to take her dose of methotrexate. She reminds herself to accept her condition with good grace. After all, it could be a lot worse. When she started losing weight a few months ago, with no reasonable explanation, she thought she might have cancer, or something properly nasty. Then her joints had started aching, her toes and ankles feeling as if they'd been stuck with glue. She progressed onto thinking that she must have Covid-19, but then, after a blood test, she was told that she had Rheumatoid Arthritis. She was stunned. She thought only old ladies got it, but apparently not.

It was Lotte, ever her princess knight in shining armour, who threw herself into researching RA, presenting Tor with several articles on cold water swimming, along with some glittery jelly shoes. It helped some people by taking down the inflammation, she explained, and was surely worth a go? After that first freezing dip in the sea, there was no turning back. The sea is Tor's drug and her salvation.

Tor feels a kind of pride in her stoicism and forbearance, especially when Alice, her twin sister, regularly declares that Tor's a 'mentalist' for going in the sea in the winter. Alice only deigns to go in the Med in August. But then, Alice has always been a hypochondriac, scamming their mother into days off school and perpetuating the myth of her 'delicate' constitution, like she's some kind of heroine from a Jane Austen novel, when actually she's as tough as old boots.

Tor could tell her the truth, of course, but she won't. She's not going to give Alice any kind of ammunition to hold over her. Besides, there's no point in bitching about her health when she has so much more to be grateful for in her life than the homeless people she deals with at work. Especially on a day like today.

There's a low rumble of voices under the awning they've rigged up, as the crowd prod the meagre contents of their boxes. The air smells of cigarettes, damp clothes and school dinners. It's impossible to tell, looking at the crowd, whether they're young or old, men or women. What unites them is their defensive body language, their mismatched layers of hoodies and jackets, and their general resignation. This is usually a jolly event, but the Covid restrictions have made everyone more guarded and ground down.

Slade's 'Merry Xmas Everybody' is playing on the van's speaker – one of the Christmas songs that particularly grates on Tor's nerves. That's one good thing about Christmas being over soon; she can finally stop playing these dreadful cheery songs, because their over-sung trite lyrics only seem to augment how strained this charity event really is. Because, no, *Noddy*, not everyone is having fun. OK, maybe apart from Vic.

She can smell him before he arrives. She knows for a fact that he used to wash every day in the public toilets on the seafront and was horrified when they closed during lockdown.

'It's Christmas,' Vic sings in a silly voice, gurning as he gives Tor his empty food box and she puts it in the black bin bag. His straggly beard is caught in the sling of a grubby medical mask and he licks gravy off his dirty finger with relish.

'Best turkey I've had in years. Reminded me of being a boy in Margate.'

'Is that where did you used to live?'

'We used to have wonderful Christmases,' he says. 'Big tree. The works.'

Tor listens patiently, knowing Vic likes to talk, knowing too that this might be the first and last friendly conversation that he'll have all day. He lost everything when his family kicked him out for drinking and, after he did time in Lewes jail, they made themselves impossible to find. Tor knows that if *her* only option was to live in a bus shelter like Vic, she'd probably drink Frosty Jack's for breakfast too. Who wouldn't? But Vic has a jolly disposition and seems to accept his lot.

A young lad she hasn't seen before nods at her as he puts his empty food box in the bag.

'You all right?' she asks. 'You got somewhere to go for the lockdown?'

Despite the PM, Boris, 'giving' everyone Christmas, the government has announced another lockdown. It's awful for people who are homeless.

The young guy nods. He's probably barely twenty, judging from his patchy beard, but his face is ravaged by familiar signs of despair, his hands shaking – possibly from withdrawal. Tor sees that all the time and her heart goes out to him. She knows how easy and alluring the drugs trap is – how young men like him are sitting targets for the scumbags who get the vulnerable hooked. She knows how impossible it is to escape. He shuffles back towards the street, and she wants to call after him and to say something encouraging, but the moment passes, and she feels the usual sinking feeling of not having done enough.

She knows these people can find shelter, although the rough sleepers like Vic baulk at what's on offer. But, even with the best will in the world, the hostels and temporary accommodation hardly constitute a home, especially at Christmas. She feels deeply for these poor people who can't put down any roots. It's so exhausting having to move on all the time.

She smiles across at Arek now, who starts to dismantle the awning. He was in the army in Poland and is a wall of muscle. She doesn't know what she'd do without his strong arms. He usually works on a building site but having been helped by the

19

charity when he first came to Brighton and got clean, he now helps other people. He's a genuinely good guy.

'I have to go soon. Give my wife a break. The baby was up all night,' he says. 'What are you up to, Tor?'

'Warming up. I'm freezing from my swim earlier. Then it's the family Zoom.'

Tor is rather dreading the forced family chat and how it will undoubtedly make things awkward with Lotte. She promised Lotte ages ago that she'll 'out' them to her family, as Lotte has to her parents in Amsterdam, but Lotte's are a liberal bunch and the opposite of her parents in Tunbridge Wells. But as Tor contemplates dropping the 'actually I'm gay' bomb into the Christmas Zoom, she already knows she'll chicken out.

Her parents still can't understand the whole thing with Mike. Her ex's parents are good friends of theirs and Tor knows that they used to plot and gossip about Tor and Mike's imagined nuptials and shared grandchildren. The disappointment of Tor calling off their ten-year relationship is still raw – even now, all these years on. She regrets carrying on the doomed relationship for so long and for not coming clean. Of course she'd known all along she was gay – and for a long while suspected that Mike secretly might be too. Their relationship was hardly sexually charged. But then Tor had started to fool around in secret and she'd plucked up the courage to leave, grabbing an opportunity to work for a charity in Africa. She'd stayed in Burkina Faso for six years. When she'd moved back to the UK, she'd headed straight for Brighton and her single life had been a whole load of much-needed fun. But then she'd moved into their shared house and Lotte had dazzled her.

It had been a laugh at first – a naughty fling. Something

serious between them was never going to be on the cards. Outgoing Lotte, with her huge personality, surely couldn't possibly be right for Tor, but somehow, against all the odds, something between them just clicked. She owes it to Lotte to tell her family, so they can potentially move on to the next stage of their relationship, but she doesn't quite have the nerve.

'Well, merry Christmas,' Arek says.

'You too.'

'Hey, Tor. Smile,' he adds. 'We did good today.'

4

New Friendship Turf

'We haven't had anyone in for a while,' the Airbnb owner tells Maddy, as she unlocks the door to the flat in the dilapidated red-brick apartment block, 'because of . . . well, you know . . . it's been tough.' Her cheeks are ruddy, her eyebrows unkempt.

If any hotels here in Brighton had been open for business, Maddy might have booked a suite, but instead she'd turned to Airbnb in desperation. Sitting in the car park in Pease Pottage services, on the way down from Cobham, she'd sent over twenty messages to various hosts and had almost given up hope, when a message for this place had pinged up. Even so, the owner had been wary of a short-term let. Maddy had persuaded her by paying up front for a fortnight. A central flat with a sea view and private parking is gold dust, after all.

She hadn't been expecting a palace, but the flat, purposely done up in neutral colours, is bleaker than she'd been expecting. It occurs to her now that maybe she's made a mistake by being so dramatic and leaving home so emphatically. Perhaps she should have gone straight round to Lisa's. Her best friend would undoubtedly have taken her in with open arms. But she knows Lisa has a houseful and Maddy's troubles are too huge to dump – even on her best friend – on Christmas afternoon.

In the kitchenette she opens the fridge and is assaulted by a blast of mouldy air.

'TV works,' the owner says, aiming the remote at the flat screen on the wall. The fairy glitter tinkle of a Christmas advert fills the room, followed by canned applause as Michael McIntyre's *Christmas Wheel* comes on. Maddy thinks of all the families around the country slumped on their sofas watching it.

She can tell the owner is itching to ask more questions. After all, there's obviously a juicy backstory to a single woman turning up on Christmas Day out of the blue, but Maddy manoeuvres her to the door, taking the keys from her.

When she's gone, Maddy sits on the thin arm of the cheap sofa bed and turns the TV off. In the flat next door, she can hear muffled classical music.

She puts her hands between her knees, her chunky diamond rings cutting into her toned thighs, and lets out a low groan. Her steely resolve has deflated on her journey here into a baggy, saggy airbag of defeat. She's being ridiculous, right? She's gone too far. What the hell is she doing here in this awful flat, in a place where she doesn't know a soul? She's fifty-two, for God's sake. She should just quit now and drive back to her nice warm home.

She can so easily picture the scene: Trent contrite and apologetic. He'll agree to therapy, he'll delete Helen's number and then he'll run her a bath. He'll bring her an iced Baileys and she will soak the day away in the Emotional Detox Bath Soak she got for Christmas in the extravagant Space NK gift box. Then she can change into her embroidered silk pyjamas, put on her lavender eye mask and pretend that today never happened.

But no. She can't. The fantasy pops. She can't pretend. Not any more.

Trent and Helen. Helen and Trent. The awful truth of it pulses in her mind.

Is it just a fling? A naughty liaison, or are they together? As in planning on being together permanently? The thought feels terrifying. Has Trent been planning to leave her? End their marriage? And what about Helen's? Alex, her husband, is not the kind of person to set the world on fire, but from the few times Maddy has met him, she can see he's a good person. He's reliable and dependable, a good dad with a successful business and an impressive golf handicap. How could Helen and Trent even think about exploding everyone's lives? The fallout is just too huge. Or do they think Maddy and Alex are just collateral damage? Because what about Helen's kids? Lois and Max? Is Trent planning on being a father figure to them? It's unthinkable.

But she's jumping to conclusions, she tells herself. It must just be a sex thing. A mistake. A silly fling that will be over just as soon as it began.

With a shaky sigh, she picks up her phone, noticing a cascade of Instagram likes and emojis for her Christmas posts. She's tempted to reply to the messages, but she can't summon up the necessary cheeriness.

There are direct messages everywhere – on WhatsApp, Instagram and Messenger, some from Trent, but most from Lisa, saying the same thing: CALL ME.

It clearly didn't take long for the jungle drums to start, then. She steels herself and presses Lisa's number.

'Oh, thank God. You're alive,' Lisa says. Her best friend does sound genuinely relieved. 'Hang on.' In the background, Maddy can hear music and the rumpus of a board game being played at the kitchen table. Tess, Jamie's contemporary, who graduated last year from uni, is home with her gorgeous boyfriend, plus Lisa's stepkids. There's a shout as someone puts down a winning card. She's always been a bit envious of Lisa's large brood.

'Maddy, what the hell? Are you all right?' Lisa asks, clearly moving out of the kitchen to the privacy of the corridor.

'I'm fine.' Maddy's voice cracks. She's not fine. Not remotely fine and hearing Lisa's voice makes tears of self-pity jam in her throat. Her concern feels like the warm hug she needs right now. But then Lisa has been through everything with her since they first met in a graduate training programme when they were twenty-two. They've shared the privilege of a lifetime having each other's backs.

'Is it true? I heard you'd . . . well, that you and Trent . . . ' Lisa starts.

Trent must have called Lisa, assuming that would be the first place Maddy would have gone. But now that she knows what a liar Trent is, she feels compelled to check.

'Who told you?'

'Helen.'

Maddy hadn't been expecting this.

'Don't talk to me about that *whore*,' Maddy spits.

'Oh God,' Lisa groans. 'Oh, babes, the thing is she thought you knew. You know . . . about her and Trent.'

25

'You mean, *you* knew? About them?' Maddy squeezes her eyes shut, trying to make sense of what Lisa has just said. 'Why would she think I would be OK about her *fucking my husband*?' Her voice has risen hysterically. 'And why didn't you tell me? Why, Lis? Why? *If you knew*?'

There's a dreadful, strained silence as Lisa realises her own culpability. Her admission has put them into new friendship territory. Maddy waits for an explanation. She can picture Lisa putting her hand on her gin-fogged brow. She, by contrast, has never felt more sober.

'I don't know. I wanted to warn you, but it's just you and Trent . . . you don't seem to . . . well, you're more focused on your career than him and . . . ' Lisa is furiously backtracking.

'And that gives Helen the right to . . . ? Jesus!' Maddy explodes, not believing what she's hearing. 'How long? And don't lie, Lis. Just tell me the truth. How long has it been going on? With her?'

'Two, maybe three.'

'Weeks? *Months?*'

There's an ominous silence. 'Lisa?'

'Years,' she says quickly and Maddy knows she's squeezing her eyes shut.

The betrayal feels like Lisa's punched her. Humiliation is the knock-out upper cut that floors Maddy entirely. A *three-year* affair, going on behind her back. So not a fling then. A relationship. A serious relationship. And Lisa let it happen without warning her?

'Maddy, please,' Lisa starts, begging for understanding, but Maddy is so furious, she throws the phone with all her might against the wall with a feral yell.

As soon as it's out of her hand, she knows this is the worst act of self-sabotage yet.

'No,' she gasps, springing across the room, seeing the shattered screen. She turns it on and off, but the phone is dead. 'No, no, no, no, no.'

There's a lull in the noise on the other side of the wall. Have the neighbours heard her?

Quietly, she gets up and puts the smashed phone on the coffee table, the parts dropping along with her tears. She takes a shuddery intake of breath and walks over to the window, suddenly needing some air.

She nudges aside the blind. There are two buildings opposite – hardly the sea view the listing had promised, but there's a sliver of moonlight on the black sea in between. She has never, ever felt more alone in her whole life.

She leans her head against the cold window as she starts to sob.

5

Pilcharding

There's a view to the pier through the chimneys on the rooftop of Helga's fisherman's cottage. As she gets up from where she's been using the last of the grout to fix the leaking skylight, she catches sight of the starlings. The murmuration is breathtaking in the dusky light. She loves how their flick-flacking antics create shadow shapes against the white sky, as they swoop and dive in unison. She knows the clever starlings group together to flummox the falcons who might otherwise pick them off, but they also look like they're having fun, and she wonders if they're swapping tips and information about their days before they settle down to roost under the shelter of the iron pier. She shades her eyes as more squadrons of starlings join the ranks and there's a huge twisting mass of them, turning the sky momentarily into the shape of a whale.

She unhooks the empty canister from the black sealant gun and wipes her hands on her canvas dungarees. She thinks briefly of Mette and how horrified her niece would be if she could see her now. Mette, with her big corporate job and perfect apartment, wouldn't countenance doing any kind of DIY herself which makes Helga even prouder of her efforts. Mette is always telling Helga she can't do things now that she's over seventy. She thinks that she needs to go back to Denmark to be near her, but much as Helga loves her, the idea doesn't really appeal. Mette is fairly controlling and Helga knows their relationship works best with some sea and land mass between them.

Remembering that she's got some bird seed in her pocket, she takes some in her fist and sprinkles it on the little patch of asphalt for the wood pigeon. His brown-grey chest has a rainbow sheen and the white ring around his neck looks like a handsome ruff.

'Night, night,' she says. The bird takes a few steps towards her, spreads his wings then folds them back, slotting them in with a little wiggle. He nods his head and makes a coo that sounds like a friendly chuckle. 'Don't take any grief from them, OK?' She nods over to the chimney stack where the seagulls live. She calls them Terry and Julie, after The Kinks' song 'Waterloo Sunset'. It used to be her and Linus's song. Terry often pecks at the kitchen door and Helga lets him in and feeds him scraps. He's particularly partial to a bit of bacon rind.

At the end of April, he and Julie will take it in turns to incubate their eggs. They usually have three or four chicks in May and then Helga won't be able to venture out onto the roof. She knows the neighbours will probably complain again about the noise. Not the nice couple next door, but the nasty woman with her no-good boyfriend on the other side. They can't stand the squawking in the morning, but, as Helga pointed out, there's no point in calling the RSPB, as the gulls are classed as migratory birds and therefore protected by law.

It annoys her that people have got it in for the seagulls. Why can't they accept that these beautiful white marauders are part of the landscape? The ways she sees it, the clever seagulls have a lot more of a right to be by the sea than the people. She's always secretly amused when the tourists get their ice creams and chips stolen, although the council bang on about the fact that seagulls can carry E. coli and harmful bacteria. But Helga can't fathom all this ridiculous health and safety nonsense. What ever happened to common sense? She often thinks the world has gone mad.

Taking care with her footing, she backs down through the hatch with her metal tool box, bolting the loft access securely above her head and holding on to the rung. She feels dizzy for a moment and squeezes her eyes shut until the feeling passes.

She thinks of *Sheelagh*, her boat, and how she used to go below deck for the night in the middle of the Atlantic. How it made her feel safe and vulnerable all at the same time. Safe because she was out of the elements, vulnerable because she wasn't in them looking out for danger. A firm atheist, she nevertheless always used to say a prayer to Poseidon, the God of the sea, to protect her, and he always had.

She glances up at the glass case full of her dusty sailing trophies, remembering the feeling of salt on her skin, her hand on a tiller, the wind in her face. She misses that feeling of sailing towards the horizon, not knowing what might happen. She might feel like she's still twenty-five, but she's old enough to know that her sailing days are sadly behind her. She can't afford it, for starters, and anyway, her confidence has gone. She hasn't got the nerve for solo-sailing any more and she couldn't sail with anyone else. It's bad enough living in a terrace with other people around; there's no way she could share a cabin with anyone.

But still her heart yearns for the sea and that's why she swims, because only by getting back to her natural element can she pretend that everything is still a possibility.

She decides to put another shout-out on the WhatsApp for a swim in the morning. Hopefully Dominica will come again. It'll do her good.

Despite her good intentions, however, Helga oversleeps. Her heart palpitations kept her awake in the small hours again, despite her trying her deep breathing tricks. She's damned if she's going to the doctor – not that they're seeing patients in the flesh. She doesn't want some do-gooder putting her on pills that will make her feel weird.

When Helga arrives at their usual spot, there's a dampness to the morning air and the sea is rougher than she'd been expecting. She already knows it's going to be chilly getting in, but that's no bad thing. She loves the sea, however its mood, and knows that its cold embrace will wash away the fears of the night.

She's pleased to see that Dominica and Tor are waiting by the groyne. She hasn't seen them since their swim a few days ago at Christmas. Not that Helga took much notice of Christmas. She'd whiled away the day painting and eating toast.

Tor is stamping her feet, keeping warm. She's wearing a camouflage-pattern sea vest over her costume.

'What do you reckon?' Tor asks Helga as she arrives, putting down her bag and already toe-heeling off her canvas shoes.

Helga can always predict the temperature of the sea within one degree and can tell which way the tide is going, and the current is running, but today is a little confusing. The sea is a foaming mass of clashing peaks. She puts her nose up, feeling the wind on her face. South-westerly. Coming up to a four on the wind scale, she reckons.

'It's a bit rough, don't you reckon?' Dominica asks.

Helga nods. 'I agree. Let's pilchard. Now we're here.'

She changes quickly and together they walk to the water's edge, where the waves are breaking, fighting each other to reach the beach, overlapping and jostling like boys in a playground around a football. The gulls caw overhead, wings out, stationary as they ride the wind.

Helga sits down on the stones and leans back on her elbows, as if she's on a sunlounger. She nods at Tor, who follows her lead and sits on the cold stones. They're freezing under her bum. She likes pilcharding, though. It's the best way of getting soaked and enjoying the benefit of going in the sea, without swimming.

Up close, the stones glisten in the weak sunshine; tan and brown and black, they seem to chatter as the sea moves them. At eye level the sea is a busy torrent of foam. She braces herself for the next wave, gripping on to the shore, the backwash dragging her in, as if the sea is trying to claim her.

'She's boisterous today.'

Suddenly, a much larger wave rolls over Tor and she's tussled in its clutches, the water going up her nose.

'It's like being in a washing machine,' she gasps, coming up for air, but she's laughing, the water plastering her long purple hair in fronds across her face, like seaweed.

Dominica has been dragged in with the backwash. She finds her footing but only just as another wave hits.

'I've got pebbles where no pebbles should ever go,' she says, laughing, when Tor finally reaches her. Walking, even in this knee-deep water, makes them both look like they are dragging ten tonne weights behind them. They hold hands with Helga too and pull her away from the clutches of the next wave. Helga loves seeing Dominica's face light up with that knockout smile of hers. The mix of laughter and the sea is the best medicine she knows.

They lie down again where the waves lick the shore, giggling like little children. Helga splashes her arms then lifts them up, unwittingly gulping in sea water as the next wave hits her in the face, but she doesn't care. This is magic.

6

Resolutions

'You're going now?' Pim yawn talks, his tone somehow accusatory. Claire used to find him so sexy in the mornings, but he's grown a beard in lockdown, which hides most of his face. Without his glasses, he squints at her across the pillows of their bed.

Pim's green irises are rimmed with a thick line of black and always used to remind her of Shah Rukh Khan, her favourite Bollywood star to whom he used to bear a passing resemblance. She wonders whether the 'King of Bollywood' has gone to seed in quite the same way as Pim has in recent months. 'It won't even be open.'

She resents him for questioning her plan. He does that a lot these days. He doesn't get it that, if she leaves now, she'll be the first person into the supermarket, and she can get back out and home before the boys are up.

'I promised Ash a fry-up and we're out of hash browns.'

'He can survive without them. We're drowning in food.'

How little he knows his own children. He doesn't know that

they have eaten every single snack in the house, as well as both tins of Celebrations (although Claire had a hand in that). So they're not *drowning* in food, and whilst he's right – Ash can survive without hash browns – Claire has a long list of other items she needs to get. It's a full-time job keeping up with the boys' voracious appetites.

'Stay,' he urges, throwing an arm across her, but she shuffles out from under his hairy embrace, feeling another flush coming on. She's spent the night veering between being as hot as the surface of the sun, and then, just as suddenly, being freezing cold. And all of that on top of the dreaded insomnia that got her in its grip again last night. She's been hatching her shopping plan since before dawn and now she can't bear to spend another second in bed.

But she still gives Pim a guilty smile and he groans again, putting his face in the pillow, knowing he's lost. As she puts on her robe, she glances back at him in bed, his arm across her sweaty side of the bed. She knows what he's probably thinking: that the boys are asleep. It's the Christmas holidays and this is a rare chance for a lie-in. A rare chance to have sex.

It's been months since they've done it, but she seems to have mislaid her libido. It's not even to do with Pim; it's just that all sexual feelings seem to have left her body. As in completely gone. Left the building. Even her dirtiest fantasies leave her cold and indifferent. And to think, she was once known as the randiest girl in Galway.

Listening to Ash's bedroom door, then Felix's, and hearing both of them snoring, she pads softly to the bathroom, noticing the loo seat is up, even though she's told the boys and Pim about this a thousand times. She notices the damp patch on the lino. *How do they all manage to miss the toilet pan?*

She tries to assert herself in these matters, of course, and to stop them all treating her like she's a domestic skivvy. Even Victorian scullery maids got time off occasionally, she often points out, but it's relentless in this household. She knows she's the one who needs to change it, but it's hard. Yesterday, she asked Felix to clean the bathroom, but he took the cloth and spray she gave him to his room and forgot all about it. She got so sick of asking him to do it that, in the end, she landed up doing it herself.

As she mops up the floor with loo roll, she realises that she's bleeding. It's her first period in almost six months. It's weird that she hasn't had the usual warning signs, but then again, her cycle seems to be all over the place. She has a love-hate relationships with periods. Having spent the most part of a decade trying to get pregnant and failing, before IVF helped her get Felix, she wept every time one of them appeared. Then Ash came of his own accord, without warning. These days, she spends just as much time wondering what happened to her regular-as-clockwork periods. She wishes she could talk to a friend about what's happening and how her erratic cycle and the hot flushes almost certainly herald the onset of her menopause. She thinks about broaching the subject with one of her sisters in Ireland, but having not seen them all year, she feels too estranged to have such a personal chat.

Anyway, she can only imagine what Siobhan would say if Claire admitted that, despite spending twenty-four-seven with Pim because of the lockdown, she feels more distant from him than ever. She's too ashamed to admit that she often feels, if not lonely, then certainly detached from the fun-loving person she used to be. Her sister would probably say that Claire's on a rocky road if she fancies going to Aldi more than she fancies her husband. And she'd probably be right.

The Brighton seafront is practically deserted apart from a lone figure who walks across the pedestrian crossing, his shoulders hunched. Claire slows down in the car and waits at the red traffic light and tunes in to the local radio station. There's an advert on. They want to find community heroes and she feels her own lack of purpose keenly as she meets the kid's eyes through the windscreen. He looks utterly dejected and, although she doesn't like to make assumptions about his status, she'd bet he's homeless.

Not that she can have any kind of conversation with Pim about someone like him, not when he's incensed at the council paying for hotel rooms for the homeless during Covid. He was appalled that one of their local hotels got trashed, the residents ripping out the fixtures and fittings to sell on, probably for money to score with.

But Claire can't help thinking of all the things that must have gone wrong for the guy to look so dejected. She watches him shuffling off up Preston Street and she feels guilty at her privilege, for her warm home, for the fact she's off to buy yet more Christmas food.

The green man on the pedestrian crossing turns to red, but just as she's setting off, she stalls the car and swears. She's glad Pim isn't here to witness her clumsiness. She thinks of her husband lying in bed and feels another guilty pang of regret that she didn't stay, but no doubt he'll have gone back to sleep, and she tells herself that he deserves to be there. It won't be long before he's back in the classroom and in front of the screen all day again.

He's found it horrible being at home all the time and, if she's honest, him being at home hasn't been a bundle of laughs for her either. She has to pussyfoot around, hardly making a sound, so that Pim can Zoom all day. It's exhausting trying to be invisible. It's only supermarket shopping that gives her a break from it all.

But even the thought that she needs time away from her family makes her feel unworthy and wretched. She knows the whole Covid thing has been much worse for the kids, although Ash says he's happy being at home. But she worries he's not developing the social skills he should. Much as she loves her baby being her baby, he's nearly ten and she knows he needs to branch out on his own. Felix is just as much of a worry, and his teenage years suddenly feel all too imminent. He only seems to communicate with her in grunts and she resents the fact that he and Pim spend hours and hours playing Fortnite. And now they've corrupted Ash too. But if blowing things up on a screen is what makes them happy and gets them through until life gets a bit more normal, then, according to Pim, they should just go with it. So Claire puts up and shuts up.

She'll make a date and walnut cake for teatime, as a treat, she decides, mentally adding baking powder to her shopping list. She's annoyed that she can't reach her handbag for her notebook to write it down. Her brain is like a sieve these days. The boys relentlessly take the piss about her forgetfulness. Even Pim had joined in on Christmas Day, when they'd mimicked her clicking her fingers and saying, 'pass me the thingummybob in the whatsit.' It has become a family catchphrase. She knows they mean it affectionately, but it stings nevertheless.

As she sets off, she glances across to the beach, surprised to see a few women playing in the waves in the distance. The way they bend over with laughter makes her do a double take. It looks like they're having fun.

On Christmas morning, when a few of the neighbours were out on the street, Claire had gone outside to catch her neighbour, Jenna, and wish her happy Christmas. She'd been dressed in one of those giant camouflage Dryrobes and was off to the beach with a gang of friends. Jenna had told Claire to come too, but Claire had declined. She's forty-four and the days of exposing her body to the public are long gone. She'd feel far too flabby and saggy in front of super-fit Jenna and her shiny friends.

Maybe she should push herself out of her comfort zone and go next time though, she thinks. With the new year coming, she needs to do something to shake things up. She can't keep on making resolutions and breaking them. Even so, she reaches across the dashboard to the cubbyhole, where she knows Ash has left half a packet of Tangfastics. The new regime can start in January.

7

Scatter Cushions

It's ridiculous, Maddy thinks, that she's become so reliant on her phone for all her basic functions that, now that it's broken, she's rendered helpless. She pays for everything on her wallet app and, having left her actual wallet in her parka pocket at home, she can't even buy a cheap replacement. She's cobbled together eleven pounds in cash from the pockets of her gym bag, but she knows it's not going to go very far and that she's going to have to face the music.

Even with no traffic it takes over an hour to get home. She'd been in such a state when she'd left that she hadn't noticed the distance, but she's exhausted by the time she gets to Cobham. She stops the car in the drive, glad that Trent's car isn't here. She notices that the wreath and Christmas lights have been left in a tangled heap by the front door. Everything had looked so pristine and welcoming on Christmas morning, but now her home looks strange and worrying to her – like a relative in a coma.

She feels her eyes fill with unexpected tears as she gets out of the car. What had she been expecting? That her home would welcome her back? That it would make everything OK? After all, this is the home that she famously built from scratch, documenting the whole process in her @made_home log and Instagram account. She's shared everything: from bidding on the ugly bungalow that had once stood on this patch of land, to driving the bulldozer that had razed it to the ground. Every roof tile, window frame, radiator fixing and light bulb she's painstakingly chosen herself, and that's all before the eye-catching décor and snazzy furniture. She knows at least five people who have used her Moroccan-inspired tile scheme in their own bathrooms.

She's made out that a project like this is a breeze. All you need is a vision and a knack for a bargain. With considerable effort, she's managed to maintain the illusion that this is a fun-filled space in which she entertains her many friends. A space that's simultaneously cosy, cool and romantic. The whole point had been to build a home in which she could live out 'her best life', as she's hashtagged so many times.

God. If only people knew the truth.

Letting herself into the silent house makes her heart physically hurt and it occurs to her that what makes a home isn't a building or a designer kitchen; it's more intangible than that. Home is the atmosphere inside the walls. There isn't a hashtag for the kind of atmosphere she feels right now. At least not one she could possibly share. She's used to constantly plumping, preening and picturing the various nooks and crannies of her home, but, for the first time, she feels a sense of shame.

She remembers now how judgemental she used to be about the kids in Jamie's class who came from a 'broken home' and how she'd encouraged him not to be friends with them, like they were unlucky or tainted in some way. Parents who'd divorced. Parents who were alcoholics. Everyone who'd distastefully outed their problems in public, lumped together in her judgemental view.

But it's easy to break a home, it turns out. It's taken until today for her to see how a home can appear to be so solid, but it's made up of the invisible strands of goodwill and honesty by its occupants. Kindness is the thing that holds it together. Kindness is its glue. Without that, it breaks.

Trent hasn't cleared up in her absence. There's washing-up in the sink. Out of habit, she steps towards the dishwasher and opens it, but then remembers the last time she was standing right here . . . and why . . . and she goes instead to the study, grabbing a few empty bags from the hall cupboard on the way.

Her old iPhone is in the drawer of her desk. She takes it, along with some carefully filed paperwork about her phone contract, her passport and car insurance. She notices the brown edges of her prayer plant and goes to fill up the designer watering can in the loo. She comes back and drenches the poor plant, wondering whether she should take it with her. It's not until that very moment that she understands that she's not staying.

Full of grim resolve, she takes the stairs two at a time up to Jamie's room. She re-decorated it when he left. It had been a disgrace, with its bongs and blimp-holed duvet cover, but maybe she should have kept it for him as it was. Isn't that what proper parents do? Keep a shrine to their absent child? Like in the movies.

She tried to picture him in the room where he must be living now. She hopes it's a nice one, but she doubts it. Since she's

42

been in Brighton, she's learnt some sobering facts about what might have happened to Jamie and it's starting to look bleak. She knows he's not living somewhere permanent. It would have been wishful thinking, but he hasn't taken out a mortgage, or registered on the electoral role. He's not paying council tax, as far as she's been able to find out. She has no way of knowing whether he's even still in Brighton at all. She picks up the framed photo of him and then puts his school photo into one of the bags too.

She steels herself and goes into her bedroom. Or 'the boudoir' as she calls it, in a slightly tongue-in-cheek way, on her feeds. She's had such fun making it a deliberately sexy, intimate, exciting space. It's even got a cute little metal and velvet bar she salvaged from Paris. Oh God. *Have Trent and Helen done it in here? Has Trent committed that ultimate sacrilege. Has Helen used her towels, her shampoo, her face creams?*

The bed isn't made, the scatter cushions falling from the chaise onto the floor with a recklessness that makes her picture Trent sitting up in bed and throwing them with force across the room. He knows how she likes the bedroom to be left tidily, as she often uses its petrol blue and gold chinoiserie walls as a backdrop for her lives and reels. There's an empty bottle of wine by Trent's side of the bed and a glass with an inch of drying claret.

Her mind can't stop picking at the fact of her husband's tawdry infidelity, as she re-stacks the scatter cushions in their careful colour order. Maybe on some fundamental level, she's never really trusted him. Not after he pulled her in a bar in Mayfair and, after she slept with him on the first night, she found out that he was already engaged. He dumped his fiancée for her, which at the time he spun as the most romantic gesture ever, but now she sees it for what it was: cruel.

She hugs a brocade cushion to her chest, as she thinks about how cruel it is too that he's shared his feelings with Helen and not her. He must have been having an affair before Jamie left. So Helen must have known how tense things had been at home. Now Maddy doesn't know what bothers her more – the fact that Helen must have been gloating behind her back, or that Trent found solace in her arms, when Maddy had been hurting so much herself.

Trent and Helen. Helen and Trent. Has he fallen in love? More in love with Helen than he had been with her? Because he must have serious feelings if it's been going on for three years. Three years. And *everyone knew*. Except her.

She thumps the pillow against the stack with unnecessary force. She's always prided herself on being perceptive, so how didn't she see what was going on right under her nose? Even in lockdown? She tries to think back over the past months and how, apart from on their wedding anniversary, there hasn't been much sex.

There used to be a lot more. Years ago, she and Trent were at it like rabbits. But not since her menopause kicked in and she went on HRT. Trent had been patient and understanding. Of course he had been. He'd been getting his end away elsewhere.

Objectively speaking, she can see how Helen might have easily lured her horny husband. She was always a go-getter, that one. Maddy saw that the first time at the PTA meeting and Helen, who only had a child in year one at that point, was already intent on bossing the school fête.

44

Oh yes, Helen must have loved the thrill of reeling him in, although it can't have been difficult. Trent was charming when he wanted to be, plus he was very generous, and he was in good shape. *Oh, God*, she thinks, remembering the cross trainer she bought him for his fiftieth. He was obsessed with it and lost nearly a stone and now she understands why. She's unwittingly trimmed him up for another woman.

She takes her trusted Paul Smith holdall from the top shelf of her walk-in closet and starts packing her clothes. She spent so long planning this little haven of a room with its purpose-built shoe racks and jumper shelves. Its movement-activated light-up mirrors have always made her feel like a film star, but now, as she catches her reflection, without the flattery of the clever bells and whistles she uses on the images she posts, she looks . . . *old. No wonder Trent doesn't find me attractive any more.*

She thinks of her forthcoming appointment with Jackie, the beautician, who comes to the house and gives her face a regular 'spruce'. She'll have to cancel the much-needed session. How can she see Jackie when she probably knows all about Helen and Trent too? It had been Maddy herself who'd given Helen Jackie's number not long after they'd first become friends, after Helen had commented on how 'fresh' Maddy always looked. Maddy had shared the secret of their inner circle, revealing that Jackie 'did' all of their friends. But Helen hadn't been admiring her; she'd just been trying to gain a competitive edge. It feels like such a gross betrayal of the sisterhood.

A little self-pitying sob escapes her as she packs her thermals, jeans, and comfortable shoes, then goes downstairs to the boot room to find her walking boots and coat. Her purse is in the pocket.

She's heaving the bags into the hall when she hears the crunch of gravel on the drive and the roar of Trent's Land Rover dying down as he turns off the engine. She sees the shadow of his body through the strip of frosted glass, the black of his leather jacket. Once, this sight made her heart race with excitement, but now it beats with dread.

'You're back,' Trent says, as he comes in, chucking his keys on the console table. He's carrying a Waitrose bag full of bottles. He must have been to the little one in Helen's village.

His tone grates.

'I just came to get a few things.'

'I was calling you and calling you.'

'My phone broke.'

'Oh. Well, you shouldn't have worried me like that.'

She used to be so enamoured with Trent. She sees this now, as he steps towards her. She flicks her arm away before he touches her. She can't look at his familiar grey eyes because she can see that he means it. She has worried him. He does love her. In his own way. And she knows this. Because they've been together for ever, which means that there's a very big part of her that belongs to him. A part, that should she detach it, might destroy her.

'We need to talk,' he says, his head cocked at a just-too-slightly-condescending angle. It's enough to snap her to her senses.

'What's there to talk about? About how you've been sleeping with one of my best friends for three years?'

'It's not three . . . I . . .' he stumbles, taken aback that

46

the frame matters. 'I meant to stop it. Honestly, I did. But Helen . . . she was just there and so willing and I . . . well, I was weak, babes. I know that. I can see that. And I didn't mean to hurt you. It didn't mean anything. Honestly, you've got to believe me.'

'I don't believe you.' Because she doesn't. She can see it in his face. He's lying. How dare he act as if he's been repeatedly lured away by some wicked sex siren against his will. It's pathetic.

She starts to walk past him.

'Maddy.' He grabs her arm and she freezes, staring down at his wedding ring. After a fraught moment he lets her go. Her heart hammers so hard in her chest, she feels sick. She moves towards the front door and opens it. 'When will you be back? We're supposed to be in lockdown. You're not supposed to be travelling anywhere unless it's essential.'

She doesn't answer him, although she's tempted to snap that this *is* an emergency; that she does have the right to travel. Because it is *absolutely essential* that she gets away from him.

'Maddy,' he calls. 'Maddy, come on. Be reasonable. At least tell me where you're going. You owe me that.'

'If you must know, I'm going to find Jamie,' she manages.

Trent lets out a snort of derision as he calls after her, 'Well, good luck with that. Isn't it a bit late to play mother of the year?'

8

The Family Zoom

Tor can't wait to get in the sea and puts a shout-out to the Sea-Gals mid week. It's been a trying few days. Lotte has been embracing her time off with relish, in the way that only Lotte can. Because the hair salon is closed, she's been home hairdressing and has embarked on an elaborate tattoo for their housemate, Declan, inconveniently setting up her make-shift studio in the kitchen. There's been a constant stream of friends coming and going to the house, drinking and getting stoned in the garden. Tor has been trying to instigate the lockdown rules, but Lotte doesn't seem to think that they apply to her. It annoys Tor that their house and their life seems to be so public. They've barely had five minutes alone together, but Lotte loves all the attention, holding court, always teetering on the edge of any gathering becoming a party.

It's a relief to get in the sea and have a break from it all. The tide's in and the water is a deep navy-blue in the winter sunshine, the sky a watercolourist's blue. Tor kicks furiously, her gloves raking through the water as she gets her shoulders under, blowing out a shocked sigh as the cold hits. Her skin stings, like the sunburn she had when she first got to Africa. She's glad of her woolly hat.

Dominica and Helga head off in the direction of the buoy, which is easily swimmable in the summer, but there's a pull in the water, the tide going out, and it looks miles away. When Tor starts lagging behind, Helga comes to the same conclusion.

'Let's head that way,' Helga says, nodding to the wooden groyne. As always, Tor is grateful to be in such a safe pair of hands. She knows it'll be a relatively short swim. They only stay in a minute per degree of temperature, which Helga says is around eight today.

'Oh, God, this is good. I can't tell you how glad I am that Christmas is over,' she says to Dominica. She means it.

'I forgot to ask the other day. How was your family Zoom?' Dominica asks.

'Awful.'

'Why?'

'Because my sister, Alice, made such a big thing of it. She was even in heels. Who wears heels on Christmas Day?'

There's a thrill to bitching about Alice tinged with a familiar guilt. They've been brought up to believe that their twin bond is sacred, but, often, it feels like that's just a slogan. They might have shared a womb once, but that's where the similarity ends.

'We had to do this synchronised present opening. God, it was awful.'

In typical Alice style, she'd sent face cream and one glance at the back of the box had assured Tor that it was definitely not vegan. She remembers how Alice had told her to use it sparingly, as 'the expensive stuff' went such a long way. She told Tor to have a go at the wrinkle between her brow.

She does an impression of Alice peering at the screen, pointing out the Botoxed place on her own face that she finds objectionable on Tor's, and Helga and Dominica laugh.

'She's so rude. And she doesn't even realise it. I mean, we're chalk and cheese. We always have been. But she always makes out that my appearance somehow reflects badly on her. It's *always* about her.' It's not until she lets this out that she realises how much she needed to purge this resentment.

'My sister was the same,' Helga says.

'Really?' Tor asks.

'Oh, she was a nightmare. She always looked down on me, even though I was the one winning sailing trophies. Didn't matter a bit to her. She never acknowledged my success.'

'I didn't know you had a sister.' Dominica sounds curious.

'She died in a skiing accident when she was forty,' Helga says. 'My niece was only young. Mette. We've become close, but it would never have happened if my sister had lived because she was such a control freak. It didn't help that she was married to an awful man. And I mean awful. I couldn't stand the sight of him.'

'I can't stand my brother-in-law either,' Tor says. It's good to admit this out loud.

'Oh. I love hearing about another arsehole,' Helga says, flipping onto her back and nodding for Tor to proceed.

She explains how it had all started because Tor had told her parents and Alice and Graham about how she'd been helping out at the charity and her mother, with an earnestness that always gets right up Tor's nose, announced that she thought it was 'commendable' that Tor was helping out 'those poor

50

people'. Tor had wanted to point out that the poor people would have been a lot better off if her simple wish had been listened to and they'd all sponsored her for her upcoming dawn charity swim instead of sending presents, as she'd requested.

And that's when Graham had chipped in.

'You say that, Rita, but I think half the people on the streets aren't really homeless.' He takes a big bite out of his cheese-laden cracker, but not before adding, 'Just putting it out there.'

Still eating, he ploughs on. 'They've got hostels to go to. That's what I pay my council tax for.' His cheeks are flushed from the champagne they've been drinking (apparently since breakfast) and now he takes a slug of port to wash down the cheese. He runs his tongue unpleasantly around his teeth. Tor happens to know that he cracked on to one of Alice's bridesmaids the night before their wedding, so she's never trusted him. She's often wished that she'd had the guts to pipe up and tell Alice the truth, but confrontation is not her forte. However, something about the way Graham's eyes glint now gives her the courage she needs.

'That's not really the same as a home though, is it, Graham? There's rooflessness, I grant you. People who are sleeping rough, but there's also homelessness. People who have a shelter, but it's only temporary.'

'It's better than nothing.'

'But only just. Don't people deserve more? How would you feel if you had to stay in a hostel? Surrounded by strangers? With no home comforts? Told to get out and move on in the morning?'

Tor doesn't point out that there are other, even more toxic forms of homelessness. Like the families she deals with who are living in insecure housing, where they're trapped by payday loans and debts, living with the constant threat of that knock on the door that means they'll be evicted. Or the youngsters she knows who are staying with family and friends, but they're stuck sofa-surfing.

'Yeah, well, those people don't really help themselves, do they? *I* don't rely on other people,' Graham says.

'They didn't become homeless *by choice*, Graham. Mostly, there are many factors involved.'

'Like what?'

He's so fucking ignorant. 'Well, lots of them got made redundant, or become unemployed in a place where there's no hope of getting another job. And once they've lost their home, they don't necessarily get access to welfare benefits, or have the education or language skills to help themselves get online. And that's all before you factor in poor mental health, or people who have come out of prison, or people who have lost their partner or the person who looked after them.'

'Well—'

'Or people who split up and have to move out of their home and they can't afford to rent somewhere else,' she says, cutting him off. 'Not to mention the people I meet all the time who've experienced horrific abuse. Would you stay in a house where someone was beating you up or raping you?'

'I'm not talking about *them*. I'm talking about the spongers.'

'The spongers. I see.' Tor wishes Alice and her parents could hear what a bigot he sounds.

'The people who come over here—'

'The refugees? Or the economic migrants? People who are fleeing persecution or war? *Those* spongers?'

'You two,' Alice interjects, and Tor sees that it's time to bite her lip.

'Yeah, well, there must be other solutions other than hand-outs. That's all I'm saying,' Graham concedes, but Tor is riled by the self-satisfied way he sits back in his chair.

'If private landlords' – Tor is aware of her flushed cheeks and shaky voice – 'didn't hike up the rents, then maybe there wouldn't *be* such a housing crisis.'

Graham owns a whole load of commercial properties and flats. He shrugs, but his eyes are steely. 'Let's not go there, Victoria. I know it might come as a shock to you, with your "hippy-dippy, right-on Brighton" ways' – he puts his fingers up to invert a phrase he's made up himself – 'but I'm not responsible for market forces.'

Dominica and Helga are listening as Tor recounts this word for word. They've turned and are heading back in.

'Yep, he's a prick,' Helga announces. 'Grade A. You're right, Tor. Good for sticking up for yourself.'

'And we'll all do the swim with you,' Dominica says. 'It's in March, right? Don't worry. We can get some sponsorship money between us.'

Tor feels more reassured than she has done all day. She slows as they get to the shore. It's too deep to put her feet down. She follows Dominica and Helga and together, they catch a wave as it barrels over onto the pebbles, depositing them into shallow water, like a mother coaxing a child forward.

'Sorry to offload all of that,' she says to Dominica as they walk up the beach. She notices her legs are bright orangey pink, but Dominica, in her light-blue swimming costume with dolphins on it, looks like a goddess.

'Don't be sorry,' she says, smiling. 'That's what the sea's for,' and Tor wonders what she leaves behind when she comes out.

9

The Extension

Claire waves her fingers away from the scorching heat and licks her finger, as she places the last mince pie on the wire rack. 'Asbestos fingers' is what Pim calls her, with her ability to withstand intense temperatures, but it's actually just laziness on her part. She's never got the correct utensil so uses her fingers instead. She wonders how long it will be before the boys rip themselves away from their screens and come down. Not long, she reckons, knowing the aroma will be floating through the house right now. She takes the last pie – the runty little one – and pops it in her mouth. Chef's treat.

She waits for the usual barrage of mental self-abuse about her inability to stick to her calorie count, but now it's the last day of the year, she's excited about starting on her new regime tomorrow. She has a whole stack of resolutions and she's been writing visualisations. She felt a bit silly writing them down, but she was listening to a podcast about putting your wishes out into the universe and so she's sent out a request for a whole new her. It's worth a shot.

It's been a bit dreary weather-wise – the long days stretching between Christmas and New Year are never her favourite – but now, as she wipes a porthole in the steamed-up kitchen window, she can see that the sun has come out.

She takes the phone out of her apron pocket and texts Jenna to tell her she's almost ready and that she's bringing mince pies. She tries to adopt a breezy tone as she writes and re-writes the text as if going for a swim is something she does every day. But a sunset swim on the very last day of the year feels symbolic and grand – two things in her life that have clearly been so lacking she feels rather giddy with excitement.

She bumped into Jenna when she came back from Aldi the other day and agreed to accompany her on a sunset swim today. Jenna is a Wim Hof evangelist and, having looked up The Iceman online, Claire has turned the shower to the cold setting for the past few mornings, although she can only stand such masochistic torture for a few seconds. But the sea? At this time of year? Can she really do it?

But then she thinks of the women she saw playing in the waves. How hard can it really be?

She presses send and puts the phone down, before taking some of the energy balls she made from her new clean-living cookbook Siobhan sent her for Christmas and wrapping them in greaseproof paper before putting them in a Tupperware box. Her phone pings.

Perfect. I'll call for you.

Claire smiles, feeling vindicated that her baking session will now have a proper purpose. She goes to the airing cupboard by the ironing board, which is stacked with a to-be-ironed pile, and pulls down a towel.

She's packed everything into her bag and is just making a flask of tea when Pim comes into the kitchen. He's wearing stained grey jogging bottoms and a hoodie. Why hasn't he put on the fresh ones from the pile of clean washing she put on his side of the bed earlier?

He waves a piece of paper he's printed off the computer in her face. She's about to comment that she can see he's used the coloured ink mode (something he's expressly banned the boys from doing) when she sees that, beneath his glasses, he's frowning heavily.

'Read it.' His tone is ominous.

Claire wipes her hands on the apron and takes it. 'What is it?'

'I wouldn't have found it,' he says, pacing across the chequered kitchen lino in front of the sink. 'I just happened to find it by chance.'

Claire tries to fathom out what she's looking at and what's made him so cross.

'Just read it, Claire,' he says sharply, and she feels a lurch in the pit of her stomach. She hates it when he uses that tone, like he suspects that she's stupid. It digs right into the psychological compost of her mind, unearthing age-old insecurities, hard and as tangible as bulbs. Because he went to university, and she dropped out. Something he's somehow never let her forget. 'It's an application for planning permission. Your friend Jenna and Rob are planning on extending their house next door. It'll block out all our light. Not to mention the noise and the mess.'

'An extension?' Claire says, staring out of the window to the cherry tree. It's on Jenna's side, officially, although most of the tree falls across their boundary. They won't cut that down, will they? She loves that tree and the robin she's affectionately named Sam is on its bare branches right now. Claire wonders if the robin looks in on her, observing her life, the way she observes his.

'Didn't she mention it?'

'No.'

'Are you sure?'

'I think I'd remember a conversation about her wanting to put an extension on the back of her house, wouldn't I?' She can't keep the resentment out of her voice. Maybe she is forgetful, but not about something like this.

'That's why she's been so nice to you.' Pim wags his finger, as if he's puzzled something clever out. 'That whole swimming thing. She's just trying to butter you up.'

His theory hurts. 'I'm sure it's not like that—'

'It's *exactly* like that. They're just people who think they can take take take. I've put up with Rob clanking around at dawn on his pushbike for the whole of lockdown, but I won't put up with this.'

'What are you going to do?' Claire asks, realising from the scorn in Pim's voice that he's just as envious of Rob as she is of Jenna.

'I don't know. But you're not to see her until we've worked out our position.'

'You can't just ban me from—'

'You're not to see her. Do you understand me?'

'But I'm going swimming with her.'

And, right on cue, there's the ding-dong chime of the door-bell. Claire and Pim glare at each other.

'That's her,' Claire says in a small voice.

She wants to defy him and go to the door to see Jenna herself, but Pim beats her to it. She shrinks out of view in the kitchen, wanting to cover her ears like she did as a child, when Da came home drunk and fought with her mother. She hates confrontation of any sort and this is making her feel horribly queasy.

Pim and Jenna are talking and then she hears Pim's tone change.

'Yeah, well, she's not coming now,' Pim says. 'Because of this. You think you can just slip this under the radar?'

'The council were supposed to put a notice up.' Jenna sounds surprised, but she's sticking her ground. Claire moves a fraction so that she can see a small sliver of Jenna standing below Pim on the doorstep. She has perfect blonde hair, poking out beneath a stylish hat. She's in her camouflage Dryrobe, but even in such an oversized garment, you can tell she's slim. Her perfect chin juts out now. She's not intimidated by Pim. 'I thought you'd have seen it.'

'There wasn't a notice.'

Claire slinks back and presses herself against the cooker and her bum makes the gas ignition click. She should go to the door. She should make peace and smooth things over but she's too frightened to confront either of them. To be fair, Pim is hardly a confrontational type. He's usually so mild-mannered and polite. That's what attracted her to him in the first place – because he was such a gentleman. But lockdown has made everyone exposed and raw and this is all escalating too fast. She has to stop it.

'There's plenty of other houses with extensions in the street, so I really don't think it's worth your time or energy making a fuss. We're going to fight to make it happen, no matter what you say.' Jenna sounds steely. Her voice has become posher.

A moment later, Claire hears the door shut forcefully. Pim goes into the den and flicks on the TV.

'Pim. Oh my God! That was so rude! Did you just slam the door in her face?'

Pim wriggles back in the recliner in a self-justified manner. He's pretending to watch a game show – the type he can't stand.

'You can't be so aggressive. She's our neighbour. She's my friend.' Claire is aghast.

'She's the aggressive one! And anyway, you're supposed to be on my side.'

Clearly annoyed that she's criticised him, he gets up and stomps upstairs. The boys are next door in the lounge on the game, oblivious to the drama.

Claire stands in the corridor, feeling the pulsing male energy of the house. She's tempted to go straight around to Jenna's to make peace. She walks into the kitchen and, on a whim, picks up her swimming bag. There's always a chance that Jenna might go to the beach anyway.

10

Luna

Maddy is on her laptop, but she jumps as her phone buzzes, and when she takes it out she sees it's a withheld number. *Please let this be the callback from the social services*, she prays as she answers.

It feels unbearable that she might be in the same town as her son, but she's been here for nearly a whole week and she can't find him. It's not for lack of trying. It's infuriating that Jamie could be in any of these buildings. He could be just a wall away.

It *is* the callback and she gushes to the woman, Reeva, about how grateful she is for her time. But Reeva – a woman who couldn't sound more bored if she tried – isn't going to be able to provide any answers either. It's the same old story Maddy has heard everywhere she's tried. Jamie is an adult. She's not at liberty to divulge if there's even any 'data' on him.

'But I'm his mother,' Maddy protests.

It's like banging on the door of a fortress. It makes her so angry that other people are now the guardians of information about her son. It makes her feel so unworthy.

'If someone doesn't want to be found, there's not much you can do,' Reeva says.

She rings off and Maddy presses her thumb and forefinger into the throbbing points on her forehead.

She keeps thinking about Jamie's message. That word: Mum. And the way he said it. She can't get it out of her head. Something primal is telling her that he needs her.

She's been feeling so bruised since she came back from seeing Trent three days ago, that she's convinced herself the only thing that will make her feel better is if she can find a way to let Jamie know she's here. But how?

The low battery message prompts her to move to plug in her laptop, but her foot is numb from where she's had it bent underneath her, and she limps over to the wall, feeling pathetic.

She opens the blinds fully to let the afternoon light in and she realises there's a small balcony off the spare room she hasn't used yet. Her stomach growls and she limps to the kitchenette, noticing that it's a bit whiffy, and she pulls out the small bin. At home it's Rey, the cleaner, who often deals with the trash and recycling. How will Trent have explained Maddy's absence to nosy Rey? Or maybe Rey is on the long list of betrayers too and knew all about Trent and Helen.

Her phone buzzes with another incoming call and Maddy feels her heart beating a little faster when she sees it's Manpreet. She lets the phone ring once, then twice more. She shouldn't appear too keen, but whatever she does it's hard not to feel uncool around Manpreet. She thinks of the expensive media consultant wafting around in her perfect Notting Hill home in something cashmere and gorgeous. She's been trying, in her own way, to emulate Manpreet, who shares photographs that look like they're from a glossy magazine shoot. Her life is filled with household-name celebrities so it had really been a thrill when Manpreet had agreed to take Maddy on as her baby client.

She feels her pulse racing as she presses the answer button.

They exchange a few pleasantries, but Maddy can hear the sound of waves crashing in the background.

'Is that the sea?' she asks, wondering whether she should share that she's near the sea herself. Whenever she talks to Manpreet, she feels the competitive urge to point out what they have in common.

'Oh, yes, we flew out to our place in the Maldives for Christmas,' Manpreet says, as if that is something everyone does. 'We just needed a break, you know?'

Don't we all, Maddy thinks, wondering how it is that the super-rich don't seem to worry about the rules or getting caught at all.

'So what's up? I haven't seen you post?'

Maddy starts to explain that she's away from home.

'Then re-post. You can't have these long gaps.'

It's only been a few days, Maddy thinks, defensively.

'If you want things to take off, then you have to feed the beast. Consistent. Constant. Remember the rules I gave you?'

'Yes,' Maddy says, inwardly squirming. She feels told off. Like she's been caught cheating on a diet plan.

'If you want people to take you seriously, that is. A brand is a constant job. And you've been doing so well until now.'

Maddy is about to explain herself – about the phone being broken and to thank Manpreet for liking her Christmas grotto post, when Manpreet's tone changes.

63

'But that's not why I called,' she says. 'It's delicate, but I was wondering why the last invoices haven't been paid?'

This is why she's a successful business woman, Maddy thinks. Because Manpreet isn't afraid to get what she wants or to ask direct questions. She's been so fixated on the fantasy of Manpreet becoming a friend in real life, but now she remembers that this relationship is just a business one.

'Oh, haven't they? I had no idea. I'll see to it,' Maddy apologises.

They talk for a minute more, Manpreet explaining that she has to dash as she's hosting a dinner. She wishes Maddy a happy new year and then rings off and Maddy imagines her bossing around her private chef and laying her perfect table.

She logs in to her bank and sees the balance of her joint account is pitifully low. Trent usually tops it up and deals with their accounts, but he hasn't this month and she thinks of the credit card bill that's about to hit the account. How is she going to settle up with Manpreet? Let alone carry on using her services?

Chastened by her call, she puts some bread into the toaster and, whilst she waits, she scrolls through posts from her key influencer accounts, careful to write nurturing, encouraging comments, knowing she'll need these accounts to reciprocate. That's the whole point of social media. *I'll scratch your back, if you'll scratch mine.* They call it networking, but everyone knows it's more dog-eat-dog than that glib corporate word implies.

She's going to have to post. She can't put it off any longer. It's New Year's Eve after all and she's been radio silent enough for Manpreet to notice. But how can she possibly enthuse about this dismal Airbnb when its character-less blandness is distinctly off-brand?

Maybe she can do something outside, she decides, even though she's all about home comforts. She can tell her followers she's on a little break. She'll work it out, she decides, opening up the travel mirror and putting her face on, tying up, then letting her hair loose, styling it beneath her beanie with a pout in the mirror, then remembering her fur-trimmed hat and putting that on instead. Fur and lip gloss always makes her feel like she's upped her game. As her grandfather always used to say, 'A little dab of powder, a little dab of paint, makes a little lady what she really ain't.'

She gathers up the bin bag and goes out of the flat and shuts the door of the apartment.

'Luuuuna!' she hears a man cry, from the crack in the door he's opened next door. A small scruffy dog with ginger curly hair has made a bolt for it. Instinctively, Maddy puts her foot out to stop it.

The man comes out of the flat and scoops down and picks the dog up. '*Gracias*,' he says gratefully. He has a Spanish accent and swarthy olive skin, his hair a mass of lustrous brown curls. He's wearing a cardigan with buttons that remind Maddy of toffees and he's wearing the kind of soft green lace-up boots that only Europeans wear. Trent, with his designer trainer addiction, is such a snob about footwear, it's always the first thing she notices about people. He must be late thirties, possibly in his forties, she reckons. At least a decade younger than her, for sure.

'I didn't realise there was someone in the rental. I'm sorry if you've been disturbed by her barking.' Bar-king. With a rolled Spanish 'r'. His voice sounds like sunshine.

'It's OK,' Maddy says, although the flat really doesn't have any discernible sound insulation and they both know it.

'I have to quarantine, and the dog just wants to go out, but I'm holding on the phone to the Embassy . . . ' He pulls an exasperated face. 'I'm trying to sort out my visa, but . . . ' he shrugs and smiles. 'And poor Luna's not very happy being inside. She's only a puppy.'

'I could take her out?' Maddy offers.

'You could? You mean, you wouldn't mind?' He smiles and Maddy instinctively smiles back.

'I'm not doing anything. Well, I'm going to the bins.'

She can see from his expression that her un-thought-out offer is a lifeline.

'I'll get her lead.'

He goes back inside, talking to Luna in Spanish, and Maddy is tempted to be nosy and look inside his flat. In better clothes, with a decent haircut and a shave, he might even be considered good-looking. She can imagine that Lisa would describe him as a 'hotty'. But even thinking about Lisa is like picking at a painful scab.

He comes back with a lead and a couple of small plastic bags. She'll have to pick up the dog's mess, she realises, recoiling at the thought, but it's too late now.

'Thank you so much . . . ?'

'Maddy,' she says, realising too late that she can't shake hands with him. All this lack of contact and unnatural behaviour – will it ever be over?

'Matteo,' he introduces himself. They awkwardly bump elbows, but he notices the hole in his cardigan's elbow. He bites his lip in an endearing way as he picks at the hole.

'Sorry. It's . . . uh . . . *viejo*. Old.'

She waves his embarrassment away, then watches as he brushes his hair from his face and she suddenly imagines that it's the exact gesture he'd probably make in bed. She swallows and smiles, tearing herself away from the sight of him standing with his hands on his slim hips in the doorway. '*Muchas gracias*,' he calls after her.

'*De nada*,' she calls back, feeling like a silly, showy-offy schoolgirl. She hardly speaks any Spanish. What must he think of her, with her clinking bin bag of bottles? Thank God she put her make-up on and he hadn't seen her in the state she was in earlier.

On the seafront, it takes a while for Maddy to get the hang of Luna's extendable lead. Jamie always wanted a dog, but they never got around to getting him one. Trent was always too busy with his business, and she didn't have the time. Now, she wonders what her life might have been like if she'd given in to Jamie's simple wish. If he had a dog to love, might he have stayed? Why hadn't she realised that she only had a finite time to parent him when he was under her roof? She could have done more. Given him more of the things he really wanted rather than the things she thought he needed. And now it's too late.

She walks past The Fortune of War pub, the fishmonger's hut and smoking shack, past the boarded-up arcade towards the Palace Pier. Above it, thousands of starlings are swooping and soaring in unison, a huge in sync ariel display, a twisting, turning cloud.

Her phone bleeps. It's Trent. He's left her several messages. A couple with a pleading tone; one that was angry. She knows

67

he's confused by her behaviour and hurt too, but she doesn't want to talk to him. She doesn't want to hear his pathetic justification for his affair. Because she knows he'll try and blame her. He'll try and spin his way out of being in the wrong. He always does. She knows the best way to punish him is to not give him the chance to talk her round. But at some point very soon, she's going to have to confront him and work out the thorny issue of their finances and she knows she won't be able to continue being angry – not when she's beholden to him.

She feels so weak and pathetic for not being more independent. She wishes now that she'd stuck at a career. She could have been the managing director of a company. She could have had her own money to pay Manpreet. She's going to have to cash in the last of her savings to sort it out, but then there will be no cushion at all and she only has herself to blame. Her big plans for her @made_home channels suddenly seem like precarious pipe dreams.

Then, she sees it – the starlings have made a massive phallus shape against the grey sky. An actual cock and balls. Talk about pathetic fallacy. She bursts out laughing. It's the first time she's laughed in days. She turns, wondering if there's anyone to share the moment with, but she's alone.

She gets out her phone and takes a picture of the murmuration, but the cock and balls have gone. It's just a huge circle, like a speech bubble. Putting a flattering filter over the image, she thinks of all the hashtags that she wants to type #fuckthatyear #fuckmyhusband, but instead she dashes off a paragraph about how she's enjoying nature and the winter sunshine by the beach. *Hashtag bollocks*, she thinks.

II

Washing Away the Bad Juju

Dominica's sister-in-law Emma is babbling on the phone from London, her soft Welsh accent reminding her so much of Chris's, it makes her feel wobbly. She's been trying an experiment since Christmas – a form of denial, she knows – to force herself to stop disappearing into her memories and to try and remain present. Except that the past is so much more appealing it's hard not to fall again into that bittersweet pit of reminiscence that's so tantalisingly soft on the way in, but lined with cruel barbs on the way out.

She remembers now hearing Chris's laugh across the hotel bar in Hong Kong all those years ago. She'd been about to go to bed. Her stopover there hadn't been planned and she'd been exhausted after a trip around Australia doing a reccy for her holiday company and hiring branch staff. Chris had caught her eye and insisted on buying her a drink.

She'd been about to refuse, but then he'd smiled and had come over and introduced himself, apologising for his rowdy mates from the rugby club, who were here on holiday supporting Wales on their tour. He'd begged her to give him a few moments respite from their relentless banter. From the very first moment, he'd made her feel that she'd been recruited into team Chris. That it was the two of them against the world.

At the time, she'd been steadfastly single and had almost given up on dating, let alone love. She was forty, resigned to being childless after a botched operation on an ovarian cyst in her early twenties had rendered her sterile. Men found her height, her success, her confidence too intimidating, but Chris had seemed to see her in a way that made her feel that she could drop her guard and relax. She remembers that once-in-a-lifetime feeling of *oh, there you are. I've been barking up the wrong tree all this time. Forelsket*, she remembers thinking, recalling the Norwegian word describing the euphoric feeling at the beginning of love.

Towards dawn the following morning – probably still drunk – she'd told him exactly that and he'd said he'd felt the same way. *Forelsket*, he'd told her, was exactly it. He didn't care about having kids. He just wanted to crack on with building the best possible life he could with her at his side. Within a month they'd been engaged. When their friends saw them together, not one person expressed a doubt that they were going too fast.

Chris had been desperate for her to meet his kid sister, Emma, who he clearly adored. After their mum had died when she was little, it was Chris who'd stepped into looking out for her. He was so proud that Emma wanted to be a doctor. Dominica never pointed out that he could have been a doctor himself, if he'd still had his parents around and had had the support he'd needed to study. He'd become a paramedic instead and it had suited him – being the first person on the scene of any crisis, his Welsh voice calming everyone down. Dominica wouldn't mind betting he'd saved more lives than most doctors ever did.

She crashes back to the present.

'Dom? New Year? Plans?'

'Oh, nothing. I'll probably go to bed early.'

Emma's getting ready for a neighbourhood street party and Dominica can tell she's excited.

Dominica's never been one to celebrate New Year. Before she met Chris, she was often travelling over Christmas. Then, in recent years, Chris was often on call. The paramedics were always in short supply, and they needed someone with his experience. So this particular date on the calendar shouldn't be a thing. Except that it is. Because what will it be like when the clocks turn at midnight and she faces a new, virgin year without Chris? It feels like an awful milestone.

'I just wish . . .' she begins, but she stalls. She's full of wishes that feel very akin to regrets.

'I wish he was here too,' Emma says and her voice cracks.

There's a moment laden with silent emotion. Dominica imagines Emma sitting on the stairs of her North London terrace house fighting back the tears. It's an awful thing, but Emma's pain makes her feel less lonely. Chris had been her big brother, her sponsor, and her parents wrapped into one and whilst Emma has a lovely husband, Jack, and her kids, Dominica knows there's a huge Chris-shaped hole in her life too.

'I wish I could give you a *cwych*. I can't bear it that you're on your own,' Emma says.

The word has a sweet sting to it: Chris's Welsh word for

71

a cuddle, although his were more like all-consuming bear hugs. 'Me too.'

'It was such a weird Christmas. Nobody brought anything annoying or impractically large.'

'You remember the voice-activated fish?' Dominica can't stop a smile forming at the memory of the present Chris had insisted on buying Emma years ago, back in the days when they'd thought his younger sister was going to be single forever and they'd scooped her up from her digs. Chris had put the fake fish on its board on the wall and it had frightened the life out of Emma the first time it had gone off, flick-flacking with its stupid song.

'And when he brought that musical floor keyboard,' Emma reminds her of the plastic contraption that had filled the entire lounge. 'And we got drunk and tried to do the scene in *Big* when they play "Chopsticks".'

Dominica laughs. 'And you got a groin strain.'

The memories help and they chat until Dominica says she has to go. She's joining Helga and Tor for a sunset swim.

'It's so good you've got them,' Emma says. 'Your Sea-Gals.'

Dominica agrees. If it weren't for them, she doubts she'd have got it together to leave the house at all.

'Next time you come up to town,' Emma says, 'maybe we could swim together in the pond in Hampstead? In the spring. It'll give us both something to look forward to? Bring them if you like?'

Spring seems a long way off, Dominica thinks. She can't seem to visualise it. She can't seem to get a grip on the future when the past looms so large.

*

Dominica spots the woman in the scruffy parka on the beach, as she, Helga and Tor pass by to leave their stuff by the groyne in their usual spot. The woman, who has her hands around the lid of a flask of tea, looks up.

'Have you been in?' Dominica asks, nodding towards the sea, assuming she has. There's a group already in and Dominica wonders if she's part of their gang. She's chubby with frizzy grey hair poking out from under her pink bobble hat.

'No. No, I was going to, but then the person I was going to swim with . . . ' she peters out. She has a lovely lilting Irish accent, but Dominica hears a catch in her voice. 'And I can't go alone. I'm . . . well, to be honest, I'm too afraid. I'm not really a swimmer, I only thought I might go today . . . '

'Come in with us,' Helga offers. It's typical of her to swoop up a stray swimmer, but the woman seems unsure.

'You'd be most welcome.' Dominica gives her an encouraging smile and the woman gets up and brings her bag to join them.

The new swimmer is called Claire and she lives just up the road on the Hove side of the peace statue. Dominica explains she cycles to this beach from her flat in Kemp Town, whilst Helga comes from the Lanes and Tor from Seven Dials.

They chat easily, but Claire is trying to wrestle into her swimming costume under her coat.

'I should have got changed before,' she mumbles, trying to balance.

Dominica smiles. Her swimming clobber is always to hand, and she has two hot water bottles and metal drink flasks permanently by the kettle.

'You'll get to learn the tricks of the trade soon enough.' It's nice to be reassuring for once, not the one being reassured. It feels kind of liberating that this woman, Claire, has no idea that Dominica is bereaved.

'See you down there,' Tor says, heading off with Helga to the water's edge, but Dominica hangs back, waiting for Claire. There's something a little fragile and unassuming about her that Dominica rather likes. Tor and Helga are so strident, but Claire has a gentleness to her that appeals. There's something endearing about someone who is clearly trying to be brave.

The sea is reflecting the steel-grey cloud above the beach, but there's a band of white and pink between the sea and the sky near the horizon. The starlings are doing their thing over the pier, huge masses of them. It won't be long before they're off.

Helga walks straight in, as she does, but now, as they approach the rippling waves on the shore, Dominica stands with Claire, watching the sun coming through the bottom of the cloud, a sudden orange football hovering above the horizon. They watch as the golden pink blush wobbles towards them across the surface of the water.

She likes getting in the sea at all times of the day, but there's something profound about going in at sunset. It makes her feel in touch with the spinning of the earth, as if, in the sea, she can ride it out, going with time, rather than racing to fight against it like a roadrunner on land. 'Shall we?' She nods to the water.

Claire stands, slightly knock-kneed with fear and Dominica wants to tell her to stand up tall and to own the space she inhabits. She remembers how Chris had always made a virtue of her height. Her height, *and* her skin *and* her smile. Without him, it's like she's permanently in shadow.

'If you're not used to it, don't stay in for long,' Helga calls out to Claire who smiles gratefully for the advice.

Dominica walks into the water. 'That's it,' she tells Claire, who follows, letting out a squeal of shock at the cold. 'Take slow breaths. Don't panic.'

The tide is midway out, so it's not long before the stones suddenly dip under foot and turn into sand. Dominica is used to it, but Claire loses her footing and cries out as her shoulders dip unexpectedly. Dominica grabs her and helps her stand up.

'Bloody hell, it's cold,' she gasps. She has that wide-eyed shock of a new swimmer.

'Just relax,' Dominica coaxes, gently. 'Breathe.'

She swims alongside Claire, who does an anxious breast-stroke, her teeth chattering. Helga swims over and they chat and Dominica nods, knowing that Helga will instantly calm Claire and give her confidence in the water. She swims further away now to join Tor.

'And . . . there it goes,' Dominica says to Tor, as they tread water and watch the sun sink into the sea. 'The shittiest year. Done.'

'It'll get better.' Tor's face is lit with a rosy glow and Dominica smiles at her. Behind her the water is a deep bluish purple. She reaches out and puts her black glove out and holds Dominica's hand under the water.

The gesture shocks Dominica – mainly because it's so unexpected, but also because it's so heartfelt.

Tor smiles.

'Let's wash away all the bad juju,' she suggests. 'Come on, you go under. I'll hold your hat.'

Dominica, seeing the challenge in Tor's face, relents and

takes off her bobble hat and hands it over. She ducks underneath the water and she kicks furiously, swimming towards the horizon, her face freezing. She comes up crying out.

'Brain freeze,' Dominica gasps.

'That'll do it.' Tor laughs, swimming over and giving Dominica back her hat where she's held it out of the water. Tor does the same and soon they are both gasping.

And, as they bob side by side, watching the last tiny sliver of sun, like a golden cursor, Dominica is buzzing all over. Perhaps Tor is right. Maybe things will start to get better.

12

Dog Ambush

Claire is a good new addition to the group, Helga thinks. She's a sweet girl. No confidence. Anyone can see that, but she has the glow now that she's been in the sea. You can slap on all the anti-ageing cream you want, but nothing does the trick of taking off the years like a dip in cold water.

Helga rubs the back of her neck with her towel, taking a moment to appreciate the sky, which is a blaze of pinks and oranges over to the west, but by the pier in the east, the dark-blue night is approaching. Day and night and her in the middle. A part of her soul yearns to be on a boat, where this feeling is always the most profound at sunrise and sunset. They always felt like the greatest privilege to witness. She remembers watching a whole school of whales off the coast of South Africa once at sunset. That feels like a lifetime ago.

She turns her attention back to the group and starts to get dressed, but it's a rigmarole. She's got four tops and a jumper and coat, plus a scarf and hat, but she's already shivering with the after-drop. She knows she'll miss this buzz once the weather gets warmer.

Dominica lies on her back, trying to pull Chris's tracksuit bottoms up her long legs, but, like Helga's, her skin is sticky and it's hard.

Once they're all dressed and wrapped in scarves, hats and gloves, there's a friendly atmosphere as they all huddle together on the stones and chat. Dominica gives her hot water bottle to Claire who really has the shivers, but she soon settles and then seems to remember something. She pulls out a Tupperware box from her bag and offers it around.

Helga peers inside. It's filled with crinkly greaseproof paper, below which is a layer of home-made mince pies.

'What a treat!' Helga takes one gratefully and passes the box on.

'Are they vegan?' Tor asks.

'I'm afraid not. I have these, though.' Claire brings out another Tupperware tub filled with what she calls 'health balls', clearly anxious to please. She unclips the lid with difficulty, her fingers numb. 'They're dates and coconut oil and raw cacao powder. Oh, and cashews. You're OK with nuts?'

'I certainly am. And I'm very OK with these,' Tor says, eating one. 'They're delicious. Wow.' Her straggly hair is sticking out from under the turn up of her thick bobble hat and she grins, the cacao powder sticking to her teeth.

'You can come again,' Helga says. 'In fact, I'll put you on the Sea-Gals WhatsApp chat if you like?'

'That'd be grand. It's nice to make food that's appreciated. I love baking, but I hate having to throw away what I make. But then the worst thing happens . . . I end up eating it myself.'

Claire pats her stomach with disdain. She's nicely rotund, Helga thinks. Solid. In a good way. She wonders if she'd ever model for her life-drawing classes. They could all do with some fresh blood, having drawn Keith over and over. She's not sure she can do better justice to his back fat wrinkles and sunken shoulders any longer. But Claire has a touch of Botticelli about her.

'Don't ever throw cakes away. I will always take them off your hands,' Tor says. 'For the food bank. I'm serious. There are dozens of people I know who'd give their right arm for a home-made mince pie like this.'

'I'll remember that.'

Helga tries to guess at Claire's background. She must be married. Only an unappreciative man could grind down a woman's self-confidence in the way that Claire's obviously is. She's a mother too. She can tell by the stickers on the top of the Tupperware boxes. Helga bets her kids don't appreciate her either. Were they supposed to be coming with her to the beach? Is that why she's got all this delicious food? But Helga is impressed by Claire and likes her Irish charm. Anyone who is willing to get in the sea at sunset on the last day of December always goes up in her estimation.

From the side pocket of her old oilskin jacket, she gets out her notebook to write down Claire's number. She likes her phone and the camera on it, but she has a cheap contract that tethers her to the Wi-Fi in her cottage and so she uses her trusted notebook for numbers and lists and drawings, as she has done her whole life. A pen and paper are invariably the only things that work at sea. She can never get why people become so obsessed with modern tech. It always lets you down. One day, the internet is bound to crash and Helga can't help thinking what a good thing that will be for humanity. Everyone was much happier before all these apps and games and the constant 'look at me' jumping up and down, which Helga can't bear. She refuses to have any social media, much to Mette's annoyance.

She turns to the page where she did a quick sketch of the great tit on the bird box earlier, with its stripy wings and white cheeks. She's chosen her ancient yellow jumper today to match his impressive chest.

But Claire is just saying her number for her to write down, when a small, curly brown dog comes bounding across the pebbles and jumps onto Helga's lap, spilling her tea. Then it scurries around the others, its snout in the box of mince pies. Claire makes a grab for them.

'I'm so sorry,' the dog's owner apologises. She's wrapped up in a designer windcheater and a fur hat. There's something very put together about her. She has that pinched look of a woman who's had work done to her face, which is pale, the flawlessness of her forehead only serving to accentuate the lines around her eyes. Why do women do that to themselves? Helga thinks. It must be the biggest con ever invented, mostly because the result is so contrary to the intention. This woman might as well be carrying a neon sign above her head saying 'insecure', not that she realises it. Helga's sick of everyone being so against ageing. What's not to love about the sweet spot of maturity when you don't give a shit about what anyone else thinks?

'Can you try and control your dog?' Helga tries to lift her mince pie away from the jumping, yapping hound. She's not a dog lover. She doesn't like the way they chase the birds.

'It's not my dog, you see. I'm so sorry. Luna. Luna!' the woman calls, making a grab for the dog.

Dominica laughs at the carnage the dog has caused. 'He's a determined little thing, isn't he? Is it a he? A she?'

The dog jumps onto Dominica's lap. She holds its ears and makes a soothing noise, getting the dog's attention.

'She. She's a puppy. She belongs to my new neighbour.' The woman bends down to try and lean across and pick up the dog from Dominica. But she loses her footing and overbalances. She stumbles then sits down on the pebbles with a thump.

'Hey, are you OK?' Dominica asks her. She's stroking the dog, who has curled up in her lap. They look very cosy, but then Dominica has that way about her, Helga thinks. She's tall and serene and Helga always feels calm around her too. 'This is better than a hot water bottle. She's so warm.'

'I should never have agreed to walk it . . . her. She's mental,' the woman says, almost to herself. She sounds cross and Helga can't bear the stress-energy she's exuding. Feeling so mellow after the swim, it's hard to be around someone so highly strung. The woman looks at her hands, as if she's horrified that they've touched the ground. She rubs them together and checks the back of her coat. Helga sees she has had her nails professionally painted in a serious maroon varnish. Helga, who generally grubs out the dirt from under her fingernails with a screwdriver tip, wonders how much this woman spends on her appearance – and why. No good ever came out of looking in a mirror too much. Especially sober.

'Take a breath,' Helga says, before she can help herself.

The woman looks startled. She's clearly not used to being told to do anything by anyone else. *One of those*, Helga thinks, remembering her sister's ghastly set of friends. She covers the moment with a smile. 'Would you like a mince pie? There are plenty.' Claire nods in agreement to this offer and Helga holds out the box. She wonders whether the woman will make a fuss about sharing food and all the silly Covid rules they're supposed to follow, but, to her credit, the woman smiles.

'Are you sure? That's very nice of you.'

Helga can see that she finds it just as delicious as she did. The woman's eyes widen in delight as she takes a bite. 'So much for the diet,' she says, with a weak laugh, as if they all must know what she means, but Helga is confused. She looks like she barely eats, her skin stretched across her bones. Claire stares at her, confused too, but in a way that looks more like envy to Helga.

'I can't believe you've all been in,' she continues, trying to save the moment. 'I mean you must be mad. You'd never catch me . . . ' she peters out, when she realises they're all still staring at her. 'It's so cold.'

Helga shrugs. 'The sea is always cold. It's just a matter of degrees.'

'Honestly, I'm buzzing,' Claire says, readjusting Dominica's hot water bottle against her chest. 'You should try it.'

'Me?' The woman is shocked. She laughs. 'No, no, I couldn't.'

'Why not?' Helga asks.

'Because . . . because, despite what you say, it's freezing.' She laughs as if this is a crazy fact they've all overlooked.

'It's only cold water. We're not dying of hypothermia,' Helga points out. 'In fact, it's quite the reverse.'

'Well, you might be right, but the sea is not for me.'

'How can the sea not be for you?' Helga has never heard anything so ridiculous and the woman blushes.

'If you must know, I'm scared of fish,' she admits. 'I watched *Jaws* at too tender an age.'

'Oh, well then, I agree it's not for you,' Helga says, pretending to be serious. 'There are eels under the pier.'

'Well, exactly. Who knows what lurks under the water?'

A line of kittiwakes with their black-tipped wings fly across the beach towards the horizon.

Helga wants to tell her the truth: that there's a whole wonderful world out there – garfish, blennies, dogfish, starfish and seahorses. Instead, she smiles.

'You know the best way to get over a fear?'

'No.'

'Conquer it.'

'You make it sound easy.'

'I bet you'd enjoy it. If you were brave enough to give it a go?' Helga shrugs again and side-eyes the woman, wondering whether she'll rise to the bait. It's no skin off her nose whether she swims or not, but Helga has a feeling that it might do her some good.

13

The Promise of Fireworks

Maddy is feeling in a decidedly better headspace when she gets back to her apartment block. She feels silly doing it, but she checks her hair and puts on another slick of lip gloss before Matteo opens his door.

'How did you get on?' he asks, taking Luna's lead.

Maddy has been planning on recounting what a nightmare Luna has been, but she can see that he's so grateful that she doesn't want to make a fuss. Behind him, she sees a glimpse of his apartment. Unlike her drab living accommodation, she sees that his is cluttered with low furniture and retro lamps. She sees a record player and a stack of records leaning up against it. It's decidedly male. A bachelor pad, she concludes. She can't see any female shoes in the stack of trainers and boots below the hooks full of coats behind him.

'It was lovely being on the beach. I got talking to some sea swimmers.'

'Oh, yes, I see them all the time. My colleague has a vendetta against those funny coats they wear. He thinks we're being taken over by mad people. Especially the camouflage ones. He and his friend play a drinking game where they have to drink every time they spot someone wearing one.'

'That's perhaps a little mean. I wouldn't say the women I met were mad, just brave. Swimming in this weather . . . ?' She rubs her arms as if just the thought makes her cold.

Even so, she's surprised that she feels defensive that there are men taking the piss out of the swimmers on the beach. She can still taste the hot mince pie, but something stronger has stayed with her – that, for just a few minutes, she felt part of a little gang. Perhaps it's just that having been so starved of company over the past few days, she enjoyed this social interaction much more than she normally would. She's not met a group of random strangers – well, not in actual real life, that is, for as long as she can remember. She's surprised by how easy it was to talk to them and how they gave off this earthy, happy energy. She remembers the friendly woman with grey hair saying how amazing she felt. The old one with the white hair and funny accent was quite a character, too.

'Yes, well, my colleague is . . . well, shall we say . . . someone who is never going to get a girlfriend,' he clarifies and she smiles, glad that he's distinguished himself from them. 'I would ask you in . . . '

'But it's against the rules. I know.' She smiles.

'You know, if you go on your balcony, I could go on mine? That way we could each be in our apartments and talk.'

'Oh!' Maddy is surprised. 'You mean now?'

'Or later?'

'Later?'

'For new year.'

'Oh.'

'Shall we say a quarter to twelve on the balcony?' he asks.

She wants to tell him that she had been planning on putting her earplugs in and eye mask on and taking a sleeping pill. That she really has nothing to celebrate, but something stops her. She doesn't want him to think that she's no fun. Besides, she's intrigued to find out more about him. And if he's on his own balcony, then it's hardly a date. *Is it*?

The second she's inside her apartment, Maddy immediately regrets agreeing to the rendezvous. Why is she even thinking about talking to another man, when her head is in such a mess? She has no idea how to behave, or how to strike up a friendship with a member of the opposite sex. She doesn't have male friends. Ironically, Trent was always too jealous for her to hang out with any single men. Or even married ones, for that matter. So the fact she's seeing Matteo later fills her with a sense of guilt. *Which is ridiculous.*

Why shouldn't she have a drink with Matteo? The fact that Trent would be jealous of someone younger and with much better hair than him makes it feel even more illicit.

But, at the same time, paradoxically, the one person she wants to tell about her new neighbour is Trent. After all the years they've shared, being cast adrift from him is deeply confusing. She thought it would be easy to let go, but the white-hot anger has morphed into another more difficult to pin down emotion. It feels like grief. She misses the safe haven of her marriage. She misses her home. And she has nobody to comfort her. She can't turn to Trent or Lisa. The idea that Matteo is even vaguely interested in talking to her is more comforting than it ought to be.

She pours a large glass of white wine and reminds herself that Trent is probably spending tonight with Helen and bile rises in her stomach. This flick-flacking of emotion is like being constantly seasick and she wonders when it's going to stop. She longs for peace.

To distract herself, she trawls through her phone, seeing that Elise, one of Jamie's former best friends, has just got engaged. Right at the stroke of New Year – in Hong Kong.

Maddy already knows from her posts that Elise is living in a fabulous apartment. She posted about being stuck when Corona first struck, but now she's out and about and seeing her smiling face in a restaurant, the tables crowded with cocktail glasses, balloons and streamers, Maddy is struck by how grown up she looks . . . how together. So different to the scrawny tomboy of a girl who left with Jamie for their year off after school.

She worried at the time that Elise and Jamie might get it together romantically in Thailand, although Trent was more of the view that Jamie might come home with a Thai bride. Not that there was anything wrong with Elise, but Maddy secretly had an altogether different scenario for her golden boy. With his A levels in the bag and three unconditional offers from his university choices, including the coveted place at Oxford, she knew that the right girl would be waiting for him once he followed his path and she told him as much. All he needed to do was to stay safe and have fun.

When she drove them to the airport, she was confident that, with enough money in his pocket and with sensible Elise by his side, Jamie would have the time of his life.

She'll never know what really happened that night in

Thailand at the full moon party. She only knows from Elise that Jamie had got in with some bad boys at one of the hostels and gone on an all-night bender, followed by another. He always was competitive and was absolutely at his worst at that age.

Maddy will always remember the tearful call Elise made at three in the morning, telling her that Jamie was in serious trouble and that she didn't know what to do.

Maddy flew out to Thailand herself the next day and, after a fraught eighteen-hour dash, found Jamie cowering in a hospital bed. She was horrified at the sight of him, tanned, yet gaunt, his eyes wild as he tugged the sheet up around him, his feet up, as if there was a monster at the end of the bed. He hardly recognised her.

She'll never know what cracked his brain, but it must have been some kind of bad acid trip. The Thai doctors didn't know or seem to care. Perhaps they'd seen it all before. The police were equally unhelpful.

It's still a blur – that horrible week in Thailand and the dreadful trip home. She thought Jamie would snap out of his paranoia once he came down, but he didn't and, soon, she and Trent were at their wits end. She'd never had to deal with any kind of mental health issue before and when their GP suggested a residential stay in a psychiatric hospital after evaluating Jamie, they reluctantly agreed.

It took six months to get even a glimmer of the old Jamie back, but by then his friends had moved on. He deferred his uni place, then let the whole thing drop. He stayed at home in his room, insisting that smoking weed was the only thing that was keeping him straight. He slept every day until late afternoon and Maddy didn't know what was worse: Trent's fury at their son sleeping, or the resentful atmosphere Jamie created once he got up.

She writes a congratulatory message to Elise, then deletes it. Elise won't want to be reminded of Maddy – and by association, Jamie.

Where's Jamie now? she wonders. Is he having flashbacks to that horrible New Year that everything changed too? She wishes she could go back. She wishes she'd never let him go.

At a quarter to midnight, Maddy yearns for the oblivion of sleep, but she feels she can't deal with the social embarrassment of ditching Matteo when he lives right next door. She spritzes her face, arranges the neck of her cashmere roll-neck and then goes to the spare room and fiddles with door.

Matteo is waiting on his balcony, the apartment behind him lit up. He's wearing a nice jumper and a green moleskin jacket that complements his eyes. There's some lovely Spanish guitar music playing. There's a little table and he's lit some candles in coloured jars, but he appears to be alone.

'There you are. Here. Have a chair.' He passes over a flimsy wooden and metal chair. She has no choice but to grab it and unfold it. 'Oh, and take a candle,' he adds, handing her a jam jar. He goes back inside and she surreptitiously snaps a picture of the candle and puts a filter on it. She'll save it for later and try to think of a good caption. Perhaps something about the poor people who died of Covid? Not that she was affected personally, but it'll make her sound like she's a caring person. But even as she thinks this, she hates herself for being so shallow. She feels a wave of resentment towards Manpreet and her followers and for having to feed her site with this constant show of giving a shit.

'And this,' he adds, coming back with a bottle and two glasses. He's made quite an effort, she realises. 'It's new year and I'm going early. And it's the least I can do to thank you for taking Luna out. She's been so much calmer this afternoon.'

He reaches over the balcony and gives her a glass of fizz with a smile. 'My ex insisted on getting a puppy in lockdown, but she's online all the time and it was impossible for her to work, so I've got Luna.'

So he *is* single. Single, and decent enough to help out his ex.

She raises a glass and takes a sip, then appraises the glass. 'Wow, that's delicious.'

'It's only Cava,' he explains. 'From my home town.'

He seems pleased that she likes it. The way he says 'home town' makes him seem exiled. She's not that familiar with Spain, but she imagines him with a straw hat on, tall crystal glasses and a summer lunch laid out among the vines.

'We'll have a good view of the fireworks on the beach from here.'

'Fireworks? I thought it was lockdown?'

'There'll be fireworks,' he says. 'There always are by the sea. It'll be fun.'

They both sit and, with the candlelight and the music, it feels very European – like she could be on holiday. Except for the temperature. She lets the bubbles fizz over her tongue. Trent is a snob about champagne. She has a momentary panic that Trent might have forgotten to get the bottles from the boxes in the garage at home to chill them in the wine fridge. But then she remembers. She's not going to be drinking Perrier-Jouët with him. Helen is. She hopes she chokes on it.

'So where is home?' she asks Matteo. He describes a hilltop

town inland from Barcelona and his troubles getting back there in lockdown. He tells her about how he met his ex, Shauna, when she was on holiday in Barcelona and he had a student job as a city tour guide.

'I followed her to England.' He smiles bashfully at how romantic he'd been. 'I wanted to transfer my studies to carry on studying to be a teacher.'

'You wanted to be a teacher?'

'I still do. But I had to get a job. I had to be a grown-up.'

It's funny how far people go, then get scuppered by events, she thinks. When Jamie was young, she thought that if she gave him the best education, she'd propel him into his future, with enough backing and momentum to carry him to the stars. But it didn't happen that way.

'One day, I still dream I'll build my own house on the patch of land at the edge of my village. It's got a view of the mountains to die for.'

'It sounds lovely,' she says. 'And Shauna?'

'We weren't as compatible as we thought,' he said. 'The lockdown proved that we are just too different. I loved her – and in a way I still do – but we wound each other up too much. Being together twenty-four-seven was the making of some people, but it broke us.'

'I'm sorry.'

He shrugs. 'It was a scary time. She was very, very anxious about Covid. Debilitatingly so.'

'You won't get back together?' she asks.

'No. No,' he says and shrugs sadly. 'No. It's finished.'

Maddy wonders if the girl, Shauna, regrets letting him go.

'What about you, Maddy?' he asks. She likes the way he

says her name. She likes the way he looks at her. As if he's genuinely interested. She realises that she can't remember the last time Trent has looked at her with anything other than defensiveness, or disinterest.

She fiddles with the stem of the glass. 'Oh, you don't want to know. It's a long story.'

'We have all night.'

She laughs and looks at him and she can see that he means it. So she describes the scene on Christmas Day and how she's left Trent. Saying it out loud feel liberating. All the confusion she felt earlier disappears, as she looks at Matteo's face. Trent's affair with Helen is despicable. Unforgiveable.

'Ouch,' he says, his thick eyebrows crinkling together. 'That sounds painful.'

She nods, feeling unbidden tears stinging her nose. She swallows them down.

'Thank you,' she says.

'To better times,' he says, leaning across the balcony and clinking glasses with her. She feels a tear fall as the fireworks on the beach start. She laughs at the stupidity of her emotion. It's embarrassing to cry in front of him.

'Trent is a fool,' Matteo says.

She nods and smiles. Someone at last. On her side.

14

Inner Superhero

Claire stands in her kitchen watching as the birds flit between the cherry tree and the fence, waiting for the kettle to boil. It's a non-descript dismal day and the atmosphere at home hasn't been great. She and Pim have not really patched things up after their row on New Year's Eve about Jenna and Rob, and he's retreated into a conveniently all-consuming ball of stress about his classes starting up again. She's spent the last fortnight on her new January diet, but so far she's yet to lose so much as a pound. She can feel the call of the chocolate brownies she's double taped into a tin box in the cupboard, like an evil whisper.

Pim sits with his headphones on at the kitchen table. In fact, she's entirely invisible to him, she realises. There's a staff meeting going on and she hears him laugh.

She wonders, if things had turned out differently, whether she might have been a teacher herself. Then it might have been *her* having that easy camaraderie, her belonging to a team. Back in her twenties, she used to have a good job in a recruitment agency, but she gave it up when they moved to Brighton for Pim's job and she was concentrating on getting pregnant. And then, when she had babies, they became her focus. She wanted to give her all to being a mum. But, now, all the good years have rushed by and she can't help feeling that she has nothing to show for herself.

While she waits for the detox teabag to brew, she picks up her phone and scrolls through the Sea-Gals chat. She likes the clips that Helga posts of the starlings and the gulls. Their house where she grew up in Ireland was inland from the coast and they hardly ever visited the rugged beaches. Even so, she's always thought of herself as a coastal kind of person. That's why she and Pim had moved to Brighton.

But now, she marvels at how she's lived by this huge other element for a decade and has really not taken much notice of it. How has she not known about the tides or the currents? How has she mostly ignored the sunsets and sunrises?

Now that she's started sea swimming herself, she notices women like her everywhere. She's discovered The Salty Seabirds, an offspring of a social enterprise set up by two women to help people with their mental health. She was surprised to learn that there's thousands of members on the Facebook group and she joined up herself, reading the helpful tips on swimming in cold water. It feels exciting to be part of such a big community, but she likes being part of the Sea-Gals group the best.

Today, Dominica has reposted a picture of a swimmer in a Wonder Woman cape from another sea swimmers' group, the Blue Tits. It's been so long since she's been away anywhere that Claire feels a little thrill at being connected to these women on the other side of the country.

She studies the picture – a group of women larking around

on the shore; women in costumes with wobbly bottoms just like hers, their gloved hands held aloft, grins on their faces. It's comforting to know that her tiny gang on the beach is part of a vast movement of swimmers. When everyone else is moaning half the time, the fact that there are people enjoying the benefits of cold water feels like a massive force for good. She likes to think of this veritable army around the coastline of Britain as hardy, can-do types who get things done. Because that's the gist of the post. That swimming in cold water invokes one's inner superhero.

Claire has never thought of it like that, but it's true. Not believing in a million years that you might be able to go in, and then actually doing it is powerful stuff. You may find, the quote says, that your superhero power stays with you through the rest of your day. You might find the courage to wear a brighter colour or say something daring at a meeting.

She can see that Dominica is typing and she clicks the message. She's asking if anyone is around now for a swim at low tide. Claire feels a leap of excitement. She looks at the clock on the cooker. She can do it. She can get down there and back before she really has to chivvy the boys along with their schoolwork. Pim doesn't notice as she leaves.

The tide is going out and there's a sea mist making everything slightly blurry when Claire joins Helga and Dominica on the beach.

'They must know something we don't know,' Claire says, as she puts her bag down. The surfers, clad in black, are floating on the still water by the burnt-out pier. There's not even the hint of a wave. What are they doing?

Tor comes down from the prom to join them, her feet sliding in the slope of pebbles. Apart from their gang and the surfers in the distance, there's nobody around, except for the man she can see stretching on the bandstand next to a tent. Not a very relaxing place to pitch up, she shouldn't imagine.

'Look.' Helga points toward the groyne to where there's a small brown bird on the pebbles.

'It's a turnstone.'

Claire watches as it picks over a shell then looks up to check that nobody has seen it, then puts its head down again. If Helga hadn't pointed it out, she'd have never noticed it. She can see that the bird is torn between the world at its feet and the world around it. It's fascinating to watch.

In the water, they all set off in a slow swim parallel to the shore. It's taken a will of steel, but Claire's proud of herself for getting in with the minimum of fuss, like Helga. She watches her gloves beneath the surface, still hardly able to believe they're hers. She got the neoprene boots and gloves online and she feels more like she belongs now she has the right kit.

'How are you finding it?' Helga asks her.

'Fecking cold, but good.' Somehow it feels OK to swear in front of Helga.

'Hmm, my temperature gauge says that it's *bloody* cold. Not *fucking* cold,' Tor says, and Claire laughs, realising that this is an 'in' joke between them all.

'It's fucking cold in February and March,' Dominica clarifies in a posh accent, as if that's an actual thing.

'I'm glad you've got a working temperature gauge. I don't seem to be able to control my temperature at the best of times,'

Claire tells Dominica. 'I wake up all the time in the night with hot sweats.' It's the first time she's admitted this, but she sees that Tor and Helga are listening, so she goes on. 'It drives my husband crazy. I can't bear for him to touch me and I fling off the duvet and then I lie there, feeling myself sweating from head-to-toe and it's disgusting. My nightie clings to me, my hair gets sodden, and my scalp feels like it's on fire. Then, just as quickly, I'm freezing and shivering.'

'Oh yeah. *That*.' Dominica clearly understands exactly what Claire is describing.

Claire tells them about how frustrating it is to be so clumsy and how Pim and the boys tease her for mispronouncing her words and forgetting everything.

'They make me feel like a right eejit.'

'Don't they speak menopause?' Dominica asks. 'I know exactly what a thingummy in a whatsit means in the right context.'

'At least someone does.'

'It sounds to me like you need to get tooled up. First off, you need a Chillow Pillow.'

'What's that?'

Dominica flips over on her back so that she can talk more easily to Claire. Her words mist on the water as she explains that it's a thing you put in the fridge and then under your pillow at night and then you can flip it to stop your head being so hot.

'And I've heard the magnets are great,' Dominica continues. 'My sister-in-law swears by them. Menopoised. That's the site. I'll send you the link. You put a tiny magnet in a plaster on the back of your neck on a heat acupressure point. Works wonders for some.'

'You've been through the menopause?' Claire asks.

'Yep,' Dominica says. 'I was forty-eight.'

'I'm forty-four,' Claire says.

'Yeah, well, that was eight years ago.'

Claire is stunned. She thought Dominica was younger than her, not almost a decade older. But her wisdom is comforting and she's glad she's having this chat, because it's not until this moment that Claire has considered that there may be alternative solutions to her menopausal symptoms.

'My husband says I should go to the doctor to get on HRT.' Much as she's suffering, Claire doesn't believe stuffing herself full of hormones is going to make the feeling that she's changing go away. And she's heard that HRT only puts the menopause off. She doesn't want these hot sweats when she's seventy. She tells all this to Dominica, who completely agrees. She asks Claire about the supplements she's taking and tuts when Claire tells her that she's not taking anything. There's clearly so much more she can be doing to help herself. Dominica says she'll put some links on the chat.

'When I was your age, women never talked about the menopause at all,' Helga says, joining in the conversation. She's ahead of Claire and her knees break the surface of the sea occasionally. Other than that, her head glides as gracefully as a swan. Claire has to swim a little bit faster to keep up so she can hear her. 'It came as a complete shock to me. In the space of a month, everything dried up. My skin, my vagina.' Tor and Claire laugh at how candid she's being. 'I'm serious. My libido disappeared along with my waistline. Just like that.'

'That's exactly how I feel,' Claire says.

Dominica chips in, 'I'd always been so slim and trim and

then, without doing anything differently, I put on weight and sprouted a muffin top.'

She's so statuesque and beautiful. And she certainly doesn't have a muffin top and Claire's about to say so, when Helga continues, 'But it passes. And the second act of life is by far and away the most rewarding.'

'That's reassuring,' Claire says.

'And believe me, this is the best thing you can do.'

'Is it?'

Helga nods. 'Oh, yes. For the menopause? You have to be out in nature. You see you are changing from a girl who is tied to the moon and her cycles, to the slower pace of Mother Earth. When you reach the change, it's as if you come into land like a bird. I find that I'm much more in tune with the seasons now than I've ever been.'

As Claire swims on, she chews over this nugget of wisdom from Helga, feeling it penetrate her like a warm glow. This is a new way to think about the future. She likes that idea of coming in to land on Mother Earth. It's comforting somehow. As if she still has a purpose. As if she's still relevant.

Without discussion, Tor, Helga and Dominica turn around to swim back the way they came and a little wave goes up Claire's nose. Their stuff in the pile on the beach suddenly looks like miles away, but Helga has struck out back across the width of the beach, like a mother duck leading her duck-lings. Claire is slightly out of breath, feeling her legs kick out behind her but, in the water, she doesn't feel lumpy or fat. She feels strong.

'I've always been scared of the menopause,' Tor says. 'And having that all to come. I'm scared I'll turn into an old hag.'

'Oh, I hope you do,' Helga announces. 'I totally identify as an old hag. I always draw in a new box on those government forms when they ask me.'

'That figures,' Dominica teases her.

'A hag in days gone by was a wise woman. Someone who lived independently. Who knew about remedies,' Helga says matter-of-factly.

Tor smiles. 'You're a very fit old hag, Helga.'

'You enjoy being young,' Claire tells Tor. 'With that lovely figure of yours. I'd so love to be skinny.'

'I *hate* being skinny,' Tor exclaims. 'I hate being flat-chested and having a boy's bum. Why do *you* want to be skinny?'

Claire is surprised – by her admission and by the genuine confusion on Tor's face. 'Well, to be healthier for a start. To feel attractive again.'

'You don't feel attractive? Does your husband tell you you're not attractive?' Helga asks and Claire is shocked by her directness.

'Pim?' Claire feels suddenly disloyal somehow, ashamed that Helga would think that of him. 'No . . . no . . . ' she stumbles, but the truth is that she can't really remember the last time Pim properly flirted with her. She can't remember the last time she spontaneously snogged him. It's been so long that the thought of it is preposterous. That if, say, she were to press him against the fridge and kiss him – with tongues – he'd think it was some kind of assault.

'Then who is telling you you're not attractive?' Helga asks.

'I am, I suppose . . . ' she trails off. She can't admit the truth. That she looks in the mirror and often turns sideways, viewing the flap of her stomach above her butchered double

Caesarean scar with a loathing so violent it sometimes makes tears come to her eyes. And how she increasingly wonders where her youthful skin went and what on earth she can do about her grey roots.

'Nonsense. I want you to model for me,' Helga says.

'Model?'

'I teach a life-drawing class. You're so much more interesting than Keith.'

'I don't, I can't . . . '

'Yes, you can,' Helga says encouragingly, meaning it.

At that moment, a wave comes from nowhere and crashes over their heads.

'That took me by surprise,' Claire splutters.

'There's nothing like the slap of a wave on the back of the head to remind you who's boss,' Helga says. 'Look out, here comes the break.'

She nods towards the surfers in the distance near the burnt-out pier who are all on the move.

Another wave breaks over Claire's head and she's dragged forward then gets her feet down. Tor bodysurfs past her like a dolphin, making a gleeful whoop of joy.

Claire is still smiling when she gets back to the house. Pim is already complaining about his workload, about the latest dictate from his nemesis – the deputy head, but, for once, she remembers the swimmer in the superhero cape and, before she knows what she's doing, she stands her ground.

Facing him, she tells him that before he sets up for the day on the kitchen table, it's not convenient for him to be working in her space. He's to shut the wooden doors to the dining room area, or to retreat upstairs to the small study. She can't continue to pussyfoot around.

'I need my space,' she tells him. 'And it doesn't work for me going forward that you're in it.'

He looks surprised. 'But you're not doing anything.'

She opens her mouth, shocked that this is actually what he thinks. 'Pim, I do everything. *Every bloody thing.* I clean, I tidy, I wash and iron, I think about, shop for and make every bit of food that goes into your mouth, then I clean your plate away and use my very underutilised brain to plan the next meal to keep it interesting – not that any of you ever . . . ever appreciate it.'

Her voice has risen. She can't believe she's actually said these words out loud, rather than muttering them silently to herself.

'Claire—' he says, but she holds up her hand.

'Please don't try and justify yourself. Just hear what I've just said.'

'All right. I hear you,' he says, in a slightly defeated way. 'I'm sorry. I'll get out of your hair.'

His computer makes a sound – another Zoom call. He gets up and takes his laptop and leaves her shaking in the kitchen.

She holds on to the kitchen worktop and looks at the magpies in the cherry tree. After a moment, she flicks on the radio. A pop song is playing from the nineties – the Cardigans – and she knows the tune. She hums it, letting her voice and her mind reclaim her kitchen.

'Not doing anything,' she says aloud. 'The feckin' cheek of it.'

15

Tent Call

Maddy is out with Luna for her early-afternoon stroll around the graveyard. She's been taking the little dog out every day since New Year to help Matteo out, but also because she likes having an excuse to get out of the flat. Talking to Matteo on the doorstep is becoming the highlight of her days.

She wishes she could talk to a girlfriend about this little flirtation going on. Is she being a crazy menopausal woman thinking that Matteo might find her attractive, like she finds him? There's such a big age difference between them. Surely someone as hot as Matteo would go after younger women? He's confided to her that he wants children and that's why it could never have worked out with Shauna, who didn't feel mentally stable enough to be a mother, so Maddy is at completely the wrong life stage for him. So what could he possibly see in her? Nothing, surely? But then . . . the way he looks at her . . . ? She can't help thinking that *something* might be there. Not that she would have the guts to do anything about it, but it's making her feel like a bloody teenager when she imagines what he might look like naked.

Lisa would help make sense of it all, but Maddy can't reach out to her. Lisa's deception still stings too much. The fact that she knew about Trent's affair with Helen feels too huge a betrayal. Because she must have known all the details. All the dates, all the . . . wait . . . *holidays*? Maddy can't help raking over the past for evidence, feeling a jolt each time she thinks of a new moment that she must have been lied to about – like Trent's golfing trips. How he used to tell her every boring detail so that she tuned out . . . as he knew she would. And she remembers too, at the golf club dinner – how Trent's friends were always so charming towards her. Had *they* known that he was cheating on her? One man – Geoff – sticks in her mind. How he made a joke she hadn't understood and Trent had brushed over it.

With a little distance, she can see that maybe the signs were there, but she'd deliberately ignored them. Maybe it was to do with her menopause, or just that she and Trent had got too used to each other and he'd got bored. But it's so hard to untangle it all and her feelings about her marriage and Jamie without feeling floored by helplessness and shame.

It doesn't help that it's already a fortnight into a new year and she's drawn a blank on her hunt for Jamie. She's starting to think that maybe he's changed his name. Or maybe he's not even living here. Maybe he'd just been passing through at Christmas. She's taped a hundred 'missing' posters to lamp posts around the town and in the phone box from where Jamie made the call on Christmas Day. She's shown his photo in every shop and to practically everyone she's met, but . . . nothing.

She's just taping a laminated photo to the graveyard's notice board, when she notices a woman smiling at her. She's the one with the two boys who have gone off around the looping path on their skateboards and she's coming towards her by the gate. They must be about nine and eleven, Maddy thinks, staring wistfully at the boys. They both have a mop of black hair and are clearly brothers. The older one is tall and gangly and she can remember Jamie at exactly that age. How he grew suddenly, sprouting legs and hair overnight. She remembers too, what a ninja he was – how sure-footed and daring. He'd had no fear, just complete confidence in his physical abilities.

'Oh,' the woman says, 'you were the lady on the beach. I recognise the dog.'

Maddy is startled. She doesn't know anyone here, apart from Matteo, so it feels odd to be recognised.

'Oh, Luna, yes.' Maddy remembers the woman, recognising her Irish accent. She's wearing a pink woolly coat and the wrong shade of lipstick, and her smile is friendly. She looks expectantly at Maddy.

'I was so impressed you went in,' Maddy says. 'I thought it was nice you had a gang.'

'Oh, yes. I suppose we are a gang. I guess swimming together does instantly bond you. I've lived here for ten years and being down at the beach is the first time I've really felt part of a wider community. The women in the Sea-Gals, they're really lovely.'

Maddy smiles. The Sea-Gals. She remembers the older one mentioning that now. She likes the playful pun. These are obviously not women who take themselves too seriously. 'They were very good-natured about the dog.'

'Dominica totally fell for Luna.'

Dominica must have been that tall striking one, Maddy thinks, remembering how Luna had crawled onto her lap.

'Why don't you come down and join us sometime? Helga had been about to ask you to join the group. I can take your number if you like and get her to add you?' the woman says, taking out her phone.

Maddy is about to refuse, but the woman seems insistent and, before Maddy knows it, she's given over her details.

'How long have you lived here?' Claire – as she now introduces herself as – asks.

'A few weeks.'

'Is that all?' She sounds shocked.

'Yes, I'm . . . I've . . . I've left my husband.'

Claire bites her lip, embarrassed. 'Oh, no. I'm so sorry.'

'It's been coming for a while.' It's only now that she says these words that Maddy realises how true it is.

'Are you all right? Are you staying with family?'

'No, no, I'm alone, although I'm trying to find my son. He lives here. I think.'

'You think?'

'We've lost contact and . . . ' Maddy feels her voice break and a rush of emotion, making tears spring to her eyes. She nods to the picture she's just taped up.

'Don't apologise. Honestly, I complain about those two the whole time, but I couldn't bear to be separated. That must be so tough.'

Her genuine compassion feels so comforting. 'I've tried really hard to find him, but I've drawn a blank so far.'

'Come for a swim. Or at least come down to the beach and meet the others. They've all been in Brighton for years. One of them might be able to help. We're going in the morning. Nine o'clock. You'd be most welcome.' Claire smiles brightly and squeezes her arm, as if they've already arranged it.

Maddy smiles back at her and gives her a little wave as she leaves through the gate with her sons. Where she lives, her friendships have taken years to build, alliances carefully formed through friends of friends, new women vetted for their credentials as having the right balance of looking the part, whilst being fun. All of them are wealthy. All of them have designer homes. All of them, she thinks now, unhappily skinny.

It's been a very long time since she's formed a spontaneous friendship, certainly with someone like Claire. Someone *normal*. She can well imagine the derogatory comment Trent would make about her appearance. He's always been such a body fascist – one of the reasons that Maddy's kept her figure so trim and well maintained. Because of Trent's 'high standards'. But now she knows what a wanker he is, it only makes her more resolved to take up Claire's kind offer to join them swimming tomorrow. Is she brave enough?

She walks to the end of the path with Luna, noticing there's a tent at the end tucked between the far gravestones. It's shocking that someone is camping in a corner of a graveyard in January. But Maddy has started to see helpless people everywhere. People with slumped shoulders and haunted eyes. Any of them could be Jamie. If he's homeless, that is. Because *is* he? For all she knows, he might be living in a mansion, on his way to being a tech billionaire. Isn't that what he once declared he was going to be?

But somehow, she knows, just *knows* that that's wishful

thinking. That his dreams never did come true and that it's up to her to find him and try and put that right.

On a whim she walks over to the tent, wondering how one knocks on a fabric door.

'Hello,' she calls. 'Is there anyone in there?'

She waits outside the tent. There's no answer. Luna comes over and snuffles at the zip.

There's some rustling inside the tent. A very sleepy man opens the zip and peers out. His gums are blackened, several teeth missing.

'What do you want?' There's confusion on his gaunt face as he takes in Maddy and Luna.

'Sorry to disturb you,' she says. 'It's just . . . I'm looking for my son.' As the stumbled words come out, she realises how pathetically posh she sounds. How needy and uninformed.

The man's weariness comes at her along with an atrocious smell. He's ill. Really ill. He slumps back down as if he's been expecting a fight. Now she looks inside the tent, she can see an empty cider bottle and a jumble of clothes and bedding.

'This is him.' She takes out a picture of Jamie, but her stomach is curdling with the thought that Jamie might been reduced to this state. She shows it to the man, but he shakes his head. He sways slightly and Maddy realises he's swooning with hunger.

'Can I help you at all?' she asks, but as the man meets her eye, it takes all she has not to look away in revulsion.

'You got any spare money?' he asks.

'Some. A tenner, I think.' She remembers the cash in her jeans at the same time that she remembers that it might be the last bit of actual money she might be able to get her hands on. She's liquidated an ISA to pay Manpreet and her living expenses, but it's not going to last her long. With her and Trent's joint account still ominously empty, she'll have no choice but to use her credit cards to get by. She's always found comfort in having a little safety net of her own savings, but now they've gone, it's scary that she's going to have to start budgeting and thinking about money in a way she hasn't had to for years.

He nods and she fumbles, taking the cash out of her jeans, thinking that he obviously needs it more. The man grabs the crisp note. Then he juts out his chin in thanks and she takes it as her cue to leave.

As she gets to the gate with Luna, two police officers in high-vis jackets are walking in, a man and woman. The woman bends down to pet Luna and Maddy thinks how Luna melts hearts wherever she goes. She'd never realised what a conversational ice-breaker a puppy is until now, as she starts chatting to the policewoman, but then her partner's radio goes. He turns to Maddy.

'You haven't seen anything suspicious?' he asks.

'No, I was just talking to the guy in there.' Maddy points to the tent. 'He seemed a bit unwell. I gave him a tenner.'

'That's kind of you, but you don't want to talk to them,' the policeman says, with a frown. 'Some of them really don't like being disturbed in the day. There's been some incidents.'

Maddy realises how stupid she'd been.

'Why can't they get to hostels?' she asks the policewoman.

'They can. But they can't do drugs in the hostels, so they'd rather sleep rough. Don't worry. We'll move him on.'

'No, no you don't need to—'

But they're already marching up the path.

Maddy watches the gate close and feels a spike of dread. As she walks away, she cringes at the thought that she might have unwittingly made things worse.

16

Oystercatchers

Helga can't sleep and she gets up with the dawn chorus and, in front of the heater in the conservatory, idles away a few hours working on the life drawings she's started, but she's not inspired. Keith, their model, with his thick shoulders and hairy back, is impossible to make beautiful. She wonders if Claire will be brave enough to take her up on her offer. She has a feeling that stripping off and baring all might give her the confidence she's lacking.

She goes to the bookshelf where she pressed her pictures yesterday in between two of the heavy books. They are both sailing books and, on a whim, she opens one of them. A piece of paper flutters to the scuffed floorboards and she picks it up, her heart thudding once in recognition. She's not sentimental – particularly about mementos. She throws most things away, keeping her clutter to a minimum. She likes the place to be shipshape, everything in its natural place, so she'd be ashamed if anyone knew that she's kept this note from Linus for all these years. A piece of her heart preserved on a flimsy piece of paper, yellowed and brittle by a long-set sun.

Meet me at the dock.

She sighs, putting the faded note in the book. There's no place for regrets, she tells herself. But, still, her mind strays back to those sun-filled days messing around on boats with Linus that Christmas in Antigua – oh, it must be nearly fifty years ago, but she can picture it all as if it were yesterday. She remembers his tanned, lithe torso, his floppy blond fringe, his infectious smile.

She thinks back to that day she made the choice *not* to meet him on the dock.

She'd been so headstrong. So determined to be a solo sailor and to be recognised, but the sailing trophies that had seemed so important at the time wouldn't even fetch anything at a car boot sale now. It's far too late, but sometimes she can't help wondering what would have happened if she *hadn't* let him sail away without her?

'Oh, for God's sake,' she says out loud. That is *ancient* history. She needs to get over herself.

She distracts herself by calling Mette. She left a message a few days ago, so Helga owes her niece a call. In her mind's eye, Mette is still a young teenager with long colt-like legs and blonde plaits, licking the sugar from the top of the bakery pastries in the morning. It's a surprise that it's Mette's secretary who answers her phone and Helga realises she's already in work.

They haven't been so affected by Covid where Mette is and she thinks of her in her glass office in Copenhagen, ordering around her staff. Mette has short hair these days and wears stylish well-cut clothes in muted tones of grey and black. Helga wonders where that fun-loving girl who used to make up silly dances has gone. She's so serious these days. Too serious to date. Too serious to have children. Helga respects her for being an independent woman. Of course she does. She was proudly one herself, but she wishes she was brave enough to tell Mette that forging your own path can leave you way out in front all alone.

Still, it's comforting to hear her mother tongue as Mette is given her phone and Helga listens to her giving orders to a minion. Mette's the boss at an architectural practice and Helga's always surprised by her capacity for logistics and planning. That's probably why she's got such a big job.

'There you are,' Mette says, with relief, turning her attention to Helga. 'At last. I was beginning to get worried.'

She's of that generation, Helga thinks, where everything has to be instantaneous.

'I'm fine. I didn't have my phone on.'

'But what if something happens? What if you get ill?'

'Why would I be ill?'

'I worry about you.'

'Don't waste your energy worrying about me. There's no need.'

When did their relationship shift, Helga wonders? When did she stop being the one caring for Mette, to the one being cared for? The power balance feels all wrong.

'But I do worry. I wish you had a community around you. People looking out for you. It's not healthy to be so alone. Especially in lockdown.'

'I have a community. I have my swimmers,' Helga says

defensively. She used to have a wild independent lifestyle that people admired and it annoys her that Mette finds her set-up lacking.

'Listen. I've been meaning to talk to you about something. I've been doing some work on a new development. A retirement complex. I'm going to send you the brochure. I think you'd love it. It would be nearby. I could see you all the—'

'Oh, Mette, no . . . no, I couldn't stand the other people. You know I'm no good with old people.'

'But—'

'Seriously. Save your breath. I mean it.'

Mette makes a 'we'll see about that' kind of noise. She knows Mette has the best intentions, but she hates feeling like this . . . like she's become a burden. It's a sobering thought that Mette thinks of her as old.

She gets up and looks in the mirror, but it's a mistake. The face staring back at her *is* old.

Mette tries a different approach.

'You will want to come home,' she says. 'Eventually. I know you will. And you might as well before it's too late.'

'I don't know,' Helga says. Because she doesn't. What she does know is that Mette talking about her life as if there's not much of it left is making her heart flutter unpleasantly.

'I love you,' Mette says, with sudden affection in her voice. 'I only want what's right for you. And besides . . . I miss you.'

'I miss you too, darling. But I'm fine, really. You concentrate on that wonderful job of yours. We'll talk soon.'

Helga puts the phone down, wondering if Mette is right about how she'll eventually migrate home, like the geese in Jutland. But is Denmark really home? She left a long, long time ago, making the sea her home and then she'd settled temporarily in England. She looks around her shabby cottage, thinking that she's never thought of this place as permanent. But the thought of shipping back to an end-of-days retirement home, however stylish, fills her with dread.

When she gets down to the beach for their morning swim, she's pleased to see that Maddy, the woman she challenged the other day, is waiting on the beach, the hood of her parka up and a nervous smile on her face as she chats to Dominica. Claire had excitedly written on the WhatsApp that she'd invited her.

'You came,' Helga says with a nod.

'I nearly didn't, but I'm here.'

'That's all that counts.'

Claire bustles down the beach, her new camouflage coat flapping. 'Coming, coming,' she calls.

'Oh, so you got one, then?' Dominica says.

'You were absolutely right.' Claire grins, clapping her mittens together with delight. 'I got this on Facebook marketplace for twenty quid.'

'I thought there was bound to be one going after Christmas.'

'I'd have never thought of it if you hadn't said. So, thank you for the tip-off. I love it. And with this weather, I got it in the nick of time. Oh, Maddy, you've joined the gang.' She beams a smile, then goes to hug Maddy, but remembers the social distancing rules just in time.

Helga knows it's important that they spread out. One dog walker got very annoyed the other day that they appeared to be in a group, but she told him to bugger off, which was most satisfactory. He was even more embarrassed because Claire and Dominica were laughing so much. Helga didn't care. She's sick to death of these finger-pointers. People who pretend that they follow the rules to the absolute letter, ignoring all common sense. It was none of his business, but since she only sees the swimming girls, they do count as her bubble. She's not breaking any rules as far as she's concerned, not that she could be bothered to explain that to the sanctimonious dog walker.

Helga is constantly amazed by the vitriol and indignation of the mainly white middle-aged man towards sea swimmers. Increasingly, she sees snippy clickbait articles about swimmers in the press – that always seem to be written by men – about people wearing Dryrobes for everyday tasks, as if going about your business in something cosy and waterproof is not allowed. They don't seem to approve of the Dryrobes being worn for their intended purpose either. But then, throughout history, men seeing groups of women doing something brave has always caused a rattling of sabres. Helga thinks it's rather wonderful that the sea swimming gangs on the beach are recognisable from their long hooded coats.

Helga gets changed quickly and watches as Maddy neatly stores her things in her bag.

'See. The oystercatchers.' Helga points to a group of birds with long orange beaks who land on the groyne ahead, as if they've arrived to inspect their group.

'Is that what they're called? I've never noticed them before,' Maddy says.

'Helga has taught me so much about the seabirds,' Claire confides. 'Every time we come I learn something new. Like those. Sandpipers, right?'

Helga nods, following her gaze to the speckled birds. She's

warmed by Claire's praise, as they all get undressed. It's no skin off her nose to talk about the birds. She's astounded that people don't notice the way they call out and communicate, the way they chatter and argue and play. In her opinion, watching birds is far better than watching any soap opera on the TV – the fights, the affairs, the love, the struggle for territory – it's fascinating.

'Is that all you're wearing?' Maddy asks, pointing to Helga's costume and she looks down at her blue swimsuit, thinking that she really should get round to getting a new one. Where it was once taut and springy, the elastic in the material is now revealing itself in little white worms and the whole thing is baggy and saggy – rather like how Helga feels herself.

Maddy is wearing a wetsuit underneath her sweatshirt and sweatpants. 'I feel overdressed. I borrowed this from my neighbour. It's a man's one, but it fits.' She has a trimmed, toned body and Helga remembers having one of those herself. In a shocking flash, she remembers Linus pouring champagne into the dip of her belly button.

'Whatever works for you.' Helga's not a snob about these things. People can wear what they want. Whatever gets them in the water.

Tor arrives in a hurry, clearly in desperate need of a dip, poor kid. Helga lives in fear of getting arthritis herself. Plenty of people her age are sufferers, but she hopes her lifetime in cold water has saved her that particular torment, for now at least. Something is bound to get her soon enough, though. Especially according to Mette. She still feels unsettled by their call earlier.

The tide is going out, the sun filtered behind the clouds, a shy bride behind a veil.

'I'm not really a swimmer.' Maddy sticks close to Helga, as they head off down the stones towards the sea. There are some swimmers further out, swimming with languid strokes.

'I'm not either,' Claire says. 'But wouldn't it be good to swim like that?'

'You could take lessons,' Helga says, remembering that Dominica had mentioned having some in the Queens Hotel. 'Didn't you have some a while back?' she asks her.

'Oh yeah,' Dominica says. 'With Andy. I'll give you his number.'

'Is he nice?' Claire asks.

'Oh yes,' Dominica says in a strange way and Helga remembers now that Dominica had told her that he was very attractive. 'I think you'll like him.'

'So, what's the trick? To getting in, I mean?' Maddy asks, now they're ankle-deep.

'To walk in slowly,' Helga explains. 'Which is why it's good you're going in at low tide. Just gentle steps in,' she coaxes, as they reach the water.

Tor and Dominica and Claire wade ahead, bracing their knees against the breaking waves. They're like Amazonian warriors heading off towards the sinking sun. Tor's shoulders get higher and higher as she avoids getting her armpits into the cold water, then she braves it and dives in, like a mermaid. She comes up with a whoop of joy.

'Oh my God,' Maddy says, stopping. 'Sorry,' she apologises. 'I can't do it.'

'You can. Don't be intimidated. Nothing bad is going to happen.'

'Really?'

'You're going to experience some very normal reactions. The first of which is your gasp reflex, when you'll take a sharp intake of breath. Your heart rate will go up. That's why people get in trouble when they jump into very cold water, but you doing this . . . walking slowly . . . means it's all going to be fine.'

Maddy nods and continues to walk in with Helga.

'OK, so this isn't going to be pleasant, but my suggestion is that you dunk down and get some cold water down the front of your wetsuit. Get that reaction over with.'

'And then what happens?'

'Well, just notice. You'll be fine after the initial shock.'

Maddy dips down and puts water down the neck of her wetsuit. She squeals and gasps at the same time.

'You're right. That's horrible.'

Helga's not one for wetsuits. Never has been. As far as she's concerned, the wetsuit is like a full-body condom and she's not up for total sensory deprivation, when the whole point of getting in the water is to experience your senses fizzing. The others are all in now and she glides down into the water with a smile.

Maddy is intrepidly following her, deeper now. 'What's the temperature? I mean, what classifies as cold water?'

'Well, anything under sixteen degrees is cold and under ten is really cold. I think we're at about nine today.'

'Err . . . yep. I'd say it's really cold.' Maddy lets out a shocked laugh. 'You don't have to stay in longer on my account.'

'We won't stay longer than ten minutes or so, in any case.'

'What happens if you do?'

Helga remembers that night swim when she and Linus had got into trouble. It had been summertime, but the Scandinavian nights are always cold. It was their first holiday together. She'd taken him home to introduce him to her grandmother and, with her blessing, they'd taken her beloved old camper van to the coast.

'In cold water, they reckon that anywhere between five and thirty minutes, you cool down too much for your fingers and forearms to move.'

She pictures Linus, his blond hair falling in his face, his lips blue in the moonlight as he fumbled with the keys to the van, unable to turn them in the lock and dropping them in the sand, the tide coming precariously close.

'It's scary. It happened to me once. I lost all coordination and was stumbling around like a drunk woman.' She remembers staggering to the van and how they'd moved to safety just in the nick of time, the tyres crunching over the carpet of pine needles as they'd retreated through the trees from the water's edge. How they'd stripped off and clung to each other naked under the blankets on the mattress, their lips blue, their teeth chattering. How they'd both been scared and how she'd never wanted to let him go. Why does she remember all these things so clearly, when some of the intervening decades are fuzzy and lost?

'That's it. Splash your forearms and the back of your neck.'

Dominica swims over, a few languid strokes of front crawl.

'You've put your face under,' Maddy says, clearly impressed.

'That's to stimulate the vagus nerve.'

'The vagus nerve? Sounds like something to do with gambling.'

'It's one of the biggest nerves in the body,' Helga explains. 'It runs all down here' – she puts her hand up to her face and throat – 'and right down to the abdomen. In fact, it goes everywhere. Vagus means wanderer in Latin, so it wanders all over the place to all your organs. Basically, when you get into cold water your fight or flight nervous system kicks in. But here's the thing. Cold water also stimulates the vagus nerve, which does the opposite. It kicks in your parasympathetic nervous system.'

'Did you know that pharmaceutical companies try and mimic the vagus nerve when they make antidepressants?' Dominica adds, as an aside.

Helga gives her a frown. They've spoken about the pills the doctor prescribed to Dominica, and Helga made it clear that, in her view, it's a mistake to start pills, when her grief is unavoidable. It's a process. Just like everything else in life. Taking pills for it doesn't *stop* that process, just dulls it. And what's the point of life being dull? As far as Helga's concerned, emotions are like internal weather and she's a great believer in experiencing all extremes of weather. After all, you can't go through life expecting nothing but sunny days. That's not realistic. You have to have the grey, boring days, or the relentlessly rainy ones to appreciate the sun when it comes out.

Helga keeps this to herself. It's not a popular view to believe in healing oneself, but she's told Dominica before: in her book, getting into cold water cures most ailments. Even heartbreak.

'So, this is scientific?' Claire checks. 'There's science backing up why this makes us feel so good.'

'Absolutely.'

'So, I'm speeding up and slowing down? At the same time?' Maddy asks, confused.

'Remember the baby on the Nirvana album?' Claire says

and Maddy nods. 'And how happy he looks? It's that. We have that hardwired in us.'

'Just get under. Take a few strokes and come up again to standing. Then you'll know you'll be OK,' Helga coaxes. 'Never mind the science, it's how it feels that counts.'

Maddy braces herself and dunks her shoulders under, her eyes wide, then she takes a breath and puts her head under and swims a few strokes. She comes up grinning and Helga and the others all clap. To Helga's astonishment, Maddy lets out a feral kind of howl.

'Looks like we've got ourselves another Sea-Gal,' she says.

17

Rob's Declaration

Claire is glad Maddy has been initiated into their gang and she's even more pleased when she realises that Tor works with homeless people and might be able to help her find her son. Claire's agreed to volunteer for Tor's charity and bring some cakes to the food bank she runs, but now Maddy is coming too.

She's coming back from Aldi with all the ingredients, her mind whirring with the cakes she's planning on baking. She's going to keep it simple. Sponge tray bakes with jam and desiccated coconut. Old school. There'll be plenty to go around.

As she's crossing the road, she sees Rob, Jenna's husband, coming along the pavement towards his gate from the other direction, ostentatiously swinging his leg over his bike and walking. She could hang back, but there's a car coming, so she needs to hurry with her shopping bags, the heavier one of which feels like it's about to split, so she's running with her knees bent and the bag close to the ground just in case.

She arrives at the pavement, just as Rob's blocking it with his designer bike. He should really let her pass first. That would be the polite thing to do, but he deliberately slows straight across her path and gives her a smug look as she waits in the gutter. He's got a helmet on and there are sweat streaks down his face. What do they call them? Mamils. Middle-aged-men-in-Lycra. His shorts with their obvious bulge in the front are rather distracting.

'No, after you.' Claire gestures to let him pass. He unclips his helmet without a word of thanks and Claire, stupefied by his rudeness, walks determinedly to her gate.

'I heard you put an objection in to the council,' Rob calls out, as if this justifies his behaviour.

Pim spent ages crafting a carefully worded email.

'I think it's a travesty you're cutting down the tree, that's all.' She doesn't add that she's horrified by how much light they're going to take away from the back of her house once the two-storey extension goes up. Claire has seen the plans and they will transform next door into a modern monstrosity. 'We could have discussed it before,' she adds. 'It could have been friendly.' Instead of acrimonious. She doesn't say it, but her tone implies it. She feels trembly, but firm, like a tree being shaken in the wind herself. This is not like her to be brave enough to confront anyone – especially an alpha male like Rob. But in her mind's eye, Claire suddenly has an image of Helga. She'd *never* put up with someone like Rob.

'We're neighbours. We don't have to be friends.'

'Isn't that a rather sad stance to take?' Because . . . *really*? Doesn't he care? About the environment? Or about the people around him? She hears the old song from the *Neighbours* soap in her mind. About everyone needing good neighbours. And good neighbours becoming good friends. 'Listen, Rob,

I don't want there to be any bad feeling and I wish we could sort this out,' she says and puts her bags down. 'For Jenna's sake,' she continues. 'She and I are friends, even if you and I aren't.'

'Jenna?' he says, with a snort. 'And you? Friends?'

Claire's cheeks burn at his nasty tone.

'Friends is pushing it. I think Jenna finds you a bit . . . creepy. The way you copy her. You know, the same coat and everything.' Claire is embarrassed to be caught in her Dryrobe coming back from the shops, but she hasn't changed since her swim. It hadn't crossed her mind that her robe was the same as Jenna's, but now her cheeks start pulsing. Nobody has ever said anything so downright rude to her before. *Creepy?* Has Jenna said that about her?

Is this a lockdown thing? She saw a thing about it on TV about how people are not filtering as much as they used to? Or is it just that Rob is a grade-A gobshite.

She wants desperately to defend herself, to respond with a withering take-down but the words won't come. Instead, she hurries away, the tears already brimming in her eyes, as she pushes open the side gate and lugs the bags along the tiny strip of path between the side of their house and the fence, easing past the boys' bikes and the hose that is spilling out of its plastic container by the tap. There's a tower of empty plastic plant pots from the last time she tried to garden.

A little greenfinch sits on the cherry branch. Since meeting Helga and learning about birds, Claire's noticing them everywhere, but particularly on the cherry tree. The little bird has green-gold feathers and a pink beak and there's a moment as they stare at one another. Then it flies across the garden.

Claire listens to the birdsong that fills the air. They sound like kids in a school playground at break time.

She tries to let the sound calm her and obliterate Rob's horrible words, but she's shaking as she opens the back door.

Pim is scrolling through his phone, but when he sees her he rushes over to help her with the bags.

'I'd have got those. They look heavy. Damn. They are heavy. What have you got?'

'Flour and sugar, mainly. And jam. And please, don't start. It's all on offer. And for Tor's charity,' Claire stands up and shakes out her hands. They hurt from where the handles have dug in and she's still not properly warm from the swim this morning. She's shivering, she realises. With cold? Humiliation? Or possibly both.

'Are you OK?'

'No, not really.'

'What's wrong?'

Claire jabs her finger in the direction of Rob and Jenna's. 'People like them. *They're* what's wrong.' The furious tears that have stalled now come.

'Claire?'

She shakes her head, swallowing back tears. She can't tell Pim what Rob has said. If she does, he'll cause even more of a scene.

'I just want you to know, for the record, you were absolutely right to defend us against Jenna and Rob. I'm such a people-pleaser, but not this time, Pim. Not this time.'

To her surprise, he folds her into a hug. Then he kisses the top of her head and she breathes in his comforting scent. She presses her ear against his chest, hearing his heartbeat.

They share a bed every night, but this moment of intimacy in the day is rare. She's often in her head about Pim's faults and shortcomings, but the regular rhythm of his heartbeat is a reminder that he's just human. And just as he hasn't taken much notice of her, maybe she hasn't been taking much notice of him either.

'What's happened?' he asks, pulling away, but his arms are still around her waist, their hips pressed together. This is how they used to stand, she remembers. In days gone by. When they were courting. He'd even stand like this in the pub with her. Always connected.

She explains tearfully about her encounter, making it clear that she doesn't want Pim to go into battle on her account.

'Jenna is crazy to turn down your friendship,' he says. 'Believe me, she'll regret it.'

'Thank you. That means a lot.'

'You sure you don't want me to go round there and punch Rob's lights out? Because I think I would kind of enjoy it. And he's definitely got it coming.'

She shakes her head. 'No. But thank you anyway.'

She leans over and grabs some kitchen roll and blows her nose and he sways against her, like he used to do. The very soft prelude to the foreplay from the days when sex was inevitably on the cards. Then he puts his finger on her chin to lift her face to his and they smile at each other. The familiarity of the connection feels at once thrillingly strange and so comfortingly familiar that her heart does a little skip.

She's missed this. This feeling of them being them. She's missed it so much. She's about to say it, when Felix yells from upstairs.

'Dad. Come and see this!'

He's on Fortnite and she sees Pim's eyes light up.

'Coming!' he calls back.

She doesn't want him to go. She loves the feeling of being pressed against him, but even so, she gives him a small nod of permission and he bounds out of the kitchen and up the stairs two at a time.

Claire blows her nose again. She feels better for letting out her frustrations with Rob and that, for once, Pim seemed to understand her point of view.

They're not going to cut down that tree. Not if she can help it.

18

Hard to Forgive

Since going in the sea on Saturday, Maddy has felt different. It feels as if she's had a small re-set and it occurs to her that she's never had this kind of time before – this pause to get a bit of perspective. Her days at home are usually filled with the myriad of things that need her attention: the fault in the driveway bricks, the squeaky garage door, the leaky pump on the Jacuzzi and the security light that floods the garden with light in the small hours, but it's a relief to be away from all that stuff and to take an objective view. Not that many answers are forthcoming.

Manpreet was grateful that she'd been paid at last, but Maddy had to have an embarrassing conversation about how she can't afford her any more. It feels scary going it alone without her encouraging prompts.

Before Christmas, Maddy had been on such a roll, fully focused on growing the numbers on Instagram, but without being in the home her channels are dedicated to, she's running dry on ideas. Going through old photos to re-post from a different angle only makes her realise how much time she's spent focusing on the wrong things. Surely instead of making bespoke stair rods from salvaged copper pipes, she should have been looking for her son, or noticing what her husband was up to?

Trent has progressed from being whiney and upset to aggressive and nasty in their exchanges, especially when she requested that he give her a full breakdown of their financial situation. He's always assured her that he has everything under control when it comes to money. But now she knows she can't trust him, she's worried about the future she's always taken so much for granted. With a sinking sense of dread, she keeps thinking back to some of the hints he made before Christmas, some half-conversations that she ignored because she was preoccupied with getting her posts ready. But now she wants to know just how much trouble his business is in. She's always thought of herself as well-off, but the empty account came as a shock. Trent has made her believe that everything is going to come good, but what if it doesn't? And what if he's been making contingency plans all this time to leave her for Helen?

What then? Would she have enough to live independently? It occurs to her now that she should have been more savvy. It's never crossed her mind to consult a lawyer, but she knows enough from the details of the bruising divorces that some of her friends have been through, that she should have made Trent leave the family home. She should have thrown him out, but she'd been so cross, she'd had to get away. But in hindsight, perhaps that had been rather a reckless move.

Earlier this week, on one of their swims, Dominica suggested online marriage counselling, but Maddy doesn't want to rake over their marriage with a stranger. What's the point? She can never – and will never – forgive him. Even so, having the moral high ground is a little lonely. She can't help feeling that it would feel a little less precarious if she had the moral high ground from the comfort of her own home.

But then, she wouldn't be here, she reminds herself. In Brighton, where Jamie is potentially so close. There's still no sign of him, but that hopefully might change now she's volunteering with Tor later. She's looking forward to being on the front line handing out the donations from the food bank again. Because surely someone from the homeless community will have answers. Jamie's always made friends wherever he's gone. Someone's bound to know where he is. She's set her heart on it.

She opens the door to the balcony and stands on it and stretches, grabbing a bit of afternoon sunshine. She's set her desk up in here and she likes the view. She was disappointed by the meagre sea view at first, but since she's had such a long time to look at it, she'd become rather fond of her little glimpse of ocean. It amazes her that from day to day, it's never the same colour. Today, it's a purplish blue. Little pink clouds scud on the horizon.

As she stands, the house sparrows she's been watching nesting on the floor above flutter by in a flurry of wings and she watches them.

'Hey.'

She turns. It's Matteo. He's out on his balcony, too, as if he's also taking a break from work, but she wonders now whether he's come outside because he's seen her.

'Hi,' she says, turning to face him and smoothing her hair behind her ear. 'How's your day going?'

'You know . . . the usual.' He pauses, then comes over to the side of the balcony and smiles. He's wearing a sage-green wool jumper and she has a flash forward fantasy moment of how it would be to put her arms around him. Lord knows she could do with a hug and Matteo looks like the kind of man who gives *really* good hugs.

'I'm going for a sunset walk later with Luna. You want to join me?' Matteo asks.

'I'd love to, but I'm volunteering tonight. At the food bank.' She hooks her thumbs into the belt loops of her jeans – a nervous habit of old. He's smiling, but he's looking at her lips. She remembers seeing a documentary on one of those famous Hollywood actors and how he said it was easy to do seductive acting – you just had to look from the eyes to the lips and back again. Is Matteo doing that flirty move deliberately? Surely not. Even so, it makes her feel giddy and she bites her lip, unsure of how to act in the spotlight of his attention.

'Of course. Another time.'

'Or . . . or breakfast? I saw there's a nice place for takeaway coffee on the beach?' she blurts out.

'Sure. I'll move my meeting and we'll go. It sounds good. Enjoy tonight.'

She closes the door, looking at her diamond engagement and wedding ring. She feels like she's made an illicit pact. She wonders what Lisa would say.

The phone rings again and Maddy answers, not recognising the number. This could be the man at the council who she's tasked with helping her find Jamie. She answers with an enthusiastic hello.

'What the actual?' Lisa cries. 'You're actually not taking my calls.'

Maddy is annoyed she's been duped, but her heart leaps at hearing Lisa's voice. They've always had a weird telepathy thing. How did she *know* she was thinking of her? Usually she'd comment on it, but she doesn't. Lisa doesn't deserve it.

'I've been busy.'

'Doing what? What's so important that you've stayed away all this time?' Lisa sounds indignant.

'I'm trying to find Jamie.'

Lisa is silent for a moment, letting this sink in. 'Trent is beside himself.'

'Is he?'

'Yes. I know you're cross, but come home,' Lisa says. 'You live *here*. You don't know anyone *there*.'

'I do.'

'Who?'

'My neighbour.' Maddy rubs at a smudge on her jeans, then for the hell of it adds, 'And my swimming gang.'

'Your what?'

'I've taking up sea swimming.'

'You hate the sea.'

'I don't.'

'You're far too much of a princess to get into cold water. You would only just about go in the pool when we went to Champneys that time and that was heated.'

'Well, maybe you don't know me as well as you think you do,' Maddy says, resentful that Lisa is bringing up a shared trip and all those memories that will bring them back together.

'That's it,' Lisa announces. 'I'm coming to get you.'

'Don't. Please don't. I need to be on my own. I'm too angry and cross.'

'With me?' Lisa sounds hurt.

'Yes, with you.'

'I never wanted to be caught in the middle. You've got to believe me. It's been a nightmare—'

'You weren't in the middle. You chose a side. And it wasn't mine.'

Lisa lets out a frustrated growl. 'You're so stubborn,' she snaps and Maddy is shaken to hear her voice choke into tears.

Maddy is stung by this accusation. She was in such a good mood having talked to Matteo, but this all feels too raw. 'You have no right to call me names when you've hardly behaved as a friend. Let alone a *best* friend. You knew about their affair for all that time—'

'I didn't know about it at first,' Lisa interrupts, clearly keen to get the facts straight. Her voice is still choked with tears. 'I didn't know that it was a thing until really recently. They kept it under wraps.'

'Clearly.'

This news puts Lisa's culpability in a different light, but Maddy still feels betrayed. If it had been the other way around, Maddy would have told Lisa straight away.

'And . . . I don't know, I wanted to tell you, but there wasn't ever a good time and anyway, I just got the impression that you and Trent had some understanding about it.'

'An *understanding*?'

'I was going to tell you after Christmas. When you weren't so busy.'

'Well, you're too late.'

'Jesus, Maddy. You're so black and white.'

'Well, I'm sorry, but this feels like a black-and-white situation.'

'Ugh.' Lisa is clearly exasperated. 'You know what your problem is? You're exactly the same as Jamie.'

'Jamie?'

'He was always so sure he was right, too. That's why he never came home after your row.'

Maddy's eyes are welling with tears. She ends the call, unable to speak. It hurts too much that Lisa is right.

19

A Sliver of Hope

Tor, with the help of Arek and Maddy, has set up the mobile food bank by the Meeting Place café on the seafront in Hove. Tor rotates the food bank in different locations around the city, but this one is closest to home. It's dark already and the moonlight glows on the black sea in the distance. It's hard to believe that they swim in there.

There are a few cars on the main esplanade, their lights blurring in the rain. An ambulance wails. She notices groups of people slinking out of the shadowy streets across the road.

She smiles across at Maddy. It's so sweet that she's come again. She came with Claire last week, but Claire has an online parents evening so Maddy has come by herself. Tor had had Maddy down as someone who wouldn't want to get her hands dirty, but she's been incredibly helpful.

'Where did this all come from?' Maddy asks, nodding to the sturdy green crates that they've unloaded from the van. She's wearing no make-up and a long Puffa and a hat, as she joins Tor behind the trestle table.

'From the supermarkets. They're really helpful with our initiative.' Tor picks up a can of soup and turns it round. It's Chunky Hearty Cheeseburger Soup. 'Never tried this, though. Not sure that's on the top of my go-to list. Looks like a liquidised McDonald's. It can't be that nutritious.'

'It's so awful that so many people rely on food banks,' Maddy says. 'I thought we were supposed to be a first world country? I never knew about all this and it's really quite shocking.'

'Never knew, or never chose to notice?' Tor says, wondering if she sounds rude, but she finds it easy to be direct with Maddy.

'Well, yeah, fair enough. The latter, I guess. My friends would never believe this.'

'Why?'

Maddy pauses, as if searching for the right answer. 'If I'm honest because they're like I was.'

'How do you mean?'

'It's easy to be judgemental when you're insulated in a home with an electric gate. I tell you, though, seeing this, I feel every bit the privileged white middle-class woman with absolutely no idea about what's really going on.'

'We're all only ever a couple of steps away from being homeless,' Tor says, then she waves at Vic who is coming down the pavement. 'Hey, Vic. Are you all right?'

'Chilly. I hate the rain. It's a long haul until summer.'

'I know. But the brighter days are coming.' Tor tries to be encouraging.

'I guess we've nearly done January,' Vic says. 'My mate Scotty was going to come, but he's already on the whiskey he's been saving for Burn's Night. You don't have any haggis, do you?'

'I'm afraid not.' Tor smiles at him. He's ever the optimist. 'This is Vic,' she explains to Maddy, introducing him. 'He's one of my regulars. And this is Maddy. She's a volunteer, but she's also looking for her son.' Tor nods encouragingly at Maddy who takes the laminated photograph from the pocket of her coat.

'This is the last photo I have of him,' she says. 'You haven't seen him around? I'm not sure if he's in Brighton, even?'

Vic scratches his beard. 'Well, come to think of it, he looks familiar.'

'He does?'

'James . . . Jamie?' Vic says.

'Yes,' Maddy says, stepping forward. 'Yes . . . Jamie.'

She gasps, turning to Tor, her eyes bright with excitement and hope. She puts her hand on Vic's arm. 'You've seen him? He's around here? He's near?' Her voice is shaking.

He flinches but Maddy doesn't notice. Tor, realising he's not used to being touched, steps in next to her and clutches her arm, gently pulling her away from him.

'Not for a while. I chatted to him once,' Vic says, but he looks cornered and confused by the drama his innocent comment has caused.

'Do you know where he's living?'

Vic just shrugs.

'But is he . . . is he . . . like you?'

'Well, quite a bit younger actually.'

Maddy tries again. 'No, I mean . . . '

'Yeah, yeah, I know. On the streets? Yeah, he was. At least when I saw him.'

Tor can see Maddy taking this in. They've talked about Jamie before and Tor has been keen for her to look on the bright side – and not to assume that he's homeless or in trouble – so this sighting from Vic is a body blow. Tor feels a shiver in the pit of her stomach. She can't imagine that a kid from Jamie's background has fared well out there. Not with some of the characters she knows are around here.

'But when? When did you see him? Exactly?' Maddy persists.

'Don't recall,' Vic says.

'But how was he?' Maddy presses. 'How did he seem?'

Vic sighs. 'Probably miserable. The young guys find it tough. Twenty-four hours on the street and you're a changed person.'

'What do you mean?'

'There's nothing like the terror of not having a roof over your head. Not feeling safe. Of being alone. So very, very alone. Of seeing the world for the first time as the dog-eat-dog place it is. That changes you in here, you know. Forever.' Vic taps at his temple with a dirty finger.

'Then tell me. Just tell me, where I can find him.' Maddy sounds desperate, but Vic backs away.

'I can't help you.' He turns and leaves. 'Jesus, lady. That's all I know.'

Tor puts her arms around Maddy, giving her a spontaneous hug, seeing her eyes brimming with tears.

'I'm sorry. I didn't mean to scare him off.'

'It's OK,' Tor says, but she wants to tell Maddy that she has to be gentle with people. She'll get the hang of it, Tor's sure of it, but in this crowd, they're here to help, not to ask too many questions. People are often just hanging on by a thread. They don't have the will or energy to justify themselves.

Maddy wipes at her tears with the cuff of her coat. 'At least it's something. It's so good to know he might be nearby. To know that he's . . . ' her voice cracks . . . 'well, that he's alive. That he might be here.'

'You thought he might not be?'

'I've imagined every scenario. I feel so shit about the whole thing, Tor. I should have . . . I don't know. I should have done it all differently.' She can't stop the tears.

'You shouldn't blame yourself.' Tor feels genuinely sorry for her.

'But I do. Because it's my fault. That's the thing when you're young: you think you'll have all the answers by the time you're old, but you still manage to fuck things up. I just want the chance to put things right with him. That's all.'

'We'll find him.' Tor tries to sound reassuring, but she knows how homeless people become invisible in every way. That's the thing that gets to people most – the way they're ignored and treated as if they literally don't exist. She's witnessed the humiliation and hurt of the young rough sleepers on West Street after the gangs of drunk lads on a stag party took a piss on them.

Tor isn't religious, but she can't help feeling that as a society in general, everyone has gone seriously up the wrong path. Because where has all the kindness and compassion gone? Why has it been replaced by suspicion and fear? Everyone is human, after all. Ultimately, everyone is in the same boat. Hasn't the pandemic taught everyone that?

The usual rush of regulars come and Tor is happy to check-in on them and she can see Maddy has recovered a bit and is chatting to them too.

All of the food has gone in less than half an hour and Tor starts stacking the empty crates.

She smiles at Maddy. 'You were great. Thanks for coming. I really needed the extra pair of hands.'

'You know, I can't believe that a month ago all I thought about was perfecting a perfect Instagram post and now I'm here,' she says, with a little shake of her head.

'Yeah, well, I need all the help I can get. It's going to get worse. Even more people are going to start falling through the cracks. What we're doing here is just a drop in the ocean.'

'But at least you're *doing* something. Seriously, Tor, I have to say it . . . to have organised all this . . . to help people the way you do, it's very inspiring. Your parents must be so proud.'

'I wouldn't say they're proud.'

'They must be, surely?'

'I have a twin sister, Alice. She's the golden child. The favourite,' Tor explains, noticing Maddy pausing as she packs up the boxes. 'I wish my mum was like you. She's sweet, but she doesn't notice me. It's all about Alice.'

Maddy shakes her head. 'I'm sure that's not true.'

'You don't know my family. And they really don't know me. They have no idea that me and my girlfriend, Lotte, live together. That we're, you know . . . ' Tor shakes her head. Why is it so easy to talk to Maddy and yet she still can't say the words?

'You're . . . ' Maddy prompts. Her eyes are searching hers out and Tor blushes.

She says in a hurry, 'That we're a couple, but my family . . . they don't even know I'm gay.'

'Why haven't you told them?'

'Because . . . ' Tor doesn't know how to explain about her relationship with Mike and how her parents will be flabbergasted when they realise it was all a sham. 'The bottom line is that . . . that I think they'll reject me. Judge me.'

'No, they won't.'

'You don't know them. My mum will be so "disappointed".'

'Well, I know anyone who has brought up a girl to become a woman like you must be a good person and want you to be happy. And anyway, a mother always senses when her child is lying and keeping something from them. Well, I always thought I did with Jamie. And what I realise now was that he was keeping the burden of all the pressure I put on him and how unhappy that was making him,' she says, frowning, as if she's only just realised this. 'My point is, if your mother doesn't already know, then she'll suspect. I promise you. All she'll want is for you to be happy and safe. That's all any mother wants.'

Tor nods as she lets this sink in. She's so used to seeing her mother mothering Alice that she's always felt left out, but in her own way, her mother has been supportive. She's been the one to encourage Tor to follow her path. Plenty of mothers stick their oar in when it comes to their daughter's choices, but Tor's has always let her go her own way. Maybe Maddy is right. Maybe her mother is proud. Maybe she feels that her job is done in a way that it'll never be done with Alice.

It's been strange tonight witnessing how raw Maddy's instinct is to find Jamie. Would her mum be the same if Tor was missing? Imagining her mother being hurt brings up a powerful emotion. It's the same feeling she fears she'll bring about if she spills the beans about Lotte. But what if Maddy is right and her mum suspects Tor is keeping something from her? Surely that's even more hurtful?

Finally, it's time to go home and Tor is glad. Her bones ache, in particular her little finger, where the gnarled knuckle is red. She's hoping for a dip in the morning and Maddy says she'll come along too.

Before they part, Tor asks Maddy about Trent.

Maddy shrugs sadly. 'I guess it's over.'

'You don't sound so sure.'

'It's just so sad and messy and I miss him, or at least I miss us. What we were and what we could have become. And then I remember what he's done and, well . . . that's that.'

'Yep, well, life is messy. You only have to work in a homeless charity to understand that nothing is ever just black or white. It's just a question of recognising the bright moments.'

'I suppose.'

'You know what you need?'

'What?'

'You need to go on a date with someone else.'

'How would *that* solve anything?'

'It wouldn't. But it might be fun.'

'Well, now you mention it, there is my neighbour, Matteo.' Maddy shakes her head and smiles bashfully. 'I can't even believe I'm telling you this.'

'Matteo?'

'He's Luna's owner. He and I have become, well . . . friends. But I sense a . . . I don't know . . . a vibe. We've been out for coffee twice in the last week and we really get along.'

'A vibe? That's good, isn't it? Maybe you should, you know . . . make a move.'

'Seriously? Isn't he just a distraction? Aren't I making things more complicated?'

'Well, you know what they say?' Tor remembers Alice's old phrase, from the fun days before Graham. 'The only way to get *over* someone is to get *under* someone else.'

Maddy laughs and Tor raises her eyebrows at her and she laughs even more. 'Stop it. Stop it,' she implores.

20

Snow Swim

It's Chris's birthday. He would have been sixty. In another universe, where Chris is alive and there's no Covid, they'd be having the party they'd planned at the hotel. Dominica wonders whether the rugby boys would have clubbed together for the skydive and she imagines Chris receiving the present in his new three-piece suit, his shirt cuffs turned up. She imagines the playlist he would have put together and the song he'd almost certainly whisk her out onto the dance floor to – Al Green's 'Let's Stay Together'. She can picture it all; it seems almost tangible. But each detail is a little stab to her heart.

Keen for something to distract her, Dominica starts tackling the iCloud. There have been increasingly frequent messages telling her that she's out of space and she refuses to pay for more on principle. Chris was always on about big corporations and how they suck you in and then get you by the short and curlies demanding money. What was wrong with printing out photos at Boots? she can remember him saying. Why does everything need to be backed up on a super-computer under the sea? She never asked for that. Who has paperwork *that* important?

On her computer, she realises that the space has been taken up mainly by videos, and, when she works out the way of accessing them, she's surprised by the footage that must have automatically uploaded from Chris's old phone.

She never knew these videos were here and it feels like the best kind of birthday gift. As if Chris is reaching out to her from beyond the grave. Her resentment towards the iCloud quickly morphs into humble gratitude as she trawls through the footage from 2016. It had been the year they'd been on the Honda Goldwing across the States taking the tiny fold-up tent in the panniers. Chris, ever the joker, films himself, the mirth written large across his face as he pulls back the canvas of the tent to wake her up. He was forever pranking her, she remembers.

The memories are so painful, but it's an addictive kind of pain. She can't help replaying the video clips until her eyes ache from crying. She wishes she could smash the screen and crawl through it. She misses him so much, she feels turned inside out.

Emma calls before she goes to work. Dominica has been expecting to hear from her.

'It's snowing,' Emma says. 'The kids are so excited.'

Dominica gets up from the desk and looks out of the window to the dark morning, wondering if it'll start this far south.

'Chris loved the snow,' Dominica says and her voice cracks.

'Oh, babe.'

'I found some footage. I'll send it to you,' Dominica tells her, explaining what she's been up to since dawn. 'I'm determined not to be forced into buying more storage. Not on Chris's birthday. He'd go mental.'

'I get those messages too. I dream about how there's someone at the gates of the cloud with a clipboard and I'll be ticked off for using the Earth's resources to power a super-computer that's full of photographs and videos of my children gurning.'

Dominica smiles, thinking of her niece and nephews, and then her heart hurts when she thinks about little Cerys sending a daffodil she made out of tissue paper for Dominica to put on Chris's coffin and the way her bottom lip trembled when Dominica had thanked her on FaceTime. Those kids adored their uncle. Bard and Owen had loved nothing more than being hitched over his shoulder in a fireman's lift as he spun them around.

'I wish I didn't feel so sad,' Emma says.

'I know, darling. Me too. But he wouldn't want us to . . . '

'To dwell. I know.'

There's a beat as they both accept this.

'Oh, did I tell you they've sent me an email from work? I'll be going back next month,' she tells Emma. 'They're staggering our return to the office.'

'That's great news.'

Is it? Dominica wonders. She wonders how it'll feel to pick up the old strands of her life at the travel company. She feels nervous about engaging with the customers and her colleagues. She's asked to go back three days a week, to ease herself in gently, but she knows how all-consuming it can become and how it'll inevitably spill into the other days.

'Listen. I've got to go. Are you swimming with your friends?'

'In the snow?'

'When has that ever stopped you?' Emma says with a laugh.

Dominica is tempted to go back to bed, but instead, after

Emma rings off, she puts a shout-out on the WhatsApp. Emma is right. She needs to do something today to mark Chris's birthday. Something that would have made him proud. A swim in the snow feels appropriate.

It's been a skiddy but exhilarating ride here on her bike and Dominica's breath clouds as she locks it up and surveys the view of the beach. There's a dusting of snow over everything making the still scene look like a Christmas card, the burnt-out pier standing in sharp relief against the white sky. The sea is a bluish grey – the kind of stylish colour that might grace the walls of a boutique hotel. It's flat, the waves rippling weakly along the shore, as if they too are conserving energy.

The pebbles are frozen solid as Dominica arrives at the beach. They feel weird to walk on and she laughs in surprise as she joins the others.

Helga is in a jolly mood, talking about an article she saw in the paper about some hardy types in Scotland swimming with an axe and breaking the ice to get in a freezing loch. This will be nothing in comparison, she says, as they head down. Dominica knows that Helga, with her lifetime of adventures, thinks they're all a bunch of southern wusses, but even so, like Claire and Dominica, she's made a concession to the weather and is wearing her bobble hat along with her costume.

Maddy is head-to-toe in her wetsuit and says she feels smug as she waits for them all to change. She opens up the chat on her phone and sees that Tor isn't going to make it this morning.

'You know, I was thinking…about Tor,' Claire says.

'Oh?' Dominica asks.

'I heard this thing on the radio,' Claire said. 'They're looking to award community heroes. People who have made a difference in lockdown. Maddy and I thought we should nominate Home Help – and Tor in particular.'

'That's a great idea,' Dominica says.

'If I send you the link, can you both nominate her too?' Maddy asks. 'Only don't say anything to her.'

'Sure,' Dominica says, glad that Maddy and Claire want to support Tor too. They clearly feel protective towards her, like Dominica does herself. She'd love the opportunity to do something to get Tor seen and appreciated. She's a good woman. One of the best.

They talk about Tor's upcoming charity swim in a couple of weeks and Dominica says she's already promised Tor that she'll do it. Maddy says she'll come along to it too.

Perhaps she'll be able to ask her colleagues in the office to sponsor her. Lord knows she's been strong-armed often enough into their charity endeavours.

The water is icy cold as Dominica puts one foot into the retreating wave and Claire reaches out to hold her hand. Together, they walk in slowly and quietly, each of them concentrating. Helga is ahead and even she is slower than normal, getting used to the temperature. She scoops up water and pours it over her shoulders.

Dominica inches forward, her body trying to get used to the shock. She breathes slowly, meditatively looking out at the horizon. In the distance, two cormorants are flurrying around the surface of the water, their throaty call loud across the still water.

Waist-deep now and Dominica steels herself as her shoulders go under. It feels like swimming in mercury. Her body is buzzing as the blood rushes from her extremities.

'I can't believe I'm swimming in the snow.' Claire leans backwards and opens her mouth to collect a snowflake. A few half-hearted ones are falling from the sky. Her eyes sparkle with wonder and Dominica knows what she means. Snow always can make anything magical, but in the water it feels even more special. It starts to snow more heavily now, a soft white blanket settling over the stones.

She's used to them all being noisy and chatty in the sea, but now she notices that today there's an awed silence as the snow falls gently around them. It feels very elemental. Dominica is aware of her infinitesimal smallness in the universe.

They swim silently and she imagines them like nuns gliding along a cloister. There's definitely something religious about the swim today.

But then, as they turn and head back, Dominica breaks the silence.

'It's Chris's birthday today,' she says. Somehow, in this quiet, magical space, it feels safe to share how she's feeling. 'He was such an adventurous spirit. I found footage from some of our old holidays this morning. He would have loved this.'

'Oh, Dominica,' Helga says. Her voice is full of empathy. 'Then today is hard.'

'You know, my husband, Pim, is a physics teacher?' Claire asks.

She hadn't known this, but it stands to reason that Claire is with someone bright. Despite the way she sometimes puts herself down, she's very astute.

'He's always banging on about Einstein's big ideas,' Claire continues.

'Oh?' Dominica asks, intrigued.

'That energy is constant. So maybe Chris's energy is still out there. And he talked about time too, and how the past, present and future all exist forever. So all those moments on the video? They're happening out there somewhere too.'

Dominica feels a great wave of emotion bubbling up and it comes out in a kind of sigh, up to the snow. She looks up into it, thinking that this moment – this very moment with her friends in the snow – is travelling with her in time, too. It's a comforting thought.

'I keep thinking that we'd be having a party,' Dominica says. 'I can see it in my mind so clearly.'

'Maybe Claire's right. It's all going on somewhere,' Maddy says. 'And hopefully without any bloody Covid regulations scuppering it.'

'I hope so. Although he'd have made an embarrassing speech,' Dominica says, with a smile.

'Embarrassing how?' Maddy asks.

Dominica feels her throat tightening. 'Only that he would have told everyone . . . would have said . . . ' She shakes her head. She knows the others are waiting for her to speak and the moment in the quiet snow requires honesty. 'He would have told people I was the love of his life.' She lets out a sob. 'Sorry, it's pathetic. I was always so embarrassed when he said things like that, but I should have . . . I should have . . . '

'What?' Helga asks.

'I should have said thank you, I guess,' she says.

'But that love didn't die,' Claire says. 'With him. It's here. It's in you.'

Dominica nods, her tears mixing with the salt water.

'He sounds like a really good guy,' Maddy says. 'I'm so sorry it hurts.'

'Well, if you're listening, happy birthday, Chris,' Helga says, leaning back and blinking.

'Happy birthday,' Maddy and Claire repeat, their eyelids fluttering in the snow.

Dominica nods and smiles, but she can't speak, because her heart is so full.

21

A Glimpse into Next Door

Her corner shop has gone posh in recent years and Helga feels an indignant injustice at having to wait for the guy behind the counter to serve her. He's busy with the giant hissing coffee machine and takes an age to get to her and to ring through her milk, eggs and flour. She's not religious, but she heard on the radio this morning that it's Shrove Tuesday and she fancies making pancakes. Dominica had predicted it, saying the snow wouldn't last long, but Helga can see a looming dark-grey cloud and she's not going to have long to get home before the heavens open. She knows the power of clouds like that. A few long splatters arrive on the shop front glass, heralding the start of the downpour, and she tuts, wondering whether to just dump her things and make a run for it.

Instead, she forces herself to stay calm, her mind drifting back to the 'Tweet of the Day', her favourite programme on Radio 4 and the fascinating facts about chaffinches and bramblings. She hadn't realised that the chaffinch develops regional dialects to their call, which always finishes with a flourish. The programme had pointed out that the flourish sounds to some like 'ginger beer' and Helga rather likes that description and has been listening out for her chaffinch friend in the tall sycamore at the end of the lane. She picks up a bottle of ginger beer from the shelf next to her on a whim and pays. The man watches her warily over his mask.

Outside, Helga puts her hood up on her ancient yellow oilskin coat and crosses the road to the entrance to the alley leading to the cottages. There's a young guy in a doorway, smoking a foul-smelling joint, and a whole cloud of it wafts up into Helga's face. She coughs at the offensive odour. They make eye contact.

'Why don't you stop smoking that shit,' she mutters. 'That'll rot your brain.'

'Fuck off.'

'It might improve your comebacks, too.'

She walks on, feeling his menacing stare on her back. Her pulse quickens, but she doesn't speed up. She stands by her words. She can't bear to see these young guys ravaged by drugs and wrung out with alcohol abuse. She's always taken it as a point of pride, as her defining character trait, that she's unafraid to call a spade a spade, but as she walks down the narrow alley, she can see that perhaps she's been foolish. What if he were to follow her?

And then it occurs to her . . . what if that kid is Jamie? Maddy's son? She turns, wondering whether to go back and ask, but he's gone. There's only a bit of cardboard where he was sitting getting soaked in the rain. She's shocked to think that she might have a personal connection, that the junkie might not just be 'one of them', but could actually be 'one of us'.

She's at her gate, but now she sees the next-door neighbour,

Will, coming out of his house. He's holding his heavily pregnant wife Katie's hand up as she grips on to it for dear life. Her red cheeks puff out.

'Is she . . . ?' Helga asks as Katie makes a strangled noise and her knees buckle a bit. She can see the tips of Will's fingers going purple where she's gripping them.

'We're going to the hospital, but we're going to have to take Josh with us. My mum is on a train stuck at a signal. It's a nightmare,' Will says. He sounds scared. 'Come on, Josh. Hurry up,' he urges.

Helga can see he's torn – trying to support his wife, but also not to frighten his kid. They're both getting soaked in the rain. Helga looks at the little toddler hiding behind the doorframe. He's still in his pyjamas, holding a toy rabbit, pressing the ear to his upper lip.

'That's it, buddy, come on. Let's get Mummy to the hospital,' Will tries to cajole him. He looks desperate.

'I'll watch him until she gets here,' Helga offers. 'Your mum, I mean. I don't mind.'

'You would?'

Helga tries to look reassuring. 'Yeah. Sure. I'm really happy to help out.'

Katie's knees buckle again. 'Quick.'

'Granny will be here in a few minutes.' Will kneels in front of the child and kissing him, says, 'OK? Will you be a good boy and wait with . . . '

'Helga,' Helga reminds him. 'He can come to my house if he wants,' Helga suggests, but Will shakes his head. 'Can you wait with him at ours? It's against the rules. I think. I'm not sure. This is an emergency, right?'

Helga nods and crosses over the small divide – something she's never done before, and Will kisses the little boy on the head. 'Be a good boy, OK?' He looks at Helga, nervously. 'Thank you. My mother really won't be long. Fifteen minutes, tops.'

'Wiiiiillll,' Katie moans.

'You go. Oh, what does he like? Does he need feeding?'

'Josh? No. He's eaten. He's good at drawing. He's always drawing something.'

'Then I'll show him how to draw a boat.' The little boy looks up at her with large, frightened brown eyes. 'It's OK. I don't bite,' she tells him. 'Good luck,' she calls out, as she closes the door.

Will and Katie's cottage is how her house could be if she'd made some effort to modernise it. It's bright and light and full of lush-looking houseplants and linen couches.

'Could you show me your picture?' Helga asks, as she takes off her wet coat and leaves it by the door. Josh goes to a desk in the open-plan kitchen and soberly lifts the lid, then pulls out a sheaf of A3 sheets covered in pencil and crayon and some that are crinkly with heavily applied paint. He brings them over to her and Helga carefully studies each one. She sees that the proportions are all good and that little Josh has a good eye.

Helga kneels down by his desk, her knees cracking, and she takes his crayons and a clean bit of paper.

'I had a boat,' she tells him. '*Sheelagh*. She had a big mainsail like this.'

She draws the yacht, talking about the wheelhouse, junk sails and how the spinnaker was the devil to reel in. The little boy still doesn't speak, but listens intently, watching her crayon over the paper as she describes her days at sea.

'Why don't you try and draw *Sheelagh*,' she tells him now. She gives him the crayon and he tries to copy what she's done. Whilst he's concentrating, she cocks her head, seeing his earnest expression, the tip of his tongue poking out from the corner of his mouth. She quietly takes a clean piece of paper and sketches him.

In fact, they're both so absorbed that she jumps when the door opens with a key. A woman bustles in. She looks flustered and stressed. This must be Will's mum. She's wearing a stylish trench coat and has white cropped hair.

'Josh?' she cries out. 'Josh. Are you OK? I came as quickly as I could.' She runs into the kitchen and puts the sopping umbrella in the sink. 'Oh, baby.' Josh drops the crayon on the floor and runs into her arms.

Helga gets up from the floor, her knees aching. She leaves the picture of Josh and holds on to the unit, her head suddenly spinning.

'You must be the neighbour,' Will's mum says.

'Helga. Yes.'

'I'm Judith. Thank you for watching him. Bloody trains. It was a nightmare. But I'm here now.'

Helga nods and tries to walk to the door, but she's gone stiff. 'Are you all right? You're shivering.'

'I swam in the sea earlier,' she tells Judith.

'In the sea?' Judith looks at her as if she hasn't heard right.

Helga nods. 'I try and go most days.'

'That's so impressive.'

'I haven't warmed up yet. That's all.'

She leaves Judith with Josh. At the door she turns and watches her cuddle the small boy on her lap. She's tactile and confident and Helga feels an unfamiliar wave of envy.

'Goodbye, Josh,' she says, sad at how redundant she feels.

Judith gives her a quick, dismissive smile and Helga says she'll see herself out.

She walks back to her cottage and closes the door, thinking of how Judith's life is so different to hers. She's only got her pride to blame, she tells herself. She could have made different choices. She could have had a family. She could have a loving grandchild too, but instead she's alone. And she's always been fine about being alone, she reminds herself. Militantly so. But now, as the rain splatters against the glass in the conservatory, she feels uncharacteristically all at sea.

22

Date Night

Matteo is leaning against his doorframe, looking up at the drip that's coming through the ceiling of their communal hallway.

'It's just relentless,' Maddy says, positioning the saucepan from the Airbnb's kitchen under the drip. 'And this is going to be like water torture.'

'I know.'

Even with the leaky ceiling, being inside in the warm is making her feel guilty. Is Jamie somewhere out there in the cold rain? What if he's in a tent in this? Or in some horrible damp shelter? After talking to Vic and finding out that Jamie is definitely here, she's been ramping up her efforts, hoping that every day there'll be a message. Because surely he must have seen the posters she's put up, or found out from the social services that she's here looking for him?

'Are you worrying about Jamie?' Matteo asks and she smiles sadly, amazed that he can read her so easily.

'I can't help thinking . . . what if he knows I'm here and he's deliberately ignoring me? What then?'

'I think that's highly unlikely. Seriously, Maddy. You're doing all you can. I'm sure you'll find him soon.'

She likes the way that however unhinged she sounds, he takes it all on board calmly, always giving her a rational, common-sense point of view. In the past few weeks, she's not sure what she would have done without his comforting words of wisdom.

'Why don't you come over for something to eat? Tonight?' he offers and she turns.

'Dinner?'

'Yes, dinner. I *can* cook,' he says. 'But it'll just be a simple kitchen supper.'

'Sure. I guess . . . I mean, I'm not doing anything.' She feels ridiculous saying this. Of course he knows she's not doing anything.

'So come at eight.'

He smiles and then she realises the conversation is over and she goes back to her apartment and leans on the door.

Dinner.

A date.

A dinner date.

She hasn't been on a date, or been asked out for dinner, for decades and now she's frozen with indecision as she mentally rakes through her wardrobe options and what each choice might inadvertently signify.

She picks up her phone and messages the Sea-Gals chat. 'Going over to Matteo's for supper. Help!' She sends it, then worries about how silly she must sound. She's almost old enough to be Tor's mother.

'At last,' Tor replies almost immediately. 'Go for it. Good luck.'

'I'm so nervous,' Maddy replies.

'You're just out of practice,' Claire types back. 'You'll be fine.'

Maddy laughs. Maybe it's true. Years ago, she used to be so confident when it came to men and dating. She was always the one in control, calling the shots, always flirting, always weighing up her options. She remembers laughing in the back of a cab with Lisa as they travelled across London to yet another party. Those days had been so much fun. So carefree.

After her shower, Maddy blow-dries her hair and does her nails, realising that these little personal rituals have been conspicuously absent since she's been in Brighton and has started swimming. There's been no point in blow-drying her hair, when she's been stuffing it under a cap and she hasn't had the inclination to seek out a nail clinic now they've re-opened.

She changes into her glittery cross-over top and sprays her Jo Loves perfume on her wrists. And then, for good measure, some between her breasts. She catches her reflection in the mirror. Is she planning on Matteo being anywhere near her breasts? Surely not? She's being desperate, she tells herself. Matteo is just a friend. A neighbour. And over a decade younger than her.

Even so, her heart is pounding as she arrives outside his door. She clutches the chilled bottle of Albariño she's picked up from the wine merchant in town when she was out, liking the coolness against her sweating palms.

Matteo opens the door and leans in to kiss her on the cheek. He's wearing a nice blue shirt and smart jeans, with a linen tea towel draped over his shoulder. He's clean-shaven, she notices, and his hair is neater than she's seen it. He smiles. 'You look lovely,' he says, as if he really means it. 'Come in, come in.'

She wants to hug him, or kiss his cheek, but with the wave of Covid sweeping through the nation, everyone is keeping their distance. She's done a test at home and she tells him she's all clear as she steps over the threshold.

She notices straight away that the lighting is carefully placed for a warm ambience. *Hejira*, her favourite Joni Mitchell LP, is playing on an ancient turntable and there's something that smells delicious simmering in a battered orange Le Creuset Dutch oven on the hob. She's used to being entertained in her friends' homes, all of which have a modern, chic aesthetic, but this feels shabby and a bit studenty, but in a good way. There's even a macramé plant potholder with a wildly sprouting spider plant in it.

He brings her a glass of sherry — 'real sherry, none of your undrinkable English Christmas rubbish,' he teases — in a dainty cut glass, and she perches on the retro 1970s stool by the kitchen counter as he finishes cooking and produces a plate of delicious-looking tapas – little rounds of toasted baguette topped with oozing cheese.

It's been so long since someone else has cooked for her, every mouthful feels more delicious than anything she's ever eaten in a Michelin-starred restaurant. Trent loved all those places – all that willy-waggling over getting the best table and paying through the nose for expensive wine, just to show off. In truth, though, he was never much of a foodie, but now, as she watches Matteo taste the sauce and then add a little more salt, she can see that he's a man in touch with his senses in a way that Trent has never been.

He lays out two places on the counter on stylish raffia mats and serves up the Spanish stew in earthenware dishes and gives her an ochre linen napkin.

'Do you mind if I take a picture?' she asks.

'Of what?'

She feels silly asking. 'I've got this account and . . . well, I have to keep posting. That's the whole point of it. And this . . . this looks very Instagrammable.'

Matteo looks inside the pot as if this is a surprise. 'It does?'

'Yes,' Maddy says, taking a picture, then quickly adjusting it and holding it up. She's been posting random things on her feed, constantly trying to make connections between her daily life and the aspirational lifestyle she's been promoting, but it's becoming rather desperate. Trying to be profound about 'stuff' whilst making out that she's living an aesthetically pleasing life is a strain to say the least.

She turns around her phone.

'See? It looks good enough to eat,' she says. 'Shall I tag you in?'

'Oh, no,' he says, shaking his head. 'I don't do all that social media stuff.'

'You don't . . . you mean, you don't have any accounts?'

'I did, but I deleted them all. I can't really see the point. I'm shy and it just made me stressed. And I had friends who fell out on Twitter. I think it's killing language – everything reduced to soundbites. There's no room for humour, or tone, or . . . what's the word . . . no . . . new?' He screws up his face trying to remember.

'Nuance?'

'Nuance. That's it. And also, I think my girlfriend's – ex's' – he corrects himself – 'problems were to do with being online too much. She had eating disorders and . . . ' He sighs and shrugs. 'I personally believe her obsession with Instagram made it so, so much worse. It killed her self-esteem constantly comparing herself to other people. I really don't understand what's so good about it.'

Maddy feels chastened by this honest appraisal. She knows her own self-esteem is damaged by the constant comparison too, but hearing this reminder from Matteo about the real dangers of social media is sobering. Because she's guilty of being an addict too, isn't she? The thought that he might think less of her because of it is enough to make her put away her phone and resolve not to get it out again in his company.

They chat easily and soon they're on to the subject of her hunt for Jamie and Matteo seems genuinely sorry that she hasn't been able to find him yet. She finds herself telling him about seeing his friends online and how much it hurts that they've all moved on.

She tells him the details about Jamie's trip to Thailand and what terrible shape he'd been in afterwards. She describes the tense atmosphere at home and how it had come to a head last January. She shudders when she remembers the row and how Jamie had snapped one evening after dinner, when he'd taken Trent's pleas to change his lifestyle so personally. He'd lashed out at them both, telling them they were useless parents.

Trent was furious, but she was more hurt. She remembers crying and telling Jamie over and over that he didn't mean it, but he kept on, his words increasingly vicious, as he screamed in her face that he hated everything she stood for. Trent tried to make him apologise, of course, but Jamie turned his fury on Trent and it got physical very quickly. She remembers how she tried to break it up. When Trent punched Jamie, his black eye had appeared almost instantly.

The physicality of the fight feels so shaming – even now.

'And then Jamie left. He just walked out,' she tells Matteo. 'He was always a drama queen when he was little, but it was awful. I kept thinking he'd come back and apologise, but he never did.'

'That must have been hard.'

'I felt terrible that Trent had hit him and that we'd lost control, but Trent was unapologetic. He said that Jamie had it coming, that he deserved it. That we couldn't put up with this emotional abuse from our son. And I agreed with him on that one. Trent said it was about time that Jamie took responsibility for himself, but . . . ' Maddy sighs and takes a sip of wine. It feels scary, but also liberating to let all of this out. 'I wish I could go back and do it differently. To take our egos out of it and see that he needed help. Because now . . . now I'm really worried.'

'Can't your husband help you? Can't you find Jamie together?' Matteo asks, but he's staring at her and she's sucked into his soft gaze.

'No.' She shakes her head. 'It's too complicated and . . . let's not talk any more about Trent.' Because she doesn't want Trent here in this lovely room, in this lovely moment.

'I agree.'

She can feel the fluttering in her abdomen increase as her long-dormant libido wakes up. Flashes of fast-forward scenarios fill her mind – her hand on his bare chest, her legs wrapped around him. 'Let's talk about dessert instead,' he says.

He's made Crema Catalana and it's even more delicious than the main course. Maddy is feeling utterly spoilt as they sit on the sofa afterwards and he pours her a brandy. She's already inspected his record collection and James Taylor is playing on the stereo. Luna is asleep in her basket, the rain pattering on the window. Matteo stretches his arm along the back of the sofa and strokes the hair out of her face.

There's a moment and she sees the question in his eyes. All she has to do is make the right signal and she'll be in his bed.

But panic overtakes her as she imagines how the next five minutes might play out. Because, as much as she wants to lean across and kiss him – and she knows it has to be her that makes the first move, because he's being a gentleman – she's not brave enough, or self-assured enough to follow through with the promise of the kiss.

'I had some news today,' he says.

'Oh?'

'A job back home came up and I applied and today I found out I got it.'

'That's great, Matteo.'

She's suddenly embarrassed that all she's done is talk about herself, when he's had this bit of news to share the whole time. He's not wanting to kiss her . . . *he's been wanting her to shut up*.

'When are you going?'

'Soon . . . well, as soon as I can travel. Certainly by the summer.'

'Oh.'

'So all change, I guess,' he says, rubbing his hands along his thighs. His gorgeous slim thighs, she notices.

'But . . . it's good, right?' She's trying to smile, but her voice sounds tight.

'Yes. I'm pleased.'

Their eyes lock for a second and her heart is pounding. She wants to be cool, but feels too emotional. She doesn't want him to leave. He's managed to make her feel safe here and helped her cope with this strange new, independent life she's living, but this news makes her realise that her life is horribly temporary. If he goes, she'll have no one apart from the swimming girls. She consults her Fitbit. It's half eleven.

'I should go,' she says.

There's a flicker of disappointment in his eyes. 'Sure.'

'That was a lovely evening. I really enjoyed it.'

He nods. 'Me too.'

She walks to the door, wondering what it is she's broken, or how to break the tension between them. Because she's definitely got this very wrong. She feels as if she's been rude. She shouldn't be leaving when he's told her such a monumental piece of news, but what's the alternative? She needs to be alone to be upset. She doesn't want him to see her crumble.

'We should do this again sometime,' he says.

'I'd like that.'

They don't attempt to kiss – even on the cheek – as she leaves.

Maddy tries to walk calmly to her apartment door, aware he's watching her. She opens it with the key and gives him a wave and he waves back. She imagines that he's undressing her with his eyes, before she remembers that it's just her fantasy and not reality at all. He gives her a neighbourly smile and wave.

She gets inside the door and lets out a sigh, slumping back against it, hearing the thudding of her heart. She's like a bloody teenager, she tells herself. She picks up her phone and dials

Lisa's number, then thinks better of it and presses the red button. Lisa would say she's being ridiculous. She is being ridiculous, with her stupid flirtation.

She goes to the kitchen and pours herself a large glass of wine. She slugs half of it down. Her phone buzzes and she picks it up, her heart leaping. Might it be a message from Matteo? Asking her to come back?

But it's not a message from Matteo. It's from Trent. It's late and so he's probably drunk, but even so, she's not prepared for the words on the screen.

I love you Maddy. I always have and I always will.

She feels her nose stinging with tears. How dare he? How dare he throw her this curveball, when she's confused enough as it is?

A gust of wind and rain batter the window and she crosses the room to close the shutters. Opposite, on the street, she sees the glow of the end of a cigarette as someone shivers in a doorway.

23

Quad Bike

After the grey days, the sun has re-appeared, and the sky is a dazzling blue, the sea a shimmering mass of diamonds. It could be the Côte D'Azur, except it's February and bloody freezing. Claire shields her eyes with her hand and sees that the tide is going out, but it hasn't reached the break yet. There's a funny haze in the far distance hiding the wind farm. A perfect day for a swim.

She smiles to herself. Just months ago the thought of it would have made her recoil in horror, but the more she comes, the more she needs it. Siobhan couldn't believe it when they Zoomed last night. Her sister had said straight away that Claire looked different, in that suspicious way that her sisters always have – as if Claire might be using a miracle product she hasn't shared with them. Only there's no secret. The miracle product is the sea.

It's helped that she's started taking supplements and the Menopoised magnet that Dominica bought online and gave her last week has made a big difference to her night sweats.

Pim was sceptical that it would have any effect at all, but, as a physicist, he hadn't been able to argue with the science behind Chinese medicine and the evidence that the spot on the back of the neck to treat heat has been working for thousands of years. Whether it's the magnet, the supplement, or sea, or the combination of them all, she's feeling – if not exactly like herself of old – then certainly that a new version is coming into view.

On the pebbles, dogs are running and there are some people blowing up inflatable paddleboards. With conditions this good, with this freakish sun for this time of year, who can blame them? There must be twenty or thirty people out there on boards, some kneeling, some standing. She can hear a plane and a speck in the sky comes into view from Shoreham. She looks up as it does a loop in the sky, the vapour trail leaving a fluffy line of white against the blue.

It's Claire herself who has put the shout-out for a swim and she calls out as she arrives at the top of the bank of pebbles and Dominica waves back. At first, when she met Dominica, Claire hadn't thought they had much in common, but the more they swim together, the more she appreciates her humour and kindness. They hug warmly as Claire arrives. Helga is in the sun, her back to the wall. She's sketching the scene in her notebook and Claire looks down at what she's doing, impressed.

'Oh, a seagull,' she says.

'A herring gull,' she corrects her. 'You see its pink legs? And that one, with the dark grey wings? That's a lesser black-backed gull. He's got yellow legs.'

'Why black-backed if his wings are grey?'

'Because' – Helga points, with her pencil, as the bird takes flight – 'he's got black wing tips. Not to be confused with the great black-backed gull. Those are the giant ones. With beady eyes. And that little one over there is the common gull. Dark eyes, see, and a yellow bill. It has a common name, but I think it's cuter than the herring gull.'

'Wow. I never knew the difference between them all. Can I take a look at your drawings?'

'Sure.' Helga passes Claire her notebook and she looks through it, reverentially. She hadn't realised how talented Helga was.

'Who's this?' she asks, looking at the picture of a naked man. It's a perfect sketch, Helga having captured the old guy's resigned expression in a few strokes.

'Keith. Our life-drawing model. He's the one I was telling you about. And believe me, that's a flattering version. I haven't drawn in his hairy back.'

Claire shows the picture to Dominica. 'It's amazing, right?'

'Why don't you model for us, Claire?' Helga asks. 'You'd be perfect.'

'Me? I thought you were joking? I couldn't, I . . . I'm far too shy,' Claire says, shaking her head, but she's flattered, nevertheless. She tries to imagine baring all in front of strangers and lets out a little laugh at the absurdity of the suggestion.

'You should give it a go,' Dominica says. 'Do something out of your comfort zone. You'd be a great model. You're all curves, but in a good way.'

Their attention is caught now by a dog barking and the birds all take flight. A second later, she sees Maddy arriving with Luna. At the top of the shelf of stones, Maddy lets go of the lead and the little dog bounds over the pebbles to Dominica, who picks her up.

'Hello, you.'

Maddy arrives and greets the others. 'I told Matteo I'd bring Luna out,' she explains, pushing her sunglasses up into her hair. Her eyes are shining. 'She'll be OK on the beach whilst we swim, I think?'

'Yes, you'll be as good as gold,' Dominica says, petting the dog. 'Aren't you as good as gold. Oh, look at her face. She's *so* cute.'

'So?' Claire asks, referring to Maddy's date with Matteo. 'Tell us everything. How did it go?'

'I don't know, I kind of . . . well, I ran away,' Maddy says, with her face screwed up. 'And then Trent sent me a message . . . and . . . oh, I don't know. I'm so confused.'

'But you had a good time?' Claire checks. She's surprised. She'd assumed that everything was easy for someone like Maddy, with her confidence and amazing figure and lovely clothes.

'Yes, *really* nice.' Maddy puts her bag down and strips off her coat. 'But, I don't know . . . he's younger than me and . . . I got scared of making a fool of myself. And anyway, he's leaving to go back to Spain. So there's no point in getting into anything, when it's only going to end.'

'I'd say that's a perfect arrangement if you ask me,' Helga says.

Tor arrives next. 'What did I miss?' she asks. 'What happened?'

'Maddy was just telling us about her date with Matteo.'

'And?'

172

Maddy pulls a face. 'I kind of blew it.' She tells Tor what happened.

'But that's OK. There's nothing wrong with playing hard to get,' Tor says. 'Don't lose heart.'

'I guess.'

Tor changes and Dominica is just settling Luna on her coat, when one of the lifeguards on a quad bike comes over. He's young, barely even a shaver, but he has that confident swagger of youth as he stands up on the bike.

'Morning,' he says. 'Just watch yourselves,' he says. 'The water quality isn't great today.'

Claire is confused. 'It looks glorious to me.'

'Well, there's been a spill. Don't swallow any of the water. Just giving you the heads up.'

He turns away on the bike and the stones rattle under the tyres and Luna yelps and trembles. Dominica soothes her and she snuggles into her arms. Dominica notices Maddy staring after the lifeguard, her eyes shining.

'Are you OK?' Dominica asks.

'He was exactly the same age as Jamie. For a moment I thought it might be him . . . '

'What does he mean? A spill?' Claire asks.

'It's a bloody outrage,' Dominica says. 'It means a "combined sewage overflow".' She holds up her fingers to quote it.

'A what?'

'Basically, the British Victorian sewer system is archaic, and the water companies haven't modernised them. So, we still have combined sewers, which means that all the rain water that drains off roads and roofs goes into the same sewage as everything from the loos. When there's loads of rain, the sewage plant can't process the sheer volume, so they discharge the whole lot into the rivers and the seas. Untreated. They say it's better that way, than to flood people's homes.'

'That's revolting!' Claire can't believe it. 'It's where we swim.'

'What's revolting is that it's only half the story. What's really revolting is that they're doing spills even when it hasn't rained,' Helga adds.

'Isn't that illegal?' Maddy asks.

Dominica nods. 'It should be, but there's nobody to check. The water companies get away with spills all the time. Or they just do it anyway and pay the fines, if they happen to get caught. And they're privatised, so nobody holds them properly to account.'

'A spill. That makes it sound very dainty. Like a tiny drop in a bone china saucer,' Claire says. 'When they're actually taking a shit in our bathing water.'

They head out together to the water, but Claire feels differently now that she knows the water could be dangerous. Dominica's right. It is an outrage, she thinks. Somebody ought to do something about it.

Claire is still thinking about the swim and the situation with the water quality, as she serves up lasagne later for supper. Ash is miserable as he's got to do a geography project.

'What's it on?' she asks.

'The environment.'

'Boring,' Felix says.

'It's not boring.' Claire frowns at him. He's always pouring scorn on his younger brother's ideas.

'The environment is the one thing you two can't afford to be cynical about. Because it's up to you lot to change how we all live to save it. I'm afraid we haven't covered ourselves in glory when it comes to what we've done with the planet.'

'Your mother is right,' Pim says, surprising Claire by backing her up.

'Yeah, well, I have no idea where to start on my project, let alone saving the world,' Ash says.

'Well, how about on our doorstep?' Claire suggests.

'Eh?'

'Everything you need is right there.' She throws out her arm in the direction of the beach.

She serves herself and sits down, then tells the three of them about the lifeguard earlier, and what he said about the spill. They've been a bit dismissive about her swims, as if she's taken up a crazy hobby, but she's delighted to see that she's got their attention.

She tells them about how she walked along the beach with Dominica after their swim and she got chatting to Ella at the lifeguard's office. A surfer and clean sea activist herself, Ella had told Claire about the beach clean project. She tells Ash about some sites that Ella has suggested and, to her surprise, Ash says that he wants to look at them with her after supper.

She thinks he doesn't mean it, but then Pim declares that he and Felix are on cleaning up duty and he gets Ash's laptop.

Claire pulls up the Surfers Against Sewage site and, before she knows it, Ash is delving deeper and taking notes.

'This is perfect for the project,' he declares. 'There's loads about it here. About the quality of the bathing water. And about the tankers offshore and the dredging in the marina, too. You're right, Mum. It's all right on our doorstep.'

Pim turns from the sink, the tea towel over his shoulder and gives her a wink. 'Well done,' he mouths and Claire smiles back, glad that he's noticed she's done something good for once.

24

Back to the Office

Dominica takes off her mask as she sits down at her desk, feeling the familiar leather cushion of her office chair still moulded to the shape of her bum. She adjusts the photograph of her and Chris on her desk. It was taken at a Christmas ball, and she'd felt like a film star in her glittery gown. She wipes the dust from it with the cuff of her blouse. God, it's weird being back, she thinks. Everything is the same and yet different. As if she's been in a dream, or under a spell and she's just woken up. She turns in her chair and looks out of the window at the familiar view, noticing how the tufts of grass are poking out through the paving slabs below the benches where she and her colleagues used to eat sandwiches at lunchtime.

Whilst the garden outside has grown, the cactus on her windowsill has died. When she lifts up the pot, it's feathery light. She goes over to the kitchen and turns on the tap and puts the cactus underneath it, but the water cascades out of the bottom through the desiccated soil.

'Feels odd, doesn't it?' Bonnie calls over to her. 'Being back?'

Dominica smiles and nods at her colleague. Because she's right. It *is* odd. She doesn't quite know how to fit back in.

Her phone buzzes with a message on the Sea-Gals WhatsApp. It's from Helga wishing her luck for today and she smiles.

'Come for a swim after work,' Tor has written.

'So, what's been happening?' Bonnie says, coming over and standing by her cubicle. She dips a chocolate biscuit in her tea and takes a bite. Lockdown has aged her, Dominica thinks, looking at her grey roots, and she's put on at least a stone. Doesn't she know about Chris? It's odd that she hasn't mentioned it, but then again why *would* she know? Dominica is used to a level of honesty with Emma and her friends, with all parts of her life being visible, but now she feels like she's wearing invisible armour. Her work guard is up.

'You've been keeping fit. I can see that,' Bonnie says.

'I've been sea swimming.'

'Blimey, you're brave.'

Dominica doesn't think of it as brave, so much as necessary. 'Actually, I'm doing a dawn swim for my friend's charity soon.'

'I can't believe you'd even think of getting in that freezing water at dawn. It's still *dark* at dawn.'

'I think that's the point. To do something hard. To conquer it, you know. To highlight that no matter how dark things get, there's always hope.'

'Yeah, well, good for you. Put me down for a tenner if you want sponsorship. I'll spread the word.'

'Thanks.'

The day gets underway and passes in a blur of calls and meetings. It's so strange, jumping right back in. It's as if nothing has changed, but everything has. Dominica had expected her grief to have somehow diminished her capabilities, but in some way it's made it easier to function on autopilot.

But it's also as if there's an invisible barrier between her and everything she's doing. She used to feel so needed, so up for troubleshooting, but the problems she's used to dealing with no longer seem to matter. It's depressing to discover how many of the small companies she usually deals with have folded in lockdown. The whole industry is on its knees.

By the end of the day, she's exhausted, but she heads for the sea on her bike. She's been dreading the routine of work, but going back to the empty house has been the bit she's been dreading the most and she is touched that her friends know this and that a swim will help.

The light is fading fast so they all change quickly. Dominica decides to ditch her bobble hat for her swimming hat and, as soon as she's in the water, she's glad she has, because the swell is big and she takes the opportunity to dive through the centre of the wave. The water is freezing on her nose and cheeks, but God, *she needed that*, she thinks, as she comes up the other side.

She likes it when the sea is like this at high tide. It's bouncy and you have to keep your wits about you to make sure you don't swallow too much water. The sky is mottled with almost an animal print of blues and greys.

She swims further out, greeting the others, noting that Maddy has ditched the wetsuit and is just in a swimming costume, boots and gloves.

It's windy, the waves being whipped up as if an invisible puppet master is making them dance. The sun breaks through the patch of clouds, although there's slanting rain far away on the horizon beneath a bank of dark-grey clouds. The five of them are bobbing in a wide circle.

'Oh, it's lovely,' she says, a big grin on her face. 'Whooo!' She laughs as a big wave lifts her up and they plunge down the other side.

'I love it,' Claire says, joyfully. 'I didn't think we'd be in earlier when it was raining.'

'It's still raining over there,' Tor says, pointing out the slanting cloud towards Worthing.

'It'll be here in half an hour,' Helga predicts.

'Here we go . . . watch out,' Maddy says, nodding behind her, and Dominica follows her gaze to the huge wave approaching. The swell is covered in foamy bubbles and it lifts them up and plunges them down the other side. It's like being on a fairground ride.

'How did it go at work?' Maddy asks. 'You went back today?'

She appreciates Maddy taking the time to ask, but there's no point in bitching about work. Not when there's another wave. They all get swept up on it and plummet down the other side. Her day so far – everything is forgotten as they squeal like children.

They're all exhilarated and exhausted as they struggle out of the crashing waves to get back to the beach, arms around each other as they pull away from the clutches of the water.

Claire has still got her swimming hat on above her Dryrobe and her teeth are chattering, but she looks cheerful as they get dressed. She stands up, shielding her eyes. Dominica turns, seeing a man walking across the beach and seeing Luna straining on the lead. Her heart does a little skip of joy.

'Oh, it's Luna.'

'Yes. And that's Matteo, his owner,' Maddy says, quickly gathering up her stuff, after waving to him. 'I told him we were coming for a swim.'

He's younger than Dominica had been expecting and he has swarthy skin and bright eyes. He's hot, she thinks, immediately.

Maddy turns back and grins at Dominica, her eyes widening.

'I've asked him over for dinner at mine. Well, we're watching the same series on Netflix . . . '

'So it's a Netflix and chill night,' Tor clarifies. 'You do know that's universally accepted code right?'

Maddy blushes. 'You mean . . . '

'Yes,' Dominica urges her.

'Sex,' Tor says.

'I've asked him over for sex?' Maddy checks, aghast.

'Well, you've certainly hinted at it pretty strongly,' Tor teases.

'Have I?'

Dominica grins. 'It'll do you good.'

'You reckon?' Maddy asks. 'Oh, it's all so confusing. There's this attraction, but then when I stuffed it up . . . I don't know what's going on . . ..'

'He looks very interested, if you ask me,' Tor says.

'Just do it, Maddy. The bottom line is that all any of us need is a good shag,' Helga says, making them all laugh.

Dominica watches Maddy walk up the pebbles to join Matteo on the prom. He kisses her cheek warmly. She says something to him and he lets go of the lead, and Luna runs down to Dominica.

Maddy waves and smiles and Dominica picks up the little

dog. She's touched Luna recognises her. Her little tongue pants with joy, her brown eyes bright.

'You should get a dog,' Helga says. 'Stop you being lonely at home.'

Dominica has thought about it, but she couldn't leave a dog alone all day. It wouldn't be fair. Besides, she's read about the three million new lockdown puppies and how there's been an exodus of vets because of Brexit. She doesn't want to add to the problem.

'I'm not a dog person,' she says. Because she's not. She just likes Luna who licks her face now, making her laugh. 'Now you'd better go.'

She pats the little dog who skitters back up the pebbles to Maddy and Matteo and they both wave to Dominica.

Seeing them together, she feels a little pang, not exactly of envy, but more of sadness. She can't move on like Maddy can from Trent. It's not the same for her. Not when she still loves Chris. How can she ever love someone else when that's the case?

25

The Jab

Despite what the Sea-Gals said about 'the code', Matteo clearly hasn't got the memo, Maddy concludes. He'd come round for dinner and been utterly charming, but as he'd sat beside her on her uncomfortable sofa, Maddy hadn't been able to concentrate, fixating as she had been on the expanse of green cushion between them. She'd felt like a teenager. Everything had been so relaxed, but he hadn't made any kind of move. And why would he, given she'd run out on him after he'd cooked her such a delicious supper?

She feels such a novice, so unsure of herself.

She's longing to go for a swim, mainly so that she can discuss the evening with the swimming girls, but she's been called up by her GP for her Covid vaccination. She's booked in her slot at the vaccination centre, which is being held in the local sports hall a mile away from her house in Cobham.

It's the first time she's left Brighton for ages and she feels a pang, knowing that she's missing the swim today and the Sea-Gals will be gathering without her. As she drives out of town and through the downs, there are clouds ahead and blue sky in the rear-view mirror.

She can't really believe it's March and that she's been away from home all this time. She's paid up front for another month in the Airbnb, though she can't keep on renting such an expensive place with her dwindling funds. But she can't leave until she's found Jamie.

As she drives nearer to Cobham, the familiar sights that used to feel a part of her now don't. When they'd always been on long journeys, Jamie would do a countdown to the brown Twinning sign on the edge of town that would signify that they were nearly home, but when Maddy passes it, she feels nothing.

She hasn't told Trent that she's coming today for her jab, and she feels her heart fluttering with nerves about being caught out as she drives past the road that would lead to the house. She'd eventually replied to Trent's text telling him it was too little too late. She'd pointed out that she wasn't stupid and that, judging from the hour of his text, he'd been undoubtedly drunk. He hadn't taken that well. He'd told her that she can't just call time on their relationship without discussing it. He'd told her that it was unfair that she'd just upped and left without any explanation. She'd retorted that he'd been the one to trash their relationship. He hadn't replied after that.

She indicates into the vaccination centre car park, impressed with how the system is in place to usher everyone through. She puts on her black mask, hoping that there's nobody here who'll recognise her. As she waits in line, she looks at her phone to avoid making eye contact with anyone.

Claire has posted a video of them all in the water this morning and Maddy feels a genuine pang to be back there with her gang. She's jealous of them larking around in the sea. She wants to be in the sea herself.

She wonders now why she didn't she move to the coast when she was younger and had the chance to bring up Jamie by the beach? He could have been a surfer, or a lifeguard. It could have been him tearing about on one of those beach buggies. He'd have loved that.

She likes the weather in Brighton, too. The fact that it announces itself on the horizon. When it rains, it really rains, then the skies clear. Here inland, the sky is disappointingly dull, like a whites wash that's been mixed with a rogue black sock.

There's a guy in front of her in the queue and when he reaches the marshal with the clipboard, he pipes up in a rehearsed kind of a way, 'Just here for a little prick,' with a comedy laugh and the usher, who can only be in his twenties, rolls his eyes at Maddy in despair.

Maddy walks quickly through the roped-off areas, answers her medical questions and is then shown inside to an area in the sports hall by the climbing wall. There's a queue for the cubicles and she prepares herself to wait.

And then she sees her.

It's Helen Bradbury. She's in a marshal's uniform, her chestnut hair tied back in a neat ponytail, but it's her. As if sensing the scrutiny, Helen turns and they make eye contact just as Maddy is called into the cubicle. Maddy sees her eyes widen over her mask.

Why is Helen volunteering? She's not a medic, but then she doesn't need to be, to be a marshall. She used to have a big career in an insurance company, Maddy remembers, but that must have stopped for her to be here. Or is she just trying to virtue signal? Show she's some kind of upstanding citizen? When in fact, she's a home-wrecker.

Maddy sits in the chair as directed, but she can hardly concentrate as the nurse talks her through the protocol. She winces as the needle pierces her skin, but her mind is whirring. The woman who stole her husband is in this very same building and, as much as Maddy wants to confront her, she knows this is absolutely the wrong place to do it. Everyone their age is coming for a vaccine. She doesn't want a horrible soap opera-esque scene in public, even though she's imagined so many.

'That's it. All done—'

Before the nurse has even finished the pleasantries, Maddy is straight out of her chair and heading for the exit.

'You've got to wait for ten minutes,' the nurse calls after her.

'I'll wait outside.'

'But—'

She hurries as fast as she can, without running to the exit sign, but it's too late. Helen has been waiting. *Shit.*

'Maddy,' she calls. 'Maddy. Wait.'

'I have nothing to say to you.' Maddy pushes through the double doors, but Helen catches the door before it shuts.

'Please,' Helen implores as Maddy hurries away from her to the car park. But Helen is following and Maddy rips off her mask and furiously faces her. Can't she take a hint? She doesn't want to have this conversation. Not here.

'Trent is really upset that you won't talk to him,' Helen says.

Maddy is speechless for a moment. She's got the gall . . . the nerve . . . to speak to her about how her husband is feeling!

Helen's wearing an NHS T-shirt, under which she's got

a push-up bra. Well, at least that's if she hasn't had a boob job. Maybe she has had a boob job, Maddy thinks, suddenly comparing herself. Helen's hair is enviably glossy, her skin wrinkle-free and her nails are adorned with fresh acrylics. She's attractive. Desirable.

With a sickening moment of self-awareness, Maddy realises that she has always felt as if she's had the upper hand among her peers. She's always felt the prettiest, the coolest, but right now she feels usurped. And a fool too, for letting this woman into her life.

But they'd been good friends once, Maddy remembers. Helen had been ambitious, smart and funny and, even though Maddy was older than her, they'd clicked immediately. It had been Maddy who'd invited her into the fold and Helen had played this honour perfectly, not stepping on anyone's toes, respecting the unspoken hierarchy until she'd become one of 'the girls'. A memory surfaces of how they'd been pissed one summer in the back garden of Lisa's house and how Helen had declared how much she admired Maddy, how impressed she was by everything she did. Maddy had been flattered, but she'd batted down the praise, telling Helen she'd been the impressive one. It had been a girl love-in. How long ago those days seem now.

'Look, I'm sorry,' Helen says. 'I didn't mean it to happen. I never meant to split up your marriage.' Maddy sees that Helen's not wearing a wedding ring.

'Then what *did* you mean to do?' Maddy folds her arms.

'I don't know. It was so good to be paid some attention. I never meant to hurt anyone at all. You've got to believe me. It wasn't malicious. But once I'd been out for one drink with

Trent and we got chatting . . . ' She sighs. 'Nothing happened for ages. It was just that he was easy to talk to.'

Maddy has been wondering about how they got it together, building up romantic scenarios in her head that would be impossible to forgive. She's imagined Trent making some grand gesture, but now she sees that it was as mundane as a drink in the pub that made them spark. Their mutual need for human connection. Not that this makes her feel any less jealous. She used to love talking to her husband too. Because Trent had used to listen to her, she remembers. He'd been her confidante and best friend. How did she lose that? Because she *had* lost that. Maybe even before Helen came along.

'Look. The thing is . . . me and Trent. It was out of both our controls.'

'Oh, please,' Maddy snorts.

'It's not been easy for me. All of this,' Helen says.

'You are not the victim here.'

Helen cocks her head. 'Alex won't let me see the kids. He won't talk to me, or let me back home. I'm staying at my sisters.'

Maddy can see she's hurting, but even so, she says, 'I can't say I blame him.'

Helen nods, taking this punishment and Maddy feels a horribly churning wash of emotions, because she shouldn't feel sorry for Helen. This is her fault. She's brought this on herself. But the way she looks at the tarmac and sighs is too hard to watch. 'But it must be difficult not seeing the kids,' she concedes. 'For you and for them.'

There's a beat and Helen smiles weakly, taking this olive branch. 'How's it going? Looking for Jamie?'

Maddy almost tells her. They have far more history as

friends than as enemies and normally she would happily talk about whatever was going on in her life. It had always been so easy and natural with her. But not now. She shrugs and lets the silence stretch. Helen has forfeited her right to any information.

'I want you and Trent to sort things out,' Helen says. 'Then we can all move forward. It's just too hard for him that you're not talking.'

So they're still together? Maddy feels the urge to blurt out that Trent is still texting her declaring undying love.

'Poor Trent,' Maddy says, hating the way she sounds so bitter and twisted.

She remembers reading something once about a marriage being a fortress and that it only works if you keep your walls and windows secure. But Trent left the back door wide open and now it feels as if Helen is trampling over something sacred.

Logically, she knows Helen is only being practical. She wants commitments, promises, a view of the future. What does she want to do? Move into Maddy's home? Is that her game plan?

Maddy is too unsettled by this new status as the wronged wife. A role that she never wanted. A role she hates Helen for giving her. Because now she feels on the back foot. Why should Helen get to feel clear about her future, when she feels as if her life has been ripped away from her?

She stalks to the car, pressing the blipper, but her legs are shaking. Helen calls after her as she gets in, the engine growling as she drives away. She can see Helen in the rear-view mirror watching, shrugging as if she'd tried to reason with her. Maddy drives around the corner and screeches to a halt, taking in a gasp of air. Then she hits the steering wheel with her palms and yells.

Helen is not getting her house. No way. Over her dead body.

For a moment, she contemplates driving home to tell Trent exactly that, but she's too jangled. She needs to re-group. Re-assess. Pull herself together.

She needs to get in the sea.

26

Dawn Call

When the alarm goes off at four thirty in the morning, Tor groans as she switches it off, then turns to face Lotte. She strokes the blue and blonde hair away from Lotte's face, thinking how childlike she looks when she sleeps.

'Hon,' she says.

She leans across and kisses Lotte's cheek. She smells vaguely of tobacco, mixed with Nivea cream. Lotte's not one for beauty protocols and never takes her make-up off before bed, but she does slap on a bit of cream when she remembers.

'Babes, come on. If we're doing it, we have to go.'

'Uhhh,' Lotte says and opens one bloodshot blue eye.

'Yep. It's brutal, but we're doing it.'

She thinks Lotte is going to ignore her and go back to sleep, but she screws up her face.

'OK, OK, yep,' Lotte says and Tor kisses her again, because she knows how much Lotte hates the cold and the mornings.

They get dressed, Lotte throwing jumpers over the *Fleabag* T-shirt she's wearing. Her thighs are elaborately tattooed and she stumbles, naked from the waist down, to their tallboy chest of drawers they got from a car boot sale in the marina.

'I don't know where my costume is,' she says.

'Nice excuse. Wear knickers and the wet suit.'

'You reckon?'

'You're not used to the cold.'

'You do realise how much I love you to be even considering this?' Lotte says, turning round.

'Yes. I do. I'm going to make a flask of tea. Do not go back to bed.'

There's a splatter of rain against the window and Lotte shivers. 'Is that rain? That's rain, right? Brrrr.'

Tor shrugs and pulls a face. Yesterday, she checked the weather app relentlessly, not really believing that the one hundred per cent chance of rain was true. She grew up with parents who inherently distrusted the weather predictions after the 1987 storm wiped out her dad's Volvo when a fallen tree crushed it. But the forecast has turned out to be depressingly accurate. She'd so been hoping for clear-blue skies, and for this to feel like a hopeful event, but now she worries that the charity swim is going to be a subdued affair.

In the kitchen, she checks the chat. Dominica and Claire are about to leave. Helga and Maddy are coming too. She steels herself and refreshes the fundraising page. She's fifty per cent to her target, but her family haven't put their money in yet and Dominica says some of her work colleagues have promised sponsorship.

It's eerie setting out in the dark. Lotte's bike has a flat tyre and they're the only people around as they walk along the middle of the road, the blurred streetlamps reflected in the puddles.

'It's freaky. It's like we're in a computer simulation,' Lotte says. 'It's weird being sober at this time in the morning.'

A fox is by the big black bins, where it licks a discarded takeaway box. It stops and stares at them.

The road on the seafront is empty, the traffic lights green in both directions, but it's getting lighter and the sea ahead a dark-green haze. There's no horizon.

The Sea-Gals are waiting by the groyne, their Dryrobes bright against the grey wall. Dominica has her bike light on, illuminating their little group. There's some others joining too – Arek from the charity and five or six others that she doesn't recognise, and she feels a wave of gratitude, for people getting up at dawn.

The tide is out, but the water is choppy and Tor knows already that she'll be in for more bruises on her shins getting in and out. She really doesn't want to take off her coat, but they all strip off quickly. Lotte does up her neoprene cap with the chin strap and claps her gloved hands together. She's so covered in waterproof gear, she looks like a seal. Tor introduces her to Maddy and she's pleased that they seem to get on.

'I've heard so much about you,' Lotte says. 'Tor said you were brilliant at volunteering.'

'It's nice to be able to help out.'

Arek comes down the beach. 'Oh, Maddy. I meant to tell you,' he said. 'I was chatting to one of my regulars. I was telling him about Jamie and he knew a guy that fitted the description.'

Tor stares at Maddy and they both look at Arek.

'They know where he is?' Maddy asks.

Arek shakes his head. 'No. I tried to get more, but the guy was high. He didn't speak that much English. That's all I got. I'm sorry. But they think he's here in Brighton.'

Maddy nods and Tor sees her fighting back the emotion.

'At least he's near,' Tor says, trying to comfort her. 'At least it's something, right?'

'I heard of this private detective agency,' Lotte said. 'One of my clients at the salon used them, to help look for her daughter. I've got her number somewhere. It's not cheap, but it might be worth a try.'

Maddy smiles. 'Thank you. That would be great. I'll do anything at this point.'

Tor smiles gratefully at Lotte, glad she's come.

They all set off towards the water's edge in a group. In the fine mist, they can only see a few metres in front of them.

'This must be what it's like swimming in heaven,' Dominica says.

'It actually reminds me of a spa I went to in Bali on my honeymoon,' Maddy says.

'Bali,' Tor says, teasing her. 'Exactly. Heaven.'

'I paid a bloody fortune, and this is free. And better. I don't have to put up with Trent.'

'How are things in the Trent department?' Dominica asks.

'Don't ask. I ran into Helen at the vaccination centre when I went home. She's the woman he had an affair with. Still is, by the sounds of it. I'm so angry . . . '

'Don't waste your time being angry, Maddy,' Helga says. 'It's not good for you.'

'I guess.'

'You must keep positive,' Helga says.

Lotte strides forward and lets out a yelp as she splashes through a wave. She comes up smiling.

'Not as bad as I thought,' she calls and Maddy goes to join her.

Tor stands for moment with Dominica. 'Do you remember last year?'

'Yes, of course I remember,' Dominica says, the rain pattering on their skin, the drops making them squint and blink. Tor rubs her upper arms. They'd done the dawn swim a month after Chris had died. Tor hadn't thought Dominica would come in, but she had turned up at the beach, her face drawn with grief.

'Look how far you've come,' Tor tells her.

'You think so? I don't feel any different.'

'But you've kept going. That's something right? Something to be proud of. You kept showing up.'

The water is murky, the waves peaking and, as Tor knew it would be, it's difficult to get in when it's so rough. For a moment, when she goes for it and launches herself into the shallow water and compared to the outside temperature, it feels momentarily, pleasantly warm. She ducks under a wave and Claire copies her.

'Jeez! That's one way to wake up,' she says.

There's a pull in the water and they don't swim so much as bob as they're dragged towards the other groyne, but it's fun being swirled around in the water. Arek and his friends get in and Tor realises how different it is swimming with men. As they lark around, dunking each other, they bring a different kind of energy.

She's only aware of the light changing when she sees the

other beaches coming into view. As far as Tor can see along the coast, they are the only people around.

Helga announces that it's time to head in, but Tor doesn't want to get out of the water. She knows she must, though – that the after-drop will be mega today.

Claire is slightly behind her, but she gets tumbled by a wave.

'Steady,' Tor says, catching hold of her hand as she splutters. She helps her find her footing as they time it between waves to walk up from the sea to the shore.

'Thank you. That was a bit scary,' Claire says.

Back at their pile of bags, Tor takes her towel and wipes her face. Her whole body is tingling and buzzing.

And then Lotte touches her arm and they all stop and are quiet. A dove has come to land just by them. It stands still on the stones, the white of its body somehow supernatural against the tan and black shingle.

'Is that a dove?' Tor asks Helga, who nods.

'Is it some kind of sign?' Claire asks in a whisper.

It certainly feels like one to Tor. The white dove feels symbolic somehow.

'New beginnings. And peace,' Helga says. 'That's what a dove means.'

'They let them off at weddings.' Dominica's voice is husky.

'I think it's a sign, Maddy, I really do,' Lotte says. 'I think it means you're going to find Jamie.'

Tor reaches out to Lotte. How does she always manage to say the right thing?

There's a moment as they all stare at the little bird and it feels almost religious. Then Maddy moves to take the phone out of her pocket, but the movement scares the bird away.

Tor sees Helga give her a look.

'Oh well,' she says. 'Serves me right. Maybe this is too special to put on Instagram.'

Helga nods and gives her a little smile.

27

Life Drawing

Claire stands in Helga's bedroom, not quite believing that she's actually here. She wants to be the kind of person to impress Dominica and Helga and the others, who have encouraged her to step out of her comfort zone, but she hasn't let on how terrifying she finds this whole idea.

She can't tell the Sea-Gals that since she had the boys, she mostly loathes her body. It would seem petty to admit such insecurity, when she's been stripping off in front of them for months. But body shape doesn't seem to matter when their group is all shapes and sizes. In the sea the notion of the 'perfect body' Claire has always been so intimidated by is totally irrelevant. Hand on heart Claire finds every one of the women she's come to know and admire in their swimming tribe both amazing and beautiful. Can they possibly feel the same about her? They must do for Helga to be so keen to draw her.

She walks over and strokes the soft Nordic blanket on the end of Helga's low bed and inspects the framed model of a sailing yacht on the wall. The room feels oddly masculine, with its blue rugs over the rickety exposed floorboards. Above her, the beams slope downwards. Claire picks up the framed photograph next to the bed. It's of an earnest young blonde woman. There's an old leather necklace with a shell on it wrapped around it.

'That's Mette, my niece,' Helga says, coming in with a robe. 'Just put this on and come down when you're ready. We're all set. Everyone is here.'

Claire nods and thanks her. It's too late to back out now.

She changes out of her clothes, feeling more and more nervous as she unhooks her bra. She leaves everything in a neat pile on the low leather chair in the corner and slips on the thin cotton robe. It smells of stale perfume and she wonders when it was last washed. She takes out her phone and sees the thumbs up message from Pim to her text. She's told him that she's having a drink with a friend, but he's clearly not bothered. It's been insanely busy for him going back in the classroom. She hasn't had the nerve to tell him where she is, or what she's doing. It's not that he doesn't approve of the Sea-Gals, but she knows he's a bit put out by her new friendship group and how she's doing things she never used to do. Like volunteering for Tor and getting up at dawn for a swim. When she came home and told him about her scary tumble getting out of the sea, he said he thought she was stupid for putting herself at the risk of hypothermia and that she ought to be careful swimming with strangers who he presumed weren't medically qualified.

She creeps downstairs and walks past the pushed back sofas to the conservatory, where Helga is hosting the life-drawing class. There's an electric bar heater next to a wooden stool and there's a dressing mirror along with a large spotlight on a stand. It's like a stage and Claire feels jittery with nerves.

'There you are,' Helga says. 'This is Claire, everyone.'

She introduces an elderly couple, a man and woman both with matching grey ponytails, but Claire doesn't catch their names. There's an earnest-looking young man with a waxed moustache and a girl with ginger hair. They're all behind easels.

Helga leads Claire over to the stool.

'Sit with your back to us,' she says and Claire sits down on the stool, wiggling her bottom on it to try and get comfortable. Helga adjusts the spotlight on the stand and the earnest guy asks her to move it backwards. He has an odd accent. Russian maybe.

'When you're ready.' Helga touches Claire's shoulder reassuringly.

'You want me to take the whole thing off?'

'Ideally, but just be comfortable.'

Comfortable? That's the last thing she is. This is way, way out of her comfort zone, but Helga doesn't seem to think it's a big deal. Claire realises that she has to be a grown-up and brazen this out. She presses her thighs together, aware of her nudity, of the parts of her body she hides away as she lets the robe fall, closing her eyes, waiting for what? Gasps of shock?

But there's nothing, just a scratching on paper as the group start to draw.

'Can you turn a little to the side?' Helga asks from behind her easel. If she's noticed how Claire is feeling, she's not going to mention it.

Claire turns a little and she can see her reflection in the mirror and the artists behind her. The chap with the long ponytail has already started stroking the paper on his easel with a charcoal. He stands back, contemplating the paper and then looking at Claire's back.

'What shall I do with my hands?' Claire asks.

'Just stay still. Just as you are. It's perfect,' the girl with the ginger hair says. She sounds excited.

Some lovely classical music starts playing in the studio and Helga comes back from a CD stack.

'I like this music,' Claire says.

'Debussy. "Clair de Lune". Seems appropriate.' Claire smiles. 'Just relax, Claire. You look wonderful.'

It's hard to sit still though and she tries not to tense her muscles. She's aware of her belly and her breasts and how they hang and the stool pressing into her thigh, accentuating her cellulite, but then she glances at the artists in the mirror, and she sees the ponytail woman's eyes glistening as she glances at Claire and then at her paper.

And it's this scrutiny that makes her imagine that she's one of the artists herself. She observes her smooth skin and the proportions of her body and suddenly, rather than hating herself, she remembers that this body, which five people are also appraising, is a wonderful thing. It's a body that has borne children and that has got her to this point in life. A body that is worthy of art.

Maybe getting older isn't so bad, she thinks. Maybe Helga's right. Maybe not giving a damn about what anyone else thinks is the way forward.

She's stiff, though, by the time the session has ended and she gets up and stretches and puts the robe back on, although surprisingly, she's got used to being naked. She doesn't feel shy as she turns to face everyone. The guy with the ponytail shows her the sketch he's done and she gasps. It's really beautiful. She looks like a woman in one of the famous Botticelli sketches and, oddly, like her mother. But in a good way. He's caught her profile – her chin and the slant of her nose. Even her hair, which makes her feel self-conscious, is drawn artfully.

'Maybe this is where I've been going wrong,' Claire tells him. 'Maybe, instead of photographs, which always seem to highlight my faults, maybe I should get people to sketch me.'

'You can keep it if you like,' he says.

'Are you sure?'

'Your husband would like it, I bet,' the woman with the matching ponytail says.

Claire smiles, accepting the gift, wondering what on earth Pim would say if she were to present him with this. And what would the boys think? They'd die if they saw a picture of their naked mother, wouldn't they? That she has done something so shocking feels rather marvellous.

'Do you want to stay for a drink?' Helga asks.

'I should get back. To my family.'

'You have children?' the ponytail guy asks. He sounds surprised and she wants to make a joke that he must have guessed from her stretch marks.

'I have two boys,' she says. 'They're very messy.'

'See, that's why I never had children. I can't stand other people's stuff in my space,' Helga says, taking a sip of wine. 'Children. Brrr.'

'You'll miss them when they're gone,' the older lady says to Claire. 'That's what made us take up life drawing. When we had an empty nest. Make the most of them.'

Claire feels exhilarated after her modelling session. It's not just the confidence it's given her, but the unexpected pleasure of meeting new people, as well as having a chance to see Helga in her home. It's made her feel like their friendship is even stronger. But the second she gets through her front door, the feeling evaporates. The whole place is a bombsite. She spent the morning cleaning, but now Ash and Felix have disgorged the contents of their school bags on the floor. There's mud on the stairs and, as she walks into the kitchen, there's evidence from a sandwich-making session. Their game blares from the TV in the living room, the sound of explosions is deafening.

'Where have you been?' Pim says, from his laptop at the table. It's strewn with papers and books. 'We're starving.'

'I was doing something for Helga,' she says evasively. Pim's so disinterested, he doesn't enquire further. Claire yanks open the freezer and pulls out a packet of fishfingers and a bag of frozen chips. 'There,' she says, dumping them forcefully in front of him. 'Shouldn't be too hard to work out.'

Because it shouldn't be. Why the feck can't they feed themselves if they're hungry? Why is everything always down to her? She's had enough.

Pim, shocked away from his screen, looks up at her with confusion. 'Claire?'

'I'm going to have a bath.'

'Mum?' Felix asks. 'What's for dinner?'

'Ask your father,' she says and she stomps up the stairs, feeling their shocked stares on her back, but she doesn't care. It's time they started to respect her.

28

Equinox

It's a crisp, blue-sky morning, it being early, and Helga can see other groups on the beaches towards Hove. She's noticing more swimmers now that spring is in the air. Little Luna is curled up on Dominica's coat on the shore, guarding their things. Tor comes down the stones, waving a piece of paper.

'Did you get one of these?' she asks.

'What is it?' Helga asks.

'They were handing them out by the steps.'

Helga reads the leaflet asking people to join in the beach clean. Maddy takes it and then gives it to Claire.

'We'll do that,' Claire says. 'I'm very happy to join in.'

She gives it to Dominica, who nods. 'Me too.'

Maddy is getting changed and is sporting a stylish speedo suit. She twists up her hair and expertly pulls on her swimming hat.

'How lovely to feel the sun on my skin,' she says. 'I always used to be terrified of stripping off on the beach, but it's not as cold as you'd expect.'

'Yes, there's brighter days ahead,' Helga says, pointing her nose into the light breeze. She can always smell the onset of spring. She closes her eyes for a moment, feeling the sun on her face. It's a wonderful antidote to the restless night she's spent, staring at the beams in her bedroom, wondering why her heart won't quieten down. It's like a distressed bird in a cage.

'Big day today,' Dominica says.

'Why's that?' Claire asks.

'I'm switching from boots to jelly shoes,' she says. 'I just bought these from Decathlon.'

She puts on the jelly shoes and wiggles her feet in them. They're not the most flattering footwear in the world, but the most necessary. Helga knows there's no dignity in a woman of a certain age trying to make it out of the waves and up the shingle beach without shoes. Maybe she should get some like those for herself. These old things are almost worn through. But she hates shopping at the best of times and she refuses to shop online.

'You're not ditching the swimming gloves though?' Claire asks Dominica, who shakes her head.

'No. One thing at a time,' she says.

Helga knows that Claire is still making sure she does the right thing and follows the right protocol when it comes to swimming, but Helga's noticed a change in her. Especially since she sat for the life drawing. The group had all told Helga what a find Claire was. How it surprised them all how Claire didn't realise quite how gorgeous and voluptuous she was, how luminescent her pale skin. What a delight she'd been to draw.

Helga hopes the session gave Claire something too. She certainly seems to be coming out of her shell and that timid, eager-to-please way she had about her when they first met has given way to a more secure confidence.

Today, the water is just how Helga likes it. Cold and buoyant and high. Maddy, who usually gets in slowly, strides in and dives in straight away. She tips back her head in the water with a sigh. She lies on her back, like Helga has shown her, floating on the surface like a starfish for a few moments, as the others get in.

A man is fishing off the high groyne, his lines taught and Helga can see a shoal of mackerel shimmying below in the clear water. She doesn't tell Maddy. She doesn't want to blow her confidence when she's starting to love the water so much. She sets off in the opposite direction, away from the fishermen.

'Did you know that it's the spring solstice today?' Tor says as they swim out.

'So it is,' Helga says. There's a whale-skeleton of white clouds way above. 'Funny to think that over in Australia their autumn is starting today. That they're facing the dark days ahead and getting out their jumpers and coats, whilst we're looking forward to the summer.'

Is Linus in Australia? She imagines him in a smart house with a yacht at the end of his private dock.

'It's the equinox too,' she adds.

'I like the word equinox,' Dominica says. 'It gets you a good score in Scrabble.'

'From the Latin for equal, *aequus*, and the night, *nox*,' Helga explains. 'The spring equinox is also known as the vernal because the two hemispheres of the earth are receiving the sun's rays equally. Did you know that the sunrises and sunsets are faster at the equinox?'

'I love that feeling that summer is coming,' Claire says. 'It's easier to have a brighter outlook when the sun is shining.'

'Won't it be amazing when we can get out of the sea and dry off in our costumes on the stones and lounge around in the sun?' Dominica says. 'Although I'll miss the cold buzz.'

'We certainly will,' Helga says, because it's true. It won't be the same in the warmer weather, but even so, she likes the fact that this group is a constant. That it's a given that they'll be swimming together in the months to come.

'Is the spring equinox the same as the spring tides?' Maddy asks and Helga likes that the Sea-Gals are all listening in.

'No. The spring tides happen around the new moon, or the full moon. When you look up, the moon is either invisible or you can see it, and, at that point, the moon and the sun are generally in a straight line. When that happens there's a tidal bulge, which means that the high tides are higher and the low tides are lower.'

'What's the difference between spring and neap tides then?' Tor asks.

'Neap tides are when the moon is halfway through its cycle, so it's not new or full. The moon and the sun are at right angles to each other. At those times, the forces on the sea are weaker, so there's not much difference between a high and low tide. So when you get in even at low tide, you can only just touch the bottom.'

'How come you know so much about all this?' Maddy asks.

'I learnt all about the sun and moon when I was sailing,' Helga says. 'It's fascinating stuff. And what's really weird is that, wherever you sail in the world, the sun always rises in the east and sets in the west.'

'Really?' Claire sounds genuinely fascinated.

'Each day from now, the sun will arc higher across the sky.' She points up. 'By the summer equinox in June, the sun will set over there because each day that arc will be shifting to the north.'

'I'd never noticed that before.' Maddy sounds thoughtful.

'That's why all the birds and butterflies migrate north too – along the path of the sun.' Helga watched the starlings go last week. They'd gathered in great numbers on the telephone wires and she'd imagined them chatting about the journey back to Scandinavia. How she longs to go on a journey herself.

'How have I got to nearly fifty and been so ignorant of facts like these?' Claire says.

'You know them now,' Helga says. 'I bet you know all sorts of stuff I don't know.'

'This week I'm learning about planning laws. Not the most fascinating subject,' Claire says. 'My bloody neighbour is putting up an extension and . . . ' She shakes her head. 'I'm not going to get worked up about it now. This is my break from it, but I've become rather obsessed with an appeal.'

'Nothing worse than horrible neighbours,' Dominica says.

'Rob and Jenna. They think they're so perfect. They've got this plan to build a monstrosity on the back of their house, which will take all of our light and overlook us completely, but the worst bit of it all is that they're going to cut down the cherry tree. I love that tree.'

'Surely they can't do that?' Maddy says.

'Well, you'd think not,' Claire replies, 'but I don't know how we can stop them.'

'I know a bit about planning,' Maddy tells her. 'Maybe I can help?'

'Could you?'

'I'd be happy to try. It's the least I can do to say thank you for getting me into swimming.'

Helga swims ahead with Dominica leaving them to chat.

'You're all right at work?' Tor checks and Dominica smiles. 'How's it been this week?'

'I had a meeting with my boss,' Dominica says. 'He wanted to check in to see that everything was fine now I'm back and to re-instate my targets. He was very awkward about the Chris thing.'

'You mean, you being bereaved,' Helga clarifies. Why do people pussy-foot around death?

'Exactly. You should have seen him squirm.'

'Oh dear,' Tor says.

'I just . . . it's just not the same. I can't seem to get my head into it. I don't seem to be able to care.'

'Then do something you care about,' Helga says.

'You make it sound simple.'

'Isn't it? Surely life is too short to do anything your heart's not in?'

'You should go back to the Samaritans,' Tor says. 'I'd bet your old boss Bill would have you back in a heartbeat.'

'I know. I've been thinking about it.'

'Do it. It'll give you something else to focus on.'

'Yeah, maybe you're right.'

Helga isn't so sure. She doesn't want the burden of other people's problems, but then Dominica is very different to her. She's got so much potential and it pains Helga to see her floundering without Chris. She knows she can't interfere with her grieving process, but she wants to tell her that life is short.

Way too short. Dominica certainly doesn't want to get to Helga's age and be contemplating the next ten years – if she's lucky enough to have ten years – with nothing exciting on the horizon. Apart from the bloody retirement village. She's received the brochure that Mette sent and it's made her feel profoundly depressed. You can put all the glossy covers on it you want, but surely any kind of retirement village is still a waiting room for the grave.

Helga has always shied away from people her own age. She's seen Judith, Will's mother from next door, a couple of times in the past few weeks and invited her in for coffee when she got locked out. Afterwards, at Judith's suggestion, Helga and Katie swapped spare keys. It's not something Helga's ever done before, but Katie couldn't have been nicer, gushing about the sketch of Josh Helga did and how they've put it in a frame. But as friendly as Judith is, Helga doesn't really have that much in common with her, when all she talks about is her grandchildren.

As Helga gets dressed and warms herself on the flask-lid of tea, she realises that she likes being among her younger Sea-Gals and she likes her status as the wise one among the group. At the same time, she wonders what they'd think of her if they knew that increasingly she feels a little bit afraid.

29

Home Hairdresser

Tonight, the food bank is up by the racecourse and Maddy offers to give Tor and Claire a lift home after their shift finishes. Tor's grateful to Maddy for driving and for all her help. Tor's van has been on the blink all week and she's taken it to the garage. Fortunately, the money from the charity swim will pay for it to be fixed. She's reached a hundred per cent of her target thanks to all the money Dominica raised in the office and, to her surprise, thanks to Alice, who did a whip round among her school-mother friends. Tor knows it's an olive branch. They haven't been talking that much since Christmas and Alice can't bear it when they start to become estranged. So Tor called and quickly realised that the sponsorship money was a bribe. She's been summoned to Alice's for Easter.

'Your cakes went down a storm tonight,' Tor tells Claire. 'Everyone loves them. Lotte will be gutted there aren't any left.'

'They went faster than ever. I'll have to make more.'

'They're so good, you know,' Maddy says. 'You should run a café.'

'A café? Me? Oh, no, my cakes aren't that good.'

'They are!' Tor exclaims. 'I'd pay good money for that coconut one any day.'

Claire grins. 'Well, that's lovely of you to say so.'

Tor sits in the back and watches as Claire flips down the visor in the passenger's seat.

'Oh good gracious. Look at the state of me,' she says. 'Why didn't any of you tell me?'

Maddy laughs. 'Stop being so self-critical.'

'I've been trying to get an appointment at the hairdresser, but it's impossible to get through.'

'I can get Lotte to do your hair,' Tor offers. 'She used to work in a salon.'

'Really?'

'I can ask her,' Tor says, taking out her phone and texting, as they drive into town back towards Tor's house. Her phone pings back straight away.

'She says to bring you round now.'

'Now?' Claire asks.

'Well, it's not that late. It's only half eight.'

'Well, if you're sure?'

'I can drop you off,' Maddy says.

'Oh no, come too,' Tor says. She hasn't invited people round for ages. 'Stay and have a drink. We've rigged up lights in the garden and there's wine in the fridge.'

As they walk through the front door, Tor can't help seeing her house through her friends' eyes. The messy chaos is something that she takes for granted, but now, as they squeeze awkwardly past the jumble of bikes in the corridor, the scuffed floorboards and the ancient threadbare carpet runner down the stairs, the pop art graffiti over the walls, she feels embarrassed. She's fed up with this kind of communal living. She wants somewhere where she can relax when she comes home and not have to deal with other people.

'I'm home,' Tor calls.

'In here,' Lotte calls back and she beckons Maddy, Claire and Tor to the kitchen.

'The kick-ass swimmers,' Lotte says. 'Heavenly. Come in, come in. And great timing. I've just finished,' she adds. Declan, their housemate, is on the wooden kitchen chair and Tor's Anglepoise lamp is trained on his upper arm, where Lotte has inked the last part of his elaborate lotus flower sleeve. She's carefully sticking cling film over it.

Declan stands up and Tor sees Maddy clock his lanky thin limbs and crazy beard. He's painfully shy and shuffles off.

The kitchen smells of boiled lentils and there are pots and pans piled up in the sink, but Maddy only smiles. 'Look at those herbs and your lovely garden,' she says. 'It's like being in the middle of the countryside.'

She's being nice, Tor thinks. 'Sorry about the mess.'

'It's not messy. I like it. It's homely. These old Edwardian town houses have such amazing proportions and energy about them.'

Lotte grins, delightedly, the gap between her front teeth as endearing as ever. She's wearing a diaphanous green dress with her twelve-hole DMs, her arms jangling with bangles. 'Oh, you . . . you're the one,' Lotte says, hugging Claire effusively, 'who makes the delicious cake, aren't you? You smell like a delicious cake. And look at those curls.' She fluffs out Claire's hair. 'Oh, my.'

Tor watches Claire blush and pat her hair self-consciously. She always forgets how people react when Lotte shines her light on them. It's pretty intense.

'I hate the grey.'

'There's nothing wrong with grey, but why be grey? Unless you're a statement grey. Why not go blonde?'

'I used to be blonde. Years ago, in my twenties. I really should think about it before I make a drastic change.'

'No, darling. No, you must be impulsive,' Lotte insists. 'The universe has brought you here to me and I intend to fulfil my purpose.'

Claire relents and Tor lets Lotte whisk her away upstairs to the bathroom and she takes Maddy outside.

'I love those,' Maddy says, nodding to the lights strung up in the trees. She puts another log on the fire pit and sparks fly up as Tor and Maddy sit down on the sofas Lotte made out of pallets and bean bags.

Looking up at the back of the house, Tor can see Lotte and Claire in the bathroom, Lotte standing behind Claire by the sink. She'll be doing one of her 'consultations' in the bathroom mirror. She feels a pang of guilt. Poor Claire is bound to be bamboozled by Lotte into a completely new look.

'What are you doing for Easter?' Maddy asks.

'I've had the summons to my sister's.'

'Are you going to go?'

'There's no choice,' she says. 'You?'

She shrugs. 'Not sure yet. Trent keeps saying he want to see me, so I guess I'll have to go home and face the music.'

'What about Matteo?' she asks.

'What *about* Matteo?' She rolls her eyes.

'Still nothing?'

'*Nada*. I think I've missed that boat.'

'Oh, I wouldn't be so sure,' Tor says.

'He's been away this week. I hadn't realised that I'd miss him so much.'

'That's good, isn't it?'

'Yes, if it wasn't for the fact that I fancy him. And I know it's ridiculous because I'm latching on to him, because he's near. Because I'm a desperate, lonely old lady.'

A lonely old lady hardly describes Maddy, thinks Tor, who manages to look cool no matter what she does.

'If you suspect there's a spark there, then why not act on it? See what happens?'

Maddy sighs. 'Because I don't know if I can trust my instincts any more. This whole thing with Helen has made me really second-guess myself about everything, you know? Because I thought my friends were my friends, but they were all lying to me. It's been so refreshing to meet you lot and to just be myself.'

They chat easily and then the subject of Jamie comes up. Tor knew it would. Maddy's been in touch with the contact of Lotte's – a private detective, who she's paying to try and find Jamie. She says she's using the fund that she set up for Jamie's education to pay for it. The last pot of money, as she describes it. Maddy has always come across as so affluent, so it's a surprise to Tor that she's struggling so much to make ends meet. Tor really hopes the detective works out, and it's worth it, but annoyingly there have been no leads so far.

Tor is curious. 'Did you only ever want Jamie? You weren't tempted to have more kids?'

'I wanted to, but there was a complication and I had to have an operation after Jamie was born. I thought briefly about adopting, but I was so in love with my cherubic child.' She sighs. 'He was my everything. He was always more than enough. I wish I'd told him that, though. I think he always felt that he was trying to live up to being several children.'

Tor smiles gently.

'But nobody tells you how to be a parent,' Maddy says. 'It comes as a massive shock and you have to wing it. Literally. I was making it up as I went along. And life is going by so fast and you have to make snap decisions. And by the time you realise you've said something or done something wrong, it's too late to fix it. And the funny thing is that now I'm older, I realise how easy it is to mess up. And how my mother messed up too. How she criticised me once about my grades in public. And I never forgot it. It was one of those pivotal moments and she probably didn't even notice it happening, but it shaped who I am.'

'I guess I know what you mean. I can't pick a moment,' Tor says, 'but I just have always felt my parents love Alice more.'

'Well, I bet that's not true.'

'No,' Tor says, with a shrug. 'They prefer Alice.'

'Has it ever occurred to you that your mum probably feels that Alice needs more attention, because Alice needs her, and you don't. Because you're strong?' Maddy asks.

'But I'm not.'

'Err, excuse me, but yes you are,' Maddy says. Tor is warmed by her support.

'I don't know. It's just . . . Alice has always had all their focus. Maybe it was something to do with the fact that she was really ill when we were born.'

'Well, then, that makes perfect sense. I can't imagine having two babies at the same time. But one of them being sick must have been terrifying. What if she'd lost your twin?'

Tor feels an unexpected surge of affection for her twin. Maddy's right. She can't imagine life without Alice. Maybe it won't really be so bad telling her parents and Alice about her and Lotte. She knows they love her, so surely they'll come to accept her and Lotte? And, even if they don't, she has people around her who will. She resolves that she'll fix it at Easter. She'll find a way to move forward.

It's lovely being outside by the fire bowl and Tor feels so much better for talking to Maddy. Claire comes back with foils in her hair and they chat for a while and eat a pizza Lotte heats up from the freezer.

Lotte is excited about the new look she has planned for Claire, who pulls a worried look at Tor and Maddy.

An alarm sounds on Lotte's phone and she whisks Claire away to rinse her hair and to dry it.

'Wish me luck,' Claire says.

'You don't need luck. You're going to love it,' Lotte calls effusively and Claire laughs. People are always shocked by Lotte's absolute certainty about things. It's one of the reasons Tor loves her. Because she's so decisive, so sure of her footing in life. It makes Tor feel safe.

Tor tells Maddy about her adventures in Africa and running away from Mike and is coming on to how she met Lotte, when Lotte comes into the garden. Claire has a towel loosely over her hair and a big grin on her face.

'You ready?' she asks.

Maddy and Tor both stand for the big reveal and Claire

whips away the towel. Her hair has been cut in a flattering shape around her face and coloured into natural caramel and fudge tones. She looks at least ten years younger.

'Do you like it?' she asks, nervously, patting it.

'Oh my God!' Maddy exclaims, jumping up to inspect it. 'It's amazing. Lotte, I'm booking you in right now.'

'Seriously?' Claire asks, looking to Tor.

'It's wonderful,' Tor says, kissing her cheek. Maddy takes photos of Claire for her to see.

'Well done,' Tor whispers to Lotte. 'Thank you for doing that.'

Lotte grins back. 'Pleasure. She was fun. I like your friends.'

Claire is blushing from all the attention. She studies the photos on Maddy's phone, then says, 'Goodness. It's so late. I must get home to Pim and the boys.'

Lotte wraps her in a big hug and kisses her on the cheek and Claire squeaks in surprise, then giggles.

'This has been so much fun. Honestly. Lotte, you're a genius.'

Tor likes the feeling that she's been able to make a difference to Claire's confidence – albeit vicariously through Lotte.

'You're so natural together,' Maddy says to Tor. 'Why on earth wouldn't you want your parents to see that? If you were my daughter, I'd be thrilled that you were with Lotte. You clearly belong together.'

Tor waves them off.

'Hey,' she says to Lotte, grabbing her. 'Did I tell you yet today that I love you?'

'Not enough,' Lotte says, smiling and then Tor hugs her as they go inside.

30

Beach Clean

'Oh,' Pim says, when he comes down the stairs on Saturday morning in his pyjamas and dressing gown, and sees Claire and Ash in the kitchen. He's carrying the cup of tea Claire put by the bed earlier. 'Where are you two off to? It's early.'

'The beach clean, remember?' Claire says.

'Oh, yeah.' He's clearly forgotten. He takes a sip of tea. 'You're going with Mum?' he asks Ash.

She asked Ash if he wanted to join her and the Sea-Gals today and when he said he was up for it, she felt like punching the air. He's done loads of research for his project and she's delighted that he's found something that he's interested in apart from that damned video game. Pim looks impressed as he nods.

She catches sight of herself in the hall mirror as they go out of the door. She feels different since Lotte did her hair. It took Pim a whole ten minutes and the boys an hour on Friday morning to clock it, but to Claire it feels wildly different. She feels younger. More alive. Revamped in a way she hasn't done for years. She keeps catching Pim looking at her, as if he can't quite put his finger on her transformation. Even Ash told her that she looked pretty. She's racked her brains, but as far as she can remember, her son has never, to her knowledge, used any kind of adjective to describe her. She's just been part of the furniture as far as he's concerned, so 'pretty' was fairly impactful. She'll take pretty.

She joins Dominica and Tor, Helga and Maddy on the beach and introduces Ash, and she's proud when he's polite. She can see him re-evaluating her, as he watches her with her friends, curious that Claire has a life beyond her domestic cage.

'You should come in for a swim with us one day,' Dominica tells him and the expression on his face makes them all laugh.

'So, you swim in there?' Ash asks, as if he's seeing the sea for the first time.

Claire follows his gaze to the water. She feels a physical yearning to fling herself in and she regrets not bringing her kit. She's tempted to go in anyway, but she suspects that Ash would die of embarrassment if she stripped off in front of him and swam in her pants. She never thought she'd become so addicted to the water but looking at the expanse of blue makes her feel as if she's discovered treasure.

Dominica is talking to the organiser of the beach clean, and she gives Ash a high-vis tabard and a picker-up stick and shows him how to work it and gives a plastic bag to Claire, as she struggles with her vest. Claire's first instinct on seeing that she would need to wear one was dread. There was no way one was going to fit, but the large size slides on easily over her T-shirt. Yesterday she got on the bathroom scales and noticed that she was half a stone lighter than she was at Christmas.

And it's not as if she's been particularly dieting, but she's not eating as much sugar.

It's to do with the swimming, she's convinced. The mid-morning and mid-afternoon slumps when she used to crave the kids' snacks don't happen when she's been in the water. But that's because she fills up on nourishing food when she's cold, not junk.

The crowd disperses into little groups and Claire sees them setting off along the beach in both directions.

'Which way do you want to go?' she asks Ash and he nods towards Hove and they set off together. Dominica and Maddy come with them.

Now they're searching for litter, Claire can see it everywhere. It's still weird seeing surgical masks, she thinks, as Ash picks one up and puts it in her bag, his nose wrinkling with disgust. A year ago, if she'd seen a mask on the beach, she'd have assumed that there might have been a terrible accident, involving an ambulance and that a medic had dropped one, but now she sees them everywhere. A horrible sign of the times. She hopes that, before too long, they'll be an anathema, something people remember and go, *oh yes. We wore masks*. Maybe that's why she's been so drawn to the sea. Because on the beach, by and large, she's been able to forget all about the pandemic.

Dominica chats easily to Ash and Maddy joins in too.

'Oh, I've remembered. I've got a joke. Do you like jokes, Ash? This was always a favourite one of my son's.'

He nods eagerly and Maddy's face cracks into a wide smile. 'OK, then. What's a pirate's favourite letter?'

Claire stops with Ash too, trying to think of the answer. Ash loves this kind of thing.

'I don't know,' he says, giving up.

'You'd think it'd be arr, but it be the sea,' Maddy says and Claire and Ash laugh.

'I've got to get Felix with that one,' he tells Claire, and she nods. She's glad he's having fun.

'Oh. Wait up, you missed something,' Dominica tells Ash, as they pick through the debris in the line of tangled seaweed. She points.

'That's just rope, isn't it?'

'No, that, I'm afraid, *that* is a tampon,' Dominica explains.

Ash's cheeks pulse red at the word. 'Err . . . That's gross.'

Claire picks up the tangle of seaweed and the bundle of white cotton.

'Mum!'

'It's clean. It's been in the sea. But look how much it's unravelled.'

'Ugh, stop it,' Ash begs. 'Put it down.' He hurries away to a plastic lid a few metres away.

'Sorry,' Dominica says to Claire. 'I didn't mean to embarrass him.'

'Don't worry.'

'He's a sweet kid,' she tells her and Claire smiles.

'Yes, he really is,' Maddy agrees.

Claire catches up with Ash and leaves Dominica and Maddy to chat.

'Hey, wait up,' she says. 'Dominica said sorry. She didn't mean to embarrass you about the tampon.'

He flinches at the word and Claire realises how little they've talked about anything female. She's been annoyed that her sons have belittled her, but what has she really taught them about being a woman? She's assumed that he's picked up all this stuff at school, but what if he hasn't? Pim said he would do the talking about the birds and the bees to the boys, but now she wonders how good a job he's done.

'I was shocked, not embarrassed. I hadn't thought stuff like that ends up in the sea. It's revolting.'

'It is, but that's why it's important to take part in beach cleans so that you're aware of what's going on. Because then you can change it.'

They walk along for a little bit and Claire points out the black-headed gulls flitting across the stones. 'How do you know what they're called?'

'My friend Helga has taught me,' Claire says. 'But whilst we're on the subject of tampons—'

'We're not.'

'But whilst we are' – Claire is amused by his resilience – 'let's chat about periods. I want to know what you know.'

'*Mum.*'

'This is important. Come on. Give me some facts. What do you know about periods?'

'You're so embarrassing.'

Claire stands her ground. She can't let this slip.

'It's just bodies, Ash. Fifty per cent of the population. It's not embarrassing. It's life. And it's important, as your mother, that I know you have the facts straight. So . . . come on?'

This is new turf. She's never pushed him like this before, but she feels powerful and determined. Being by the sea is giving her strength.

'Dunno.'

'Seriously?'

Claire sighs, realising that he doesn't even know the basics. Walking side by side with him, the sound of their footsteps on the pebbles, the waves breaking on the shore and the cries of the gulls, she decides that now is probably as good a time as any. She's read that it's good to chat to your kids when engaged in an activity outside and she glances across at her precious boy and the way his dark hair flops into his eyes.

Five minutes later, Ash stops walking and stands with the grabber, his eyebrows creased together in concern.

'So, you're saying girls do that every month? Girls in school? They're dealing with that all the time?' he asks.

She's touched by his concern. 'Yes. Some are at your age, but more when they get to senior school.'

'But how do you know which ones are doing it? You know, bleeding?'

'You don't. Girls are secretive. They don't want boys to know, but that doesn't mean you shouldn't know.'

He nods, then something dawns on him. 'Does that happen to you? Every month?'

'It used to, but when you get to my age, periods stop and then you get the menopause.'

'The *what*?'

Claire shakes her head and smiles at herself. It feels brave to be having this conversation. Her mother didn't ever tell her about the menopause. She'd never mentioned it once. She knows Pim will almost certainly say that Ash is too young to be receiving this information, but it's just biology. She wants him to know. Besides, if he's old enough to play Fortnite, which is technically a twelve plus, he's old enough to hear this.

'The menopause. Or the change.'

'Oh.' Ash is genuinely bemused. 'What changes?'

'Your metabolism. Your hormones. It's called the change because a woman stops being fertile and able to have babies.'

He looks at her as if this thought – that she might have still been able to reproduce – is horrific, but she ploughs on. 'So, you know I get forgetful sometimes? Or you tease me because I misspeak or get my words jumbled up?'

'Or you say Dad's name, then Felix's before you get to mine.'

'Exactly.'

'That's all part of the menopause. And I get really hot flushes.'

'You're going through all of this and you didn't tell us?'

She's touched by how genuinely worried he sounds.

'I'm telling you now,' she says.

Dominica comes back over. 'How are you getting on?'

'Fine,' Claire says, putting her arm around Ash's shoulder. 'We've been chatting.'

'Well, keep up the good work. Coffees and cakes are at ten by the peace statue.'

31

Bunny Ears

Tor has spent weeks worrying about the subject of Easter and how to bring it up with Lotte, but now she regrets not being honest from the outset. When she told Lotte she was going alone to Alice's for Easter Day lunch, she made out that Alice was paranoid about numbers and that it's just a family thing. But that only made it worse. It made it sound as if Lotte had been invited and Alice had then backtracked, when in fact, Alice has no idea about Lotte.

Of course, as usual Lotte sussed the truth and was upset with Tor for lying. Tor tried to explain that she can't introduce Lotte to her family without warning her family first, but Lotte hadn't understood, slamming the door to their bedroom. When Tor went upstairs, Lotte was red-cheeked from crying.

'Why are you acting like I'm your nasty little secret?' she said. 'Is that all I am?'

'No, Lotte, no. I will change it. I'll make it OK.'

Lotte looked at her with watery, resentful eyes and, now, Tor tries to think of that look and of Maddy and what she said about Tor and Lotte being good together as she sits in the 'event shelter' that Alice has rigged up in her large garden for the family lunch, aware that the time has been ticking and she's yet to start the conversation she knows she must have.

The tent is festooned with bunting and strings of lights and pom-pom things Alice claims she's made out of tissue paper, but they look suspiciously shop-bought to Tor. She's served up a lamb roast with all the fancy frills, but Tor's only eaten the vegetables. It wouldn't have killed her to provide a vegan option. Being vegan is hardly a 'thing' these days, but she's still been made to feel as if she's been deliberately awkward. Alice has insisted that they all wear Easter bunny ears on headbands. *For fun*.

There's one of those gas-guzzling heaters that wreck the ozone and Tor's dad huddles next to it in his bunny ears. She's reminded of Vic warming himself next to the brazier.

Thomas and Alfie, Alice's kids, high on the biggest haul of chocolate eggs Tor has ever seen, tear around screaming. Alice doesn't seem to notice. She's drinking 'lady petrol', as she calls it, from a giant glass, which she's just sloshily topped up from one of the several bottles of open Chardonnay in the ice bucket on the table. Tor shifts uncomfortably in the garden chair. It's all very well to be able to meet in person, but it was so much better on Zoom. Here, with the marquee's plastic walls flapping in the breeze, she feels trapped.

She's been trying to get on to the subject of Lotte with her mother all day, but it's been impossible to get her alone. But now, as Alice takes their dirty plates, insisting that she doesn't need help, she seizes this moment.

She smiles at her mum. She's coming up for sixty-five, and

looks-wise she could pass for a decade younger, although compared to Helga she could be decades older. She's slim and has white hair and is wearing the same smudge of blue eyeshadow on her brown eyes that she's been probably wearing since her twenties. Her reading glasses hang on a gold chain around her neck above her white polo neck. She's put on one of Alice's skiing jackets for extra warmth, which make her look bulky, when she's slim, like Tor. She laughs indulgently as Thomas knocks into her. Tor wishes that her mother would tell the truth: that she finds the fact that Alice and Graham let their boys run riot as annoying as she does, but her mother would never commit such a gross act of betrayal. She adores being a grandparent and sometimes Tor feels her over-indulgence of the boys as a personal snub. As if she deliberately has to spoil them, because they might be the only grandchildren she ever gets at this rate.

Perhaps seeing Tor's raised eyebrow as an invite for such delicious insubordination, her mum resorts to an age-old tactic.

'So you're still purple,' she says, nodding at Tor's hair.

This is a typical Rita Hathaway move, Tor thinks, remembering all at once that whenever they're alone, her mother always puts a little barb out there first. Often to do with Tor's fashion or life choices. Criticisms that she reserves for when they're alone, granted, but criticisms nevertheless.

Perhaps it was because she wanted to dress up her little girl twins like matching dollies – and whilst Alice was always so happy to comply, Tor deliberately sabotaged any efforts for them to look the same.

'Lotte did it,' Tor says. 'My housemate.'

Her heartbeat quickens. This is it. She's going to say something.

'She's a hairdresser,' she adds.

Her mum frowns and makes a noise, as if to say Lotte can't be a very good hairdresser and Tor kicks herself mentally for getting off on the wrong tack.

'It's such fun, you know, living in the house with her . . . '

Tor stops as her brother-in-law appears, waggling a bottle for a refill. Graham's wearing red chinos and tan suede shoes with tassels on them and no socks, along with a green jumper with a little logo of a polo player. Her mum puts her hand over her glass. Her cheeks are already flushed, but Graham nudges her hand aside and she simpers at his cheekiness.

'Come on, Rita. We're celebrating. Isn't it wonderful to be together at last?'

He picks up on Tor's look. 'Sorry. Did I interrupt something.'

'Tor was just talking about her housemates.'

'Housemates?' Graham says, pulling a face. 'Still living like a student, then? At nearly forty. My advice would be to get out of that terrible dive.'

'It's not terrible,' Tor says, offended. 'And it's not a dive. Those Edwardian houses have loads of space and potential.' She feels empowered quoting Maddy.

'But a shared house really isn't a home. Not a proper home.' Graham looks to Rita for confirmation. Why won't her mother defend her?

'That's easier said than done. Rents are extortionately high where I live.'

'Then live somewhere cheaper.'

'I don't want to. I want to be close to work. And to the sea.'

'Oh, the sea, yes,' her mum says in a panic, her look darting between Graham and Tor. She can't bear conflict and Tor longs to ask her how she can stand the sight of Graham, when he makes her skin crawl so much. 'How's the swimming going, darling?'

Her mum gives her a desperate smile. Behind her Graham gives Tor a look, as Alice comes over.

'Good, thank you. I go most days.'

'You lunatic,' Alice says, draping herself over Graham's shoulder. Tor feels them looming over her.

'I bet you're into all that tides and moon cycles stuff?' Graham says, as if Tor is crazy.

'I read an article in *Good Housekeeping*. People say that swimming is very addictive,' her mum says and, caught between Tor and Alice and Graham, adds, 'I tell people that you go every day.' Tor knows she means well, but the way she says it only makes it sound like she, too, tells her friends that Tor is crazy. Or, if not crazy, then unfathomably quirky.

'Well, I try.'

'Bloody masochism, if you ask me,' Graham says.

Tor has had enough.

'Actually, Graham, I try and go swimming every day, because I've got rheumatoid arthritis and the cold water helps with the pain,' she says, standing up stiffly. She hasn't meant to blurt it like she has, but only the truth will shut him up. There's a moment of stunned silence. 'You know, this has been . . . great,' she manages generously, 'but I really should be going. I've just realised the time and I don't like driving in the dark.'

'What? You're going? After . . . after announcing that!' Alice exclaims, as Tor slips around her. Alice clutches her arm. 'Tor?'

Tor sighs. 'It's not a biggie. Seriously. It's just a condition. I'm managing it.'

'Like old ladies?' Alice asks.

'Roger, Roger,' her mother calls. 'Come quickly.'

Tor's dad gets up from where, for no apparent reason, he's been sorting out a deck of cards on the garden table.

'What did I miss?' he asks, and her mum reaches up to grab hold of his hand, clearly not able to receive this information alone.

'Victoria is poorly,' she says. 'Oh, love.'

'What is it?' her dad asks, confused.

'Arthritis.'

'Oh. Rum luck,' he says. 'Sue had that.'

'Aunty Sue?' Alice pipes up.

'She was the one in the wheelchair?' Graham checks.

Tor watches them all staring at her, her cheeks burning. She longs for Lotte. Lotte would know what to say.

'Oh, so there was a reason. I knew it,' Graham says, as if he's sussed out why she's been self-flagellating.

Tor can't bear it that he's so disparaging about something she loves so much. Something he clearly doesn't – and won't ever – understand. He nods at Alice as if he's been particularly clever. She shakes her head and makes for the door of the 'event shelter'.

'Do you know? I'm just going to go.'

Alice catches up with her when she's halfway across the garden. It's drizzling and cold. 'Why didn't you tell me?' she demands. 'I'm your sister. I'm your *twin*.'

'Because you're married to that insensitive arsehole.'

'He's not . . . he's . . . ' Alice tries to defend him, but Tor doesn't want to stay and listen to her sister's justification. 'You should have told me.'

'Why? What's the point? It's not exactly as if you can do anything about it.' Tor isn't used to taking this tone with Alice, who backs away.

'But . . . I would help. I can't believe that you've kept it all to yourself.'

'Well, now you know.'

There's a beat and Tor sighs. Alice's chin is wobbling indignantly.

'You could have rung, or texted, or something. You didn't have to drop it like bomb into Easter. When I wanted it to be so perfect. I tried to make it so lovely for everyone and you . . . you . . . ' She's started to cry and Tor looks up to the sky.

'Alice . . . ' She sighs. 'I'm sorry.'

'Too late,' Alice says, weeping openly now as she struts back to the event shelter, her bottom wiggling in her skirt as she negotiates the damp grass with her heels.

She probably expects Tor to follow her and to apologise publicly and make the peace, but she wants to go home. She carries on to the side of the house, where the car she's borrowed from Declan is parked on the road, already pointing out of town for a quick getaway. She manages to get in and is about to start it when she sees her mother hurrying down the drive, waving.

'Tor,' she says, knocking on the glass, and reluctantly Tor winds down the window. 'Come back inside. Let's talk about this.'

Tor stops clenching the steering wheel and turns around to face her mother. She's still wearing her bunny ears.

'Darling,' she says. 'Darling. Don't stalk off like that.'

Stalking off. That was always something her mother had accused her of. Even as a child.

'I'm not stalking off, Mum. I'm leaving. Because it's impossible to have a conversation in this family.'

'You always expect people to have perfectly rational reactions when you give them news.'

So now her expectations are too high? She tries not to react to prove her mother's point.

'But I'd like to help. I'd like to talk,' she says. 'Are you getting treatment? For you know . . . for the condition? Is there anything I can do?'

Tor softens. She does sound like she's genuinely concerned. 'The sea swimming helps. It's not all about moon cycles.'

'Oh, ignore Graham. He's only trying to be funny.'

'He's not funny, Mum. Do you have any idea how offensive I find him?'

'Oh, come on. Try and get on,' her mother says. 'For Alice's sake.'

And . . . *there it is*, Tor thinks. The first honest conversation she's had about herself with her mother for decades and it's swung right back around to being about Alice.

32

Bombshell

Maddy drives along her lane on Easter Monday, wondering exactly what Trent's going to propose at this 'summit'. Because that was the subject header of his email. He's told her that they have to talk about something urgently.

Hopefully he'll have some good news about their financial affairs – at long bloody last. He's been avoiding her probing questions and she resents the fact that she's not only used the last of her savings, Jamie's education fund, but also has had to borrow a couple of grand from her brother to pay for basic living expenses. It was so humiliating having to ask.

She's assured Toby that she was only suffering a temporary cash-flow problem until Trent's business gets back on track. She didn't tell her brother that she's left Trent. It would take too much explaining. Because if she tells her brother that they've separated, then her parents will find out too and there'll be uncomfortable conversations. She's not strong enough to cope with their upset or concern.

Seeing the sleek glass and steel lines of her house, she thinks of everything she's built and how much it once impressed her family. She remembers posting a series of Instagram videos of the crane lifting the colossal joist into place and how it had felt so scary. She remembers how her sister-in-law had commented that Maddy really knew how to style-out a hard hat. She'd felt daring . . . important.

How full of dreams she'd been back then, she thinks. How excited about the home she was creating.

And this *is* her home, she remembers. Her self-inflicted exile has only made her see what a huge achievement and asset it is. Maybe now she's clearer about her feelings for Trent, they can come to some kind of arrangement about the future of the house. As Helga told her yesterday when then all met for a late-afternoon swim, Trent was the one who did the dirty and so it stands to reason that he should be the one to move out. Maddy appreciated the wise counsel of her swimming friends. Once she's found Jamie and brought him home, she's going to miss them.

She thinks about going to the front door, but having not seen Trent for months, it feels too invasive to open it with her keys, so she goes instead to the side gate, like she always does when she comes back with the shopping. As she pushes through it, she notices that the small box hedges have yellow patches, and the grass is weedy and overgrown. Trent clearly hasn't been doing much upkeep.

She sees him through the glass of the back door. He's sitting at the kitchen counter, the reading glasses that he hates being seen in perched on the end of his nose. He stares down at a sheaf of papers. From outside, she notices that his face is more drawn and lined than she's realised before. She slides open the door, surprising him. He snatches off his glasses and stands up.

'You came,' he says, as if he hadn't believed she would.

The kitchen is unkempt, although it's passably clean. He's swept the white floor tiles, although leaving the mound of dust in the corner. One of his more annoying habits.

'You said you wanted to talk, so I'm here,' she says, walking towards him and standing against the end counter, placing her handbag on it.

Do they kiss on both cheeks politely like strangers? she wonders, but Trent doesn't move and the awkward moment passes.

'You look well,' he says, as if this is a surprise. 'Glowing.'

'The sea air, I guess. And I've been swimming.'

'In the sea?'

'Yes.'

'Alone?' He sounds horrified.

'No, I go with friends.'

'What friends?'

The Sea-Gals have become friends, she realises, at the same time as she realises that she could never introduce them to Trent. He's always striven to have friends who are the most similar he can find. Or, even better, ones he feels are similar and yet slightly aspirational. Maddy has found it a breath of fresh air to meet people with utterly different lives and backgrounds to her.

She tells him a few facts about her life in Brighton and he listens, as if he can't quite believe she's not been at home. He doesn't ask about Jamie. His lack of curiosity speaks volumes of how much he doesn't care.

Trent faffs around putting a Nespresso Pod in their expensive machine, although he hasn't asked if she wants a coffee. He curses when the pod jams and she points out that he needs to empty the cartridge holder. Another thing she's always done. She wonders how he's coped without her and feels a frisson of satisfaction that he must realise now how much hard work it's taken to live somewhere that looks this good.

When he's made her the coffee, he retreats around the counter and hitches his buttock onto the white stool. He's put on weight, she notices, seeing a bulge beneath his white shirt at the waistband of his jeans. In fact, those are his baggier jeans. He's usually so put together and slick, but he reminds her of a teddy bear that's losing its stuffing.

'What have you got there?' she asks, out of curiosity. He usually works in the study. It's unlike him to bring papers through to the kitchen.

'Oh, these, well, um, you know . . . stuff to do with Fairfax.'

His eyes dart towards hers then off to the side. His shifty look.

What's he been up to? Trent has always insisted that once the Fairfax building contract came good, he'd re-fill the accounts and buy back the shares.

'The contract's through, right?'

He rubs a spot on the counter top and winces. 'No, it's all gone rather tits up.'

'What do you mean, tits up?'

'Just . . . ' He shrugs and she suddenly understands the magnitude of what he's saying.

'How long have you known? That it wasn't coming good?' she asks.

'A while.'

'And you haven't said anything?'

'I would have if you hadn't have stormed out.'

He says 'stormed out' as if she's flounced out on an unjustifiable whim and she remembers Tor talking bitterly yesterday about how her mother accused her of 'stalking' out of her twin sister's lunch. Perhaps that's why she likes Tor. Because she sticks up for what she believes in too and doesn't put up with other people's bullshit.

She glares at him. She's not going to let him blame her. 'What's happened?'

He sighs and she sees he's defeated. 'I, well, the thing is, Maddy . . . '

She feels her throat go dry at his tone and the way he says her name. He twists his lips and then his voice catches as he starts to speak. She puts her coffee cup on the side.

'I've tried, you've got to believe me, I've *really* tried, but . . . well, there's no easy way to tell you.'

'Tell me *what*?'

He shrinks, closing his eyes, as if he's expecting a bomb to go off. 'The house is going to have to go. I've got to repay the loan. It's the only way.'

There's a moment of silence, but it resonates like the aftermath of a bell being struck.

'Go?' Maddy asks, not quite understanding.

'I put some . . . there was some legal clauses in the loan I took out and I used the house as collateral—'

'You said that it was nothing. Just a formality. That there was no risk,' she reminds him, her mind laser sharp now as she remembers him cajoling her into signing some papers two years ago, over a candlelit dinner. 'You said . . . ?' She walks away, her palm on her forehead. She feels dizzy at the bombshell he's just dropped. 'Jesus!'

'Maybe sit down—'

'I don't want to sit down,' she screams at him. 'You've fucking *lost our house*?' She wants to throw something at him. She wants to hurt him. 'After everything . . . ' The tears of outrage spring now and choke her.

'Maddy,' he says. 'Maddy, please—'

'I won't let you,' she snaps, cutting him off. She doesn't want his pity. 'I'll find a lawyer and . . . '

Trent shakes his head and picks up the papers in front of him. 'It won't work. You signed these. We both did. I didn't think—'

'No, you didn't think.' She cries out now, an agonising, seething wail that seems to come from the pit of her stomach.

'Being hysterical won't help,' Trent says. His shoulders slump and he mutters, 'I knew you'd be like this.'

Even though she hates him in this moment, he's right – being hysterical won't help – but, even so, she feels better for screaming. She watches him, his head bowed like a little boy.

She forces herself to change tack. 'OK, then explain.'

'Explain?'

'Yes, all of it. Explain it to me. Explain why we're in this mess.' She sits down opposite him at the counter. 'Don't leave anything out,' she warns him. 'Anything at all. I want the truth for once, Trent. All of it.'

She listens, shaking in stunned silence as he begins to tell her the debacle of the business deal that went wrong and, as much as she tries not to, Maddy can't help being staggered at the series of thoughtless blunders that have led to this moment. She wants to know why Trent hasn't told her, but, as he describes trying to shore things up in the background and to stop her finding out the truth, she suddenly understands what a toll having her Instagram ambitions tied up with the house must have taken on Trent. No wonder he couldn't say anything, when she was spending all day bragging online about her perfect home. As his voice wobbles, she realises what a terribly big secret he's been carrying around with him. As angry as she is, can she really blame him for it causing such a rift? They used to talk about everything, but, looking back, she realises that those conversations stopped long ago. Why hadn't she noticed that he wasn't sharing anything with her? Why hadn't she questioned him more?

Because she'd been looking at her phone. That's why. Because she hadn't wanted to know that everything might not be perfect. She'd let herself believe that everything would be all right. That she was safe in the fortress of her home.

But that's clearly all bullshit and now her mind is scrambling ahead, trying to find a solution, a way out, but when she studies her signature on the legal papers and the various letters from the lawyers, she can see that Trent is right. They have to repay their colossal loan. The only way to do it is to sell. And, as much as she knows she's a little bit culpable in the whole disaster, it still feels like she's been stabbed in the guts.

'Jesus, Trent. I can't . . . I just can't believe it.'

'Yeah, well, it's not my fault. There's been a pandemic and—'

She stares at him, aghast. How can he blame outside forces when this is absolutely his fault?

'Are you not even *sorry*?'

'God!' Trent explodes. 'How many times do I have to say it?'

'Once,' she shouts back. 'Once would be nice.'

'I've been doing nothing else but saying sorry to you for

the past twenty years,' he rails. 'I've never been good enough for you. Never enough.'

This feels horribly close to the bone. They haven't ever really had the vocabulary to talk about their relationship. At the beginning, when they were young, they used to talk about 'them' as an interesting subject, checking in with each other's feelings, making sure they were on the same page. But then they got married and they stopped having any kind of conversation about their relationship. She just assumed everything was OK. But she'd been kidding herself. Everything was not OK. Especially if he's been feeling like this.

'That's not true,' she says, because it isn't. Of course it isn't.

'Yes, it bloody is.' His voice really cracks now and she can see tears in his blazing eyes. She's only seen Trent cry once, at his mum's funeral, and she's startled by this show of emotion.

He growls with frustration, embarrassed. He wipes his face and composes himself, the barrier suddenly drawn up, this brief glimpse into his inner psyche back behind steel doors. He steps away from her, his face making it completely apparent that the subject is closed. The tense silence between them stretches and she imagines all the conversations stalled and trapped in it.

'I've got a valuation happening on Wednesday. Then it'll go on the market by the end of the week.'

Her house is being sold by the end of the week?

'The estate agent says he'll get a good price. He's juicing up some cash buyers from London. A place like this will shift straight away. The market's boiling hot. If it was ever a good time to sell, it's now.'

It's typical of him to try and put a positive spin on this.

'You can't ice a turd, Trent,' she snaps, firing a phrase that Jamie used to say back at him.

They both realise the significance straight away. Of the ghost of their son being in this moment.

'And then what?' Maddy asks, her voice husky. Her chest feels tight with an emotion she can't name. It's too raw. Too new. 'We'll be homeless. Homeless.'

'This isn't exactly a home, though, is it?' he says, his eyes boring into hers. 'It's just your backdrop.'

He says it in such a sneery, nasty way, she thinks he must have felt like this all along. He's made noises about supporting her, but he's been resenting her this whole time. This beautiful home. That he's had the benefit of living in.

'That's mean.'

'But true. You just posted away to impress your friends.'

'The friends you shagged,' she snaps back.

'Oh, here we go,' he says, throwing up his arm. 'I wondered how long it would take you to bring that up.'

'*That*? Your affair with Helen, you mean? Your ongoing affair? I saw her, you know.'

'She said.'

'So it's still a thing? You two? You're together?'

He shrugs. 'At least Helen likes me,' he says.

Maddy stares at him, her eyes filling with tears. Because with this irrefutable truth, he's won the argument.

33

The Nightingale

Helga pauses in the bathroom, her heart leaping as she hears it.

It's back. The nightingale has returned.

He usually comes in April and stays until June, if she's lucky. She pulls the light string to switch off the overhead light, then pushes the window sash up, but it'll only budge a little way. She kneels down, so that she can lean on her forearms.

There's a tiny yard at the back of her cottage, the back wall of which is covered in an overgrown tangle of plants, half a metre thick. Despite being an 'eyesore', according to the neighbours, Helga preserves the brown branches and thorns, so that the little reclusive bird can nest down in its impenetrable depths.

This sound was the only thing she ever really missed when she'd been at sea, and the only thing worth being on land for. She can hear the nightingale, but she can't yet see the little bird, although, to be honest, a nightingale is not much to look at. No bigger than a robin and without a red breast, it's just a plain little brown bird, but its song announces its presence to the world in the most astonishing acrobatics. The nightingale is living proof that you should never judge anything by appearances only.

She closes her eyes, listening to the rippling, trilling whistles, astonished by the range of his tone. There's a good reason why the little bird has been celebrated in song and literature for centuries.

The cool dawn air is chilly and she opens her eyes as other birds join in the dawn chorus in the pink sky. She can identify a chaffinch, a blackbird and maybe a lark, she thinks, but her knees are hurting from kneeling on the tiles. Behind the hedge, she can see a tiny line of blue sea between the buildings and she wonders how long it'll be before she can put out a message for the others to join her for a swim. This damn insomnia is driving her to distraction. She doesn't know why she can't sleep, only that her heart beats fitfully, like she's been running, even when she's resting, her mind worrying over the knots of the past and the tangle of the future. Hopefully, once she's swum, she'll be able to have a snooze.

She gets up too fast, the action making her feel dizzy, and she curses, holding on to the window frame. The same thing happened at Will's house when she got up too fast. What would happen if she fell backwards and smashed her head on the bath? Who would find her?

Downstairs, there's a big brown envelope on her mat along with a smaller airmail packet. She opens the envelope and inside is a child's drawing of a boat. The latest one from Josh. Helga smiles and puts the drawing on her fridge with one of the magnets along with a few of the others he's done for her. The one good deed she did keeps on giving, she thinks, touched that the little boy wants to impress her. Or maybe the pictures are payment for her not complaining about the screaming newborn. Who knows? She stands back to admire the yacht he's drawn, hoping she's inspired the little boy to take to the sea one day.

She opens the airmail bag, already knowing that it'll be from Mette. Inside is a little cardboard box with embossed letters on it. Inside is a gold necklace with a heavy grey pearl on it. Helga lifts it out.

I know you don't usually like jewellery, but I saw this and thought of you.

Mette always remembers her birthday, Helga thinks, even though Helga herself never celebrates it. She never tells anyone, and she weighs the heavy pearl, sensing her obligation to her niece.

She puts it back in the box. It'll go in the drawer with all the other gifts Mette has sent over the years. She thinks of her niece in an expensive jewellery shop, or in one of those posh places in the airport duty-free, pointing to the necklace and opening her leather wallet full of credit cards.

Mette had never been decisive as a small child. Helga couldn't stand her saying that she 'didn't mind' to every question she asked her about what she wanted to do, or what she wanted to eat.

'You should mind,' Helga had told her. 'You should mind very much about your choices. You mustn't leave it up to anyone else. Decide what you want. For you.'

How easy it had been to give such worthy life advice back then. She thought life would get easier as she got older. She assumed her choices and what she wants would always be in sync. But they're not.

The promise of the earlier dawn materialises into a sparkling day. When Helga gets to the beach, the sea is blue and clear and cold, the sea peaking in a million dazzling crests. The sky is striped in a lazy wash of greeny-blue.

Helga yawns as she stretches towards the horizon where there's a soft, pink haze. A flock of black and white terns swoop and duck. The breeze is the warmest it has been for months and Helga turns her face into the sun and closes her eyes.

'Oh, she's not coming,' Claire says from beside her, looking at her phone. They've been waiting for Tor, but now it's time to get moving. Helga yawns again.

'OK, let's go,' she says.

'Stay there,' Claire tells Luna. The little dog is sitting on Dominica's coat.

'You seem tired?' Claire says.

'I was up at dawn. The nightingale is back in my yard,' Helga explains.

'A nightingale? Aren't they rare?'

Helga nods and tells Claire to look up the BBC recording of a cellist playing the 'Londonderry Air' with the nightingale singing along.

Dominica and Maddy have gone ahead and are already fully submerged. Dominica waves as Claire and Helga arrive at the water's edge.

'Get in. It's wonderful,' she calls.

The water is cold, but not as cold as it has been and it's calm and clear as they swim out.

'Helga's got a nightingale in her garden,' Claire tells the others, who are all impressed too.

'I like the sound of your place,' Maddy says.

246

'You'd love it,' Claire chips in. 'It's so quirky and character-ful.'

'Yes, well, it could be way nicer, but I don't have the inclination or the money.'

'Join the club.' Maddy's voice catches.

'Are you all right, Maddy?' Dominica asks. Maddy usually looks so vital and clear, but today she has the weight of the world on her shoulders. 'You seem a bit low.'

'I don't want to bore you,' she says.

'We're not bored,' Helga says. 'This is as good a place as any to chat it out.'

'Aren't we supposed to be swimming?'

'We can, but we can take a breather for a little while.'

Helga lies back in the water, seeing the town laid out on the shore in the sunshine. She likes chatting to her friends. She likes it that they confide in each other, but she's shocked as she listens to Maddy recounting the latest drama with Trent.

Maddy starts to cry as she describes losing her home and the terrible fight with Trent about it. Helga rarely cries herself and she can see that it's the same for Maddy. She tells them about the unbearable tension of the last few days as she's tried to make her house ready for the valuation. She says she had to leave yesterday, as she was scared that she might be physically violent to the estate agent.

'I'm sorry,' Maddy says. 'I'm just so bloody angry.'

'It's OK,' Dominica reassures her.

'If it's any consolation, the same thing happened to me,' Helga tells Maddy.

'Really?'

Helga sighs. She's never admitted this shocking fact about

herself to the Sea-Gals, but now is as good a time as any and she realises that her shame is dwarfed by her urge to make Maddy feel better. She wants to prove that anyone can be duped like she has been. Even so, it feels bigger than she realised to open up like this.

She tells them about her last long-term relationship, the one that put her off relationships forever. Generally, she likes to paint herself as having been single for her entire life, but that isn't true. There was Linus, of course, but, long after him, she met Paul on an airplane between London and New York. He was an American gallery owner, suave, sophisticated and rich. They bonded over art.

He was perfect, except for the fact he was married, although he claimed he was estranged from his wife. That, like so many other facts she later found out about him, was untrue.

She'd thought he'd been joking when he'd offered to show her the sights of New York. Excited by his flattery and attention, she'd found herself naked on a hotel room bed with him two hours after landing.

She'd convinced herself that it was fate and that they had a special connection, but with hindsight, she can see that she was just living out a silly fantasy of having an international lover.

The scamming had started innocuously at first. They'd met in Paris and he'd been stressed. The bridging loan he'd needed for an art purchase had fallen through. Helga offered to help him out. He pretended to be surprised that she had money. She lived frugally enough, but told him how she'd invested her sailing prize winnings well, then she'd been left shares in her father's business and that, along with the couple of art pieces she'd sold, had resulted in a considerable nest egg. Money didn't bother her. It wasn't something she either noticed or cared about. She didn't mind paying for the hotel, or his flights, if it meant they could meet.

'And so it went on, until he'd drained me dry. It took about six months. When I tried to challenge him about paying me back, he was charm itself, promising me that he would, begging me to understand,' she told them, remembering all those phone calls that had made her feel as if she was going crazy. She'd tried to go after him with lawyers, but he'd covered his tracks. It turned out that he wasn't even an art dealer. And Paul hadn't been his real name. She'd been taken for a ride.

'Oh, God, Helga, that's awful,' Dominica says.

'You were catfished,' Claire says.

'I'm sorry, Helga,' Maddy says. 'Truly.'

Helga nods, grateful for their sympathy. Grateful that they haven't judged her like she constantly judges herself.

'It wasn't the money. It was the shame of it that got me. I'm amazed I've even told you,' she says. 'It's taken me a long time to get over it, but I've realised that, at one point or another, people make bad decisions. It's life. You might not feel like it right now, but you'll find a way through all of this, Maddy, and come out on top. You're a smart woman,' Helga says, reassuringly.

'I don't feel very smart. I feel wrung out.'

'Then let the sea give you her energy,' Helga says. 'Come on. Head under. Leave it all here.'

Helga is surprised to see Claire swimming in an efficient, languid front crawl.

'Look at you,' Helga says. 'Mrs Speedy.'

'I had my first swimming lesson.' Claire seems proud that they've all noticed.

'With delicious Andy,' Dominica says.

'Oh God! Isn't he?'

Helga smiles as they giggle like schoolgirls about the handsome swimming instructor, who appears to be working wonders with Claire. And she remembers Linus diving into the sea and coming up grinning, flicking his hair and declaring that he'd race her around the yacht and how she'd swum for her life and still hadn't beaten him. How invincible they'd been. How beautiful and young; and her heart aches for that golden moment.

Back on the beach, Claire has brought some flapjacks, which she's made with seeds soaked in orange oil. They sit in the sunshine, talking and sipping their flasks of tea.

The conversation turns back to Maddy and how she's going to have to go back home and sort out the house if they get a buyer. She's panicking about where to put all of her stuff and how much hard work it's going to be.

'Sorry,' Maddy apologises yet again. 'Dumping all this on you.'

'It's OK,' Dominica says, stroking the little dog in her lap, 'we've got time to talk. And besides, I don't want you to go when Luna is keeping me warm.'

Maddy sighs and ruffles Luna's soft ginger ears. 'The worst thing is that I can't help thinking that I deserve this. All of this. Trent, Jamie, the house . . . all of it.'

'Why do you think that?' Claire asks.

'Because . . . because I'm a fraud.'

Helga is surprised at the self-loathing in her voice. 'A fraud?'

'It's true. I'm making all this content and you know what? It's all bullshit.' Maddy pushes the cuff of her coat to her eyes. 'You know, actually, it feels very good to say that. To let that out.'

'If you feel like that, then why not be honest? Why not report on what's real? What you're going through? How it feels?' Helga says.

'Because . . . ' Maddy sighs. 'People expect me to be perfect and I'm not brave enough to admit the truth.'

'Oh, I think you're brave, Maddy,' Dominica says.

'It's so easy to see with hindsight where everything went wrong. I wish I could go back. Unmake the mistakes.'

Helga shakes her head. 'No. Keep flying forward,' she says, meaning it. 'We're Sea-Gals, after all.'

34

Destruction

Claire comes up for air in the pool and waves at Andy where he's standing in the shallow end, his muscled torso rising up from the water. Dominica is right. All he needs is a trident and he'd be a good model for a water deity. She knows that it's completely wrong to sexually objectify him, but it's hard not to.

He smiles beneath his swimming hat and applauds. Buoyed up by his praise, she clings on to the side and prepares herself to set off again. He's certainly given her power today. That's her first ever full length of front crawl in the twenty-five-metre pool, breathing every three strokes and remembering to twist her body in the water and glide, stretching her arm out. It feels great and she pushes off now, determined that this length will be even better. She wants to impress him, just like she impressed Helga and the Sea-Gals yesterday.

She thinks back to her half-arsed, ill-fated attempts at getting fit in the past. There was that costly gym membership that just became embarrassing, a spate where she was determined to run, until she got painful shin splints, and the spin classes in which she was the fattest and nearly had a cardiac arrest.

But this is different. And necessary. She's signed up with the others to swim around the pier in July. Dominica presented it to the group. It's the annual gathering of all the sea swimmers along this bit of coast in aid of a mental health charity. Having helped out Tor with Home Help and raised money for her charity with the dawn swim, Claire was a little bit surprised that she might be involved in another fundraiser. But then again, she likes it that the women she swims with have a social conscience. They are, as Dominica says, the kind of people charities rely on. As Claire doesn't have a paid job, being a force for good and helping people makes her feel like she's contributing to society in a good way.

But still. Round the pier? It feels like a long way. Helga says they've done it a few times and it's easy and that Claire can do it, but she wants to be sure she can. Pim told her she was mad and the boys clearly think she's too old to attempt anything like that, so she's going to prove them all wrong. And, since she met Andy at the pool at 6.30 a.m. and it was still dark, her family aren't even aware that she's out of the house. So what's it to them?

'Well done,' Andy says, as she joins him at the other end. 'You've got it.'

They get out of the pool and he puts his hand on her shoulder as they walk to the changing rooms, but not in a creepy way. 'Shame the sauna isn't open. It's always good after a swim.'

She walks through the female door and catches sight of herself in the full wall mirror. Her cheeks are glowing and, for once, her mind doesn't fall into negative hate thoughts about her tummy or arms, because her mind is occupied by what Andy has just said. Was he flirting with her? Was he saying that he wanted to have a sauna with her?

A sauna? Christ, that would be sexy.

She hasn't had a sexual thought about anyone other than Pim (and not really about Pim either) for so long that it's a shock to feel her libido saying hello. But there it is.

Wow.

She's home from the pool in plenty of time before school starts. The boys are still asleep, by the looks of it, as their curtains are shut.

'How was it?' Pim asks, coming up behind her as she puts her bag in the utility room. 'You went at the crack of dawn.'

'Hard,' she admits. 'But good.'

Dare she tell him about sexy Andy? That he'd been flirting with her? Might he see her differently if he realised his wife was admired by another man?

She suddenly decides that this is it – she's going to press herself against him and kiss him. She's going to get their sex life back on track. She steps towards him.

'It's nice to feel healthy. More alive, you know . . . '

He smiles and she reaches out to touch his ancient towelling dressing gown, letting her hands loosen the belt. He looks surprised, but happy about it. She takes a step closer, revelling in how thrilling this unexpected bit of foreplay is. She knows that it's crazy . . . absurd to arouse her husband when the boys will be down any minute, but her hand starts to travel south.

But suddenly there's a deafening noise of a chainsaw right outside and they stare at each other.

'You've got to be kidding,' Pim says, stepping away and re-knotting the dressing gown cord. He flings open the back door. The noise is horrific. Sawdust fills the air.

Right above them, there's a workman in a harness sawing through the branches of Jenna and Rob's cherry tree. Seeing them he grins and touches the rim of his red hard hat. As if he's doing them a favour. Claire tries to shout at him, but he can't hear her, so she rushes upstairs to the landing window.

It takes her a while to locate the key to open it, but then she flings it open. She's now more on a level with the workman.

'Stop,' she shouts. 'Stop it right now.'

The workman puts his hand to his ear, as if he can't hear her, but she waves at him and the noise of the chain saw cuts out for a moment. 'You can't chop it down. The birds are nesting there.'

She sees that Rob has come out into his garden, holding a cup of coffee.

'What's going on?' he calls up to the workman. 'Why have you stopped?'

Then he sees Claire in the window and he rolls his eyes. 'Oh, here we go.'

'You can't just chop down the tree,' she shouts at him. 'The birds live there. They've been building their nest. This is the wrong time of year. And anyway, you can't . . . you can't just—'

'They're birds. They can live anywhere. They make too much noise anyway and that pigeon craps on my wicker sofa.'

Claire is so cross; she feels close to tears. 'You really don't care, do you? About anyone other than yourselves.'

'This is none of your business.'

'It *is* my business. It's my view.'

255

'That I've been providing free of charge.'

'You don't own nature,' she shouts then slams the window shut.

'That went well,' Pim says, but she growls at him furiously. She didn't see *him* trying. She stomps downstairs. There must be something they can do? But calling the police seems a little reckless, when Rob isn't breaking the law. Is he? It feels like he is.

She picks up the home phone.

'What are you doing?' Pim asks.

'Calling the police.'

He gives her a look as if she's crazy. 'Don't be daft. The police can't do anything. Just let it go.'

He shakes his head and goes upstairs to get dressed. Claire stands with the phone in her hand, the sound of the chainsaw filling the hallway.

She hears the ping of a message on her phone in her pocket and she replaces the receiver. It's Maddy on WhatsApp. She's has to drive back to Cobham, but she's got a few things she wants to give Claire for when she volunteers for Home Help. 'I'm on my way,' Claire types back. 'I'll be there in five.'

She's still seething as she arrives at Maddy's apartment block. It's the kind of place that you'd never notice and she has to double-check the pin Maddy has sent. It looks rather run-down for someone posh like Maddy.

Claire texts her and a few moments later, Maddy comes out of the building, carrying two black plastic bags. Claire gets out and opens the boot of the car.

'Some jackets,' she explains, 'and some sanitary products from Lidl.'

'Tor will be pleased. That's very generous of you.'

'It's the least I can do. I keep thinking how Jamie would want stuff like that.'

'Still no word?'

'This guy that Lotte's friend used. He's on the case. He called to say that Jamie stayed in a hostel in Oriental Place last year. I've talked to the warden there who doesn't remember him. But then, they have people coming and going all the time. She didn't have any idea where he might have gone. But it's a start. A timeline at least.'

Claire smiles, but Maddy frowns. 'Hey? Are you OK?'

'Not really.'

Claire explains what has just happened.

'They can't do that,' Maddy says, and Claire is touched that she's just as indignant.

'Well, they're doing it.'

'Right now?'

'Yes, right now. I'm glad you texted. I couldn't bear to watch.'

Maddy takes out her phone and squints at the screen and dials. 'Let me see if I can help?'

'Help? But how?' Claire asks.

'Matteo.'

'Matteo the sexy neighbour?'

Maddy laughs and holds up a finger.

'Matteo, it's me. Can you do me a favour?' she asks. She walks a few steps up the pavement and then back again to the car. Claire hears her explain the situation to him.

'I know! Exactly.' She smiles and Claire sees Maddy's whole demeanour change when she listens to him. 'You would? Seriously? Oh, Matteo. That's great. Thank you. I owe you.'

She rings off, her eyes bright. A second later, a text pings up. 'Here we go,' she says, but Claire still doesn't understand.

'What are you doing?' Claire asks.

She presses a number on her phone and raises her eyebrows at Claire and then nods as she gets through to someone on the other end. And Claire sees why it is that Maddy has been able to build a home from scratch. She's rather formidable.

'Hi,' she says brightly. 'You don't know me, but I'm Maddy Wolfe. Matteo, my next-door neighbour, gave me your number.' There's a pause and her eyes shine. 'Oh, did he?' She laughs. 'Well, he said you'd help.' She turns away and Claire hears her explaining about Jenna and Rob's property and the tree on the boundary wall.

'Yes, they're there now,' Maddy says. 'What's the address?' she mouths to Claire, who tells her. 'Fourteen Waterloo Drive,' she repeats. 'Yes, that's right. You'll go right away? Oh, that's great. Thank you.'

Claire stares at her in amazement as Maddy explains that Matteo's colleague from the council will be paying a visit with an order to stop the destruction of the tree.

'I cannot believe you just did that,' Claire says. 'Thank you.'

'No problem. You got time for a quick coffee?' she asks.

Claire nods and locks the car and they go up the stairs a few flights to Maddy's floor. Only a few months ago, Claire would have been completely out of breath, but to her surprise, she keeps up with Maddy who takes the stairs two at a time. She's wearing old faded Levi jeans that make her bum look great.

She hasn't got any make-up on and, in her baggy jumper, she looks effortlessly cool. Even with everything going on, she looks a lot more relaxed than she did when Claire first met her.

They get to the apartment and Luna comes over from her bed in the corner.

'Oh, hello you.'

'I said I'd watch her whilst Matteo is at the office.'

'So what's the deal with you and Matteo? If you can just call in a favour like that?'

'He's still just a friend,' Maddy says, smoothing the hair behind her ear.

'But you want it to be more?'

Maddy lets out a strangled laugh. 'Oh God, Claire. I don't know. I definitely fancy him, but I'm too shy to make the first move. It just feels like such a huge step to take.'

'You're overthinking it,' Claire says.

'Am I?'

And as Claire sits, watching Maddy make coffee for them, she feels like she used to with her sisters when they were teenagers. She loves it that Maddy values her opinion and wants her advice.

'God, I don't know what I'd do without you lot to keep me sane,' Maddy says.

35

Home in a Box

Thanks to Maddy's @made_home Instagram fame, there's been a flurry of interest since the house hit the market. It's on for a healthy price, but once Trent has paid back the exorbitant loan he's taken out, there'll hardly be anything left over.

Trent's excited about the cash buyer from London and Maddy has only been home a few hours when he announces that they're coming for a second viewing and 'today will be the day'. She hates him wanting the sale to happen so much.

Nevertheless, Maddy steels herself, trying to present a united front with Trent, when the banker and his Melania Trump lookalike younger wife arrive in a Ferrari, scattering the gravel over the flower beds.

They wander slowly through the rooms, Melania running her talons over Maddy's carefully selected furniture, her face impassive and unmoving. She leans in close to the banker, her hand on his shoulder as she towers over him. Maddy can't hear what she's whispering in his ear. Do they like the house or don't they? What gives them the right to sneer? She feels her spine tingling with indignation.

She's about to snap, but Trent stops her. 'Be patient. Please,' he hisses, through the side of his mouth. 'They're our best hope.'

Trent invites the couple to join them on the patio for a glass of bubbly, although it's rather premature. It's all Maddy can do not to flinch when Trent puts his hand on her knee, as if they are the perfect couple. It's a sunny spring day – the kind that promises summer. The kind that would be perfect for a swim. She pictures her friends striding into the sea without her.

The bird of paradise plants she's been waiting for to bloom are finally out, their orange flowers bright against the blue sky, and she realises that all of her careful garden planning is going to be enjoyed by someone else. That's if they don't rip out all of her planting and the sapling trees that cost a fortune. These two look like the type who might concrete over all the beds.

Trent is giving them the kind of charm-offensive schmooze that always makes her want to dial out. So she almost chokes when the banker suddenly breaks into a smile and announces that they'll take the house for the asking price. Cash. And they'll negotiate for the furniture. She can see that it takes every ounce of self-control for Trent not to punch the air, but she has to turn away to stop them seeing the tears in her eyes.

The next days are a blur, as Maddy starts to pack up the house. She makes a point of spending as little time as possible with Trent, communicating with him in terse texts about the arrangements necessary for the move. He's cross with her that she's not more delighted he's managed a quick sale, but when the first of the boxes leave in the van for the expensive storage unit, his precious golf clubs rattling in the back among them, reality seems to dawn. They're actually leaving.

'Can't we talk?' he asks, coming into their bedroom where she's putting everything in her bedside drawer in a box. It's stuff she hasn't thought about for a while. Her grandmother's dainty nineteen thirties watch, a folded piece of Filofax paper with a note from Jamie telling her that he loves her, her first Glastonbury wristband. She used to find it comforting having these keepsakes near to her as she slept, but she can't connect to the person to whom they mattered so much. She can't imagine that they'll mean the same thing, or ever be in a space again in the same way. She's written so much about the energy of spaces, about the synergy of objects and emotion, but now she sees that she was grasping at straws. Trying to find meaning where there wasn't one. They are just things now that this is no longer a home.

'What's there to talk about?' she asks, and he sighs and gives her his give-me-a-break look. Since she's been home, she's slept in Jamie's room and Trent has been on the sofa in his office. But the sofa has gone and, in the bedroom, only their marital bed remains. The new buyers have bought it and she hopes it doesn't bring them bad luck. Its presence and what it represents feels radioactive as they stand with it in between them.

'I know there have been some things that have been said, but . . . ' he pauses. 'But the thing is, I think we should start again.'

Maddy can hardly believe what she's hearing. 'Start again?'

'Couldn't we be how we used to be?'

She almost reacts with sarcasm, because that's never going to be possible after what he's done.

'You can't go backwards,' Maddy says, shaking her head, remembering Helga on the beach.

'Don't you love me any more? Even a little bit? Because I still love you. I want to make things work.'

She stares at him, seeing the flirty look on his face. In a moment, he might suggest that they give the bed a go for old time's sake. Where has *this* curveball suddenly come from? And why now? When they've almost moved out?

'What about Helen? And you? You're together with her. You chose her.'

'She's not important.'

Maddy can't believe what she's hearing. 'And she knows that, does she? You've told her?'

Because he'll be hedging his bets, Maddy thinks. As much as she hates Helen, this from Trent, at this late hour, is such a betrayal. Of them both.

He doesn't answer.

She feels her heart breaking a little bit more as she remembers the moment she said 'Yes' in New York when he'd asked her to marry him outside Tiffany's. How she'd jumped into his arms and the doorman had clapped, before opening it so that Trent could buy her the diamond ring she'd set her heart on. How she's so rarely ever said no to him since. Until now.

'No. It's too late,' she says. 'I can't come back from this.'

And then she sees it in his eyes. He doesn't want love, she realises. Or even her. He just wants someone to soothe his ego. He wants not to feel humiliated that he's lost their home. He wants someone to make it OK that he hasn't managed to salvage a business situation. That hasn't turned out to be Trent Wolfe, the big I am. What she's looking at is a rare thing: Trent with a crushed ego.

'Where will you go?' he asks.

'Back to Brighton, I guess. And you?'

'To Dad's, just for a bit,' he says. And although he doesn't deserve it, Maddy feels a bit sorry for him. 'Until the money comes through and I can decide what's next . . .'

He stiffens and draws himself up, as if braced for a fight, but Maddy has no fight left in her. And now, when his eyes meet hers, she understands that their business is done. That moment was just it. The end of her marriage.

She stares at him, feeling as if they should mark the moment with a handshake or a hug, but neither of them move. After a moment, he turns and leaves and she falls on the bed and looks up at the ceiling, a sob escaping her.

36

Back on Call

Dominica cycles up to Hove station and parks her bike outside the bridal shop for her first shift back at the Samaritans. The girl in the window who is dressing a new mannequin waves to her. It's a lovely dress, but Dominica knows that it's a difficult business to keep afloat in these testing times.

She's half an hour early, as is the custom, so that volunteers can seamlessly overlap and now, as she pushes in through the glass door of the Samaritans' office, it's as if she's never been away. Jasmin waves from where she's on the phone in one of the glass booths and Bill claps and comes over to kiss her. He's bought her a welcome back cake. They have tea and she enjoys catching up with him, although hearing about how much pressure he's been under to run the office himself, she's glad she's come back into the fold. Good guys like Bill shouldn't reach burnout. She's grateful that he's waited for her to be ready. Not that you're ever exactly ready for this stuff.

'Have you been going in the sea?' he asks.

She nods. 'Most days.'

'You look good on it,' he comments with a nod. 'I haven't been in since Christmas when I saw you.'

'You should go,' she says. 'It does wonders for my head.'

'And how are you?' he asks.

She sighs. 'I'm getting there. As I said, the swimming helps. I've got a good bunch of friends I swim with. They stop things becoming too bleak. And work has been . . . well, work.'

Ever perceptive, Bill cocks his head. 'You're not enjoying being back?'

'It's OK. It's just that my heart's not in it,' she says. 'But I'm not sure what choice I have. I've got a bit of a cushion from Chris's savings, but, financially, I can't afford to give up work. I'm too old to do anything else.'

'Nonsense,' Bill says. 'I didn't come to work at the Samaritans until I was fifty. You're never too old for a new direction.'

'I don't know what that direction would be.'

'I'm sure you do. If you really think about it.'

Dominica smiles and she remembers Tor in the sea saying how she should be a counsellor.

'It has crossed my mind to retrain,' she says, feeling silly for admitting this. 'Be a professional therapist of some sort.'

'I can't think of a finer idea. You'd be perfect.'

Jasmin comes out of the booth and hugs Dominica, warmly, delighted that she's back. She's always had youthful good looks, but her black hair is streaked with grey and there are bags under her eyes. She has a little bit of cake, but she's tired and needs to get back for her kids.

Dominica heads to the booth, knowing that there'll be callers waiting. She signs into her account and then switches her status to 'available' and the phone immediately rings.

Bill gives her a thumbs up and smiles as she answers.

There's a young girl crying on the other end of the phone. Dominica makes soothing noises and gives the girl the time to stop crying. Once she has, Dominica gently tries to find out what's causing the overwhelm. It doesn't take long for her to start describing her situation. She's caring for her disabled mum, there's an alcoholic abusive father in the mix and she's fallen out with her best friend over a boy. There's an eviction order too, and a dangerous dog that had to be put down. It's that bit of the story that has been the most heart-wrenching, so far.

During all of this description, the girl stops talking for minutes at a time, but Dominica knows to expect the silences. Her job has been to keep asking open questions, so the girl doesn't shut down the conversation. There've been times that Dominica was worried she might be losing her, but she's experienced enough to really listen to the silences. It's so important not to jump in and fill the gaps, because that's when people are often processing their thoughts.

Over time, she's learnt that people are nothing if not expert in their own problems and she knows that, on a call, people are often just trying to work something out for themselves. Her role is to give them time and help coax it out of them, rather than to shut them down by offering her advice, although sometimes it's tempting. People rarely see their choices as clear paths, but a blurry mess. She hopes to help the fog clear enough for them to see a road forward. Whether it's the right one or not is often unknowable.

And now she's rewarded with the eureka moment. The girl finally opens up about the reason for her call: she's found out she's pregnant and the father of her baby is her best friend's boyfriend. Dominica takes a sip of tea, waiting for the girl to calm down as the grief for her mistakes and bad choices washes through her like a storm. She sobs and sobs.

Dominica is used to this. Used to being able to witness other people's emotions.

She was always told she was a good listener when she was young, but that was only because she found it difficult to concentrate on what people were saying when there was a radio on, or music in the background. She's never been able to multi-task listen like Chris could. He could have the TV on as well as rugby commentary on the radio at the same time as being on a phone call, but Dominica can only listen to one source of information at a time. She never knew this was a requirement of being a good listener, until Bill told her so in training.

She sits back and tries to be still.

'I haven't told anyone. I'm so ashamed,' the girl sobs.

'It's OK,' Dominica says. 'Really. Take your time.'

'Do you think I should tell her what I've done?'

'It's not about what I think. You know your own situation so you're the best person to find a solution.'

'I suppose.'

'You have a lot of things to consider, and I get that it's hard. Of course I do. But I know from talking to you that you're a good person and you'll do the right thing.'

And the girl stops crying and Dominica can feel that she's coming back down now, a little step at a time, back down into a clearer, calmer space. It never stops being a gift witnessing this happening.

Tor was right. She should be doing this. This is her calling.

37

Upfront and Honest

It's a starlit night and the moon hangs between the dip in the downs as Maddy drives south, her possessions loaded haphazardly in cardboard boxes in the back. She feels utterly wrung out. Leaving the house for the very last time was much more of a wrench than she'd expected, especially as Trent refused to say goodbye to her or see her off.

It felt frightening driving away from her home for the last time. Not least of all because if Jamie were to go back there, strangers would be living in it. It feels as if she's done yet another thing to hurt him, even though it wasn't her fault. Wherever he is, Jamie truly is homeless now.

She parks outside the flat on the road and goes inside and up the stairs with one of the cardboard boxes from the boot, balancing two of the houseplants. She gave the big ones to Rey, the cleaner, who turned up to help do the final clean. It had been awful saying goodbye to her too.

'Hey,' Matteo says, coming out of his flat. He rushes over

and takes the box before it falls. 'It's heavy. Did you carry it up the stairs?'

'I've been lugging boxes like that all week. I've got loads more like that in the back of the car.'

'I was worried you weren't going to come back.'

She remembers now the text she'd sent him after the house had sold. Trent had opened champagne, but she couldn't drink it. She's only been able to think about Matteo and how he'd given her cava at New Year.

Has he really been worried? She wishes she could tell him how lovely it is to see his friendly face.

'Where else have I got to go? Besides, I've got to find Jamie. Because if he were to go home . . . it wouldn't be there any more. I know it's silly, but that's the bit that gets me the most.'

Her voice breaks then and, despite wanting to be strong, she starts crying, more from exhaustion than anything else.

'Hey,' Matteo says, and he puts down the box. He pulls her into a much-needed hug. And now, it all comes out – all the sadness, and pent-up fury as she sobs against his soft cashmere jumper.

'It's going to be all right,' he tells her, over and over again, rubbing her back.

Finally, she manages to pull herself together and steps away. She apologises for falling apart and for making a mess of his jumper. It's covered in mascara and she tells him she'll pay to get it dry cleaned, but he waves her suggestion away with a gentle smile.

'I'm sorry, Maddy. It sounds like you've had the week from hell.'

'That's an understatement,' she says.

He helps her move the boxes from the car into the flat and she parks in the car park. The flat is a mess and Matteo helps her stack the boxes up against the wall. He leaves the heaviest one with some of her ceramics pieces in it until last and almost drops it. They push it to a safe position amidst the teetering pile of boxes.

They are standing side by side and they are both out of breath. She instinctively puts her hand over his.

She turns to him. 'Thank you,' she says.

'You're welcome.' He doesn't move his hand. Then she sees a question in his eyes and, before giving herself time to think, she kisses him.

He responds, pulling her towards him, and all the sexual tension between them bursts out into the open, as he holds her hair, kissing her hard.

It's as if a firework has gone off inside her. He lifts her up, kissing her as if his life depends on it and she doesn't care, there's no control left. She's only vaguely aware that he's carrying her to the sofa and then he's on top of her and she looks into his deep brown eyes.

'I have wanted you for so long, Maddy,' he says. He strokes her hair away from her face. 'Do you want this too?'

'Oh yes,' she breathes, feeling his hardness against her jeans and how she's already melting. 'Yes, yes. Oh God, yes.'

Maddy wakes up in her bed, a smile on her lips. There's a weak morning light coming through the shutters. She stretches, feeling the novelty of her nakedness between the sheets. She feels centred in a way that she hasn't done for a very, very long time.

As if sensing that she's awake, Matteo stirs next to her. He opens his eyes and smiles.

'*Buenos dias*,' she says, remembering how she drunkenly practised her Spanish on him last night.

She must look a complete state. She didn't ever get round to taking off her tear-streaked make-up from yesterday, but he's seen her at her most raw and she realises she doesn't care. The sex had been amazing – far too frantic and fast the first time, but then they'd had a bottle of wine and he'd made her lie on her bed and insisted on massaging her, his hands stroking away the stress and the heartbreak. It had been amazing. Then they'd had deep, slow sex, kissing and talking and exploring.

'Impossible, but you're even prettier in the morning,' he says.

She feels a girlish thrill at his compliment. Nobody has called her pretty for a long time. Stylish maybe, and before she came to Brighton and before lockdown when her standards were much, much higher, certainly 'put together'. But this compliment feels more natural. Like he's describing her in her raw state. Not her make-up, or her hairstyle or her clothes. None of the things that she normally throws money and time at. And it's this – this acknowledgement of how she is right now – that feels almost more intimate than the sex they've shared.

She feels him stirring against her and a wave of desire comes over her as she leans in to kiss him. How had she forgotten how wonderful kissing is? How spectacular sex makes her feel? It's like she didn't realise she was thirsty until she had a drink and now she feels insatiable.

Suddenly, there's a yapping and Luna jumps on the bed, surprising them both.

'Oh! Luna. Hey you.'

Luna nuzzles in, breaking them apart. 'OK, OK,' Matteo says, stretching. 'This is my cue to get up. I should go and shower before my meeting.'

She watches him admiring his olive skin and pert bum. He's in good shape and she likes the dark curly hair on his legs and chest. He's manly in a way that Trent never really was with all his preening and waxing.

'But this is to be continued. I *will* see you later,' he says.

When he's gone, Maddy contemplates the cardboard boxes. She's spent her entire life rushing to re-cycle all the cardboard boxes that things arrive in, but now she has a wall of the bloody things. There's no way she can even start to unload all her stuff when there's nowhere to put anything.

She hears the buzz of her phone on the coffee table and opens up the screen. Her heart leaps when she sees there's a new message. It's from Neil Watson. He's the guy she's hired to find Jamie. Does he have news?

She sinks down on the sofa to read his message.

'I've looked everywhere. I'm sorry. I don't think there's any more that I can do. Usually there's a lead, but I haven't been able to find one. Perhaps we should start searching internationally.' Internationally? Surely Jamie couldn't have gone abroad? No one has been travelling in Covid, have they? But then she remembers how resourceful Jamie can be. What if he'd found a way to go back to Thailand? Is he locked down abroad? Is that why she can't find him?

It's been hard enough looking for him in Brighton, but how will she find him anywhere else in the world?

She closes the email and then opens her Instagram account,

but she can't really focus on the jolly colourful posts from the people she's following. Sighing, she clicks on her messages. There are dozens that she can't find the energy to deal with. Mostly they are from people wanting follow-up information about some of the suppliers she's recommended, some wanting her to like links and pages, but she leaves those and opens one from a girl she did a course with a while ago.

Everything OK? You haven't posted anything new for a while?

Her followers have noticed her re-hashed posts, then. She's about to respond, give an excuse, when she stops herself.

She can't post anything about her life at home when it doesn't exist any more. Those chairs and sofas belong to the Melania Trump lookalike. Having not told the truth about the house being sold, she feels more of a fraud than ever.

And she thinks of Helga and, all of a sudden, she knows she's going to do it. She's going to take the plunge. Before she gives herself time to chicken out, or has even looked in the mirror, she presses the Live button and starts talking.

'So . . . this is me,' she says to the recording phone screen. 'Raw and, as you can see, pretty much unfiltered.' She can't believe she's actually doing this. 'As one of my followers, Hayley, pointed out, I haven't posted anything fresh for a while. But that's because there's been a lot of change going on for me. Changes that I didn't think would happen to me at my age. But you see, it seems that I've unexpectedly found myself homeless. This is what's left.' She scans round to the wall of cardboard boxes.

'I know I always said that I didn't want to move again, having made my dream home, but I had no choice in the matter. So here I am. And I feel like I'm at a crossroads in my life and, well' – she pauses – 'and I think I need to talk about how my home became *un*-made.'

She feels butterflies in her stomach. It's so utterly new being this real . . . this honest . . . that it makes her feel shaky.

'I have been so driven in my quest for perfection, but the truth is . . . my perfect life wasn't perfect. Far from it. I was living a lie. But now that my home has gone and I'm on my own and I'm starting all over again, I want to be honest. Because I can't pretend that I live this glossy life when I really don't. Because the reality is that my marriage has broken down and I've lost my son. And when I say lost, I mean lost. He's really gone.'

She feels tears coming now and she tries to swallow them down.

'And I . . . just . . . if there's any way this gets shared and Jamie sees this, by some kind of miracle, I want him to know, I've tried to put it right. I've tried to find him, but maybe he just doesn't want to be found. And I've realised that I have to accept that. That sometimes you have to accept other people and situations as they are. Even if you don't like it.'

She squeezes her lips together and smiles. 'So, if you're in your home with your husband or partner, or your kids or your cat or dog, and you're coming to my feed for inspiration, then I have to tell you this: life doesn't have to be perfect. Making something look gorgeous doesn't make it gorgeous. Life – real life – is messy and disordered and unfiltered and often a bit shit, but also magnificent and joyous. It can't be snapped or defined. So, forget about striving for perfection. Do something instead. Do something that makes you happy. And on that note, I'm signing off, because I'm going for a swim in the sea.'

38

A Trip to Hampstead Pond

It's a beautiful early May morning as Dominica arrives to pick up Helga to take her on their trip to Hampstead. Emma has insisted that she come up for a visit now everyone is allowed to mix. She should really have gone before, but Dominica has thrown herself in at the Samaritans and her dates and Emma's have clashed until now.

She's asked the rest of the Sea-Gals to come along too, but everyone is busy, except Helga who said she could do with a change of scene. Dominica is pleased she's coming, not least of all because she hasn't driven to London for a long time and she could do with the company.

Despite seeing Helga several times a week for over a year, Dominica hasn't ever been to her home, but as she goes down the lane and knocks on the door, her shabby, ramshackle cottage makes perfect sense. There's a purple magnolia tree, which fills her tiny front garden, and there's a scattering of petals in the stone bird bath below it. A baby magpie washes, oblivious of Dominica's presence.

When she opens the door, Dominica sees that Helga is wearing holey tracksuit pants, her worn canvas shoes and a long coat that looks as if it came from a charity shop. What on earth is Emma going to make of her?

Dominica follows her inside. 'Oh my God!'

She takes a step back, her hand on her chest. There's a huge seagull in the kitchen. It paddles its feet and flaps its huge wings. Helga laughs at her shock.

'It's only Terry,' she says, bustling the seagull out of the kitchen door and locking it. 'He came in for his breakfast.'

'You feed him in the kitchen?'

'He and Julie – that's his wife – they've had chicks. He's got a lot on his plate.'

Dominica laughs and follows her through to the sitting room. There are two low sofas and worn silk rugs on the wooden floorboards. It's got a very artistic vibe. A huge model of a sailing ship dominates one wall, along with Japanese glass floats in worn rope, then the room opens onto an arty studio space with a glass roof and glass doors to the overgrown garden. It feels like a forgotten cottage in the middle of the countryside.

'I love it,' Dominica says.

'My niece Mette wants me to move. To some dreadful retirement village.'

'*You?*' Dominica can't help laughing.

'Exactly. She thinks I'm old.'

She knows she's being nosy, but whilst Helga runs upstairs, she walks into the conservatory where there are several easels and canvases stacked up against the wall. She spots some sketches pinned to long looping string across the ceiling, like photos in a dark room, or T-shirts on a washing line. She walks along, studying them, realising with shock that one of them is Claire.

She knew Claire had modelled for her, but she hadn't seen the result. This is gorgeous. It captures Claire in all her curvy glory.

'Helga, these are amazing,' Dominica says when she comes back.

'She's a good model, right?' she says, grinning. 'My friend Rutger's sketch was even better. I think she's got that one.'

'Do you think she's shown Pim?'

'I doubt it. But she should.'

Helga locks up and they go down the lane to where the car is parked.

'It's weird,' Dominica says. 'I hope I can remember how to drive.' She smiles over the roof of the car at Helga. She means it. She's travelled the world, but after lockdown her horizons have shrunk so much that going to London seems like a really big deal.

'Me too,' Helga says, settling into the passenger's seat. She picks up the bag on it. 'What's this?'

'That's for you. Don't be offended,' Dominica says.

Helga looks inside. There's a new swimming costume with lots of technical-looking labels attached to it. Not cheap then. 'You're too embarrassed by the old one?'

'I hope it fits.'

'It's lovely and very thoughtful,' Helga says. 'Thank you.'

They drive out of town and when Helga asks how it's going at work, Dominica tells her the big news of the week.

'I had a meeting yesterday with my boss.'

'Oh?'

'They want me to consider early retirement.'

'I hope you bit their hand off.'

Dominica glances across at her with a frown. She's been feeling churned up about it, so Helga's no-nonsense reaction is a surprise. Although, knowing Helga, it shouldn't be. 'I don't know. Retirement makes me feel old. The word . . . I can't believe it might actually apply to me.'

'Oh, rubbish. It's just a word. If someone is fool enough to fund you doing what makes you happy then grab the chance,' Helga says. 'I've still got my pension from my last teaching job.'

'I didn't know you taught?'

'Art. At a secondary school. For a few years.'

'You? With children?'

'Exactly. Teenagers,' Helga says, with a mock shiver. 'Hated the vile little bastards, with their petty hang-ups and silly language. When they asked me to leave, I did a little jig.'

'Yeah, well, you suit retirement. You're practised at your own company. I don't know what I'll do to make me feel useful.'

'Of course you do. You should be a counsellor or a therapist, or whatever they call them. I admire you volunteering, but you should get paid for it.'

Dominica speeds up on the road ahead as they hit the motorway, seeing the countryside unfurling on either side, the trees bursting with buds. She admits to Helga that she's already been looking at the various courses she's found for retraining. The more she looks into it, the more excited she is about taking a step in this new direction.

They get on to talking about the others in the gang and how

terrible it has been for Maddy to lose her home. Dominica has been intrigued about Helga's admission in the sea. She so rarely gives anything personal away, but her confession clearly helped Maddy. 'I was sorry to hear what you said the other day. About your boyfriend. About how he ripped you off.'

'It doesn't matter. That whole episode is ancient history.'

'Were you desperately in love?'

'No. Not really. I thought I was . . . but that's the thing about hindsight . . . I can see that it was always doomed.'

Dominica is intrigued by the way she says it. Helga mostly holds her cards close to her chest, but she senses that she means that she was desperately in love with someone else. 'So he wasn't the one?' she takes a punt.

'Which one?'

'You know, they say there's "the one".'

But Helga doesn't answer.

The traffic is heavier now, people driving more erratically, and Dominica has to concentrate to get around the roundabout.

She thinks Helga has forgotten about it, but still looking out of the window the other way, she says, 'No. Paul wasn't the one. And what about you?'

'Me?'

'Will you move on from Chris? Find someone else? He'd have wanted that for you, surely?'

'I haven't thought about it.'

'Haven't you?'

'No!' Dominica says, trying not to sound as offended as she feels.

'You're not lonely?'

'Of course I'm lonely!' It feels good to admit it. Because it feels so pitifully self-indulgent.

'Then you need a companion at the very least.'

'Why? You don't have one.'

'I have my birds,' Helga says. 'But you don't want to end up like me.'

'I'd be happy to end up like you,' Dominica tells her, meaning it. 'You're independent and strong.'

'But you're too good a person not to love and be loved in return.'

'I thought you didn't believe in love,' Dominica teases her.

'What on earth gave you that idea?'

Emma bounds out of the mansion block as Dominica parks the car on the London street. She's a shorter, female version of Chris and Dominica's heart lurches with genuine love as she gets out of the car and Emma pulls her into a hug.

'You came, you came,' she cries. She smells of fabric softener and Dominica slumps for a moment against her voluptuous curves, feeling tears spring to her eyes too. It's just so damn good to get a hug. Emma pulls away, wiping her eyes. 'Oh, oh,' she says, flapping her hand in front of her face. 'Sorry. I just can't help it. It's so good to see you.'

'Aunty Dominica,' she hears, and now Cerys and the boys are bounding towards her too, and Dominica cries out with delight as they fling themselves at her. They have all grown an astonishing amount in the past months and it's this – seeing Cerys with her front teeth missing – that makes Dominica realise how much time has passed without her noticing.

'This is my friend, Helga,' Dominica explains, once she's

hugged and kissed them, and Helga gets out of the car and they go towards the house.

'What are your grandchildren called?' Cerys asks, with her usual directness, as they walk up the path to the house and around the back to the garden.

'Oh, I don't have any grandchildren.'

Cerys's blonde eyebrows crinkle up together in a frown. 'You don't? Why not?'

'I made bad choices,' Helga says. 'It's easy to do. You'll find that out.'

Emma raises her eyebrows at Dominica.

'So, what do you like doing?' Cerys asks, confused, as if being Helga's age can only involve tending to grandchildren.

'Cerys,' Emma scolds. 'Don't be nosy.'

'It's not nosy,' Helga says. 'It's a good question.'

Cerys flashes a 'told-you-so' look at Emma.

Helga smiles. 'I like birds. I like watching them and drawing them.'

'We've got a bird box.'

'I'd like to see it,' Helga says gravely, and Cerys leads her away.

'She's quite a character, isn't she? Your friend Helga. How old is she?'

'I don't know. Seventy something.'

She can see Emma is confused that they're friends, when there's such an age difference, but Dominica never notices it. She knows Emma will get it once she sees Helga in the water.

'She's not everyone's cup of tea, but she's a good friend. She's had my back, since . . . well, you know . . . '

'Anyone who gets you back in the sea gets my vote.'

They only stop at the house for coffee and then it's time to walk to the pond. Emma always swims with a gang and her friends arrive and all six of them set off down the road.

'We'll talk later,' Emma promises Dominica, squeezing her hand. 'When we've done the swim. Oh, I can't tell you how much I love having you here. Can't I kidnap you? Can't you stay over?'

Dominica laughs. 'This is just a day trip, but now I know I can still drive, I'll be back. I promise.'

She is so used to Helga leading the way in their group, it's weird to see her at the back, looking her age.

'We've been swimming all winter,' Dominica tells them. 'We even went in the snow.' It's strange having this conversation – like she's a clanswoman from another tribe.

'Yes, these guys are the professionals,' Emma says, proudly.

Dominica smiles at Helga. 'You hear that? We're the professionals.'

Emma squeezes her arm. 'It's so good to hear you laugh.'

39

That Unmistakeable Profile

It's certainly not the same as the sea, Helga thinks, as she lowers herself down the steps after Dominica and Emma, and into the bathing pond. It feels colder for a start, which she hadn't been expecting, but there are other ways it's different too. The texture of the water feels silky on her skin, not salty. She's not as buoyant either, and she's surprised that she has to kick harder to stay afloat.

She puts her mouth under the surface, feeling the coolness on her chin and seeing little flies jump on the surface. A skein of ducks fly low and land gracefully on the lake in the distance beyond the line of white markers in the water. There are lots of swimmers dotted around and she watches Emma and her friends in the water, like a little flock, as they swim out.

She's glad she came for Dominica's sake, but today has made her feel more self-conscious than she's felt for a very long time. She'd never normally admit such weakness, but she's been nervous all day. It started with the drive here, which freaked her out – all those suburbs, all those people. In the comfortable rut of her simple life, she's forgotten about the wider world, about the sheer grubby scope of humanity. She guesses it's why she's always been drawn to the solitude of the sea.

She's not used to strangers either, even friendly ones like Emma and her friends. They're city people and, next to them, she feels old and shabby. She's obviously frayed at the edges in a way she hadn't realised that other people noticed. Why would Dominica have taken it upon herself to get her this lovely new swimming suit?

Once she's moving in the water, though, she starts to feel calmer, as she taps into that delicious feeling of freedom that cold water inevitably brings. She sees a vapour trail across the blue. It's been a while since she's seen one of those. She rather liked it when the skies belonged only to the birds. God knows nature needed a rest from all the pollution, but she suspects mankind will be back to its vile old ways before too long.

This really must be a lovely place to swim every day, she thinks. You don't get the trees at the ocean. There's a resplendent bank of them in their full May majesty and Helga sees how beautifully they are reflected in the still water.

Her gaze strays to a group of people talking on the jetty and Helga is about to turn around and continue onwards with the others, when the sound of laughter reaches her on the gentle breeze and something about it makes her turn her head to look.

One of the guys talking on the jetty is blurry at this distance, but there's something about his profile, about the shape of his head . . .

Her heart thuds once, very hard. She suddenly stops in the water. She sinks slightly, then scrambles to keep afloat.

Oh, for God's sake, she tells herself. She's just latching on to objects and people to make sense of this unusual environment.

It's not him. He lives in Australia.

Doesn't he?

But before she consciously realises what she's doing, she's swimming back towards the jetty, as if pulled by a higher force.

'Helga?' Dominica calls. 'Helga? Where are you going?'

She turns her attention back to Dominica and the swimmers who are heading for the far bank, but there's shivers running up and down her spine.

Dominica swims some crawl over and surfaces with a frown on her face. 'Are you all right. Do you feel OK?'

'I'm going to . . . I'm getting out,' Helga says.

'I'll come with you.'

'No, no, please don't. Carry on. I'm fine.'

'But—'

'Don't worry, honestly. I'll just be on the side.'

She smiles reassuringly at Dominica and squeezes her arm, before turning away.

'Helga?' Dominica calls out. 'Are you sure?'

'Quite sure,' she calls, but she doesn't turn. Her heart is hammering, as she breaststrokes fast, like she used to, dipping her head way below the water undulating her body and coming up for air, treating herself to the sight on the jetty each time. Her heart is going mental now, as she gets closer. *It can't be*, she says to herself, as she frog-legs powerfully; it can't be, *it can't be* . . .

Soon she's at the metal steps at the jetty and she climbs out, feeling the water dripping from her hips down her legs. The group have moved away now to the other end of the jetty and she's telling herself that she's being ridiculous as she pulls up her goggles onto her hat and feels the wooden slats beneath her feet. She feels self-conscious in her figure-hugging swimming costume as she walks towards the changing area as if she's on a catwalk.

And then she hears it again.

His laugh.

A man in jeans with shoulder-length silver hair is standing with his back to her, his hands in a padded black gilet, but she'd know that unmistakeable profile anywhere. She's sure of it. The boy she didn't meet on the dock nearly half a century ago, all grown into a man. An old man. As old as her.

Helga approaches, hardly able to breathe as she reaches him and touches his arm.

As he turns, it's as if the whole world has gone into slow motion. She drinks him in, the water droplets dripping from her eyelashes, as her mouth opens in a gasp.

It *is* him.

Linus.

Time has been kind to him in the way that it is to men. His tanned skin is lined from years in the sun and he has a silver goatee beard, a leather band around his neck with a silver pendant on it. He always wore a necklace. She has the original one he gave her on the photo frame next to her bed.

'Linus.' It feels like her body is being flooded with light, just saying his name.

'Helga?' he asks, as if he can't quite believe it either.

She's aware of the skin on her arms and thighs. How she must look so saggy and old.

'I was in the water and I thought it was you. I can't believe it. I can't believe you're here.'

'My daughter's friend swims here,' he says, but his blue eyes are locked with hers. And the golden energy is now surging between them.

She nods, as her brain scrambles to catch up with the facts. He has children. *That figures.* And now she sees a wedding ring on his finger. *Of course he has a wife.* Who wouldn't have snared a catch like Linus? She's always known this, logically, but now she understands that there's a childish part of her that has always wished he'd been waiting for her.

'I followed your career. You were so successful. I always knew you would be. It's no surprise you're in the water. You always were a mermaid.'

My little mermaid. His nickname for her. His eyes glitter as he says it and her stomach erupts with butterflies – old, girlish emotions that don't belong in an old woman, but they are there just the same. Just as strong.

'You're cold,' he says, and she realises that her teeth have started to chatter.

'Yes, let me get my towel and coat. It's just over there.'

He walks with her as she goes to retrieve her coat from where she's left it in the changing area. She shrugs it on over her wet costume, knowing that she should get changed, but she can't waste these moments.

'Do you live here?' he asks, as she joins him outside.

'No, I'm just visiting. With a friend. I live down in Brighton. By the sea. What about you?'

'I'm over for a visit from Oz. I got stuck here for the

lockdown. It's been a crazy year, but there are worse places to be stuck. I'm going back. Won't be long now.'

He's been here the whole time? Her Linus. In easy distance? And now he's leaving to go to the other side of the world?

She reaches into her coat and takes out her notebook, but she drops it, her hands are shaking so much. He bends down to pick it up at the same time as her and their heads are so close together she can breathe him in.

'You still take a notebook everywhere?' he asks. He smells the same.

She never takes much notice of this vital sense, but her olfactory memory is stirred now. She can't pinpoint a place or a time, but she remembers an atmosphere. An atmosphere of youth and sunshine and endless sex. She's touched his skin more than anyone's in her life and she remembers how they were permanently draped around one another. As if they couldn't bear to break skin contact. She runs her eyes over his face and hair and imagines pressing her forehead against his. The urge to pull him inside her is almost overpowering.

'Take my number. If I ever get down to the South Coast, I'll be sure to come and say hello.' He stands, breaking the moment.

Does he feel this too? This familiarity, this unfathomable sense of ownership after all this time?

'I'd like that,' she says, but she can hardly get the words out.

He flicks through the pages.

'All these beautiful birds. You always were so talented. Look at this,' he marvels. She's so private about her notebooks, but she's handed it over to him without a second thought. She's proud that he likes what he sees on the pages. She watches as he points to a clean page and writes down his mobile number and she knows that, from now on, this will forever be the most precious of all her notebooks.

'You should get in the warm,' he says. His eyes lock with hers. Those little freckles near the bridge of his nose are still beautiful.

From further along, towards the entrance, a woman calls out. 'Dad? Dad, you coming?'

He waves and Helga follows his gaze to the blonde woman. She must be in her forties and she has an athletic figure and wide smile, just like his. She's very attractive, Helga realises. Linus's genes were always going to produce splendid offspring, though. That was a given. Helga wonders how it would feel if that confident young woman was her daughter.

He passes back the book. Helga is trapped in his gaze, but it's too bright, too exposing. Because he's cracked something open inside her, something long buried. It's desire, she realises, but it's something more, too, a heart ache that feels so strong, she worries that she might actually be having a heart incident.

'It's so good to see you again, Helga,' he says. 'So good.'

She nods. 'You, too.'

'I'm sorry I've got to go, but my daughter is in charge today and if I don't do what she wants . . . ?' he confides with an old Linus grin. He doesn't look as if he really minds being bossed around. She feels a childish sense of loss that he's going. She wants to be introduced to his daughter. She wants him to tell her that she's his long-lost lover.

'Please call me, Helga. Please. I'd so love to talk to you, but I can't here.'

'I will. I promise.'

'Will you?' he asks and his blue eyes bore into hers.

She sees a flicker of doubt. He doesn't believe that she will. And why would he, when she let him down all those years ago? But she solemnly promises.

He leans forward and kisses her on the cheek, but she remains motionless. As he walks away she almost calls out after him because she *has* to know. Did she break his heart? Like she broke her own? Did it hurt as much for him as it had done for her?

The rest of the day is a blur and she hardly registers it when Dominica announces that it's time to go back to Brighton. Helga can tell that the day has done her the world of good and that she's been cheered up by seeing her family and swimming in the pond, but she knows, too, that she's let Dominica down, by being weird and quiet.

But she can't help it. She can't help going over and over the encounter. *Linus is here. In the UK.* She clamps her hand around the notebook in her pocket. She has his number. And he wants to talk. She can hardly believe it.

She feels very strange, her chest tight with a knot, right in the middle. She knows there's been a seismic shift, like an earthquake under the seabed and she's grateful that Dominica doesn't press her on the drive home. But as the familiar shape of the South Downs come into view, she finally cracks, when Dominica says, 'So, are you going to tell me what's going on?'

'Sorry.'

'What's bugging you?'

'Oh . . . I don't know. Everything. The past.'

'The past?' Dominica asks, confused.

Today has made Helga feel old in so many ways but seeing Linus has been like she's been thrown a rope back to the past. Back to the daredevil, risk-taking girl she used to be. 'I thought I was scared of the future, but maybe it's the past that's the difficult thing to face . . . '

'You want to stop talking in riddles and tell me what's going on? I'm guessing it's something to do with that guy you were talking to?'

Helga nods and she watches the rosy hues of the sunset as she tells Dominica about Linus and how she'd always wondered about him, how there'd always been a flame in her heart for him.

'Oh, I see. So *he* was the one,' Dominica says, referring to their earlier conversation. 'You never answered before.'

'Oh, yes,' Helga admits, because all of her seems to be leaking out. Everything that has been brittle and icy is suddenly water. 'He was the only man I ever truly loved.'

'I'm glad it was that. I thought you might be having a heart attack.'

'I thought I was when I saw him.'

'So, what happens now?'

Helga sighs. 'He's going back to Australia as soon as he's able. He told me to call him.'

'And you're going to, right?'

Helga sighs, her heart torn. 'I want to. I said I would, but is there any point in raking over the past? I'm not sure if we'd have anything in common. He's got a family and . . . ' She shakes her head. 'I feel so nervous. Like a silly girl when I'm an old woman.'

'Oh Helga,' Dominica says. 'Don't be scared. Call him.'

'You think I should?'

'Yes,' Dominica shouts. 'Hell, yes. Because if you don't, I will.'

By the time they're back in Brighton, it's dark. Dominica drops Helga at the end of the lane, making her promise before she gets out the car that she's going to go home and call Linus straight away.

Helga puts her notebook in her bag for safekeeping and her keys too, then kisses Dominica before getting out of the car. She's been a good friend today.

'Promise me?' Dominica says.

'I promise.' It's the second promise that she's made today.

As she walks up the lane, she feels lighter, buoyed up by Dominica's confidence, like a balloon that might take off. She's so excited, she starts walking faster towards the hot shower she needs, before she'll make herself a tea and ring him. She *will* ring him now because she's promised Dominica. And they'll talk for hours. She already knows they will. His blue eyes fill her mind.

She doesn't notice the man on the corner turn to follow her.

40

Full Moon Swim

Claire is sweating as she parks and bustles across the road to the bandstand. She's worn far too many clothes under her Dryrobe and, even though she knows the water temperature will be the same as it was yesterday, there's always the fear it'll be much colder in the dark, so she's layered up.

It's the first time there's been a mass gathering of swimmers for a full moon swim for a long time. After the shout went out on the chat a couple of days ago, Claire has been excited and nervous about tonight's swim. There's the promise of a supermoon when it rises at nine twenty-five, but there's fairly thick cloud cover and she's not sure they'll even see it. Pim was alarmed that she was going out after supper on a Wednesday night and was worried about her swimming in the dark. He rolled his eyes at the boys and Claire knew that, given the chance, Felix would have added to the gesture and twirled his finger by his temple to signify she was mad, but solidarity came from Ash, who, to her surprise, asked her to say hello to Dominica. It felt good to know he was on her side.

She knows it's because his geography project earned him the best mark in the class and he's setting up a school beach cleaning team. He's asked to join the lifeguard training team, too. She never thought he would get into cold water, but he went on Saturday morning in the new wetsuit she'd got him and he came back buzzing. It seems that he's caught the water bug too.

Pim admitted to Claire the other morning that he was 'gobsmacked' that Ash had got so involved so quickly, but she can tell that he's impressed.

There are people – mostly women of a similar age to her – walking from all directions to the beach, like iron filings drawn to a magnet. As Claire gets to the pebbles, it really does feel as if she's joining a flock. Usually their Sea-Gals gang gather alone by the groyne, but this evening there are little groups of swimmers strewn out across the pebbles, greeting each new arrival with a hug. The sky is dappled with a full array of fading pink, purple and grey hues as night approaches. She's so used to this bit of beach, but the atmosphere feels more charged. There's a sense of occasion, but it's the deep purple of the sea that feels the most different. It's alluring, like seeing a friend you're used to seeing in tracky bottoms dressed up for a night out.

Dominica and Tor are already on the beach, changing. Maddy has sent her apologies, but she's not going to make it, and Helga is late, which is unusual.

As they change, they discuss the tide.

'What does peregrine mean?' Claire asks. She'd told the boys that she was swimming at the peregrine tide, quoting the WhatsApp message as if she knew what she was talking about.

'It's the point where the moon is closest to the earth in its orbit, so if we see it, it should look big,' Dominica says.

'Low tide was at six,' Tor says, 'so it's coming in. It looks just right.'

Around them, the swimmers are collectively stripping off, their Dryrobes falling to the beach, the hats and boots and gloves going on next, and then there's a whole mass of bare thighs and arms. Dozens of women of all shapes and sizes, and a few men too, approach the water, tiptoeing across the stones.

Claire smiles as she hears the screams of delight as the swimmers get in the water and she remembers reading that someone had described the collective noise as 'sea opera'. There's certainly something grand and musical about the sound as the crowd bounce around in the bobbing waves. There's a collective whoop as a big wave breaks over their heads.

'You coming?' Dominica asks, noticing that Tor is lingering, but she's looking at her phone. 'I'll wait for Lotte and the others,' Tor says. 'You go.'

'Keep an eye out for Helga, too. It's not like her to be late,' Dominica says. 'Come on then, Claire. Let's do this thing.'

It's not as cold as Claire has been anticipating and, with so many swimmers in, it feels like a party in the sea, as if everyone is dancing around each other in a disco. To her surprise, Claire recognises quite a few of the faces among the swimmers. There's the owner of the café, who smiles and says hello, the lady who works in the physiotherapy department at the hospital who helped sort out her knee years ago. She's wearing a jaunty retro swimming cap with purple flowers on it and Claire wonders again where Helga is. She'd love this.

A memory surfaces of going to a water park with Pim

and the boys once, and how the wave machine jostled them and they'd all squealed with delight. It feels a little like that as they drift further away from the shore towards the pier. Ash has always liked the water, she remembers. She'd just forgotten.

She smiles at Dominica as some spontaneous singing breaks out and Claire joins in, amazed by how unselfconscious she feels. It's Blondie first, 'The Tide is High', then 'Blue Moon'. It feels crazy to be singing in the sea.

The light fades quickly now and the streetlights and hotel lights come on along prom. From out there in the water, it's weird to see this night perspective of the town, the i360 all lit up in red and blue. The tow floats that some of the swimmers are wearing glow against the darkness of the water.

Years ago, on their honeymoon in India, Pim and Claire went to a festival and there were candles in lotus flowers floating on a lake and this is similar. There's something of a religious celebration about this.

She rarely thinks of Pim's Indian heritage, but now she thinks how lovely it would be to go back to visit his extended family with the boys. They've talked about it, but they've never made the trip happen. They used to talk about their dreams and their future all the time. Has it just been Covid that has made them stop and stall? Not able to see past the next government announcement? Claire has been happy to be at home, keeping her family together, but being here tonight is connecting her to that sense of wonder, that feeling that something extraordinary is happening. She only usually gets that when she goes abroad.

And then, suddenly, momentously, there it is.

Over by the burnt-out pier, there's a break in the cloud and the majestic crown of the moon pokes out. Claire is already facing it, but the call goes out among the swimmers and soon everyone is facing the same way. They all bob in the waves, watching the moon rising, the mood of jubilation subdued now to one of momentary awe.

It's quite something – the blood moon. It's like a huge swollen mandarin in the sky, as if it's risen just for them. It feels exotically foreign and the atmosphere in the water is suddenly one of jubilation. A spontaneous howl breaks out. Claire howls too and then laughs.

She spots Tor and then sees Lotte in the water.

'My beautiful blondie,' Lotte says, effusively. Her hair is piled up in two bobbles on her head, like Minnie Mouse ears, and her copious eye make-up is running, but the joy radiates from her. 'Are you ready to go more daring? I was thinking that pink would suit you.'

'You've gone far enough. But it's definitely made me feel more confident,' Claire says. 'It took a while for my husband to notice, but he likes it too.'

'At least you *get* noticed,' Lotte says.

'What do you mean?'

'Nothing,' she says, glancing across to where Tor is laughing, greeting some other swimmers. 'It's just that it's hard being hidden away by someone you love. Like you're a dirty secret.'

'You're not a dirty secret, Lotte,' Claire says, shocked by this rare insight into Tor's relationship. 'You and Tor are great together.'

'Yeah, well, tell her that.'

They get split up and Claire turns away and heads for the

shore and she sees that Dominica has drifted with the others in the pull of the water. There's another group of swimmers and Claire suddenly sees that one of them is Jenna. She's laughing with her friends, but her smile fades when she sees Claire.

'Oh,' she says in a haughty way. 'It's you.'

'Hi Jenna,' Claire says. She tries to keep her voice neutral. 'I'm glad we got to see the moon.'

'Yes, well, I've seen the full moon loads of times before,' she says in a snotty way, as if Claire seeing it too has somehow spoilt it. How exhausting it must be, Claire thinks, to have to turn everything into a competition. 'I've done this loads of times.'

'Good for you,' Claire says. And suddenly she realises that she doesn't need to justify herself. She's not going to give Jenna what she wants – which is an opportunity to put her down. She's done with people-pleasing. She's never going to be Jenna's friend and that's OK. She remembers Pim saying that she was silly to reject Claire's friendship, and he'd been right. What a shame that Jenna can't see past herself to the community spirit of this swim. How sad that she's missed the whole point.

'You got your way about the tree. I hope you're satisfied,' Jenna calls after her.

Claire smiles and swims on.

On the beach, they get dressed, quickly pulling on their clothes in a haphazard way, and huddle around the camping light Tor has brought. Claire tells Dominica about seeing Jenna in the sea. She can't wait to tell Maddy about it.

'I nearly said something,' she confides to Dominica, 'but

you know what? There's no point. She'll never see our point of view. And so there's no point in arguing with her. I see that now. I'm so bloody glad Maddy got the council to shut her down; that she and Rob weren't able to bully their way into something that was going to have a negative impact on us, just because they wanted it.' She thinks of Sam, the robin. 'I'm so glad the tree is still there.'

'You did a good thing,' Dominica says.

Someone has lit a bonfire and the woody smoke mixed with the briny air reminds Claire of being on holiday. There's something very simple about being under the night sky that makes everything else fade away. She feels salty and tired, but in a wholesome way. All around, swimmers are huddling down to get warm, like the gulls who ruffle out their feathers and bed down on the stones. There's the murmur of voices and the occasional sprinkle of laughter.

Tor passes her a silver hipflask, and she takes a sip. Usually by ten, she's tucked up under the duvet, watching Netflix in bed, but now she's on the beach in the dark with loads of women drinking rum. It's making her feel more alive than she has done in months.

'Isn't this fun?' Claire says, passing around the box of the cake she's made.

'Oh, tell me it's your carrot cake.' Dominica grins and takes a big piece. 'I love your cakes.'

'Me too,' Tor says, grabbing a big piece too.

Claire smiles. It's lovely that her baking is so appreciated.

'It's a shame Helga didn't come.' Dominica frowns. 'I wonder what happened to her?'

'She's probably turned her nose up at the thought of

the crowds,' Tor says, but Claire isn't so sure. She's with Dominica. It's really weird that she hasn't turned up. Something is off. She can feel it. Because come to think of it, it was Tor who'd replied on the group chat saying they'd all be coming, when the post went up about the full moon swim, but had Helga actually replied herself? Claire is sure now that she hadn't.

They don't stay too long on the beach, as the after-drop is making everyone shiver. It's dark, the clouds obscuring the blood moon they'd glimpsed earlier, as they walk up the shingle to the promenade. Claire's shivering and it's very late, but even so, on a hunch, she takes a detour on the way home in the car to Helga's cottage.

There aren't any lights on inside. She knocks on the door, then she crouches down and nudges the letterbox flap, but Helga's place is empty. She stands up, feeling silly. She's just being nosy. Helga doesn't need to explain herself. What is she even doing snooping around here? She should just go home and warm up.

Claire is turning away when, just over the path, the door in the next cottage opens a crack. A woman is behind it, looking out suspiciously and Claire smiles, hoping she can help. She has a baby nestled against her chest and she puts her finger to her lips to signal Claire to be quiet. The baby is asleep and the woman, her hair in a messy ponytail and dressed in linen dungarees, looks beautiful in an exhausted kind of way. Claire smiles at her and the baby, noticing its cherubic pursed lips. Her stomach flips with a strange emotion. It's amazing to think that she was once a mother to newborns herself. It seems so long ago.

'I'm so sorry to disturb you. I'm looking for Helga,' Claire says.

The woman's tired eyes change now. 'You didn't hear?'

'Hear? Hear what?'

'We think Helga was attacked in the alley at the weekend. She certainly fell and had a heart attack. That's what they said when the ambulance came. She's still in hospital.'

41

The Unexpected Cwych

That night there are dozens of messages on the Sea-Gals WhatsApp chat between Tor, Maddy and Claire as they all express their upset and discuss what to do about Helga, but it's Dominica who is the first one to get through to the hospital the next morning.

She finds Helga's ward, but the sister explains that there are six beds in her bay and only one visitor is allowed per bay. And, if she does get a slot, she's only allowed to stay for an hour maximum. Dominica books her slot for the next day.

At the hospital on Friday, it's quite a rigmarole to get admitted to the ward. She has to put on gloves, an apron and a surgical mask and, seeing the staff trying to cope and do their jobs in their suffocating protective equipment, Dominica feels slightly ashamed for feeling so claustrophobic.

Whilst she's waiting to get onto the bay, she stands by the nurse's station. The young registrar is looking at her clipboard and Dominica asks her about Helga's diagnosis.

She asks if Dominica is a relative and, knowing this might be the only way to get information, she nods.

The registrar doesn't look as if she believes her but gives her the benefit of the doubt. She explains that after the incident when she fell in the alley, she had a heart attack, which had been coming for some time, judging from her bloods. The doctor is perplexed, though. She suspects that someone must have resuscitated Helga before the paramedics arrived. Helga is stable, but they're keeping her in for a bypass, the registrar explains. She's on the surgeon's emergency list and will be getting the op as soon as he can fit her in. She's lucky in a way, the registrar tells them. If Helga hadn't fallen, she'd never have got into the system and might have had to wait months and months for the op. Months that might have proved fatal.

Now, as Dominica approaches Helga's bedside and sits down, she looks anything but lucky. Her face is swollen on one side and there are stitches on her hairline from a nasty cut where she fell. She reaches out to hold Helga's hand and her plastic glove crinkles.

'Hey.' Helga smiles weakly. 'You came.'

'Oh, Helga. I'm so sorry. I would have come before. I can't bear it that you've been on your own,' Dominica says. She feels choked up.

'I've been well looked after. Besides, I couldn't contact you. It's so hazy, but I heard footsteps and then when I fell, someone had my bag and I couldn't stop them. There were two men and I called out and tried to move, but then my heart . . . there was so much pain and then . . . I can't remember much else.'

'Oh, Helga. I'm so sorry,' Dominica says. She remembers Helga getting out of the car with her bag on Saturday night.

'It's bad enough being in here and feeling so foolish for having fallen, but to be robbed when you're feeling that vulnerable feels doubly unfair. They took my phone. And my book.'

'Do the police have any leads?' she asks. 'Do they know who stole your bag?'

'I suspect it was the junkie on the corner. I've had words with him before. He probably wanted money.'

'Your next-door neighbours are really upset. Katie says if there's anything she can do to let her know. Will is getting the neighbourhood watch group to put up CCTV. They seemed pretty shaken up. They were the ones that found you.'

Helga nods. She's usually so strong and strident, but she seems crushed. Seeing her so vulnerable is horrible. 'What about Linus?' Dominica asks.

'They took my book,' Helga says, with a sad shrug. 'I put it in my bag, remember? Before I got out of the car.'

'Oh God. Oh, Helga. I'm so sorry. I'll try and find him,' Dominica reassures her.

'I don't know how you will, though. That's just the problem,' Helga says. 'And maybe it's for the best that you don't.'

Dominica tries to be cheerful and tells Helga about their full moon swim, but all too soon their time is up and she has to leave. She promises to come back and explains that the others are going to visit too. Helga smiles weakly at this, but Dominica can tell she's exhausted.

She asks Dominica to message Mette, her niece. 'There'll be hell to pay if she finds out I've been in hospital and she didn't know,' Helga says as Dominica writes notes in her phone. She hopes she's got the spelling right and she'll be able to find Mette's company.

She gets up to leave. Her overwhelming urge is to kiss Helga's forehead, but she's wearing a mask. It breaks her heart to leave her.

She walks to the end of the ward of beds and sees the nurse.

'I'm so glad I got to see her,' Dominica says to her. 'I didn't think I'd be able to.'

'You're lucky. It's been so hard on this ward,' the nurse says. She has beautiful eyes above her mask. 'But we're muddling through. Just bracing ourselves for another wave. I was in the Covid ward just before the first lockdown. It was so grim not knowing the scale of what we were facing. We were all terrified.'

'My partner, Chris, he was in that ward,' Dominica says. 'You weren't with him? Chris? Chris Barratt?'

'No, no, I don't think so.'

'He was a paramedic.'

She sees the nurse's eyebrows draw together. She stops.

'Oh, hang on . . . the paramedic guy? *That* Chris? I think I know . . . hang on.'

She walks back towards the nurse's station, leans over the desk and picks up a phone. 'Is Alison there?' Dominica hears her say.

She waits for a moment and then turns away and Dominica can't hear what she's saying.

Then she's coming back. 'My colleague, Alison. She's coming now. She wants to have a chat with you.'

Dominica waits by the door to the ward, watching the busy comings and goings of the staff, the clanking trolleys and the incessant beeping of machines. What can Alison tell her? Does she remember Chris?

It's been so hard to imagine him alone at the end. At night, when she can't sleep, she thinks of him in his hospital bed, alone and abandoned. She can't get past the guilt of it. But now she's here, she realises that Chris wouldn't have been thinking about home. When you're here, it's hard to imagine anywhere apart from these hospital walls.

The wooden ward door buzzes and a short nurse comes in. She squeezes some hand gel from the dispenser, then puts on a new apron and gloves. The nurse behind the desk nods over to where Dominica is standing. Her eyes twinkle in a friendly way.

'Are you Dominica?' she asks and Dominica nods. 'Then in that case, come here.' She opens her arms. Dominica is shocked to suddenly be in her embrace.

'It's against the rules, but I promised Chris I'd give you a . . . coo . . . a . . . kitch . . . ?'

'*Cwych?*' Dominica says, feeling choked up.

'That's it. He said a big cuddle. But it was so busy and, I'm sorry . . . '

'You were with him? With Chris?' Dominica asks, hardly able to believe she's having this conversation. Her heart is hammering.

'Yes, I was. He was a wonderful guy. So strong. So brave.'

He *was* strong and brave. It feels so comforting to know that Alison saw him and knew him. That this lovely nurse recognises how wonderful her Chris was feels vindicating somehow.

'I feel . . . ' Dominica says, her voice choking, 'just so bad about the end. It's all I've been able to think about.'

'I'm not surprised. It was bloody terrible for the loved

308

ones,' Alison says. She means it. 'But you have to know that we gave him all the pain relief we could and, unlike a lot of the others with Covid, he knew what was happening. He wasn't scared.'

'Wasn't he?'

'No, honestly, I was with him. The last thing he said was that he wanted to give you a cooch.'

'*Cwych*.' Dominica's voice breaks again and her nose fizzes with tears.

'And to tell you to move on and to be happy.'

'He said that?'

She nods and Dominica lets out a little sob.

Alison's buzzer bleeps. 'I'm sorry, I've got to go. But I'm so glad we finally got to meet.'

'Me too,' Dominica says. 'Me too. And . . . thank you.'

Dominica walks out of the ward and down the stairs and she throws away the mask and gloves in the sanitary bins. She walks straight out of the hospital and gets on her bike and rides down to the sea.

She doesn't have her stuff with her, but the urge to get in the water feels too overwhelming. The beach on this side of the pier is wide and she leaves her bike on the stones and walks down to the water in the sunshine. She doesn't care who's watching. She strips off until she's in her vest and pants and, keeping her sockettes on to stop her feet from hurting, she walks straight into the water.

The waves are bouncy and crisp, but she doesn't care as she gasps at the cold, the surf breaking over her waist and filling her face with water as she splashes through it. She swims towards the horizon, then flips onto her back, her skin tingling all over. And now the tears come. Big, gasping tears – although she can't tell if they're happy or sad.

Because Chris wasn't alone when he died. Alison was holding his hand. Hearing the selflessness of his last words only makes her love him more, but it's also lifted some of the guilt she's been carrying – about her being the one to live, when he had died. Somehow, hearing about his last moments has made him feel more alive and real than he's been in her mind for months. The *cwych* from beyond the grave has given her strength.

'I will carry on,' she says aloud. 'I will, Chris. I promise.'

42

Caught Out

Maddy and Matteo have been in and out of each other's apartments since she came back from Cobham and they slept together that first night. She's unsure what exactly is going on between them, but the sex is amazing. It's feels so exotic to be having such an unexpected affair that she often finds she's giggling to herself.

Matteo comes up now from underneath his duvet and grins at her. She has to hand it to him: he's great at giving head.

'That was possibly the best way to start my birthday,' she says. 'Thank you.'

He kisses her. 'I have to go to work,' he says, 'but I'll come back at lunchtime. Shall we picnic in the park?'

She watches as he gets up and puts on the shower, then, smiling, she gets up and joins him and they make love in the steam. So much for being menopausal, she thinks. Her libido seems to have returned with a vengeance.

When he's gone, she goes back to her apartment and puts out the message for the others to join her for a birthday swim.

Then she goes online, seeing if there's any emails about Jamie. She hoped when she woke up this morning that today would be the day. Finding him, after all, is the only present she wants.

She arrives at the beach in a good mood, but it's weird without Helga, and when Dominica recounts how vulnerable she was at the hospital, Maddy feels terrible. Claire has brought a cake to celebrate her birthday, but they're all rather subdued and she doesn't tell them about how glorious her time with Matteo has been. It feels too cheeky. Too indulgent.

She meets Matteo at twelve and they stroll to the sandwich shop. Usually on her birthday, she has lunch in a swanky restaurant in town with Lisa and her friends, but this feels just as lovely.

When they get to the park with their brown paper bag full of lunch, the horse chestnuts are in full bloom and Luna gives chase to a baby squirrel. They choose a patch of grass and Matteo lays out his jacket in the daisies for Maddy. She unwraps the sandwiches they've bought.

Matteo's tanned hairy legs are stretched out in front of him. She flips off her shoes and crosses her feet and rocks them towards his.

'Are you OK?' she asks. 'You seem quiet.'

'I wasn't going to tell you, but it's been confirmed this morning.'

'What has?'

'The start date for the teaching job.'

She knows that this has been coming. She's known all along that he'd be leaving, but she hadn't expected it to hurt like this. 'Wow, that's great,' she manages, but she feels tearful.

'I know. But it's going to be hard.'

She nods and swallows down her tears. It's ridiculous to be upset when she should be pleased for him. This is what he wants. But even so, she knows that this is the start of the end of 'them'.

She leans over and kisses him and it feels more bittersweet than any of the times she's kissed him before. She feels him responding and she pulls away, knowing they must look like teenagers to everyone else with him almost on top of her.

'Let's go,' he whispers, his eyes burning into hers and she nods, answering their question.

They both race up the stairs to their floor as they get back to the apartment building. Matteo lets Luna scamper ahead and stops at the top of the stairs, where he presses Maddy against the wall and kisses her and she wraps her leg around his. He's already got his hand inside her T-shirt.

'Wait,' she giggles, running around the corner to their corridor.

But she stops, with a gasp.

Trent is standing by her door. He's carrying a bouquet of pink roses. The same kind that she had in her wedding bouquet. How much has he seen? How much has he heard?

Matteo hasn't got the message and Maddy yelps away from his next ticklish play. She pushes her hair behind her ear as she tries to walk calmly towards Trent, but her knees are shaking.

Trent is dressed in skinny jeans and a seersucker jacket, the sleeves rolled up, like he's from that old show, *Miami Vice*. She knows this outfit has been chosen for him by Steve, who runs Paynes in town, the designer shop where Trent gets most of his outfits. He rarely wears the same thing twice. But here, next to Matteo in his leather sandals and faded cargo shorts and ancient T-shirt, he seems overdressed and squeaky clean. He stares at Maddy and then at Matteo, his mouth falling open with shock.

'Trent,' she says. 'This is a surprise.'

'I found out your address from the Amazon account.' He says this as if he's cleverly caught her out. She hears the questions in his tone. His eyes dart towards Matteo and she knows she needs to tread carefully. She can already see the colour rising in Trent's cheeks.

She hasn't exactly been keeping her location a secret from Trent, but she's surprised he's bothered to track her down.

'This is Matteo,' Maddy says, introducing Trent. She squirms inside with embarrassment as Trent stares at him with unfiltered fury.

'I'll see you later,' Matteo says, his eyes locking with hers as he gets his key out and opens the door to his apartment, but she's acutely aware that Trent is absorbing it all.

'You'd better come in.' She opens the apartment door.

Trent looks at her and the piles of boxes behind her, but he doesn't step over the threshold.

'I was coming here to . . . ' he begins. 'And you've been shagging the next-door neighbour?' There's colour in his cheeks as he points in Matteo's direction. '*Him? He's a child.*'

'He's forty,' she says, defensively. 'Anyway, you have no right to judge me.'

Maddy resents being told off like this when he's been the one having an affair. She's also painfully aware that Matteo must be able to hear every word. Trent always did have a voice that carried, and the walls are paper-thin. She's got used to him being in a detached house, which can accommodate his large personality, but everything about his presence feels wrong in here in the shabby apartment block – like a shark that has just cruised onto a reef.

'Why are you here?'

His eyes blaze and he runs his tongue around his teeth, as if he's weighing up whether to tell her or not.

'I . . . ' he begins. 'Fuck!'

'What? Just tell me.'

He looks cornered and she knows him well enough to know that his plan has crashed.

'I was going to tell you that I've heard that the money is coming through from the sale. We could split it, but after I've paid back the loan, it might be better to use the rest of it to rent. Together. We could make it work, I'm sure. And I've found a house. It's right near a pool so you can carry on swimming.'

Christ, he has a thick skin, Maddy thinks. Has he forgotten that it's over between them? Or has it just dawned on him that he needs her half of the money in order to be able to afford to live somewhere near his mistress? And what about Helen? Does she know he's here on this ridiculous mission? Because is he seriously expecting her to live with him, after what he's done? Does he think that a bunch of roses will turn them into friends? That a smelly swimming pool will be a big enough draw? It's not until he's suggested this, that she realises that she's going to stay by the sea. No matter what.

Right now she has no money, but she's going to get whatever is left and make a new life for herself. Somehow. She'll make it work. On her own terms.

'Trent. I'm really not sure what you expect me to say.'

'Do you love him?' he asks. 'Just tell me the truth?'

His foot taps nervously like Jamie's used to do when he was cornered. It's typical of Trent to turn this into some male macho thing. Matteo has nothing to do with this.

'No,' she says, but she's blushing.

He yanks open the door and stalks out. He hears him slap Matteo's door.

'She doesn't love you, mate,' he calls out. 'But that's because she's a heartless bitch.'

She watches from the door as he throws the roses on the floor and stamps on them, then he walks away. Maddy stares after him, astounded that she hadn't realised before how emotionally immature Trent is. Because he's been so childish, his plans so ill thought through.

The thought rings out in her head. A kind of an epiphany. *She's better off without him*.

It's a shock, but she knows she'll come out of the end of their marriage in one piece. She might not have found Jamie, but she knows she's going to survive. And that's the best birthday present she could have.

43

Shallow Water

The weather gets steadily better all week, until by the weekend, it's a scorching June day. Claire can't believe the scene on the seafront when she arrives to meet Tor for a swim. Maddy is busy helping Matteo pack up his apartment and Dominica has gone to see her sister-in-law for the day. Pim and the boys are glued to their game with the curtains shut. Despite the crowds, it's a relief to be out of the house.

'Jesus, look at all the people,' Tor says, as she arrives, kissing Claire on the cheek.

The bandstand café is packed, whilst above it on the bandstand itself, there's a salsa group dancing, the couples gyrating to the Latin music. They pass a gang of students playing a frenzied game of ping-pong on the public tables, and a girl in sequinned hotpants circles in an elegant *plié*, oblivious to the teenage boys who are attempting parkour between the concrete walls. Longboarders zoom past and the playground is packed with screeching toddlers splashing in the paddling pool. Parents drink pints as they lean against the fence around the edge. Brazen seagulls peck at the rubbish spilling out of the bins.

They cross the ambling crowds to the beach, but there's no way they'll be able to get anywhere near their usual spot. There are people on every inch of the pebbles, all of them in various states of undress. Claire knows she's going to have to share the beach with the tourists now for the rest of the summer, but she hates seeing such a big crowd.

This is *her* patch of paradise but seeing the faces of the people basking in the sun and staring at the water, she can't begrudge them the collective joy of being near the sea. The air is thick with the waft of barbecue smoke, the sound of beer cans opening, reggae coming from a sound system.

There's a wide expanse of sand, reflecting the sunshine. She squints, watching a couple of dogs bound joyfully over it. Further out, there's plenty of paddleboarders and a couple of jet-skiers churning up the water past the buoys.

They find a spot where the pebbles stop and the sand starts, knowing they have a while before the tide turns.

'It's weird to be going in without gloves. I never thought I'd miss the cold water,' Tor says, 'but I really do.'

'Me too. I'm glad Helga isn't here. She'd hate these crowds.'

'How is she? Do you know?'

'Getting better, I think, according to Maddy,' Claire says, switching her phone off and putting it in the tow float with her keys. Tor does the same. Now it's so crowded, they can't leave valuables on the beach. 'They say her surgery went well.'

'Is she still being a good patient?' Tor asks. 'She was complaining when I went in.'

'I hope they let her out soon,' Claire says. 'It's driving her nuts.'

The sun is belting down and she knows that the crepey skin on her chest is burning. She frowns at Tor and they both pull a face at how awful it is now that there are so many people in the water. They stride in further and then Claire gives up when the water is thigh deep and starts swimming. They both swim right out and don't stop until they get to the buoy.

By the time they get there, Claire is out of breath, but it's good to swim and it's good to be away from the crowds.

'Oh, I needed that,' Tor says, leaning back in the water. Her hair floats around her. She reminds Claire of the famous painting of Ophelia, her hair spread out in the water. 'It's been a tough week.'

'Oh?'

'Lotte.'

'What's going on?'

Tor explains that they've been scratchy and tense with each other. 'It's the usual thing. She's cross about me not talking about us to my family. But she doesn't understand.'

Claire thinks back to Lotte and what she said about not being noticed. 'You know, I remember when Pim and I got together, he wouldn't tell his family about me. It really upset me. I just wanted to be accepted, you know?'

'And did they accept you?'

'Eventually. But it took a while. It made things really tense between me and Pim, until I realised that even if they hadn't, it wouldn't have mattered.'

'Why?'

'Because Pim was adamant that he didn't care how they

felt. That what we had was bigger for him. He was happy to sacrifice his family for me.'

'He was?'

'Yes. And actually, it was seeing that love and how he felt that brought his family round.'

As they swim together, Claire thinks that she hasn't thought back to those early days for so long. She'd struggled so hard to come to terms with his family's rejection, not just of her, but of Pim, who she knew it had hurt far more. But Pim had been steadfast and true and had stood by her and he'd turned things round. His love had been so strong. So noble. It still is, she thinks. Just a bit covered in dust.

'You know, if you love Lotte, then you have to make it official,' Claire says. 'Because they might surprise you . . . your family.'

'Graham will be horrible. He's my idiot of a brother-in-law.'

'So? Who cares what he thinks?'

'Alice does.'

'But she'll care more about you and how you feel. I've got two sisters and the one thing I know is that our relationships are complex and ever moving, but the love is there. Alice will only want that at the end of the day.'

Tor takes a moment to consider this. 'Maybe. I'm so used to thinking about Graham and how much I hate him, but you're right. The sister thing is complex. And actually, when the chips have been down, Alice has always been there for me.'

'So give her the benefit of the doubt,' Claire says and Tor nods.

They swim on towards the shore, but suddenly, something brushes Claire's stomach.

'Oh my God,' she says with a yelp.

'What?'

'There's something . . . ' Claire stops and let out a snort of laughter. She puts her hands down, realising that she's beached herself. 'I thought . . . I thought I was being attacked by a fish, but look.' She stands up. The water is ankle-deep. They both crack up laughing.

They're still smiling as they get back to their stuff and Tor gets her phone out of the rolled-up float to take a picture to send to the group, but she frowns when she turns it on.

'Three missed calls,' she says. 'That's weird.'

'Who are they from?'

Claire watches her as she stares at the screen. 'What is it?'

'Home Help has been nominated for a Community Heroes award.'

'Tor, that's fabulous,' Claire says.

'Oh my God, I can't believe it!'

'Well, you deserve it.' Claire hugs her and Tor lets out a squeak of excitement. It's wonderful to see her so happy. She wants to tell her that they've nominated her, but she'll wait until the others are there.

'I've got to tell Lotte,' Tor says.

'Go on then.'

Tor calls her number, but Lotte doesn't pick up. 'Oh, I can't bear it. I really want to tell her.'

'I reckon this calls for a celebration,' Claire says. 'Let's get the gang together and go to the pub.'

They hug again.

'Oh my God, I just can't believe it,' Tor says again. She can't keep the grin from her face.

When Claire gets home, she's still thinking about her encounter with Tor, and she goes to find Pim in the living room. He's marking and he barely acknowledges her when she comes in.

'Can I talk to you?' she asks.

'What about?' He flicks over another page.

She walks over and shuts the folder in front of him. 'Hey,' he complains, frowning. 'I was reading that.' He folds his arms defensively. 'I'm listening. What is it?'

'Well, it's about the way we communicate.'

'Communicate?' he asks, as if checking that she knows the meaning of the word. She ignores his intonation, which is usually the thing that scuppers her.

'I want us to chat about the things that are important.'

'We chat all the time.'

'Do we?' She stares at his familiar face, seeing the surprise registering. He shifts in his chair uncomfortably. 'Because I don't think we do. I mean, in all honesty, I don't know how you feel about me, or this marriage.'

She hasn't meant to say something so big – so profound. It feels like she's treading on sacred turf, asking him to discuss their marriage, but now that she's said it, it feels like she's switched a light on in a forgotten room.

'What? What on earth makes you say that?'

'A lot of things.'

'Like what?'

Claire sits down on the chair next to him.

'Like . . . I don't know. When was the last time we had a conversation – just the two of us – that wasn't something to do with our domestic arrangements?' He looks startled. 'And

I'm not blaming you. I guess you're probably feeling lonely and isolated too.'

'You're lonely?' he checks. 'But we're together all the time.'

'Are we, though? Because, if I'm honest, I've been feeling a bit lost. Like I'm invisible.'

'But you're not. You look after us all.'

'Exclusively. I shop and cook and clean, but it feels like half the time I'm a domestic slave whilst you get to work and then play Fortnite the rest of the time.'

'I was just trying to keep the boys occupied.' He's defensive and she sighs.

This isn't going as she'd hoped. She's just come across as jealous. But then she remembers what Dominica said: that all emotions are valid and that she has to own them. She's not going to apologise. Even so, she's annoyed that she's brought it down to specifics, when she was trying to have a chat about the bigger picture. She's determined to persevere.

'And what about you?' she asks.

'What about me?'

'From your point of view? What's been going wrong?'

'Wrong?'

'Well, come on. We're not firing on all cylinders, are we? Not like we could. Not like we used to.'

He sighs. 'You seem . . . I don't know. Distant. I've been wanting to give you space. You're hard to cuddle at night.'

'I know,' she says. 'It's these hormones. It's the menopause.'

'Aren't you getting HRT?'

'I might, but I want to try other things first. But this is all bigger than my body changes.'

'What is?' Pim is confused. 'Just tell me what you're trying to say.'

'Well, I've been thinking a lot lately. I'm entering the second half of my life. I love you and I love our boys, but I want more. I want to feel fulfilled. I want my life to mean something. I want to help people and do things and make a difference. Not just clear up after you lot.'

She hasn't said what she wants out loud for so long, it feels scary, but exhilarating too. Like she's on a water slide and she can't stop.

'And I want to feel respected. As a woman. Because, in this house, I feel undermined all the time and I don't want to be shouted down. I want us to parent better together because I can't bear clashing with you.'

She's shaking. Pim stands up, taking all of this in, but he doesn't say anything.

'You've been bottling all this up?'

She nods.

'Anything else?'

'Yes,' she says, standing up too. It's now or never. She has to get it all out. 'You know we haven't spontaneously snogged for . . . for so long, I can't remember when it was. You used to kiss me all the time. Even when the boys were little.'

She feels fluttery inside, saying these words. His eyes are large and focused on her.

'And I'm not blaming you. I'm to blame too, but life got in the way, didn't it, and we stopped trying?'

She feels the tears she longs to shed choking her, but she's determined not to break down. A stray tear falls anyway, and she swipes at it, angrily.

'Claire,' Pim says, gently.

'And I don't want to get emotional about this stuff. I don't want you to think that I'm just some menopausal, hormonal mess. Because I might be that at times, but I'm not all the time. And certainly not now. I'm just trying to tell you how I feel and it's hard, because I haven't told you for so long.'

'I'm sorry.' He walks towards her. 'I had no idea.'

'You must feel it too? That we've drifted away from *us*. That we've drifted away from what made us so great. Because we were great, Pim. Really great.'

'I know.' He's standing in front of her now and she sees that he's hearing her.

'I get that there's been a pandemic, and everyone has found everything hard,' she says, 'but I don't want us to lose each other.'

'Neither do I.' He holds her hands and rubs the wedding band around her finger. 'How do we fix it?'

'By talking. By making plans. Discussing dreams.'

'I don't know if I have any dreams any more. I feel like they've been beaten out of me.'

'Then let's make some. Let's do what we used to do and think about all the things we could be. And how we live our life so we grow together, not apart.'

He nods. 'I'd like that. But I'm worried that I've forgotten how.'

She touches his face. 'You haven't forgotten. You're Pim. My dreamer.'

And, as she stares into his eyes, she sees how vulnerable he is and how scared and she understands the barriers they've both put up, just to get through the terror of the world changing around them. But this is her Pim – the man who was prepared to turn his back on his own family for love. He's her rock and she might have drifted away from him, but now she feels the pull of him stronger than ever.

She steps towards him and he folds her into his embrace.

'I've missed you,' he whispers and suddenly her tummy flips in anticipation because she knows he's about to kiss her.

Behind them the door opens and Pim pauses. It's Ash.

'Gross,' Ash says, staring at them.

Pim gives him a look and he backs through the door, which Pim reaches out to kick shut with his foot.

'Now where was I?'

He pulls her into his arms again and then his lips are on hers. They are tentative at first and then they properly kiss and it feels like a first kiss. A teenage kiss. A kiss that's been filmed in slow motion for the good bit of a movie.

'God, you're right. Why haven't we snogged? We're so good at it,' he whispers.

'I know,' she says. 'I know.'

44

From The Pier

In the loo at the Samaritans, Dominica is putting on mascara for the first time in over a year for the Sea-Gals night out, although it won't be the same without Helga who is still recuperating but in good spirits. Dominica has talked several times to Helga's niece, Mette, who wants to come over, but Helga has strictly forbidden it.

Dominica understands Mette's frustration, but she also understands why Helga wants her to stay away. She is full of plans to 'solve' Helga, like she's a problem. She's determined to get her back to Denmark for a start. Shouldn't Helga have a choice in the matter? Mette's view of Helga and Dominica's couldn't be more different. She can't help feeling that if Helga's niece ever got in the sea and saw her aunt in action, she'd think differently. But then, as Dominica has been reminded from doing this volunteering, families are often places where people don't see each other at all.

She surveys herself in her tiny compact mirror, trying to wipe away the smudge. She used to be so good at putting on make-up, when she and Chris used to go out all the time. She thinks about the couples they used to do the pub quiz with, who have drifted away over the past year. Back then, she used to be queen of the quick turnaround. As she got home from work, she could be changed and in full make-up in ten minutes. She prided herself on her decisiveness, but clearly that skill has gone right out of the window. She can't even control a mascara wand.

It's only a night out at the pub, but she went through four outfit changes before cycling here for her shift. The problem is that there are so many clothes that remind her of Chris. Going through her wardrobe was like time travelling. There's quite a few that need to go to the charity shop and she's made a pile that she's left in the middle of the bedroom floor. She's not looking forward to sorting out that lot after the pub. But at least she's made a start.

She gets back to her cubicle and quickly looks at her watch and then at Bill. It's twenty past nine and only another ten minutes until the end of her shift and maybe he won't mind if she slips off now. She thinks of the others in the pub and how much she is looking forward to chatting to them and celebrating Tor's news. But Stuart, the next volunteer taking over her shift is late, although he should be here any second.

She stares at the console, knowing there are calls stacking up, knowing there are desperate people waiting. She knows it's a risk to flick her status to available, but she knows it's the right thing to do. One more call can't hurt, although conversations at this time of night are rarely short.

There's a young guy on the other end and he says hello and then he's silent. Dominica can hear seagulls in the background. He's calling from outside. That's never a good sign.

She listens and then she hears the caller sob. She's used to people ringing up in tears and she gives the caller space before she speaks.

'Can you tell me a bit about what's making you sad?' she asks.

'Everything.'

'I'm sorry to hear that.'

'You don't understand.'

'I'd like to, though . . . '

'Everything . . . everything is fucked.'

'It's OK. We all get overwhelmed sometimes. Where are you? You sound like you're outside?' she asks.

'I'm on the pier.'

She picks up her pen and pad to make some notes. Mostly the calls are anonymous, and they're encouraged not to enquire about names or locations. Locations don't really matter, since the calls all go through a national number, so she gets callers from all over the country. She's had callers from abroad too. Despair knows no physical boundaries. It's everywhere.

Dominica looks at her watch. She knows that most piers close in the evenings – those that are still open.

'I like piers. There's one in Brighton,' she says.

'That's where I am,' the guy says.

Dominica's pen stops moving on the page. 'You mean, you're on the Palace Pier?'

There's a long silence. Dominica can hear the sea more clearly now. 'It's . . . I can see the water . . . just it's so dark . . . '

Her heart rate jumps. Is he looking down into the water? Because if he is, he must be either leaning over the railings, or be on the wrong side of them altogether.

'Is anyone with you?' she asks, forcing her tone to stay calm.

'No.'

He lets out a little sob and Dominica grips the phone. She mustn't lose him. She must keep him talking.

'Will you tell my mum . . . tell her, I'm sorry,' he says.

Dominica feels the hairs on the back of her neck stand up. She stands, holding the phone with both hands. She's heard this kind of desperation before. She has to keep calm. She looks desperately across at Bill, but he's in the other booth, his back turned to her.

'Can you tell me about your mum?'

'She's . . . '

He stops talking and she can hear the sea suddenly loud, the seagulls crying.

'How would you feel about speaking to her yourself?'

'It's too late.'

Dominica can hear the desperation in his voice. 'This was never meant to happen. I was supposed to . . . '

'Supposed to . . . ?'

'She wanted so much for me, but I fucked it all up. I fucked it up and there was no way back. And . . . '

'OK, I get that you're upset, but we can sort this out. Slow down a minute . . . '

'Just tell her . . . tell her, Jamie says sorry.'

'Jamie?' Dominica feels her heart thudding. It can't be . . . it can't be Maddy's Jamie, can it? 'Is that your name? That's a really nice name.'

She knows she's not supposed to ask, but she does before she can help herself. 'What's your surname, Jamie?'

'Wolfe. My mum is . . . ' He gulps. It's like a sob. 'Maddy.'

It's him.

It's Maddy's Jamie. *Shit, oh shit, oh shit . . .*

Dominica pictures Jamie on the pier looking down into the dark water and her heart thuds so loudly, she can feel it in her ears.

He's alive.

But he's in danger.

She looks at Bill who now faces her and will be able to read her expression, so she quickly turns away, trying to think. She knows that if this is as serious as she thinks it is and that Jamie might be a danger to himself, she has to pass it up the line. Bill will need to call the police and the coastguard, but, instead, she takes her mobile out of her back pocket. Silently she presses the WhatsApp icon. She knows it's against every rule, against every protocol. She knows that she might be asked to step down as a volunteer after this, but she can't help herself.

'Urgent.' She types to the Sea-Gals chat. 'Am on call with Jamie. He's on the pier. NOW. Get help.'

And then she presses send.

45

Taking Flight

The bartender comes over to their table with another bottle of wine, replacing the one in the cooler on the wooden table, but Tor isn't keeping track. She feels fuzzy and drunk and happy. It's so lovely to be out in a pub, where there's happy chatter coming from the other tables. The sky has darkened and the string of pub lights twinkle between the trees. Maddy and Claire clink glasses with her and Tor feels a rush of affection for her friends. Maddy looks amazing in a blue jacket and a lovely necklace and she hardly recognised Claire when she first came in earlier. She's wearing flattering jeans and a floaty top that shows off her impressive cleavage. She looks sexy and at least ten years younger than when Tor first met her. Lotte's hair style really suits her and Claire has blow-dried it especially for tonight. She certainly turned a few heads when she came in earlier. When Tor asked her what her secret was, Claire replied that Helga had been right and all she'd needed was a good shag, and they all fell about laughing. She's been regaling them with stories of how she and Pim first met. Tor can't remember her being so animated and fun.

They've just poured more wine, when Maddy and Claire's phones ping at the same time. This will probably be Dominica telling them she's on her way, Tor thinks. It's a shame she missed the first bottle.

Tor realises that her phone is vibrating too. She picks it up and reads the message from Dominica and her smile fades.

'Oh God,' she says, reading her message.

Maddy is reading it too, already getting up. She knocks over her wine. 'Oh . . . oh . . . '

'She's got Jamie. Oh . . . oh!' Claire says, putting her hand over her mouth. She stares up at Maddy who lets out a little yelp. The atmosphere around them changes, the other people in the pub turning to their table.

'Keep calm,' Tor says, seeing her about to lose it.

'Oh my God, oh my God,' Maddy cries. She's shaking.

'Listen, we've got to act quickly,' Tor says.

Claire looks as if she's sobered up very quickly. 'I'll call the coastguard.'

'I'll call the police,' Maddy says. 'And a cab . . . I need a cab . . . a cab . . . ' Her voice has risen hysterically.

'I'm going now,' Tor says. 'Right now. I'll see you there.'

Tor has Lotte's bike with her and even before Maddy has got through to the police, she's already hotfooting it to the pier. She's hoping Maddy will be ahead of her, but she's the first to arrive at the entrance to the pier, with its boarded up food vendors and big black gates.

Where the hell is the security when you need it? Tor thinks, getting off her bike and rattling the gates. The pier is closed and there's no one around.

'Hello? Anyone?' she shouts through the gaps, but the pier is dark. 'Shit.'

She looks for a way onto the pier, but here, from the front, there's no way. She goes past the telephone box, quickly locking up her bike to the balustrade and racing down the steps. The pier looks huge, rising out of the sea on a lattice of black metal. The Palace Pier lights are off, only a few security lights eerily lighting up the dome and the silhouettes of the rides at the end. She runs down the rest of the steps to beach level.

She's going to have to climb up. She clambers onto the nearest hut, then on all fours, across the roof of the next building. She's going to have to stretch it, but she crosses the gap and her fingers find the edge of the pier. *Thank God her fingers are working today and she's not in the middle of a flare-up.*

'Don't look down,' she tells herself, dangling precariously in mid-air for a moment.

Then she's on the pier and swinging over the railing. She's sweating and panting as her feet touch down on the wooden boards. She waves up at the CCTV cameras. Hopefully someone is watching. Hopefully someone can help.

She checks the WhatsApp again. Is Dominica still talking to Jamie? She messages to say she's here. Dominica texts back straight away: 'He's at the end, I think.'

Tor sprints along the gang plank. It always makes her feel queasy, looking down the gaps between the boards to the sea below. It's eerily quiet, the white doughnut stalls ghostly in the dark. The bellies of the gulls are white against the sky.

A yellow moon throws a runway of light across the dark sea below. She runs past the lurid front of the ghost house, past the roller coaster and the waltzers, but there's no sign of Jamie. She stands by the end ride – the giant yellow arm towering above her. Where is he?

'Jamie?' she calls out, but there's hardly any wind. Her voice sounds loud and flat and she knows it hasn't carried. Only the cries of the gulls come back.

She runs the other way, past the trampolines and the log flume, her eyes scanning the gaps. She's panting now and she's frightened.

Please God, let her find him.

She sets off past the coin kiosk and the Dolphin Derby – and then something catches her eye. Over by the carousel, there's a telescope and she can see the shadow of a figure next to it. There's a person sitting on the top of the railings, facing out to sea.

She approaches cautiously. She can see that it's a man. He's holding a phone to his ear beneath the hood of his cotton zip top. It's him. It must be him.

'Jamie?'

He turns as Tor approaches. He has straggly long hair, his face not fully stubbly. His eyes look hollowed out. He looks vaguely familiar.

She's behind him now and his hips are so thin, he looks like a shadow, like he could just slip away and float like speck of soot.

She stops, scared he'll fall. 'Jamie,' she repeats.

'How do you know my name?'

'Just come back over and I'll explain,' Tor says, calmly,

although her heart is pounding. She holds out a hand to him, to come back to safety on the other side of the railings.

She can tell that she's confused him. He looks at the phone and then at Tor, as if he can't connect the two. And why would he?

'Please, just come back this side. And we can talk,' Tor says, but now, up close, she can see the terror in his face. He looks like Maddy, she thinks, seeing the resemblance and she just wants to grab him and hug him and keep him safe until she gets here. She wants him to know how much they've longed to find him and she smiles, still holding out her hand, but he shakes his head. He drops his phone, which falls by Tor's feet.

'It's OK. It's OK, I've got it.' Tor bends down to retrieve the cheap phone, but at that moment, her attention is caught by Maddy who now arrives, running breathlessly up the gang-plank with a security guard behind her.

'Jamie!' she screams. 'Jamie!'

'Mum?'

Tor sees Jamie register Maddy for a split second. He reaches out, but he loses his balance on the railing and, suddenly, he's gone.

'No!' Maddy howls.

She runs over to Tor, who springs up and leans over the balustrade. Way below there's a splash. Tor leans right over the edge, her eyes scanning the water in the dark, waiting for Jamie to come up.

'Oh God,' she says. 'Oh God, no . . . '

Tor turns to Maddy, but she's already scrambling up onto the balustrade.

'Hold this,' she says, shrugging off her jacket.

336

'Maddy, wait,' Tor urges, trying to restrain her, but Maddy brushes her off.

'What are you doing?' It's the security guard, with a flashlight, running towards them.

'I can't lose him again,' Maddy says. 'I can't, Tor.'

'No!' Tor cries, but it all happens in a split second.

Maddy has taken flight.

46

Eels

There's long enough during the time that she's falling through the air for Maddy to register the barnacle-encrusted black ironwork under the pier and for her to remember Helga's stories about the eels that live in the water. And then she hits the water with a thump so hard it's like hitting a wall.

She's under the water for ages and she kicks furiously to the surface. Her lungs are screaming as she comes up and gasps for air. It's freezing, and she's hyperventilating, but she hardly feels it. One of her sandals slips off as she's lifted up on the swell.

'Jamie,' she shouts, as soon as she can get her breath back, but she sucks in sea water and she gasps and coughs. Her hair is in her eyes and she brushes it away. 'Jamie?'

The moonlit sea seems vast and dark. She's never felt tinier – or more afraid. Her body is fizzing with adrenaline and her teeth are chattering as she scans the water.

She becomes vaguely aware of someone shouting in the distance and she looks up to see Tor and the security guy she'd outrun leaning over the railings. Tor is shouting, but Maddy can't make out the words. The security guard throws down an orange life ring and she swims over to it, grabbing it with difficulty.

Tor is screaming louder now but she can only hear it faintly, but she's pointing and Maddy follows her outstretched arm and for a split second, she thinks she can see a hand above the surface of the water, but in an instant her view is obscured by the swell.

She swims, kicking off her other sandal so that she can go faster, dragging the buoyancy float and then she sees bubbles on the surface of the water and, taking a deep breath, goes under, groping in the dark, her eyes open, burning in the salt water. She comes up again, choking and spluttering, but beneath her, her bare foot touches something. There's something – or someone below her. She goes under again, her ears in agony with the pressure, but she forces herself deeper, her arms outstretched, groping as she internally prays. Please let it be him. And this time she feels something that feels like hair, but it's too late. She has to breathe.

She comes up for air, rearing out of the water, her lungs screaming and she treads water for a moment, then gathering herself, she goes back down again.

It's Jamie. It must be Jamie.

She's fighting against the current and she can't see anything, apart from a dark shadow, then clawing around, she catches hold of cloth? A hoodie?

She yanks with all her might.

She's got him.

It takes all she has to get below him and push him upwards, up and up through the dark swell, and she's reminded of giving birth to him, that all-consuming need to push. As if her life depended on it. She's screaming underwater with the effort and she doesn't think she's going to make it, but then she breaks the surface, gasping for air and swallowing seawater and coughing, her strained lungs on fire. Jamie slips away from her and she grabs onto the float, hauling it under his arms and flopping his body over the top. His eyes are closed. His lips are blueish in the faint light.

'No,' she cries. 'No . . . no . . . no . . . '

She smacks his cheek. 'Jamie. Jamie! Wake up.'

He slips again under the surface of the water. She can't hold him.

She can't save him.

She's panicking now, furiously kicking, trying to keep him afloat.

She hears the sound of a boat and she's blinded as a light shines directly at her face. Then she hears Claire shouting.

'Maddy! Maddy! She's over there.'

The engine of the boat cuts out and then she hears the voices of the two lifeguards. They both lean over the side of the large inflatable boat and Jamie is being wrenched from her grasp. They haul him up and over the large orange side. She grabs on to the rope, choking on the water as the waves splash her. Then she feels strong arms grab her too and, in a second, she's slithering into the bottom of the lifeboat beside Jamie.

'You got him,' Claire says, crouching down next to him. 'You got him.'

'Jamie,' Maddy croaks, seeing her boy lifeless and still next to her.

'Move aside,' the lifeguard demands, and Claire pulls Maddy into her embrace as she wails in despair.

47

Facing Facts

Helga sleeps fitfully, but she's woken by a banging on the door. For a moment, she doesn't know where she is and then she remembers that she's home and stares at the ceiling, trying to make sense of the last few days. She gets up, surprised to find that she isn't dizzy. She doesn't hold on to the bannister in the same way either as she goes downstairs.

It's only now that she realises how much she's been compensating for her undiagnosed heart condition – deliberately not admitting that there'd been a problem to herself. Or anyone else. Mette had given her a right dressing-down on the phone about how scared Helga had made her. In a rare show of emotion, she'd started crying.

'I was so scared,' she'd said in a small voice that had made Helga think of her as a child and how she used to have night terrors. 'You're all I've got.'

Helga knows this isn't true. She's got her good-for-nothing father, but Helga used the opportunity to say something to Mette that she hasn't had the courage to before.

'I don't want to be all you've got,' she'd told her niece. 'You must find someone of your own. You must stop being scared of love.'

'I'm not,' Mette had said tearfully. 'I just haven't had time.'

'Then make time. For me. Promise me.'

And Mette had promised that she'd make more of an effort.

Helga can't imagine she'll have a problem finding someone with her intelligence, her looks and money being the icing on the cake. Mette's promised Helga she'll keep her posted on her forays into dating, although Helga can't bear the thought of those terrible dating apps and her being exposed to all sorts of crazy people. She's told Mette to do something out of the ordinary, something she loves. Because that way, she'll meet the right person and, for once in her life, Mette has taken her advice and booked a walking holiday.

It's Dominica at the door. She's grinning behind a big bouquet of flowers. She flings her arms around Helga and embraces her and Helga wants to cry. It's so good see her without her being covered in all that hideous plastic PPE.

'I called the ward and they said you'd come home. This is easier without all those damned masks,' Dominica says.

Helga is so touched that her swimming friends have looked out for her. She couldn't believe it when she got home earlier in the cab and there was a flask of soup waiting for her and a cake from Claire and the house had been cleaned and her bed freshly made. Claire and Tor had got the spare key from Katie and had come in to clear up and prepare it for her return.

Helga unpacks the delicious-smelling croissants from the bag, along with the butter and jam. She puts on a pot of coffee, delighted to see her friend, but she can tell that something is bothering Dominica.

'So? What is it? You've got something on your mind. I can tell.'

'Oh God, Helga. You have no idea.'

It's not like Dominica to be dramatic about anything, so Helga is intrigued by her tone.

'Go on. Tell me?'

Helga listens, aghast, as Dominica tells her about the call with Jamie on Friday night and how Tor, Claire and Maddy went to the pier. Bill, her supervisor, is not happy with how things went down, but Dominica is unrepentant. What else could she have done? Knowing it was Jamie?

'You did the right thing,' Helga assures hers, but now the doorbell rings and Dominica smiles.

'It'll be the others. I said on the chat I was coming round and they all wanted to see you too.'

Claire, Maddy and Tor all bustle in and hug Helga warmly and soon they're all sitting on the sofas whilst Dominica puts the kettle on to top up the coffee.

Helga won't countenance any talk of her operation or recovery. She needs to know what happened on the pier.

'You went in after him?' she asks Maddy. She can't believe all of this has happened whilst she was lying in that damned hospital bed.

'Thank God Tor was there, pointing. I saw him and I managed to get a life ring around him.'

'And Jamie? Is he OK?' Helga can hardly bear to hear the answer. Oxygen starvation? Brain damage? She knows what happens to people when they end up in the water.

'They revived him in the lifeboat.'

Maddy starts to cry.

'We thought for a moment . . . ' Maddy says, then shakes her head. 'Claire kicked up enough of a fuss to get the lifeguard out straight away. If she hadn't have got there in time . . . ' Maddy takes a hiccuppy breath. 'That's all I keep thinking about. How close it was.'

'You did the right thing. You all did. I told you the Sea-Gals were invincible. Look what you all did.'

Helga holds Maddy's hand too and Maddy gives her a watery smile. 'Thank you. At least *you* think so. Everyone else has told us off for trying to save him.'

'So what happened then? Once the lifeguard got him?' Helga asks.

'They took Jamie straight off to hospital in an ambulance,' Tor says.

'Good. Don't want him at any risk of secondary drowning,' Helga says.

'What's that?' Tor asks.

'When you've been in water, even if you've been revived, a couple of days later, your lungs can fill up. They call it secondary drowning. It's a real risk. They must have told you about that?' She checks with Maddy, who nods, but she can tell it's news to the others.

'They mentioned that, but so far he's OK. Hopefully he'll be out by the end of the week.'

Helga nods and pulls Maddy into a hug.

'You all saved him,' Helga says decisively to them. 'Together you saved him. That's quite a thing. I'm so proud of you all.'

They eat some of Claire's cake and the mood lightens, and Dominica changes the subject on to Linus.

'I still want to find him for you, but I'm going to need more details,' she says. 'Emma has put a shout-out to all the groups who swim in Hampstead, but so far nobody has come forward.'

Helga sighs. She's thought about it a lot – how Linus had been that day and how she'd felt when she'd seen him. And how entirely futile her feelings are. Because he has a family. A life. A *wife*.

'I want you to stop.' Helga sighs.

'Stop? But—'

'There's no point in contacting Linus. If I'm going to move away.'

'Move away?'

'I'm thinking of going back to Denmark. To be near Mette. I'm warming to her idea of the retirement village. I'm not getting any younger. I can't be a burden to other people.'

'But you can't move. What about the Sea-Gals?' Dominica sounds upset.

'You'll be fine without me. It's time to move on. To face up to the future.'

48

Breakfast of Champions

Maddy sits on the edge of her bed, watching Jamie sleep, remembering how she used to do the same thing when he was a baby. She reaches out and touches his hair, smoothing it away from his forehead. She and Trent used to lie with Jamie in between them, staring at him for hours.

She listens to his soft breathing, studying his face illicitly and the remnants of a black eye. His skin is still so sallow and dry, his frame terrifyingly thin and sunken.

She's glad he can sleep. She's finding it hard, not just because – having insisted on giving him her bed – she's been trying to sleep on the sofa bed, but also because every time she closes her eyes, she sees him falling and she sits up, heart pounding.

Jamie was given fluids and loads of checks in hospital and yesterday they allowed him home. He slept all day and Maddy was scared to leave him, even for a minute. She stood outside in the corridor with Matteo, not wanting to let him into the flat when Jamie was sleeping. She was so grateful when he brought supper round – a delicious chicken and chorizo stew, which she knew he'd made with love, but Jamie only had a few mouthfuls of it.

But now, as he stirs, she knows that he can smell the bacon she's cooking for breakfast. He always used to call her bacon butties the breakfast of champions.

There's so much Maddy longs to know – about where he's been and what's happened to him, but she knows she must be patient. She gets up and walks to the kitchen to butter the rolls.

'Hey,' she says, as Jamie shuffles into the kitchen area and sits on the bar stool by the counter. He has the duvet wrapped around him.

'Hi.' They smile at one another and Maddy forces down the urge to cry. He's really here. In her kitchen.

'I should tell your dad,' she says. 'I should tell him that you're safely home.'

'He won't care,' Jamie says.

'He will,' Maddy says, feeling defensive on Trent's behalf.

She'd rung him after she'd rescued Jamie from the pier, but she'd told him not to come until Jamie was out of hospital. He'd wanted to drive down straight away, but she's persuaded him not to and he's been ringing her phone non-stop since. She knows she owes him an explanation, but she needs to straighten things out with Jamie first. 'Your dad was worried sick. About you.'

'That's a first.'

'Jamie.'

'I don't know why you defend him, Mum.'

She needs to tell Jamie that she and Trent have separated.

'About your dad,' she begins. 'There's some things I need to tell you.'

'Yeah, I know,' he says.

There's a beat as she meets his eyes. 'You know?'

He gives her another meaningful look and she realises that he means he knows about the affair. And this fact clunks into her head, like a new record slotting into a juke box. Maddy flips the bacon in the pan.

'You mean, you knew? About Helen? About their affair?' she asks.

'He was a dick about it. I threatened to tell you and he . . . well, that was the end of the line for us.'

'Why didn't you tell me?'

'It felt too mean . . . and I wasn't sure you'd have believed me. And Dad . . . Dad said that, if I did, he'd never speak to me again and that I'd ruined his life.'

'Jesus.' Maddy can only imagine Trent saying this. No wonder he was so adamant about Jamie leaving and Maddy not searching for him.

'When did *you* find out?' Jamie asks.

'Not until Christmas Day. The same day as I heard your message. That's when I left to come to look for you.'

'But it's June.'

'I know. You've been very difficult to find.' She takes the pan from the heat and turns off the hob. She walks over. She cups his face. 'But, believe me, I've really tried.'

She tells him about the posters, the viral posts on Instagram and the private detective and finding out about him staying in Oriental Place. She tells him too about volunteering at Home Help and meeting Vic and how her hopes were raised, briefly, but how Vic had said how tough it was being homeless and it had made her feel sick.

'That's an understatement. Oh, God, Mum . . . you have no idea.'

'Then tell me.'

He shakes his head. His eyes are bloodshot. 'I can't . . . I'm ashamed.'

'Don't be. No more shame. Only the truth, OK?'

She sits on the bar stool next to him and takes his hands in hers. She notices black tattoos on his knuckles, but she doesn't say anything.

'I don't know. I don't know where to start.'

'Thailand?'

'Yeah, there was Thailand, but I was smoking weed behind your back long before that.'

'But you got your A levels.'

'By some kind of fluke. Everyone smoked, but it always affected me more.'

'But you were at school . . . at a *good* school . . . '

Jamie shakes his head and smiles sadly at her. 'Mum, one sure-fire way to turn a competitive child into an addict is to send them to a private school. Especially an expensive prestigious one like that. That place was full of drugs. You have no idea of what I was exposed to.'

She shakes her head, reeling. How had she not known?

'Then in Thailand the wheels *really* fell off the bus.'

'I remember. You didn't . . . I mean, I don't know what you took, but . . . ' she steels herself, fearful of the answer, but now they're being honest, she has to know. 'Was there heroin? Did you inject?'

'No, but it was everything else. Acid, MDMA, Skunk . . . loads of it. Every day. And the sicker I got, the more I needed it. I couldn't see a way out. Everything was so foggy. I felt so lost. And when I got back, I felt that I was letting you down the whole time.'

'You weren't.'

'I thought we were being honest,' Jamie reminds her. 'I was a shit.'

'You were a shit.' Maddy concedes.

'I guess I pushed it to the point where you and Dad had no choice but to throw me out. I see that.'

She nods. It feels like balm to hear him tell her this. To know that he can possibly see it from her point of view. 'I'm so sorry about that row. That it got to that point. I wish I'd been able to handle it differently. And, to be fair, you were right what you said – about me being always fixated on my phone, on my perfect life. Only it wasn't perfect. I was far from a perfect mother.'

'I said that?'

'You don't remember the fight?'

'Only Dad's right hook,' Jamie said. 'Which I probably deserved.'

'Oh, Jamie.'

'I thought that things would be OK when I left. And for a while they were. I met some good people when I first got here, but the situation was always fluid and we got thrown out of places continually. By the time it got to Christmas, things were bad. I'd met a girl by then and we moved into a squat in a derelict betting office. It had running water and intermittent electricity, but it was horrible, Mum. But I had nowhere else and no money and I was reliant on the food the restaurants threw out in the bins. And then I got Covid and was so ill.

That's when I rang. I should have left more of a message, but I lost my nerve.'

'Oh darling.'

'But then the girl . . . Martha . . . she was Martha.' His voice catches. 'She . . . died of a heroin overdose.'

'Oh God.'

'It was so . . . ugh, you have no idea seeing someone hooked on that shit. When we met, I said I'd help her stop and she really tried.' Maddy can tell he's in real pain. 'She must have done some in the night when I was asleep. She was in the next sleeping bag next to me. When I woke up she was blue.'

'Oh my God. What did you do?'

'Scully, who was in charge of the squat, refused to call the police or the ambulance. We put her body in the little park by the church where we knew the community officers would find her. I felt wretched. I should have gone to the police, but I was so ill and I wasn't thinking straight and Scully threatened me.'

'Oh, darling.'

'I couldn't sleep for a week. I needed for her not to have died in vain, you know? I knew the only thing I could do about it was to stop using drugs altogether. To turn things around. I decided then and there to stop everything, but it was the hardest thing I've ever done. It made me so sick. I didn't go outside for weeks. Months maybe.'

No wonder she couldn't find him, Maddy thinks. She sees the despair in his face and she longs to hold him.

'It just got worse and worse. I'd been clean, you see. Off the hard stuff. Then . . . ' He squeezes his eyes with his thumb and forefinger. 'Then, well, some bad shit went down.'

'What kind of bad shit?'

He shakes his head. He's not ready to tell her. She can see that, but his eyes are full of fear and shame and they meet hers. 'I got hold of some vodka and prescription pills and I was so cross with myself for cracking and so scared.'

Maddy feels a tear falling down her face. Her gorgeous boy. In despair. It breaks her heart.

'I don't even think I consciously planned to go to the pier. But I was there, with Martha's phone.'

'Thank God you called the Samaritans,' she says.

'It happened to be the last number on her phone. The last number she'd rung.'

'And you got Dominica,' she manages. 'That feels like fate. It really does.'

'She was nice. Calm, you know. I don't really know what I was doing up there, or what I intended. There was no plan, but if I'm honest, I . . . ' He pauses and Maddy waits. 'I just couldn't see a way out.'

'Oh, darling. I'm so sorry you got to that point.'

'I'm the sorry one. I've let you down. I know that.'

'You haven't let me down. Christ! I'm the one who should be apologising. I've pushed you all your life. I've piled on the pressure for you to be a perfect son, so that I could boast to my friends about it. I see that now. And if I could go back, I would. I'd do it all differently, Jamie. I would, I really would. I'd be a better mum, a better wife, a better person. I'd stop being such a . . . well, such a stupid, vain idiot wanting everyone's approval at the expense of everything else.'

'Wow, that's quite an admission,' Jamie says and his eyes are soft.

'Well, I've had a lot of time to think about it. But the point I'm making is that you've always been enough. More than enough. Just as you are. Just as you are right now. If you only knew, Jamie, how much I love you and how sorry I am . . . ' She can't say any more. The tears are coming too fast and she cries out, cross with herself. 'And I'm making this about me, when it's not about me.'

He stands and folds her into his arms. His chest is bony, his neck sinewy, but he's her boy. 'It's OK. I'm here. We've got each other.'

And he's crying too now and they both weep and weep until they start laughing and then Jamie gets up to try and find some tissues. It feels as if they've been tumbled over in a wave by the time they give up on the tissues and wash their face with cold water in the sink. It feels like that moment when she first went in the sea with Helga. The cold water feels like a baptism of sorts.

'I guess we've got a lot to unpick,' she says. 'That's all I'm saying.'

'Well, yeah. We've made a start, right?'

'I guess so.' She nods and smiles. And there he is. A flash of her boy and she recognises an emotion she'd forgotten about – but now it hits her squarely. It's pride. Because this is the kid who always used to make her believe he could do anything. Maybe he still can.

'So . . . first things first. Let's start with the breakfast of champions,' Jamie says, walking to the pan.

'Good idea. I'm bloody starving.'

49

The Betting Shop

Tor calls Maddy after work. She wants to tell her how happy Vic is that Maddy and Jamie have been reunited. She agrees to pop round to Maddy's flat for a cup of tea in the morning.

She arrives and knocks on the door, shocked to find someone as glamorous as Maddy living in such chaos. There are cardboard boxes everywhere.

'Hey.' Tor smiles at Maddy's son. He's looking significantly better than the last time she saw him. He's in clean jeans and a T-shirt. He's shaved too and cut his hair. Apart from being thin, you'd never guess he'd been through such a trauma. 'I've heard so much about you, Jamie.'

'Tor is the one who runs the charity,' Maddy explains to her son.

'One of the Sea-Gals?' Jamie checks and she nods.

Tor wonders if he remembers that she was the first one on the pier. She decides not to remind him.

'Can you come for a swim? Claire is heading down soon. I thought I'd join her.'

In the small kitchenette, Maddy talks to Tor in a hushed whisper. 'I can't. Not this morning. Jamie wants to go back to the squat he was living in. To collect his bag, but I'm scared to let him out of my sight. He doesn't want me to go with him. He says it's too awful for me to see. I don't know what to do.'

'I'll go,' Tor says.

'You'd do that?'

'Sure. Leave it to me.' She's seen squalor. How bad can it really be? Besides, she might know half the people in it.

It takes a while for Jamie to agree to let Tor come with him. He refuses to let Maddy drop them in the car and Tor texts Claire, telling her she can't meet for the swim, but hopefully she'll get to go later.

On the way, Jamie asks Tor all about her charity and, as they chat, she realises that he was the young guy she'd seen on Christmas Day when she'd been giving out Christmas meals and Vic had been talking. He'd been so tantalisingly close all along.

Jamie stops her on a scrubby patch of London Road, outside a shop front. It used to be a betting shop from the signage, but there are graffiti-covered metal grills over the windows and doors. Jamie takes her down a narrow alleyway to the small service cul-de-sac behind. He shows her the way in through the hatch behind the industrial bins. Her skin prickles all over as they creep through the gap in the loosened grill.

Inside, torn posters are peeling off the walls. The ancient carpet is horribly stained and Tor pulls the cuff of her jacket over her nose to mask the stink of squalor. There's a muffled beat of drum and bass and, as her eyes adjust to the gloom, she sees a pile of bare mattresses and filthy bedding along one wall. She has a horrible feeling that the lumps on them are sleeping people. In the other corner, she sees a man on his haunches, rocking. He's emitting a low, guttural noise that signifies pain and her instinct is to check that he's OK, but Jamie shakes his head and pulls her away.

He leads her downstairs past a kitchenette where there's a weak flickering overhead light. A rat is on the counter and she yelps. Jamie walks further down a dark corridor and pushes back the door to a store cupboard. On the floor, there's a rancid-looking sleeping bag on a stained mattress beneath some metal shelving. There's a large ashtray, which is overflowing with roll-up stubs and several bottles covered in wax from burnt down candles. He crouches and reaches right in the corner, beneath the mattress and, with a sigh of relief, pulls out a flattened backpack.

'You have to keep everything hidden. Everyone steals everything from each other. Just look at this,' he explains.

She goes with him to a black recycling box in the corner on a metal shelf. It's full of torn, emptied wallets and purses and discarded phone cases.

'That's all stolen?'

He nods.

'I don't believe it.'

'What is it?' Jamie asks.

'That,' Tor says, pointing, and Jamie reaches in and pulls out a notebook. He flicks through the pages. 'Actually, these drawings aren't too bad. Lots of birds.'

'Give me that.'

Tor snatches it, her heart leaping. Because it's Helga's

precious book. 'I know who that belongs to,' she says. She thinks of Helga sketching on the beach. Is this the book with Linus's number in it? Did Jamie have something to do with it being stolen?

'Hey!' She turns at the sound of a voice. A rough-looking man smoking a foul-smelling cigarette is approaching through the gloom. 'What the fuck do you think you're doing?'

'Run,' Jamie says, grabbing Tor's wrist.

They race down the corridor and past the stirring bodies and scramble out the way they came.

'Oi. Come back,' the man shouts, but they run fast down the road, not looking back. They don't stop until they run to London Road and manage to get straight onto the bus. Tor doesn't care which direction it's going in, only that it's going into town. Away from that terrible place.

They both swing down onto a spare seat. Tor feels shaken and she can tell Jamie is too. They're both out of breath.

'Who the hell was that guy?' she asks.

'Scully. He's in charge. You don't want to get into any kind of conflict with him. Believe me.'

'You've been living there?'

He nods sadly. 'I wouldn't exactly call it living. More like not dying.'

Tor looks down at the book. She's still gripping it tightly.

'What did you mean about that?' he asks. 'Whose is it?'

'It's Helga's,' she says. 'Our friend. From swimming. She really needs it. And I think it would mean the world to her to get it back.'

She stares at Jamie and he nods, taking it from her. He looks through the pages.

'Then I'd better make sure she gets it,' he says.

'You sure? You'll do it? You'll give it back?'

'Yeah. I will. I want to. I want to do something to put things right.'

50

A Promise Kept

He's a scrap of a lad, Helga thinks. Way too thin and too pale. He needs some sea air and feeding up. Maddy smiles at him as Helga lets them in. She hasn't been expecting their visit and she tries to tidy up the pile of papers on the coffee table and sofa. Her breakfast dish is still on the side.

'I love your place,' Jamie says.

Helga has spent the last few days trying to work out in her head where she's going to put everything when she moves. Mette, who is thrilled Helga has relented and is moving back to Denmark, is coming over to help her start packing up. She knows she's going to have to start throwing things away, but, somehow, she's not quite ready to make the first move to dismantle everything.

She regards her living space with the detachment she's been feeling since she came home from hospital. The heart attack and the operation has rattled her in a way she couldn't have foreseen. She doesn't feel quite the same as before. It's as if she's lost her nerve. The slightest noise in the night wakes her and she lies awake worrying about people breaking in.

Mette has convinced her that she'll feel safe once she's at the retirement village, but it's still unsettling leaving everything she knows for a fresh start. Mette's sent her pictures of the giant pool with its steam rooms and saunas, but it won't be the same as swimming in the sea every day.

Jamie and Maddy come to stand in the kitchen doorway, as Helga puts on the kettle. She looks up at the ceiling, cursing that the glass ceiling tile has started dripping. She's been thinking of a way of getting up there with her grouting gun, but she won't have to worry about home repairs in the retirement village. There'll be people for that. And what will Terry do? Her seagull? Will the next people who live here let him into the kitchen? She doubts it.

'Jamie,' Maddy prompts, nodding towards Helga. 'Go on.' Helga can see her eyes shining.

Jamie takes something out of his pocket and thrusts it towards her.

It can't be her notebook . . . can it?

She takes it from him and runs her finger over the cover. Then she opens it and there it is: Linus's number. In his handwriting.

'Are you OK?' Maddy asks, and she realises she hasn't said anything.

'Yes,' she says. 'It means a lot to get this back. But how? How did you get it?'

'We'd better sit down and then Jamie can explain.'

Helga sits down on the sofa, still amazed that she's holding her book.

'I found it in the squat,' Jamie explains. 'Where I was staying.'

Helga glances at Maddy. She can't be happy that her son has been staying in a squat.

'There's this guy – Scully. He steals from people all the time. He's a dealer and . . . well, you don't want to know what he's like. I went back to get my bag, you see, with Tor. He was there and he scared us stupid.'

'You went back with Tor?'

'She recognised your book.' He glances nervously at Maddy. 'I didn't realise until we were on the way here just now, but I've been here before.'

He looks worried and Maddy takes over for a moment. 'Jamie was there that night you collapsed.'

'You saw it happen?'

'I tried to stop Scully following you, but it was over so quickly. He was cross with me and he ran off with your bag, telling me to follow, but then you were on the ground and clutching your chest and I . . . I was so scared. I didn't think you'd make it. So I . . . I did the CPR thing.'

'It was you?' Helga asks, aghast.

He nods. 'Well, I tried. Then I knocked on one of the cottage doors and then I ran. I thought if the police found me I'd be in real trouble.'

'I had no idea you knew how to do that lifesaving stuff,' Maddy says.

'What do you mean? You made me go to Cubs,' he says, with sad smile. 'Then Scouts. Then Duke of Edinburgh, then that cadet thing. I guess I was equipped to save someone.'

'I guess you were.'

'And it was this Scully guy who made off with my bag?' Helga asks.

Jamie nods. 'I'm really sorry,' he trails out. 'I thought if I stayed . . . I don't know what I thought. But I was scared of Scully.'

'You gave me CPR?' Helga says. She tries to imagine him blowing breath into her body. 'They said at the hospital that was what saved me.'

Jamie shrugged. 'I felt bad I didn't do more.'

Jamie and Maddy don't stay long and, after they've gone, Helga stares out of the window, going over everything Jamie has told her. She has him to thank for her life, it seems. She could see the terror in his face as he told her about seeing her falling and clutching her chest.

Maddy insisted that they call the police together and Jamie bravely explained everything on the phone. The police are on their way to the squat now. She hopes they find Scully.

The light is coming in through the window and she watches the birds chirruping. There's a pair of collared pigeons on the stone bird bath, rubbing their necks together, and she feels the decision rising up in her.

So what if Linus has a family, a wife? She made him a promise, didn't she?

She turns and picks up her book, then her home phone and dials the number Linus has written down. She hears it connect. The ring tone seems to resonate right in her heart.

'Hello?'

It's his voice. The hairs on her arms stand up and she feels fluttery and light. She tries to speak, but the words won't come.

'Helga, is that you?' He sounds cautious.

'Yes,' she manages.

'It's about time. I thought you weren't going to call.'

'There was . . . I had . . . ' Helga says, but she's so glad to hear his voice, she can feel tears threatening to take her voice away.

'Are you all right?'

She tells him about losing her bag and phone and how she's been in hospital and how, thanks to a miracle, she got her book – and his number – back.

'I couldn't bear the thought that you might think I didn't want to call. That was the worst bit of the whole ordeal.'

He chuckles softly. 'Helga, I seem to have spent my whole life waiting for you to call. I've learnt to be patient.'

'But what about your wife and—'

'My . . . ? Oh, Helga, I'll tell you all about that later, but I'm on my own. I have been for five years.'

He's single? But he was wearing a wedding band? Helga feels so much joy radiating through her that she can hardly take it in.

'You've called me just at the right moment. I was meeting some people interested in buying the boat today. I thought there was no point in keeping it. I'm going back to Australia. Well, I'm meant to be—'

'Don't go,' she blurts. 'At least not until I've seen your boat,' she adds, and Linus laughs.

'Oh, she's a beaut.'

Helga's heart soars at the thought of seeing Linus on a boat. It's like she's manifested her most secret, treasured dream.

'So, if I come for one last sail. Will you be there?' he asks. 'Will you come and meet me?'

51

A New Companion

'I feel completely different,' Claire announces, as she changes on the beach with Dominica. She's wearing a lovely red polka dot swimming costume and she stretches her arms up and out to the horizon.

'You look completely different,' Dominica agrees, folding up her T-shirt. She grabs a squirt of sun cream and rubs some on her shoulders. It's already a scorcher. Ahead, the sea is turquoise blue and green, the sky clear except for a few clouds on the horizon.

'I just needed to reconnect with Pim, you know? It seemed so complicated, but actually it was very simple.'

'What did he say when you gave him the picture?'

'I was so nervous, but he loved it. He cried. He said it was the best present he'd ever had.'

'Oh, Claire. That's wonderful,' Dominica says. Because it is.

'I'm not sure where we're going to put it. I don't want the boys to see it just yet. Pim's sent it to the framers and he never gets things framed.'

Dominica's delighted for Claire.

'It's like we're on to a whole different chapter. We've booked a holiday with the boys and we're going paddleboarding in the Lake District.'

'That sounds fun.'

'We've ordered blow-up paddleboards to practise and we're going to have a go at the weekend.'

'Hello, hello,' Helga calls, waving. She strides down the beach and the others get up to hug her.

'You came.' Dominica smiles. It's so good to see her out in the sunshine.

'I wouldn't miss it for the world. I've missed it like crazy.'

'It's a perfect day for it,' Claire says, hugging Helga too.

Dominica helps Helga with her jacket. She's worried about her scar, but Helga has checked with the doctor and it's safe to swim.

'What's happened to you?' Helga stands back, admiring Claire in her new costume.

'I've been swimming every day. Those lessons with Andy really paid off.'

'Didn't they just. It shows.'

'I'm doing the swim round the pier. You're doing it too, right? It's in a couple of weeks.'

'No, I won't be here,' Helga says, shaking her head.

Dominica feels suddenly bereft, the joy of the day popping. Helga has become not just a swimming companion but a proper friend. No, more than that. She's like family. She can't believe she's going home. 'You're really doing it? Going to the retirement village?'

'No,' Helga shouts. 'No! Fuck that.'

Claire and Dominica laugh and Dominica puts her hand to her chest. 'Good. Because you really gave me a shock just then.'

'There's so much to tell you. Linus is coming to get me,' Helga announces. 'He's sailing here right now this minute.' She stares out at the horizon as if she can make his boat materialise.

'What? Oh my God, Helga.' Dominica whoops and then Helga is telling them about her call. Tor arrives and then Maddy and both are keen to hear what the excitement is all about.

'We were on the phone for hours and hours,' Helga says, her cheeks pink. She's radiating joy. 'He told me all about his family. His wife was a sailor, but she died five years ago. He's had this wildly successful business in Australia, but he's retired now and has been feeling at a loose end too. It's like we've collided at the same life stage. It was like all the years just melted away.'

Tor and Maddy are as excited as she is and they are all talking over each other, as they walk to the water's edge. As they stand in the shallows, it's clearer than Dominica has seen it. The pebbles under the water glint in the sun. Now that they're all back together, it feels like a new start.

They walk in and Dominica puts her head under, seeing the pebbles below through her new goggles as she swims. It always fills her with wonder to be taken to the world below the sea. It's escapism on a grand level. There's a shoal of whitebait flick-flacking in the water.

'I don't know how you can do that.' Maddy shudders as Dominica comes up. 'Look underneath.'

'You're kidding me?' Dominica says. 'You can't still be afraid?'

Maddy shrugs.

'Come here.' She swims a few strokes over to Maddy and puts the goggles on her face. 'Go on. Take a look.'

Maddy puts her head under, seeing that Dominica isn't going to let her off the hook.

'No monsters, see?' Dominica assures her as she comes up, smiling. 'It's beautiful, right?'

'I guess,' Maddy concedes.

'Keep an eye out for dolphins, though,' Claire calls over. 'Ash saw some when he was out with the surf school yesterday.'

Maddy smiles at Dominica. 'Claire's in a good mood.'

'She's sorted things with Pim,' Dominica says. 'And what about you? How are things?'

Maddy shrugs. 'Getting there, slowly. I'm just sad because Matteo is leaving and then I'll be on my own.'

'But you won't be. You have Jamie and you have us.'

Tor swims over. 'You look very jolly,' Maddy comments.

'I've got the Zoom ceremony tomorrow for the community award.'

She still doesn't know that they all nominated her and Dominica almost tells Tor, but Maddy shakes her head. It doesn't matter that it was Claire and Maddy's idea. Dominica's sure other people will have nominated Tor too. She's just glad she's got some much-needed recognition at last.

'You deserve it more than anyone I know,' Maddy tells her.

'You can watch if you want. I'll send you the link. My parents and Alice are watching. For once I've done something to make them notice. Mum has been bragging to everyone. Even Graham has had to wind his neck in and admit that the charity is a good thing.'

They swim for a while and then go back to the towels, where Dominica stretches out, letting the water droplets dry on her skin. It seems amazing that not so long ago they swam in the snow.

It's such a gorgeous day, they could be abroad. And she considers how much she always used to live for time away with Chris, but now she's quite content being here with her friends. She can't imagine feeling happier anywhere else.

Maddy sits up and waves as Matteo arrives with Luna.

'Hey,' Dominica says, as the little dog bounds over to her. 'I've missed you.'

Matteo sits down with them and has some of Claire's cake. Dominica's only seen him in passing, so she's surprised when he smiles at her. He's wearing khaki shorts and a white T-shirt and baseball cap and cool sunglasses, which he now takes off to reveal his lovely eyes. She can see why Maddy is so attracted to him.

'It's Dominica, isn't it?' he asks. She likes his Spanish accent.

Dominica nods and glances at Maddy, who is listening in to this conversation. She sees a flash of sadness cross her face.

'Well, it was Maddy's suggestion, but I came to ask you something,' Matteo says.

'Ask me? Ask me what?'

'I'm going back to Barcelona. It's been difficult finding somewhere to stay and I've finally found somewhere, but it doesn't allow pets. And in any case, I'll be out all day. I've asked Shauna, my ex-partner, but she's not in a position to have Luna back. So, sadly, I have to re-home her.'

'Re-home her?'

As if sensing this, Luna crawls right onto her lap.

'I thought you might . . . ' Maddy nods at Matteo.

'I thought . . . we thought . . . could you take her, Dominica?'

'She loves you and . . . well, you can think about it. If she's going to get a new home, I know her first choice would be yours,' Maddy says.

Matteo smiles nervously. 'It's a big decision, though, and I wouldn't ask if—'

'Yes,' Dominica says, without hesitation. She's astonished at her knee-jerk reaction. But actually . . . *why not?* If she's not going into the office and is retraining, then there's no reason why she couldn't have a dog? And what better dog than this one? Maddy's right. There was a mutual love thing straight away. She holds up Luna, then cuddles her in tight. 'We can't have you homeless, can we?'

Maddy takes Matteo's hand and smiles at him.

'You're sure,' he checks.

'Of course, I'm sure.'

They discuss all the details, but Dominica is smiling the whole time. Luna is going to be hers. She doesn't have a shred of doubt that it's the right thing for both of them.

52

Adios

Maddy links arms with Matteo as they walk past the peace statue along the prom towards Hove. It's late afternoon and he has an evening flight back to Barcelona so they've come out for a final walk, but it's strange without Luna who is happily settled at Dominica's flat. They dropped her off earlier and the little dog hardly noticed Matteo leaving. Maddy knows they're only putting off the inevitable goodbye. She's offered to take him to Gatwick, but he's booked a train.

Summer has really set in. There's a gang of twenty-some-things playing frisbee on the lawns, a fire juggler is practising, a couple of girls boxing and further along there's a yoga class going on and the roller-bladers are out in force. There's a huge family group on the beach around a wood burner, the smell of curry wafting on the air. Dogs scamper over the tarmac, school children squealing as they strip off and head into the sea. A busker with a guitar plays 'Moon River', and Maddy marvels at the people doing things that make them happy, but she feels heavy of heart and not just because Matteo is leaving.

This morning, the landlady of the Airbnb told her that the bookings have started again and so Maddy has to leave. Even though this was the arrangement, it still feels like a wrench. The fresh start she'd hoped for with Jamie feels like it's off to a very shaky beginning.

She hasn't got the nerve to tell him they're about to be homeless and need to move on again, not when she knows he likes the apartment and being by the sea. But the fact is, she can't afford a place anywhere like the one they're in. She's come clean and told her family about leaving Trent and finding Jamie, and her dad has lent her a few thousand to keep her going until she gets settled, but the rent prices have rocketed. She's asked Trent for an update on exactly how much money will be left to divide once he's paid off the loan, but he's yet to give her an exact figure, or a date as to when she might expect it.

But this is her problem to work out. And not one she can share with Matteo.

Halfway along by the café on the lawns, they stop and lean on the green balustrade, taking in the view. The water is a shimmering pale turquoise green streaked with pink where the waves are breaking. The horizon is a dusky purple blending to the softest blue above, the old burnt-out pier picked out in gold relief from the setting sun.

Matteo has suggested that they stay in touch and try and carry on their relationship when he's in Barcelona, but Maddy knows they're both grasping at straws. He needs to find the right woman and to start a family. And he needs to do that sooner rather than later. And he can't do that with an older lover in tow. She's told him as much, but he refused to hear it. But Maddy is old enough and wise enough to know what distance will do.

'I'm going to have to go soon.' He checks his watch.

'I know.'

'Listen. Why don't you stay here? Wander back in your own time? It'd be nice to think of you here. I don't want to leave you in the apartment.'

'OK, maybe you're right. I don't want to be sad on Jamie.'

In their new mode of complete honesty, she's told Jamie all about Matteo and they've met properly, although whilst both of them were charming, Maddy found it embarrassing. Seeing Jamie and Matteo together only emphasised the age difference between her and Matteo. It didn't help that afterwards Jamie jokingly called her a cougar. She tried to explain that Matteo had been a friend first, when she'd needed one most, but all the time he'd had a playful twinkle in his eye and she could tell that he wasn't going to take her seriously.

'I don't want you to be sad, full stop,' Matteo said. 'It's not goodbye. We'll see each other.'

'But not for a while and I'm sorry, but I can't help it. I am sad.'

He kisses her and she holds on to him as tears make her chin tremble.

'I don't want to say goodbye.'

'Then I shall say it. *Adios*, my lovely neighbour.' He puts his finger under her chin. 'Take care of yourself.'

'I'll try.'

'You're going to be fine, Maddy. Better than fine. I promise.'

Despite Matteo's comforting words, Maddy feels her heart hurting as he walks away. She sits down on the bench and watches his silhouette getting smaller and smaller and then he's out of sight, blending in with the crowd.

She sighs, knowing she should get back to Jamie, but, instead, she gets up and walks down to the water's edge. The tide is going out and the sand is golden. She takes off her Converse trainers and feels the cold sand under her soles. She needs a bit of time, even though she knows Jamie will be waiting for her. She needs a bit of time to process her feelings and there's only one person who can help.

She takes her phone out of her pocket, finds the contact and presses the call button.

Lisa picks up after one ring. 'Maddy?'

There's a silence. Maddy thinks back to the last time they spoke, when Lisa accused her of being stubborn. She thinks of all the hurt she's caused her friend. She tries to remember the anger she felt, but how it's all gone.

'Can you talk, Lis?' she says.

'Sure.'

There's another pause. Maddy imagines the phone pressed to Lisa's face. Her friend's dear face. It's only now, hearing her voice, that she realises how much she's missed her.

'I just need . . . I just want to talk through something. And you're the only person . . . '

'Shoot. What's happened?' she asks in that breezy yet interested way that is all Lisa's. It's their phrase of old, from when they were in their twenties and would ring each other up, night or day for advice. And in that moment, Maddy knows that all is forgiven. They're still them. Still friends for life.

Maddy feels the sun dry her tears as she tells Lisa about Matteo and how sad it has been to say goodbye.

'So, a hot Spanish lover?'

'He was kind when I needed kindness.'

'You don't want to carry it on?'

'I want to, he wants to, but I doubt it's going to work,' she says. 'Not the long-distance thing. And not with Jamie. Besides, Matteo needs someone his own age. And he wants a family.'

They talk some more about Matteo and then Maddy tells Lisa about finding Jamie. She doesn't hold back as she describes pulling him out of the sea. It feels good to tell Lisa all the scary details, some of which she's already heard from Trent.

'God, Maddy, you're so brave.'

'I'm just so thankful that . . . that, well . . . I'm grateful for a second chance. That's all.'

There's a pause, then Lisa says, 'Do we get a second chance too? Because I'm so, so sorry for letting you down, Maddy. For not being brave enough to tell you the truth.'

'It's OK. I understand,' Maddy says, with a gentle laugh. 'You were in an impossible position. And I was awful to you. And I'm really sorry.'

She stops for a moment, staring out at the sea and the amazing colours of the sky.

'I guess in the general scheme of things, we're allowed a blip or two, right?' Lisa says.

'I guess.'

'I feel really bad you've been through such a shit time and I haven't been with you.'

'It's OK. My swimming gang have been keeping me sane.'

'I want to meet them.'

'I'm doing a swim. Round the pier. If you come then, you can meet them.'

'I'd love that. I'm there.'

And just like that, there's a date to see each other and they chat and chat. As she strolls along the sand, Maddy is hungry for Lisa's news and is delighted that Tess, her daughter, has moved in with her boyfriend.

'When are you coming home?'

'I'm not sure where home is any more. And I like being near the sea. But,' she sighs, 'I have no idea how I can afford to stay. Not after losing the house. Not to mention the fact that my career is in tatters. I'm done with it, Lis. I can't put myself out there any more. I can't be the person I was trying to be.'

'Then don't be. Just be you. You know that everyone wants to know if you've found Jamie, right?' Lisa says. 'So, for starters, you should definitely do an Insta live about that.'

'I don't think so. After my last honesty splurge.'

'Which got so many comments. I saw them,' Lisa says. 'People were so grateful to you for being real.'

Maddy couldn't bring herself to read all the comments. She's barely been on Instagram since. She's been too worried about Jamie. But hearing this from Lisa makes an old flicker of her on-line vanity flare up.

'Why not think about it? Why not get Jamie to help? Use your platform to help others in your situation?'

'I'm not sure he would,' but even as she says it, Maddy wonders if that's true. Jamie has been a source of constant surprises since she got him back.

She watches the tide ahead of her as her mind starts mulling on what Lisa is suggesting. There's a ripple of golden water coming towards her and she watches how it comes and goes, always an ending, always a beginning.

53

A Family Celebration

Tor had hoped there'd be a fancy event, but even though the radio station's community awards are online, there's still a sense of occasion as she sits beside Lotte in their living room in front of the screen. There are quite a few contenders for the community awards and she starts to feel very unworthy as she hears about the bravery of the other nominees.

Hearing about how tough it's been during the last year for lots of people and how so many have fallen through the cracks is a familiar story, but she's amazed by the positivity and resourcefulness of the people who have been determined to make a difference. There's one woman who sacrificed everything to keep her care home going in terrible circumstances, a head teacher who kept several schools going for the vulnerable children during the pandemic. There's a lovely woman who has kept her choir for dementia patients going online and then it's Tor's turn.

The presenter introduces Tor and talks about the Home Help charity. This is being broadcast on the radio, but she's talking on Zoom to the presenter in the studio. He announces that there's a short video interview he'd like to play her.

She's surprised to see Arek and she blushes as she listens to him speaking about his involvement in the charity's work and how much Tor does. Then Vic joins in.

Tor's touched to see that Vic has smartened himself up.

'I don't know what I'd have done, if it hadn't been for Tor. Especially at Christmas.'

Lotte squeezes Tor's hand.

'She's always friendly. When her friends, Claire and Maddy, told me about the awards thing, I said I couldn't imagine anyone deserving it more.'

'Oh my God,' she whispers. Because now she realises that it's Claire and Maddy who have nominated her. The penny drops now, as Tor remembers Claire and Maddy talking to Arek and Greg. And she picked up something in the sea the other day between Dominica and Maddy. They all knew about this? This is happening because of the Sea-Gals?

'Did you know about this?' she whispers to Lotte, who nods.

'We all voted,' she says. 'It was Claire and Maddy's idea. We talked about it when I did her hair.'

All that time ago? Tor thinks.

'Tor . . . Tor, are you there?' the presenter asks, and Tor grins.

'Yes, I'm here. Thank you so much.'

'No, it's us who need to thank you,' she says. 'Your award and a thousand pounds towards your charity will be coming over to you later.'

'That's amazing, but I really need to say some thank yous. To the people who nominated me – my swimming friends, the

Sea-Gals Helga, Maddy, Dominica and Claire. But I also want to thank the one person who's kept me going. Who's made me believe in myself.'

She turns to Lotte and smiles. 'I want to thank my girlfriend – my partner – Lotte, who's right here. I love you. I couldn't have done this without you.'

Lotte's eyes fill with tears.

'That's so lovely. Thank you, Tor,' the presenter says. Then before she knows it, the interview is over and they're off air.

'I can't believe you said that,' Lotte said. 'On air. Everyone is listening.'

'I hope so,' Tor says with a grin.

And then her phone buzzes and she gives Tor a look and turns the phone round. It's her mum ringing.

As she goes to answer, Tor asks, 'Can I ask them over? To spend a day? To meet you properly?'

'I thought you'd never ask.'

Lotte insists on spending a fortune in Waitrose for a celebratory picnic the weekend after the awards ceremony. She's nervous and Tor has never seen her so skittish as she sets up the deckchairs on the beach. Tor checks her phone, knowing her parents are having a nightmare parking. She finally sees them and waves to them as they come down to their spot on the beach.

'Relax,' Tor tells Lotte. 'I promise. It's going to be OK.'

Because she means it. She's been so worried, but getting the award has somehow given her the boost of confidence she needs. When her mum rang straight after the awards, she sounded shocked about Tor's acceptance speech, but Tor cut her off, inviting her for a picnic and her mum agreed.

Alice called immediately afterwards.

'Lotte?' she said. 'Lotte your flatmate is your partner?' She sounded excited and Tor put her on loudspeaker.

'You're on speaker. Say hello.'

'The famous Alice,' Lotte said.

'Well, this is amazing,' Alice says. 'At long bloody last.'

'What do you mean?' Tor asked.

'Do you think I didn't realise you liked girls? I've known since we were about seven.'

Lotte bursts out laughing. 'Oh my God, Alice. You should see her face.'

'I don't know if Mum and Dad know,' Tor said, confused. How had Alice known all along?

'Oh, don't worry about them. Leave them to me. Oh, Tor, I'm so proud of you.'

Tor put down the phone and Lotte pulled her into an embrace. 'Why do you bitch about her the whole time? She sounds great.'

Now Tor wonders what Alice has told her parents as they arrive. She hasn't seen them since she dropped the bomb about her having RA at Easter and her mum has sent several envelopes full of pamphlets. She know she's worried and wants to help, so she's glad she's here. She's glad she'll be able to see for herself how well Tor feels. It helps that they're all by the sea. It feels like the best space to be having this meeting rather than in the house.

Tor kisses both her parents and, after her mother has offloaded about the parking situation, Tor introduces Lotte.

'Mum, Dad, this is Lotte,' Tor says. 'Lotte – Rita and Roger.'

'Pleased to meet you,' Lotte says.

'You're partners?' Tor's mum checks, her eyes darting between her and Lotte. 'You're the one who does the hair?'

Lotte glances nervously at Tor. She's had a cut and Lotte has dyed her hair back to its natural chestnut colour for the photo for the awards she had sent in.

'Yes, that's me,' Lotte says.

Tor feels a stab of nervousness. Her parents aren't going to be snobs about Lotte being a hairdresser, are they? When that's the very least of all of her considerable talents.

'You did a very good job,' Roger says. 'She's very pretty when she doesn't have purple hair.'

'She's very pretty even with purple hair, in my opinion,' Lotte says, and Tor could kiss her for standing up for her in such a charming way.

'I'm sorry I didn't tell you before,' Tor says, 'about us. But I want you both to be happy for me. Because I'm happy. Really happy.'

She smiles at Lotte.

'I love her,' Lotte blurts. 'Unconditionally. Completely. I will take care of her, make sure she has everything she could possibly need and everything she wants,' she adds, shaking Tor's dad's hand, then grabbing him in a bear hug.

'Goodness. Just as well I've brought champagne,' Roger says, 'because this certainly calls for a celebration.'

'We're so glad you're happy, darling. Really. I mean it,' her mum says. 'And you look so well.'

'I am well. It's so much better now that it's not so cold.'

'Have you been in swimming? Only I bought my bathers. I thought I might go in? In with you, both, I mean,' her mum says, nervously.

'Then what are we waiting for?' Lotte exclaims, already stripping off. 'Come on, Rita, I'll race you to the sea.'

Tor's mum, clearly surprised at Lotte's enthusiasm, starts to get undressed too.

'Oh, isn't this fun!' she says to Tor with an excited smile.

54

Towards the Horizon

When Linus phones to say he's arrived at the dock, Helga orders a cab straight away. She's so nervous, she calls Dominica with her new mobile.

'It's happening. I'm going to meet him,' she says, excitedly, as soon as Dominica picks up. 'He's here. At the marina.'

'Oh goodness, Helga. How are you feeling?'

'Like a giddy schoolgirl, if I'm honest. And so scared.'

'Scared?' Dominica laughs. 'You?'

'What if it doesn't work? What if he doesn't feel the same?'

'You'll know,' Dominica says. 'Don't worry. You'll know straight away.'

They chat for a while longer and Helga is glad of her reassurance. She remembers that Dominica has had a big week too. 'How did your course go?' she asks. She knows Dominica is starting her counsellor's training this week.

'I met a lot of lovely people, even though for the time being it's still on Zoom. It's fun to be learning again, though, and using my brain. And Luna is keeping me occupied, obviously. It's so lovely having her.'

Helga smiles. 'I told you you needed a companion.'

'Everywhere I go people stop me. I've got to know loads of neighbours I've never met before. They've invited me for drinks tonight.'

'That's wonderful. Oh . . . here.' She taps the glass partition for the cab driver to turn for the marina. 'I've got to go.'

'Good luck. You're a Sea-Gal, remember. Whatever happens . . . you've got this.'

Linus has given her his berth number, but the marina is busier than Helga has been expecting. The docks are crowded on both sides and she walks along the slatted boards, noticing the rainbow sheen of diesel on the surface of the water and the sloshing of the water against the hulls of the boats. She remembers the hustle and bustle of all the marinas she's sailed into in the world and how it feels to moor to the dock, exhausted but safe. She's so excited about being on a boat again – about sailing. Because that's what Linus has promised her.

Her heart is hammering. It's really happening. *She's actually meeting Linus.* She wants to pinch herself.

'Hey, Helga? Over here.'

She hears a call and shades her eyes. Linus is standing on the back rail of a yacht at the far end of the dock. He waves and she grins and runs towards him.

She stops when she's parallel to the white yacht. It has its sails half winched in and it rocks in the water. Linus is wearing a blue fisherman's smock and he takes off his cap.

'Welcome aboard,' he says and he reaches out for her hand and helps her hop from the dock. For a second, they are pressed together. Although the years have shrunk them both, their proportions are the same. She doesn't see an old man, but the boy she fell in love with all those years ago.

'Helga. You came.'

And she feels a huge wave of relief sweep over her, because she *knows*. It's just as Dominica said it would be. She knows right in her core that this is where she's meant to be. That her and Linus were destined for each other and that, from this moment on, her life will be inseparable from his.

'I have something for you,' she says, taking the note out of her pocket. He takes it, recognising his own faded handwriting, and his eyes widen. 'I know I'm fifty years too late, but I want you to know that it's my biggest regret that I never showed up that day,' she says. 'And that's why it's so good to finally be meeting you on the dock.'

He looks at her, sunlight dancing in his eyes, then he pulls her close and hugs her. She hears him sigh. 'Better late than never,' he whispers, and he kisses the top of her head. Helga feels as if a hatch door has opened somewhere inside her and she's like a bird that has been set free.

He takes her on a tour of his yacht and Helga is already in love with it by the time they get to the neat cabin, where he goes to the small fridge and gets two beers for them. Her mind is already racing ahead to them playing Scrabble at night, as she sees the battered box behind the elastic netting. She can't believe she's back on a yacht. It feels as if her soul is singing.

They go back on deck and talk about Linus's journey here and she listens to his adventure, more sure than ever that she's going to be on the next one with him. She asks if he's tired and when he says he's not, she asks him if they can go for a spin.

She loves watching how nimble he is, as he pulls in the bulky white fenders.

'Can you grab that rope?' he asks, and she pulls in the tow line, instinctively remembering what to do, the muscle memory of holding a rope so strong, it instantly makes her feel young. They work effortlessly as a team, as they used to long ago.

He reverses out of the berth and they motor out through the harbour walls.

'Where are we going?' she asks, as she stands next to him at the wheel, her arms around him, her face turned to the sun and the salty breeze.

'Let's sail to the horizon and see what happens,' he says.

'Sounds like a good plan to me.'

55

The Windfarm

Through her goggles, the water is green and opaque whilst she's near the shore, but as Claire swims further out it clears. She can see the rippled sand way below and a crab scrabbling across it as her shadow crosses. Who needs to go abroad when it's like this?

She's motoring now and she notices the bubbles as she blows out through her nose, rhythmically breathing every third stroke. She's heading for the furthest swimming buoy and she feels giddy with her own bravery. Claire felt the call of the sea so strongly this morning, she had to get in. This is the first time she's swum on her own. Dominica is busy, Tor and Lotte have gone to see Alice, and Helga should be on her way to see Linus. Maddy says she's flat-hunting with Jamie, but so far it sounds has if it's been a bit stressful trying to find somewhere they can afford.

At water level, as she turns her head one way, she can see the wind farm turbines, and, to the other side, she can see the Grand Hotel like a big vanilla ice cream cake. The pier is in the distance, the rides whirring and she can hear the faint screams of delighted thrill-seekers on the breeze. It's horrifying to think that Jamie fell all that way.

She's so glad Maddy has got her son back and she thinks about her boys Ash and Felix at home cleaning, hardly able to believe it.

'Saturday when you swim is going to be our cleaning day,' Ash announced this morning. 'Dad, Felix and I agreed. We're going to put on really loud music and we're going to clean while you're out.'

'We thought about what you said,' Pim said. 'We've decided it's about time we pulled our weight.'

Claire finishes her swim and feels tired, but exhilarated when she gets home. She's expecting to hear the boys in the living room, but instead, the house is gleaming. Pim greets her with a herbal tea. 'Have a quick bath,' he says. 'Then get dressed. We're going on a trip.'

'A trip?'

'We're going on a boat to the wind farm,' Felix says.

'Are we?'

'And we're taking a picnic,' Ash announces and then remembers something and runs downstairs. She can hear the timer on the oven.

Claire pulls an impressed face at Pim as Felix follows him.

'We were talking about careers,' Pim explains. 'Felix is serious about engineering.'

'Oh?'

'And Ash quoted you.'

'Me?'

'Yes, something about just needing to look outside our own front door for all the answers.'

'I said that?'

'You did. You're very wise,' he says, giving her an affectionate squeeze and then pushing her into the bathroom. 'Hurry
up. We're leaving soon. I'm getting the bikes ready.'

Forty minutes later, as Claire locks the front door, she sees
an estate agent is knocking a 'For Sale' sign to Rob and Jenna's
fence and she smiles at Pim, who beams back. She'd heard
a rumour that they were moving, since they couldn't get planning permission, and she listens briefly for a second to the birds
chirruping in the tree she saved.

'Good riddance,' he tells her.

They all set off together, cycling down to the marina. It's
been so long since they spent a whole day together that it feels
as if they're on holiday. She takes a selfie as they wait in the
queue for the boat that will take them out to the Rampion
Wind Farm and puts it in the WhatsApp chat. She's so proud of
Pim and his initiative, she wants to share it with the Sea-Gals.
Helga gets straight back: 'I'll be in the marina later. Come and
meet Linus. We'll be at the end of the dock. Everyone come.
I want you to meet him.'

The trip to the wind farm is magical and the boys are utterly
enthralled. Claire takes lots of photos as they glide around the
huge sails. The land looks miles away, Brighton just a tiny
dot in the distance. It's good to get this perspective. It's been
a while since she had it.

Felix talks to one of the other people on the trip and then
comes and joins Claire where she's standing with Ash.

'Look at the water. It's so clear,' she says. 'I just want to
jump in.'

'Those people were telling me about the swim,' Felix says.

'The swim?'

'There's a swim out here. It's a relay apparently. You should do it, Mum.'

'Me?'

'If you can swim round the pier, then why not?'

Claire laughs, but she can tell he's serious and it makes her proud that he thinks she could do something so daring.

'You're always telling us to challenge ourselves. Why don't you have a go?'

'Let's see if I can get round the pier first,' she says, looping her arm into his and grinning at Pim, who takes a snap of them.

By the time they chug back to the marina, it feels as if she's been abroad. It helps that, as the sun lowers, Ash spots a pod of dolphins. It's magical watching them play in the wake of the boat.

Back at the marina, the boys cycle home together and Pim comes with her to meet Helga and Claire is excited to introduce him to her friends. Somehow having him with her makes everything complete.

Helga messages directions and they find the yacht at the end of the dock. Maddy is already on board with Jamie; Dominica is sitting with little Luna on her lap, and Tor and Lotte are squished in too.

'More wonderful Sea-Gals,' Linus says, welcoming them and shaking Claire's hand and then Pim's.

He's lovely, Claire thinks, immediately. He's tanned, with twinkly eyes and silver hair and, as he puts his arm around Helga, she can see that he adores her. Helga looks radiantly happy as they describe their day sailing. He fiddles with a leather pendant on his neck and Claire realises it's the one she saw in Helga's bedroom wrapped around the photograph.

Claire tells them all about their trip to the wind farm and seeing the dolphins.

'It sounds much better than flat-hunting,' Maddy says, with a sigh.

'No joy?' Claire asks.

'No,' Jamie says. 'Although we did have some good news. Go on, Mum. Tell them.'

Maddy smiles at him. 'Well, it's nothing . . . well, it might be something.'

'Mum's got a consultant.'

'Had a consultant. When I could afford her. Manpreet.'

'She's big in social media,' Jamie explains. 'She loved the post Mum did and when Mum explained about finding me, she's going to help us find a new direction.'

'New how?' Dominica asks.

'Jamie has agreed to help me,' Maddy says. 'We're going to talk about our journey together. Try and help other people in the same situation.'

'We want to reach out to people who weren't as lucky as us,' Jamie adds.

'That's great,' Claire says, meaning it.

'It's going to be hard work, but Manpreet is going to help us. And best of all she's not charging us. Well, not for the first few sessions at least. She'll want something if it takes off, I'm sure, but we'll cross that bridge when we come to it. I'm not convinced we can make much money, but something has to happen. We've been looking at places to rent and . . . '

Her shoulders slump and she pulls a desperate face.

'No joy?' Claire asks, and Maddy shakes her head.

'Everything is ludicrously expensive. At this rate, we'll have to live in the car.'

'Well, we had an idea,' Helga grins at Linus and then at Maddy. 'Why don't you both stay at mine?'

'Yours?' Maddy asks.

'I'm afraid I have a plan to whisk this salty Sea-Gal away,' Linus says.

'Away?' Dominica asks.

'We're sailing to the Channel Islands first. Maybe to France. We'll see where opens up. We'll be away for . . . ' Helga smiles at him and he shrugs.

'Who knows?' he says. 'Let's see what happens.'

'What? But surely you can't just go?' Maddy says, looking at Claire, who knows what she's thinking . . . that this is all rather sudden.

'Why not?' Helga says. 'We both feel the same. We've been waiting for an adventure for so long. Why wait?'

'If I can have your permission,' Linus says, although he's only half-joking, 'I promise I will take very good care of her.'

'You'd better,' Dominica says and they talk excitedly as Helga opens the huge icebox and hands round beers, like she's already the owner of the boat.

Maddy looks like the weight has fallen from her shoulders too when she realises that Helga is serious about her and Jamie staying at her place.

'We'll take good care of it,' Jamie says. 'I'll fix that tile in the kitchen for starters.'

'Do what you like,' Helga says. 'I'm happy you'll get to

enjoy it and it won't be empty. But you'll have to promise to feed Terry.'

'Terry?' Jamie asks.

'My seagull.'

'He comes into the kitchen,' Dominica says. 'I'm serious.'

They stay until it's getting dark and then Claire insists that they have to go home, as they have no lights on their bikes.

'That was quite a day,' Pim says, as they cycle home along the prom.

'A brilliant one,' she says. 'Thank you.'

'I'm jealous of Helga and Linus. Off on a new adventure.'

'Me too. They looked like teenagers.'

'Didn't they? It got me thinking – about what if you and I did something crazy.'

'What? Take off on a yacht?'

'No, do something else. To combine our skills workwise. Do something for a living together.'

'For a living?'

'Yeah. I just think it would be fun to be partners in a new enterprise.'

She smiles. 'What did you have in mind?'

56

Round the Pier

Looking down from the top of the steps by the pitch and putt, Maddy can see that there's quite a crowd on the beach already and, even from here, she can sense the jolly mood as the swimmers start disrobing for the round-the-pier swim. There's a smell of doughnuts and candyfloss in the air.

The lifeguard boat bobs in the foam and she can see the markers out in the water. She was worried that it would be odd for Jamie coming back here and now she follows his gaze as they walk down the steps. The counsellor Dominica has recommended for Jamie has been working wonders and she's happy to see him getting stronger every day, but she knows difficult stuff comes up all the time. The counsellor has told Maddy to acknowledge it when it does.

'Wow. It's a long way down.' He's sombre as he nods to the end of the pier.

She nods. 'I know.'

'If you hadn't . . . '

He turns to her and she sees the gratitude and the fear in his eyes. 'I know. It's OK.'

'But you saved my life, Mum.'

She smiles at him and his eyes twinkle in the sunshine and she shudders, because what if she hadn't saved him? Because she's only a beginner at going in the sea? She's only a beginner at saving lives.

'Anytime,' she says, smiling back.

He nods and carries on down the steps and, as she watches him and the scruffy hair on the back of his head, which was the first thing she noticed when he was born, she knows he's going to be OK. That they're both going to be OK.

It's been a whirlwind twenty-four hours getting the boxes out of the Airbnb and moving into Helga's cottage and helping her pack up for her trip with Linus. But it's meant that she hasn't had any time to train for the swim and, now she's here, she's nervous about the challenge ahead.

'It's really far,' Maddy tells Jamie, now reaching beach level and seeing the crowds of swimmers getting ready. 'I have no idea if I'll make it.'

'You will. You can do anything. You're my super-mum.'

He hasn't called her that for years and she laughs. She's going to have to try her best to live up to his expectations.

'Where are Helga and Linus?' she asks, and Jamie looks along the crowded promenade.

'They were just behind us.'

Her phone pings now. It's a text from Lisa.

I'm stuck in traffic, but I'm on my way. Good luck with the swim. Can't wait to be there.

Jamie gives her an enquiring look and she explains that Lisa

394

is coming down and will be here in time for the party. Because she's hoping that's what today will turn into, once they've done the swim. Dominica is bringing loads of beers and Claire and Pim have offered to do the catering. They're all determined to give Helga and Linus a good send-off.

Maddy and Jamie spot Tor, who is already in her costume. She's with Lotte and another girl and waves Maddy over. Tor introduces Alice, her twin sister. Alice has the kind of polished look that Maddy used to have, she thinks, recognising her Botoxed skin and pristine eyebrows and highlights. But, next to Tor, who is so natural and fresh, she looks older and somehow more pinched. She's a good-looking girl, but all her interventions haven't actually enhanced her beauty, but rather ruined it. She smiles, her teeth whitened and straightened.

'Oh my God,' Alice says. 'Tor has told me all about you. You're *the* Maddy. Maddy from @made_home?'

'Yes.'

'I love what you do. Honestly. When I decorated my house, I followed all your advice.'

'Thank you.'

'I'm not joking,' Tor says, as Maddy puts down her bag. 'She's, like, a super fan.'

'I can't believe I've only just found out that Tor is friends with you.'

'I'm flattered,' Maddy says with a laugh. She talks to Alice for a while who wants advice on her new conservatory plan.

'I loved that fern-shaped shelf you featured.'

'I've still got it. I've just moved it.'

'I'd happily buy it off you.'

'Really?'

Maddy has been wondering what to do with all of the stuff she couldn't bear to put in storage and is now in Helga's conservatory, but this exchange suddenly sparks her interest. She could sell it all. To people like Alice. Why hasn't it occurred to her before?

When Alice turns away to talk to Lotte, Maddy leans in close to Tor. 'How's it going with those two?' She knows how nervous Tor's been about Lotte meeting Alice.

'They seem to have hit it off. Just like that. She came yesterday without Graham and the kids and it feels – I don't know – like we're all a family already. And Lotte thinks she's great. It feels as if we can move on to the next stage. Lotte and I have been talking about finding a flat together, for just the two of us.'

'That's great, Tor. Honestly. I'm so pleased for you.'

She waves now as Claire and Pim arrive with their boys, who are loaded with a table and cool boxes.

Jamie is soon chatting to Claire's boys and he helps them set up the table and deckchairs.

'I'm so glad you're here,' Claire says to Jamie. 'I want to ask you something.'

'Oh?' He looks at Maddy and then at Claire curiously.

'Pim and I have been talking,' she announces. She sounds giddy with excitement. 'We've decided on a new direction. We want to run a café. Tutors and Tea we're calling it. A place where students can come and have a coffee and a half-hour tutor session.'

'There's a place that we've been looking at by the station,' Pim says. 'It's a bit run down, so we're going to need help

396

getting it up and running. We need someone young and fit to help us deck it out. And tutors.'

'And we thought of you, Jamie,' Claire says.

'Me?' Jamie is surprised, looking between them and then to Maddy.

'Yes. We need a hand setting up.'

'That's a fabulous idea,' Maddy says. She's genuinely touched that Claire wants to help Jamie get back on his feet. 'And you know, Jamie would make a good tutor too. You did that once in the holidays, remember? When you started your A-levels,' she says to him.

'Yeah,' Jamie says. 'I'd forgotten, but yeah, I liked it. Helping the kids with maths.'

'Perfect,' Pim says. 'Even better.'

She leaves Pim and Claire talking to Jamie and runs to help Dominica, who is carrying a heavy cool box. Luna is tucked under her arm and she lets her down on the pebbles.

'Here, let me help,' Maddy says.

'What a day for it,' Dominica exclaims. She's wearing a long kaftan and a floppy hat. She looks like she's on a photoshoot for an exotic holiday destination.

'Well done for lugging this lot down. It's going to be a lot easier doing the swim knowing there's a cold drink at the other end.'

Dominica hugs Tor and says hello to Lotte and Alice, Pim and the boys. It feels like a party already, Maddy thinks, pleased to see that Jamie and Pim are getting on so well.

'Oh look,' Dominica says. She points to the steps. 'Here comes love's young dream.'

'Ain't that the truth,' Maddy says, looking at Helga and

Linus. She's always thought of Helga as so independent, but she and Linus really do look like the perfect couple. She's talked to Linus quite a bit whilst they moved in and she had no doubt that Helga's feelings for him are entirely reciprocated. They are as giddy as kids going on holiday preparing for their trip on the boat.

The swimmers are gathering now by the water and Claire gets changed and walks down with Tor and Maddy to the water's edge. A girl is standing by herself looking at the sea, her arms wrapped around her body.

'You OK?' Maddy asks.

'I was going to swim with my friend, but she hasn't come.'

'Come with us,' Maddy says, and the girl tags along gratefully. It feels good to be the one gathering her to the flock, just like Helga gathered her all those months ago.

'It's cold,' the girl says, as she dips her toes in the water.

'Yeah, but it's only cold water,' Helga says, arriving and grinning at Claire. 'Just walk in slowly and remember to breathe.'

The girl walks in nervously next to them, glad to have company.

'Do you really think there are eels?' Maddy asks Helga, nodding to the dark water under the pier.

'No,' she says. 'Not today. It doesn't really matter what's underneath. It's not going to drag you down. You've learnt that by now, right?'

'I know, but I should have trained more. I'm nervous.'

'Don't be,' Claire says. 'We've all got each other's backs. You'll be fine.'

Maddy looks at the glittering water ahead, hearing the cries of the swimmers as they start the swim. She hates it when people crow on about feeling blessed when they're humblebragging on social media. Since she's stopped doing it herself, she's noticed how false it sounds, but nevertheless she feels gratitude, like it's a physical force, as she watches the powerful, amazing women stride into the waves. She feels part of a tribe. Part of a revolution.

'Here we go,' Tor says. 'Let's do this thing.'

She follows Helga, who slips into the water, and Dominica skips in beside her, splashing her arms. Tor's next to her, laughing with Claire, and Maddy thinks that nothing needs to be any different to how it is right now in this moment with her friends and the horizon, as she plunges into the cool embrace of the sea.

Acknowledgements

After writing *The Cancer Ladies' Running Club*, I was half-way through another novel when Covid struck. As the weeks unfolded, I realised that the whole emotional landscape of our world had changed and the novel I was writing no longer chimed with the times.

I am very grateful to my clever agent, Felicity Blunt at Curtis Brown, who supported me changing tack, and her assistant, Rosie Pierce. I'd like to say a huge thank you to my brilliant editor Emily Kitchin and everyone at HQ, especially Lisa Milton who kept all her authors updated during some tricky times. I'd like to thank Katie Seaman who also helped edit, Sarah Lundy in PR, Melissa Kelly in marketing and everyone in production. I'm super proud to be an HQ author and I'd like to thank all the other authors who support me on the socials and all the booksellers and libraries and book clubs who champion authors like me.

They say that the first rule of writing is to write what you know and so I turned to my own doorstep for inspiration.

I wanted to write about what we gained during lockdown, rather than what we lost – and for me, that was a renewed appreciation of nature and a deeper sense of community.

I'd been living in Brighton for twelve years and had plunged in the sea at the end of the road in the summer, lazily bobbed around in our blow-up kayake and fallen off a few paddle-boards in that time, but I'd never considered swimming out of season. But when Covid struck, the sea took on a whole new significance.

As Claire says in the book, I really did have an epiphany, wondering how on earth I'd lived by this whole other element for over a decade and never taken any notice of the tide times, or the currents. I started swimming regularly and quickly found a new tribe of plucky bobble-hatted, Dryrobe wearing, tea-drinking super-women (and men) and together we took the plunge in the rain, snow, frost and sun, at dawn, at sunset. I soon became an addict for the cold-water hit and the sense of camaraderie.

The sea-swimming community in Brighton and all along this bit of coast has expanded massively thanks mostly to Cath and Kath who run Seabirds Social Enterprise – a shop and seasonal swim school that champions sea swimming as a way to be happier and healthier, so I'd like to give a big shout out to them, for their incredible achievement and starting the ever-growing Salty Seabirds Facebook group of which we're all proud members.

I'd also like to thank the inspirational Jo Godden from Rubymoon for her sustainable and ethical swimwear and also for organising the Full Moon swims. I'd also like to thank Lorelei Mathias, one of my fellow swimmers for her writing support and to everyone involved with The South Coast Sirens – a group we set up to try and tackle the water pollution issue. I also like to give a huge shout out to the team at the Lifeguards office in Brighton. I'd also really like to thank the amazing folk at Knight (knightsupport.org.uk) a wonderful charity making a huge difference to the homeless and rough sleepers in Brighton.

I'd really like to thank my own swimming gangs to whom this book is fondly dedicated – The West Pier/Bandstand Saltys and The Splash and Bobbers and The Brunswick Bathing Beauties, especially Katy Whelan for weathering over thirty years of friendship. I'd also like to thank Sophie for her beautiful Lunar Tidal Calendar, Sheelagh for her swimming lessons, Tara for her invaluable insight into Homelessness, Alice for always adding a touch of glamour, Anita for being the life and soul, as well as Helen and Michael, JP and Thiago (and Walt, of course) and the lovely Steph. Plus a big thanks to Michaelino for the intel on the Samaritans.

As well as writing about community, I really like writing about female friendship and I'm lucky enough to have a tribe of women in my life who mean the world to me. I'd really like to thank Bronwin Wheatley and Eve Tomlinson, along with Shân Lancaster and Louise Dumas, my ever-supportive early readers. A big thank you to ever-supportive Harriet Rees and also to Dawn Howarth, who has held my hand now through all my books – this being my twentieth novel. Thank you, too, to Dinah, Clare-Bear, Ruth and Orshi. Thanks too, to Lesley Thomas as well as Alice from Posh Totty Designs, Jenny Dunn for her wonderful yoga lessons and Jo Darling for her acupuncture.

Lastly, thank you to my wonderful family for always keeping me afloat with your love and humour, especially my sister Catherine Lloyd – my fellow swimmer and Christmas Day dipper (I promise I will get you a more flattering swimming hat), Kirsti, Dad and Dianne, Aunty Liz and to my intrepid water babies, Tallulah, Roxie and Minty. Thank you to Ziggy, for standing guard on the shoreline and making sure I get back to dry land safely, where his best friend Frankie Knuckles is often to be found helpfully keeping my towel warm.

Most of all, my love and thanks to my husband and literal lifesaver, Emlyn Rees for everything – and for coming up with a cracking title.

Reading Group Questions

1. How does the author create a sensory experience of swimming in the sea using language? Do you ever swim in the sea? Did reading the book make you want to?

2. Did you particularly identify with any one of the Sea-Gals, and what they are going through, over the others? If so, which one, and why?

3. Homelessness, and the struggles the homeless community faces, is a strong theme in the book. How did you respond to this theme? Did it shed light on any aspect of being homeless that you may not previously have considered?

4. 'At its essence, this is a novel about female friendship.' How true is this statement? Discuss how the author creates a sense of camaraderie between the Sea-Gals.

5. 'She often feels, if not lonely, then certainly detached from the fun-loving person she used to be.' Can you identify with Claire's feelings of detachment from her younger self? Why do you think she's feeling this way?

6. What do you think of Maddy's decision to post so honestly on her Instagram account about her experiences? Do you think that Maddy has changed by the end of the novel? If so, how?

7. The novel is set during the Covid lockdown of 2021. What impact does this have on the story?

8. Discuss the author's portrayal of grief and loss. Do you think that by the end of the novel, Dominica is starting to come to terms with her loss? If so, what do you think has helped her the most along her journey?

9. Would you say that body-positivity is a theme in the book? What did you make of Claire's decision to pose for Helga's life-drawing class? How do you think this decision impacted her confidence?

10. 'I totally identify as an old hag. I always draw in a new box on those government forms when they ask me.' What was your response to Helga as a character, and her attitude towards growing old? Did anything about it surprise you?

11. In the novel, the characters learn about the impact of pollution in the sea. Did any of the information shock you? Does it make you feel more inclined to get involved in campaigning for change?

12. 'When I was your age, women never talked about the menopause at all.' Do you think that this has changed? If so, what positive effects does this change bring in society?